CLAWS. WHAT CREATURE WAS THIS?

Fast as only a Vampire could move, Weiss attacked, fangs at the ready, leaping forward into a burst of flame.

His scream echoed in his ears as pain tore through him.

This had to be the destroyer! Whatever infernal creature it was, he'd discover later—for now, with a screech of agony, Weiss fled, knowing he had to find shelter, and fast.

He buried himself in the first patch of turned ground he found. As the healing earth and dark soothed his pain, he swore vengeance.

Once he had enough strength to restore himself and identify his attacker.

Also by Georgia Evans

BLOODY GOOD

BLOODY AWFUL

Published by Kensington Publishing Corporation

BLOODY RIGHT

GEORGIA EVANS

KENSINGTON BOOKS
http://www.kensingtonbooks.com

KENSINGTON BOOKS are published by

Kensington Publishing Corp.
119 West 40th Street
New York, NY 10018

All Kensington titles, imprints, and distributed lines are available at special quantity discounts for bulk purchases for sales promotion, premiums, fund-raising, educational, or institutional use.

Special book excerpts or customized printings can also be created to fit specific needs. For details, write or phone the office of the Kensington Special Sales Manager: Attn.: Special Sales Department. Kensington Publishing Corp., 119 West 40th Street, New York, NY 10018. Phone: 1-800-221-2647.

Kensington Books and the K logo Reg. U.S. Pat. & TM Off.

ISBN-13: 978-0-7582-3483-4
ISBN-10: 0-7582-3483-X

First Printing: August 2009
10 9 8 7 6 5 4 3 2 1

Printed in the United States of America

Chapter One

Guildford, November 1940

"Something the matter?" Paul Schmidt asked Weiss, looking across his unheated sitting room.

Something the matter? Hans Weiss wanted to spit. He'd say there was. Their masters in Germany were baying for results and blood—he gave a twisted smile at that last thought—and here he was, facing the hardest assignment they'd been given, with the last and feeblest member of their cohort as his only help.

The nagging knowledge that someone or something in the area had the power to annihilate Vampires didn't add anything but another layer of anxiety to his prospects.

The world was wrong. He'd been the next thing to invincible for five centuries and now he was reduced to serving his petty masters in Adlerroost and watching his fellow Vampires disappear among the accursed peasants. "We need to take action," he said.

"I wouldn't argue with that," Schmidt replied, "but what? Do we have orders?"

"We do."

Schmidt raised a blond eyebrow. "And?"

"Our masters are changing their plans and our mission." Weiss paused, as if considering the impermanence of mortals. "With the onset of winter, the invasion is postponed until the spring."

Schmidt nodded. He'd worked that much out for himself. "So what do they ask of us now? To keep on sowing discontent and unease?"

"That's a given but, naturally, there is more. The High Command have decided the best way to disable this wretched and stubborn country is to remove the leader."

"Kill the king? That's regicide!"

Weiss permitted himself a little smile. "Indeed it is, but the King here counts for nothing. He is a figurehead, a tool for propaganda. They mean the leader: the one who has convinced these Inselaffen, these puny island monkeys, that they are of the fabric of heroes, that their pathetic armed forces will prevail against the might of the entire German war machine, and getting bombed out of their homes is nothing more than a mere inconvenience."

"Gott!" Schmidt leaned forward, his eyes wide. "You mean Churchill?"

"Yes," Weiss replied with a nod. "We are to kill Churchill." And sat back in the lumpy armchair to enjoy Schmidt's surprise.

He was not disappointed.

Consternation, incredulity, utter amazement, and finally stunned disbelief played across the younger Vampire's face. "They are insane!" he said at last, shaking his head.

Weiss inclined his head. "Think it would be wise to share that with our masters? Would the Führer welcome your candid opinion? There are how many of your blood kindred in their hands?"

Frustration blocked out Schmidt's other emotions. "It is

close to impossible, even for us," he replied, shaking his head again. "He'll be protected, surrounded by police—or the army—at all times."

"I note you said 'close to impossible,' not impossible," Weiss replied. "Nothing is truly impossible." Not even learning who or what in that village could destroy a Vampire. "It will not be easy, but it is possible. Attacking in London would be reckless and suicidal. Instead, we will strike when he is less defended."

"And that will be when?"

Weiss paused. Pathetic really, almost mortal to go for effect, but since he could . . . "Soon. He frequently spends weekends in the country, at Wharton Lacey with his loyal friends, Sir James and Lady Gregory."

Schmidt's jaw dropped in a highly gratifying manner. "The old fool who commands the local Home Guard?"

"The same, although 'old fool' might be less than accurate. But fool or not, he is trusted. He and Churchill were at school together. The prime minister takes his secretary and a couple of policemen for protection. Sometimes cabinet ministers and representatives of friendly nations join him."

"And you know this how?"

Skepticism was to be expected. This had not been part of the master plan. "One of the parlormaids at Number Ten is our agent, plus I have suborned the family cook at Wharton Lacey. She's told when and what to cook, as seems the prime minister is a hearty trencherman."

"Brilliant, but how did you manage it? Surely she didn't volunteer."

The creature had his moments of wit. "Hardly! Propitiously, she is a native of Jersey and has relatives who did not flee before the invasion. She will provide the information I ask, to protect her family left behind."

"You don't have the power to protect them!"

"She believes I do."

Schmidt had to smile. There was a reason, other than his age, that the mortals at Adlerroost chose Weiss as their leader. He was devious, focused, and implacable. Not that Schmidt felt sorry for the duped cook, or the damned Inselaffen. But he made a mental note to never earn Weiss's enmity. "Excellent!" He meant it too. Eliminating Churchill would definitely leave the country in chaos and was the perfect opening for the Vampires to take the upper hand. "You will kill him?"

"Quite possibly."

"Only possibly?" What did Weiss have in mind?

"Eliminating him would send the country into confusion, which would be admirable, but if we could control him it would be even better."

Better but far riskier. But Schmidt would keep that to himself. "Do we have instructions?"

Weiss raised an eyebrow. "We followed instructions before and look what happened to Eiche and Bloch."

In point of fact they did not know what had happened. "You are convinced they are dead?" If such a word was precise enough to describe the extinction of an immortal creature.

"It appears they are no more," Weiss replied, "and that, in itself, is worrying. I intend to find out what happened to them while you ready the way for Mr. Churchill."

He might have guessed this was coming. "And I do what?"

Weiss smiled, always a bad sign. "The undergardener at Wharton Lacey had a most unfortunate accident early this morning: multiple fractures to his left leg. Tripped, careless man. He will be incapacitated for weeks, and you, my dear Schmidt, will fill the position."

Just like that? "How do we manage that? I'm an ambulance driver."

"Not any longer. You are now the good cook's cousin, who had his lungs severely damaged through childhood pleurisy and therefore cannot serve in His Majesty's Armed Forces."

Marvelous. Working as a laborer by day and a rescue worker by night. The things he did for the fatherland. "Wharton Lacey is a good distance away. How am I supposed to get back and forth, and where do I live?" He did not want to sound desperate, but a Vampire needed shelter and if he was expected to work out of doors . . .

"Your dear aunt, the cook, will arrange for that."

Indeed. "And have you considered the daylight factor?" Most likely not.

"Of course, my dear Schmidt. Firstly, I do consider your age. The Crusades, wasn't it, when you were turned? You can endure a little sunlight. If you're not impaled on a tree." Nasty that, but he'd let it pass. "In any case, sunshine is so unusual at this time of year and the days so short, I think you need not worry. You are in chronic poor health. The mortals will expect you to be weak."

There was something wrong with this entire scenario. Several somethings in fact. "How close is this Wharton Lacey to Brytewood?"

Another smile. A good reason to be cautious. "Four miles, my dear Schmidt. Four of their English miles. Distant enough for you?"

It was going to have to be. The last thing he needed was encountering that good Samaritan doctor. "I hope so. Doubt I'll have any reason to go into the village anyway."

"Better you do not," Weiss replied, "unless summoned. I will be there, from time to time, investigating this Vampire killer."

A shiver snaked down Schmidt's back. Not many things gave a Vampire anxiety, but those with power to destroy could. "Anything else?" Might as well hear the lot while he was here.

"Not altogether." Which meant there was. "Except . . . that Fairy creature who works for our masters?" So Weiss had noticed too, had he? "Has been conspicuously absent, hasn't she?"

And he hadn't missed her poking in his mind one little bit. "Yes. I wonder why?"

"Most likely they killed her."

"Why would they do that?"

"Beats me. I can't read mortal minds. Perhaps she refused to cooperate. Maybe her powers waned over time. How should I know?" Or care. "If she's not prying into our minds, the less the mortals in Adlerroost know about us."

"Damn good thing too, if you ask me." Not that Weiss had or was likely to.

Weiss stood. A clear signal the summons was at an end. "You have ambulance duty tonight, I believe. I suggest you miss it and use your time to study your new cover." He nodded at a thick envelope on the table. "Should be simple enough."

Paul Schmidt stood and picked up the envelope. Weiss wasn't telling him everything, that was a given.

He wished Weiss luck in that village that had already consumed two Vampires, Eiche and Bloch. Still, with Weiss occupied, he'd have the field clear for his own ambitions.

Chapter Two

Brytewood

"Here you are, Nurse, with Lady Gregory's compliments," Edith Aubin, the cook from Wharton Lacey, said as she handed Gloria a large hamper.

"This is so incredibly generous," Gloria Prewitt replied, as she lifted the lid and saw two roasted chickens, a good-sized ham and an almost complete Cheddar cheese. No wonder Miss Aubin had needed the driver's help to carry it into the village hall from the car.

Miss Aubin nodded in agreement. "Not too much for a returning hero," she replied. "Lady Gregory said to let me know if you're short on bread or tea."

"We should be alright, Mr. Whorleigh has donated tea." From under the counter, Gloria suspected, but she wasn't going to quibble over that. "Bread, someone is fetching from Leatherhead."

"Of course," Miss Aubin nodded. "Your baker disappeared, didn't he?"

He'd disintegrated at Gloria's hand, or rather under her teeth, when she'd been in fox shape, with a little help from

Andrew Barron, her intended. Not that she was ever mentioning that to anyone who didn't know already. "We certainly miss having fresh bread." But disposing of a Vampire of nefarious intent made the whole of England safer.

"Would you believe it, he did a moonlight flit?" Mrs. Chivers, mainstay of the Women's Institute and Mrs. Burrows's knitting circle, added her ha'pennorth. "Shocking, just walked out and left. Obviously forgot there's a war on."

No, he certainly hadn't. He'd been a very real part of the war but that, too, Gloria kept to herself. She was keeping a lot to herself these days.

But despite the war, the heavy black curtains that covered the windows and doors, and the scrimping and saving to put together the wartime equivalent of a groaning board, Brytewood was ready for a party.

No doubt the women in ancient Greece or Babylon put on feasts to welcome home returning warriors. And here they were, following the ways of countless women who waited and wept and wondered if their sons and brothers and lovers would return from the wars.

She was getting positively maudlin. Her lover, fiancé and light of her heart, was brushing aside the blackout curtain that covered the door.

"Andrew!" She restrained the urge to rush across the hall and wrap her arms around him. Didn't need to really, just meeting his eyes and knowing that smile was hers was enough.

"Hello, Gloria." And that was a smile and a half. "Brought you something." He placed a battered cardboard box on the table.

She lifted the top and peered inside. "Corned beef?"

He grinned and a sexy grin it was. "Best I could manage."

"Purloining government stocks?" Mary LaPrioux, the evacuated schoolteacher, asked.

"What a suggestion!" Andrew managed to look shocked whilst grinning. "It fell off the back of a lorry."

"Never mind where it came from," Gloria said. "We can use it to make shepherd's pies. Someone brought in a couple of sacks of potatoes, or we could try that rissole recipe from Lord Woolaton."

"Stick to shepherd's pie. You know what's in that," Andrew said. "Or better still, what's wrong with bully beef sandwiches?"

A lot easier too. "Pity we can't make chips with the potatoes."

"Have Mrs. Burrows organize a dripping drive around the village. Bet you'd have enough to fry several hundredweight of potatoes."

Behind Gloria, Mary laughed. Andrew was right. Mrs. Burrows was a force of nature—of course few people knew the doctor's grandmother was a Devon Pixie. It rather gave her the edge over mere mortals.

"How about . . ." Andrew went on, but broke off at the crash of a breaking window.

Miss Willows, one of the schoolteachers, looked up from counting out cups and saucers at another table. Her eyes met Mary's.

"Bet it's one of mine," Mary muttered, and ran out of the door.

The cold, damp, night air hit her immediately, but she wasn't going back for her coat. She ran forward, looking around as her eyes adjusted to the dark. She caught sight of two boys running, and set off after them, knowing she hadn't a hope of catching them unless one or both of them tripped. Until a tall man stepped out of the shadows and grabbed them both, hauling them, squalling and wriggling, back to the village hall.

He set them both on their feet a few yards from Mary. "Here you are, Miss LaPrioux. What do you want done with them? Should I boil them in oil? Send them to the coal mines? Or would the galleys do better?"

She had never appreciated Tom Longhurst's wit, and most likely never would. "Thank you for nabbing them, Mr. Longhurst," she said, eyeing the pair of them and noting, with a wave of relief, that they were village boys. She shouldn't be pleased, but she was. Seemed her Guernsey evacuees and the few remaining London ones got blamed for almost everything. "What are your names?"

They hesitated, looking at each other, obviously debating silently the wisdom of answering. "Well?" she asked, tapping her foot. "You do have names, don't you?"

"Jim Polson."

"Mike Polson."

Brothers, or maybe cousins of some sort. "So Messrs Polson. Who broke the window?"

"Didn't mean to, miss," said Mike, the taller of the two. "I was aiming at the drainpipe."

"And you had a good reason to throw stones at the drainpipe?" The scuffed toes of their shoes became of paramount interest to the boys. "Trying to get a stone to rattle all the way down, were you?" Mary suggested.

Two pairs of eyes snapped open. She'd almost swear she heard them gulp with surprise. Did they never realize that teachers had once been nine years old too? The trick of getting a small stone over the top and into the drainpipe so it rattled all the way down wasn't exactly their personal invention. "Besides, shouldn't you be home after dark?"

"Mum's in the hall, helping," Jim said. "She told us to play quietly."

So they weren't even June Willows's responsibility. "Then I suggest you go right into the village hall and explain to your mother what happened."

They didn't exactly rush to follow that direction.

"Better get a broom and clean up the broken glass too," Tom Longhurst added.

Good point. Mary watched the two boys drag themselves toward maternal retribution. It was getting downright chilly. She wrapped her arms around her chest as she followed the boys back inside.

"Take my coat," Tom Longhurst said, unbuttoning his tweed jacket.

"No, don't bother. Thank you, but I'll be inside in a jiffy." She darted forward and grabbed the door. "Were you heading here?" She hoped not. On his way to the Pig and Whistle most likely.

"Yes, I was. Mother wanted me to check numbers. She's baking apple pies."

As if Mrs. Longhurst couldn't guess how many pies might be needed. Honestly! Flimsy excuse wasn't the word. "How kind of her. She's a wonderful baker." He'd nipped ahead of her and had the door open and was lifting the blackout curtain. Would be downright rude and silly to not go in. "Better tell Gloria or Mrs. Chivers," she said quickly. "They're organizing this shindig. I'll keep an eye on those boys."

She darted across the hall, full steam ahead as the irate teacher, to find that Mrs. Polson had done the job for her. The two boys were fairly quivering under the scolding. "And now you'll clean up the mess and cover the broken pane and on top of that, pay for the new glass out of your pocket money."

Mary almost began to feel sorry for the pair of them, heads

hung and shoulders slumped under the weight of guilt. "Clean up and find a piece of cardboard to cover the hole and I expect Mr. Simmons could fix it," she said. The school caretaker was pretty adept at replacing panes broken by cricket balls, and other flying missiles.

"He's expert. Mended a couple my brother and I broke over the years."

Darn, it was Tom Longhurst. Right at her shoulder.

"You think he would, sir?" Jim Polson asked, eyes aglow with relief.

"Best ask him in the morning and cover the pane for now. There's a gale blowing through."

Mary tamped down her irritation. She and Mrs. Polson made the same request and the boys stood there. Tom Longhurst tells them and they hop to it. Alright, she was being unfair. There were precious few men left in the village and Tom was a favorite of most of the boys. And a good many of the women as well. She darn well wished they'd get his attention instead of her.

"One good thing," Tom went on, giving her his most appealing smile. "They proved that the paper strips on the glass really do hold the pane glass together."

"Yes," she replied. It certainly did. When Jim lifted the curtain the shattered fragments hung on the strips of tape that crisscrossed the window pane.

"Put that curtain back down!" a voice called across the hall. "Or we'll have the air raid wardens down on us."

"No point in inviting Jerry to the party," someone else added.

Nothing more she could do here. Might as well head back to the table where Gloria and Mrs. Chivers sorted food donations.

Only Tom tagged along. "You know Peter Wills is playing the piano for tomorrow night."

Of course she knew. She and Gloria had been in on the planning for Gryffyth Pendragon's return since the very beginning. "Should be fun." Although she rather questioned the tactlessness of dancing at a party for a returning amputee. But it seemed no one else had any qualms.

"So," Tom went on, with another too charming smile, "will you promise me a dance?"

Damn! She was not a swearing woman, but really. She'd gone to the pictures with him once (grave error of judgment that had been) and now he laid claim to her. "I'll give you one dance, Tom."

"Just one? I'm being rationed?"

Heaven help her! She'd turned him down twice already. Maybe she was too tactful. "Tom, I'd better let the other women have a look in. Can't monopolize you, can I?"

He actually paused to ponder that, which gave her a moment to get back to the table by the door. Once she was behind that . . .

"Wouldn't mind," he said, grabbing her hand.

She would. "One dance, Tom," she repeated, taking her hand from his and feeling the eyes of half the assembled company on her. "Why don't you check with Mrs. Chivers and see how many pies we need?"

"Excuse me," a voice, to her left, said. "Sorry to interrupt."

Thrilled to be interrupted, Mary smiled at the speaker, the cook from Wharton Lacey. "Yes?"

"Just wanted a quick word. If you don't mind."

"By all means. Miss Aubin, isn't it?" Mary stepped to the side and Tom moved away. To ask someone else for a dance, no doubt. "Can I help you?"

"Just wanted to introduce myself properly. You're the Guernsey girl, am I right?"

"Yes, I'm Mary LaPrioux. Evacuated here with my class."

The woman held out her hand. "Edith Aubin. From St. Clement's Parish on Jersey."

Mary clasped her hand. "I'm from St. Martins. It's good to meet someone else from the Islands." Even if she was from Jersey.

"Just wanted to say hello."

"I'm glad you did. Home seems a long way away these days. Have you been here long?"

"Fifteen years. Used to be I went home every holiday, but now . . ."

Who knew when they'd be home? If ever. "I alternate between homesickness, being glad I'm safe, and worrying about everyone left behind."

"You get news?"

"Yes," Mary replied. "But how much can they say on those Red Cross forms? We set up a code before I was evacuated, so we could let each other know if anything dire happened."

"I've an old mother, I worry about her," Edith Aubin said. "Didn't have much schooling so she never did write much. I've a married brother and sister but seldom hear from them."

Worrying. Had to be. "I think there's a limit how many of those letters they can send."

"I know," Miss Aubin replied. "I tell myself he uses them to write to his wife. She and the children went back to her family in Devon. But I can't help but worry."

She looked more than worried. She looked downright haggard. "Do you know where in Devon? The doctor's family are from that way and so's her new husband. Perhaps if you ask them."

"Miss LaPrioux!" a voice called across the hall.

"Sorry, I'd better go," Mary said. "I'll talk to Alice."

"Come up and have tea one day. I'd enjoy talking to someone from home, or at least close to home."

"Thank you, I will. I'll stop next time I'm over your way."

"Please do." With a nod, the older woman buttoned up her coat and left.

Mary went over to see what Mrs. Chivers wanted.

"I think you're breaking Tom Longhurst's heart," Gloria said, as she and Mary walked home, their shaded torches lighting the way.

Mary assumed she was teasing. "He'll survive."

"You really don't fancy him, do you?"

Good question. "He's a nice enough chap." And, she had to admit, one of the few single men left in the village, now that Gloria and Alice Watson, the doctor, had snagged the nicest two. "But he's just not my type."

"He's smitten, sexy, intelligent. If you gave him just the weeniest come-hither he'd be yours for the taking."

Maybe. But he was clearly and unmistakably human, and Mary wasn't about to tangle with him. Going out to the flicks once had been an error in judgment she was not likely to repeat. He might have a hammerpond on the edge of his land, where she bathed when the need for water overwhelmed her. But she could just imagine the look on his nice, human face if she said *Oh, by the way. I'm a Water Sprite. You don't mind if I go off in the moonlight and swim in all weathers, do you?*

Might almost be worth it to see the shock in his big blue eyes, but no. She'd been trained from childhood to keep her nature a secret, and a secret it would remain. Unless she met another of her kind, and the odds of meeting another in landlocked Surrey was about as likely as the Germans deciding they didn't want to invade her home after all.

"A penny for them?" Gloria asked. "Tom on your mind?"

"Gloria, he's just not my sort. He really isn't."

"I didn't say he was your Mr. Right, but how about a Mr. Right Now?"

Mary shook her head. "No. Someone else can have him." They were practically lining up after all. Of course, there was still the problem of the damn dance she'd promised him.

Maybe she'd stay home tomorrow night. Fat chance of that. Sensible, oh-so-human Gloria would nag her into going. There was no way out, short of breaking a leg or developing some contagious disease. She was going to have to brace herself to dance with the most eligible bachelor for miles around.

Chapter Three

"Dad, I'm not going tonight. I can't. And that's flat!"

Howell Pendragon looked up from filling the teapot, almost baptizing himself with boiling water at the sheer panic in Gryffyth's eyes and the sweat beading on his forehead. "Right you are, son," he replied, putting the lid on the pot and covering it with the knitted cozy Helen Burrows made out of Air Force Blue wool. "Tea'll be ready in a minute. Want a piece of toast with it?"

"Did you hear me, Dad?"

"Yes, I heard you." Would have been impossible not to, given he'd as good as shouted. Another mark of how keyed up he was. "You don't want to go to the party tonight."

"That's all you've got to say?"

Howell put two mugs on the table and reached into the bread bin. "What do you expect me to say, son? You said you won't go. You're a grown man. I can hardly wallop you on the bum and tell you, 'yes, you are!' The way I did when you refused to carry your cousin Bronwen's train at her wedding."

"Dad, I was six at the time."

"And now you're twenty-six. So you won't come. Want one slice of toast or two?"

"I don't want any toast!"

Silly git! Not that he'd say that aloud. Howell shook his head and put four slices of bread under the grill. He was hungry and he bet Gryff was. He fetched the week's ration of cheese from the pantry and started slicing. The lad had always had a weakness for cheese on toast. (He damn well wasn't calling it Welsh Rarebit the way the English did.) And they had two hours to go before Alice Watson would pick them up.

Howell busied himself with plates and filling the milk jug, all the time casting glances in Gryffyth's direction. He understood the lad's reluctance. It was no joke for him, hobbling about on his tin leg while everyone else, old fogies to little nippers, skipped around on two. But dammit, Gryff had done nothing but mope and frown since he came home, aside from one trip down to the Pig with Andrew and Peter. He'd gone the once and refused ever after. It wasn't good. Not at all.

"Here you are." Howell slipped two slices onto a plate and put it on Gryffyth's side of the table. "Come and get it while it's still warm and bubbly."

"I'm not hungry, Dad."

"Maybe not, but that's your cheese ration for the week so best eat up, or you will be." He set to pouring tea and made himself not watch his son. But nodded with satisfaction as Gryffyth walked over to the table. He managed that far without his stick. Good. "Here's your tea." Howell put the mug by the plate and sat down himself.

The lad got himself into the chair, but pulling it up to the table was another matter. Howell knew better than offer to help. What grown man wanted to be pushed up to the table like a child? He took a drink of tea, noting with pleasure that Gryff was already picking up knife and fork.

He let him eat, topping up his tea and not saying much until he cleared away the plates and produced the remains of the blackberry-and-apple tart Helen Burrows had brought over yesterday.

"This is delicious," Gryffyth said, between mouthfuls. "Just as it was when we were children. Remember how Alice and I and her brothers used to play together? Her grandmother used to bake the most smashing cakes and tarts."

"The Pixie touch, eh?" No joking there either.

"That's what she used to say. Said it was Devon magic."

Good opening, that. Not what he'd planned on saying right this minute, but never mind. "Why not? Ours isn't the only sort of magic, lad."

"Oh! Dad! Fat lot of good that magic did me, sitting here with my tin leg."

"Dragon magic's no use?" Howell almost laughed. "Then how is it you were the only one picked up alive?"

He wished the words back the minute Gryffyth's eyes brimmed with tears. Tears he blinked back with a snarl. "That's the whole point, isn't it, Dad? I was their sergeant and I couldn't save them!"

Howell reached across the table and grabbed both his son's hands, squeezing until he opened his eyes and glared his fury at his father. "Right there, lad. You couldn't save them. There were men in the trenches died and I couldn't save them. They'll haunt me until I die, just as your men will haunt you. But that's the way it is. You survived, just as I did."

"You came home with both legs."

"True, but seems to me, son, it's coming back that matters. Surviving. Don't think your fighting's finished just because they invalided you out. It's not. We've had our own war here and it's not been nice."

"I heard about the vicar's wife getting hurt in the bombing, and Miss Waite being arrested as a spy."

The lad didn't know the half of it. "There's a lot more, son, much more. You need to know it all, but now's not the time. If I started we'd be here until midnight and never get out of the house."

At least that got a bit of a smile. "Sounds like a good idea, Dad. Since I'm not going."

Time to get down to brass tacks. "Yes, you are, Gryff, and I'll tell you why. First off, they've worked and planned this for days and you can't let them down. People have given up their food rations and done without to put this on for you. Second, everyone needs a party. You've had it rough, so has everyone here. Not just the bombs and the worry about invasion. We've done without, made do and mended, seen friends killed or missing, and Brytewood needs a party. And this, third and final," he went on as Gryffyth opened his mouth to speak, "you're their hope."

He let out a cynical laugh. "Some hope! I come back hopping on a tin leg!"

"Yes, son, but *you came back*. That's what matters. Now that you returned alive, they can hope their sons and husbands and brothers will too."

"Hope they come back crippled?"

"Better come back like you than as a name engraved on the War Memorial on the village green. Too many damn names on that already."

Gryff went silent, holding his empty mug in both hands. "Dad, I just dread sitting there. What the hell am I going to do?"

"You're going to come along, meet your old friends—those who are still here, that is. Have a couple of beers, maybe a bit more, and come home again. Tomorrow we'll have a long talk." Time he knew what had been going on in Brytewood. Might just be a gift from the heavens that he was back. Another Dragon couldn't do anything but weigh the odds in their favor. "Tell me, son. When did you last shift? Been awhile, I bet?"

Gryffyth stared at his father. "Last time was with you, just before I left."

He'd expected as much. "Tomorrow night, we go up on Box Hill and we shift together. You need to be reminded what you really are."

"Yes, Dad, a three-legged Dragon!"

"Bet you amazed the doctors. No trouble with infection in your stump? No fever? Healed faster than anyone else?"

"Yeah!" Another slip of a smile there. "Didn't want them wondering too much. Used to joke and say we Welsh were made of stone from our mountains."

Not too far off the truth when it came to Dragons. "Alright, then. I'll clear the table, you go and spruce yourself up. Best put on a tie. Show everyone you made an effort."

He actually had made a pretty good effort. Put on a clean shirt and was brushing his jacket when Alice walked in the back door. Howell smiled and restrained a sigh. He'd had hopes for her and Gryffyth. The lad needed a wife who was Other, and Alice's Pixie blood certainly would have fitted the bill, but she was well and truly married to young Peter Watson now. And already fielding the inevitable jokes about Dr. Watson. Gryffyth would have to look elsewhere.

Once he found peace with himself.

"Good evening, Sergeant, Gryffyth. Everyone ready?"

"Evening, Alice." The boy even managed a smile. "Thanks for coming."

"My pleasure. It's good to see you back. Besides, it's not every day we get to throw a party. Ready?"

"Give me couple of ticks." Gryffyth shrugged on his jacket, Howell fisting his hands to resist the urge to help. The lad had to do it for himself, and wanted to. And managed, even throwing on his top coat. "Cold outside?" he asked.

"Not too bad," Alice replied, "given it's December. But the village hall is like a tomb. I think they're counting on body heat to warm the place."

And a room full of sweaty dancers, but that Howell kept to himself. "All set, son?"

Howell hoped the Jerries hadn't invented a system to measure noise. Of course if they had, they'd be on them already. The music greeted them long before they pulled up in front of the darkened village hall. There was a flicker of light from the door. Someone watching for them, no doubt, but Gryffyth missed that in the effort of getting out of the car.

But no one could miss the opening bars of "Men of Harlech" as they stepped into the hall. Nice touch, that. Howell blinked back a tear or two even if it was a trifle off-key. Best one could expect among the English, after all.

"Lovely," he said to Reverend Roundhill as he came up to them.

"We thought the Welsh national anthem would be a nice tribute," he replied.

Howell hadn't the heart to tell the well-meaning man that "Land of My Fathers" was their national anthem, but Alice knew—she met Howell's eyes and smiled. "They must have been practicing for ages."

"They have," Reverend whispered back as the music ended, and someone at the back started three cheers for Gryffyth.

There was no backing out after that.

He'd been right, Howell thought, as one by one and in little clusters the villagers came up to shake Gryffyth's hand. The village needed a hero and, willing or not, Gryffyth had been cast for the role.

One he seemed to accept gracefully enough as he settled down with a beer and a plate of food.

"I think Tom Longhurst's playing hard to get," Gloria whispered to Mary as they cleared the buffet table.

Mary looked across the hall at Tom dancing with one of the land girls. "Good," she replied, hoping his version of "hard to get" would soon become "no longer interested."

"Why don't you young things go and dance?" Mrs. Chivers said, bustling up to both of them. "I know that young man of yours, Gloria, is getting impatient. You've both been such a help. You go and have some fun."

Dragged onto the floor by Gloria, Mary ended up Stripping the Willow with one of the workers from the munitions plant on the heath. As she reached the end of the line, and her partner swung her around, she looked toward the side of the hall and met Gryffyth Pendragon's eyes.

Chapter Four

Mary let out a gasp. She must have stumbled, tripped or missed her footing. Her partner caught her and a moment later he had her right hand and she was back in the rhythm of the dance. Or at least her feet were keeping time with the music as she and whatever-his-name-was made their way down the dancers to the end. Now she had her back to the dark-eyed man. She wanted so much to turn and look at him again. But she wasn't that rude, was she? Her partner was a nice lad, pleasant, polite, and about as exciting as peeling a sack of potatoes.

While behind her was . . . God! She felt his gaze like a fire up and down her spine as she moved up the dance as another couple took off down the line. Utter nonsense. Was it? She swallowed hard. She wanted so much to turn her head. To prove to herself she was imagining things. That Gryffyth Pendragon (she knew it was him from the triumphal entrance engineered by the village worthies) was not watching her every step and breath, and the heat in his glance as she met his eyes was a figment of her imagination. But without turning her back on her partner and the dance, there was no way she could be sure. Besides, that would be rude. She caught the hand of the next man coming down the line. She had to concentrate, pay attention, smile at her partner.

While behind her, his eyes boring a hole between her shoulder blades, was the guest of honor who had umpteen old friends here and knew everyone and . . .

Mary stepped up as another couple reached the bottom.

Two more couples and the dance would be over. She must be out of condition. That was it. She needed to get herself up to the hammerpond and immerse herself in the water to restore her equilibrium. Why else was her heart racing like this?

The last couple reached the end. The music stopped with a flourish. She honored her partner with a bob of a curtsy, thanked him, and avoided Tom Longhurst's glance as he came toward her.

She didn't remember crossing the length of the village hall—no doubt she'd walked on toes, tripped up children and pushed aside old ladies. She just made a beeline to where Gryffyth Pendragon sat, watching her approach.

He smiled as she reached him.

Her mouth went dry.

What the hell was she doing? Approaching a virtual stranger, and the guest of honor into the bargain, when she'd promised to go back and help with the tea urn.

"Hello," she said, holding out her hand. "I'm Mary La-Prioux."

"I know," he replied, moving a coat off the chair next to him. "Have a seat. Want a beer?"

She loathed beer. "Thank you." He filled a glass from the almost empty jug in front of him. She took a sip. Yes. She loathed beer but it wouldn't kill her. "How did you know my name?"

Easy enough, really. Most of the village knew who she was by now.

"I asked Tom Longhurst."

Spluttering beer down her nose would have ruined the moment. It was a near thing. "Tom?"

"Yes." She noticed his eyes weren't dark. His long lashes were, but his eyes were the blue of a Guernsey sea in June and crinkled at the corners as he gave a slow, almost twisted, smile. "He told me you were taken."

"What?" Yes, she had no trouble believing it. "Not by him, I'm not!" That was it. He wasn't even getting the promised dance now.

"Good," Gryffyth replied, taking a deep drink of his beer.

They sat in silence. Not an awkward one, but it did go on too long.

"I know your father's glad you're back safely."

He nodded. "He keeps saying that."

"You doubt him?"

He drained his glass. "No." The empty glass made a soft, dull thud as he put it down on the table.

Odd wasn't the word. He was abrupt, almost off-putting, but she didn't want to leave him. Something about him kept her here, sitting so close their knees almost touched while she sipped on the beer that tasted worse with each mouthful.

"You don't think much of the beer, do you?"

Why lie. "I don't usually drink it. But I've never tasted Surrey beer and thought it was time I did."

"Or," he said with an edge in his voice, "you didn't want to ask a cripple to hobble across the room for a glass of orange squash."

"Of course not." That earned her a scowl. "I loathe orange squash."

His laugh was gloriously deep and earthy and sent warm shivers down her back. It took all she had not to rest her hands on his chest and feel the ripples coursing in his muscles.

She meshed her fingers together and clasped her hands tight.

"What do you like, Mary LaPrioux?"

"Moonlit nights, warm breezes, running across the countryside." And bathing naked in the hammerpond, but the latter she'd best keep to herself.

"Bit late in the year for all that, isn't it?"

And no doubt tactless of her to mention running. "It'll be spring before you know it." Unless they had a winter like last year's to get through.

"Are you always this cheerful?"

"Not really. It's a front I put on. I get pretty dismal when I let myself go."

He chuckled. Not quite as sexy as his laugh but very nice all the same. "That makes two of us. Maybe we should get dismal together."

Not quite knowing why, she reached over and took his hand. "Best not," she said.

He closed his fingers over hers. "What do you want, Mary LaPrioux?"

She had absolutely no idea. Other than to sit beside him and try to make him laugh again. "I wouldn't mind a cigarette." He reached into his jacket pocket, flipped the pack open and offered her one. Then produced a silver lighter. "Thank you."

"I'll swap you for the beer."

"Go ahead, but I drank out of it."

"Not got anything contagious, have you?"

"We've had problems with headlice in the school." Dear God! He was wonderful when he laughed. Wonderful but so melancholy.

"Nothing worse than that?"

"Terminal homesickness." Now why had she said that? She was saying nutty things. Stupid things.

He nodded. "I know what that's like."

Another odd, but not uncomfortable silence. Then he squeezed her hand, his fingers strong and warm around hers. She met his eyes and his odd, twisted smile. Very sexy, odd, twisted smile.

"Looks like Tom Longhurst is heading this way. I bet he wants to ask you to dance."

She bet he was too, dammit. "You'd better ask me first."

His smile faded as if snapped out. "Take your jokes somewhere else."

Hurt wasn't the word, but darn it, he'd walked into the hall and . . . "I'm not joking, funning, or teasing. It's a waltz, nice and slow." She stood, only half aware what she was saying and doing. But she kept hold of his hand. "Come on."

The woman was loony. Expecting him to dance when he could barely walk.

"It's a really slow one," she repeated.

Gryffyth glanced up. Longhurst was definitely heading his way. Damn. "If I fall and measure my length, you're going to swing for it."

"You won't."

He stood. Had to be as insane as she was. Except she walked slowly, keeping pace with his hobble, and the look on Longhurst's face was almost worth the risk of humiliating himself in public. Side by side they walked to the middle of the dance floor. He couldn't help noticing that everyone stepped back, scared he'd land on them when he toppled, no doubt. It was on the tip of his tongue to tell this woman she was mad as a hatter and go back to his beer. But she rested her hand on his shoulder, his arm curled around her waist and she smiled up at him. "Want me to lead?"

Hell, no! He took a firmer hold of her waist, clasped her right hand in his left one and, on the beat, stepped forward.

With his tin leg.

He didn't fall, didn't topple in a heap, but it wasn't exactly graceful as they bobbed and stepped. She was surprisingly strong for her slender build. When he wobbled, she steadied him. When he lurched, she added balance and held him strong. Forget fancy twirls and reverse turns. This was simple, straightforward, tread-on-your-partner's-toes waltzing. He managed to miss her shins most of the time but her toes had to be black-and-blue.

Not that her toes were really foremost in his mind. She was warm and so obviously woman, as he held her close, but not too close. Better not.

They didn't talk. He couldn't concentrate on his wayward limb—to say nothing of wayward other parts—and hold intelligent conversation at the same time. She was so intent on keeping him upright, and doing a damn good job of it too, she had a little crease between her eyes.

He'd been right from the start. This was nuts. But sheer heaven to feel her warm body in his arms. He wanted more of her. Much more. That was utterly insane.

The music stopped.

He threw sanity to the four winds. "If I had two good legs," he said, "I'd ask you to step outside with me."

"You have two good legs," she replied. "Just part of one isn't the same leg you were born with."

"It's not that simple!"

He'd snapped, but damn . . . how many people had heard?

"Nothing's simple," she replied.

He was about to snap again, but his father put his hand on his arm. "Excuse me, Miss LaPrioux, but the vicar has a few words to say. I need Gryffyth."

Thank heaven for that. Mary gladly stepped away and made a beeline for the ladies'. What had possessed her? She'd never asked a man to dance in her life. She'd said some of the most tactless, blunt and rude things possible and, dear heaven help her, she missed him already. Something deep and visceral drew her to Gryffyth Pendragon. Seemed her brain switched off and her hormones took over.

He'd as good as asked her to step outside and she'd have gone with him if his father hadn't arrived. Good thing he did, too. Or she'd have made an even bigger spectacle of herself.

And wouldn't have cared one iota.

Time to get her brains and sanity back.

Pushing open the door to the ladies', Mary bumped into a woman busy applying makeup in the mottled mirror. "Sorry!" She stepped aside and headed for the toilet.

"Hello," the woman said. Seemed rude to step in and latch the door, so Mary hesitated. "You're the new teacher, aren't you?" Mary agreed she was. "Such a brave and kindly action that was. Taking pity on that poor young man." For a few seconds, Mary stared at her, confused. "So good of you to act out of the kindness of your heart like that. I hope other young gels follow your example."

"I certainly don't," Mary replied, stepping into the cubicle, almost slamming the door, and latching it with a trembling hand. The woman thought dancing with Gryffyth Pendragon had been an act of pity! Stupid old bison! Who in their right mind? Oh, dear heavens! A shudder went down to her toes. Did everyone think that? Did he?

Why had she done it, anyway? Never, ever in her life had she approached a man so brazenly. Was it because she saw him as crippled? No! A million times, no! But why? Excessive hormones? Wildness? Stupidity? The entire village had to be talking about it! She couldn't go back out there, knowing she was the subject of wild gossip. She was being ridiculous thinking anyone really noticed. Only that woman had.

Mary's heart thudded and she was close to shaking.

What had possessed her?

And why, oh why?

Refusing to even think about it anymore, Mary emerged, thankful that now the only other occupants of the ladies' were a pair of workers from the plant, and nipped out the door. She found her coat on one of the hooks and slipped out the back entrance.

Once out in the cold, she stood looking across the church-yard in the night. Behind her were the sounds of music as the piano started up the "Dashing White Sergeant." She could either go back, or go home.

Without thinking twice, she set off down the lane toward the cottage she shared with Gloria.

Sir James Gregory meant well, Gryffyth conceded, but why all this fuss? Was coming out of that fiasco alive, apart from a missing leg, such an accomplishment? A lot of good men, his good men, were dead or prisoners of war. Seemed a travesty to be standing here in the limelight while others shuddered under fire, or rotted in prison camps. But mindful of his father's words, Gryffyth thanked everyone for the won-derful party, expressed his joy at being home again and as soon as he decently could, made his way back to his table and looked around for Mary.

Who was nowhere to be seen.

For one crazed instant of rabid jealousy he imagined she'd gone off with Tom Longhurst, but no, there he was, old Tom chatting up a redheaded woman.

Mary had disappeared. He half imagined he'd dreamt her,

but noticed the stubbed-out cigarette with her lipstick on the end. She'd been here, alright.

Peter Watson, Alice Doyle's new husband, and a nice enough chap it seemed, came up with a fresh jug of beer. "Thought you could use this," he said, putting the jug down.

"Thanks. Have a seat." Didn't look as if Mary was coming back.

"Just a tick. We'll be off home soon. Alice was out on a call last night and she's half dead on her feet."

"Didn't stop her dancing, did it?"

"You're a good one to talk. You and Mary pretty much took over the floor."

They had, hadn't they? He couldn't help the smile at the thought and the frown that she'd scarpered so thoroughly. Thinking better of her impulse, no doubt. Damn. "Been here long, has she? I don't remember her." Sounded nicely casual. He hoped.

Peter grinned. "Didn't get around to talking much, did you?"

No, she scarpered too fast.

"She's a schoolteacher. Evacuated from Guernsey with a bunch of school children. She's billeted with Gloria Prewitt, the nurse. You remember her?"

Gryffyth nodded. "Yeah."

"Fancy her, do you? Mary, I mean. Gloria's already taken."

No point in admitting he did. She'd shown clearly how she felt. He gave Peter a grin. "Gloria's taken. You grabbed Alice. All my old girlfriends gone for a burton." He took a swig of beer. "The place has changed."

"That's the war. It's changed everything."

Was that what Dad had been on about?

Chapter Five

A partisan camp in southeast Germany

Angela looked up as Bela Mestan walked into the cave hideout. "Your sister is useless. She does nothing but eat our food."

Bela looked Angela in the eye and glared. She hadn't escaped the Nazis, rescued her sister from Flossenbürg, and fled into the mountains to put up with this. "My sister cooks and tends the fire." When she wasn't sleeping as she was now. "She was near death when we came here. As you would be if you'd been treated as she was. I do enough for you to repay her food." Scanty as they were, the partisans' meager rations were slowly restoring Gela's strength.

Angela was unsatisfied. She scowled at the others clustered around the fire. "We cannot afford to feed useless mouths."

Spiteful, stupid human! Bela wanted to shriek into Angela's piglike eyes that Fairies were never useless. That they could do far more than humans, run faster, hide unnoticed, and move silently where mortals tramped and tripped.

She didn't have to.

"Leave her be, Angela," Rachel, the other woman in the group, said. "Rolf and Hans are coming back."

Rolf was their leader and his support and acceptance of Bela and her twin rankled with Angela but she went quiet, seemingly contenting herself with scowling at the fire.

The fire that Fairy magic kept hidden from mortal eyes. Bela dreaded discovery even more than her mortal companions.

Both men came in, shaking the snow from their shoulders and depositing a large bundle on the floor.

"Turnips," Hans said. "There's not much else out there. We need to take Bela with us next time. She can always find something."

Steal it, he meant, and yes, she could, sneaking into barns and villages unnoticed.

"We're hungry and cold," Rolf said, looking at the pot on the fire. "Stew?"

"Rabbit," Angela replied.

"That Bela caught," Rachel added and got a snarl for her pains.

The two men picked up enamel bowls and filled them from the pot resting on the campfire. Rolf sat beside Bela. "You and your sister speak English, don't you?"

Bela nodded. "Among other languages." French, Czech, German, and Romani, the language the Fairies shared with the gypsies. They, too, were being slaughtered by the Nazis.

"Who speaks it better, you or Gela?"

"English? Gela. My French is better than hers."

"We'll need both soon."

"What's going on?" Angela asked.

"We have two visitors headed our way. Coming from the group over by Tiefeswasser. They've been keeping them, now it's our turn."

"Visitors? Do we run a hotel now?" Angela asked.

"They're escaped prisoners of war," Rolf replied, almost snapping. "We'll house them a few days then they move on. They can't walk nonstop. They rest in safe places in between."

"Heading for Switzerland?" Rachel asked. "They have a hard walk ahead of them in this weather."

She was right. In summer the trip would have been long, but pleasant enough. This time of year it would be a very strong human who managed it on foot.

"So we've told them. They seem to think it would be easier to evade pursuit in this weather."

"They are fools!" Angela muttered. "Idiots!"

"It's worked for them so far," Bela pointed out.

"Only with help from the partisans and underground."

"How else would they escape?" Rachel asked. "We help them, they get home. After all, the British send us supplies." She looked at Rolf. "Isn't that how it works?"

Rolf nodded.

Angela let out a laugh. "We shall see. We do nothing but take in waifs who eat our food." She looked across at Gela sleeping under a rug. "Look how much good taking in these two has done us."

"Stop!" Rolf so rarely raised his voice that she went quiet. "Bela does more than her share, and now we need Gela."

"To entertain visitors."

Why did Rolf tolerate Angela? Bela wondered. Because they couldn't afford to have her leave? She knew where they and other groups hid out in the mountains.

"Two escapees from a prisoner of war camp?" Bela asked.

Hans nodded. "I spoke to one of Klaus's group. An Englishman and a Frenchman. The Frenchman is in a bad way. He'll need to rest for a while when he gets here."

Angela muttered something about the unit turning into a rest camp, but only Bela, with her heightened sense of hearing, caught it. She was wearied by the constant carping, and if it wore her down, how about Gela, who spent all day listening to the complaints and gripes?

"When will they get here?" Rachel asked. "We'll need more food. Men eat a lot." She gave Rolf a grin.

"Once we know they're coming, I can set more traps," Bela volunteered. Her traps seldom stayed empty for long. If they had noticed she never came back empty-handed, no one said anything. They were too glad for the meat.

"Let someone else take care of them," Rolf said. "We'll need you to come with us, once we get word."

Chapter Six

Brytewood

Mary made it to three-thirty, but between arch comments from Mrs. Spriggly, who cleaned the school, good-natured teasing from the other teachers, and even Petey Cannock's "Cor, Miss, never knew you could dance," it had been a long day.

But playing unconcerned and casual, and answering comments with *Yes, it was a lovely party, wasn't it?* she got through it. With a bit of luck in the next day or so, there'd be another German pilot bailout, or the buses would be cut because of petrol shortages, and the village would have far more interesting topics of gossip than her waltzing with Gryffyth Pendragon.

If only she could get over it as easily.

Just thinking about him sparked a memory deep in her body that was best forgotten, or at least totally ignored.

She'd made an exhibition of herself Saturday night but was not about to do that a second time. Ever.

Of course there was still Gloria to be faced, who'd been conspicuously absent until late Sunday evening, when Mary was on her way to bed. She'd cope. Gloria was a friend, not a village gossip.

Mary saw the last child out onto the playground, wrote the next day's date on the blackboard, sorted papers for the morning, and left with a sheaf of essays under her arm.

It was her turn to stop by Whorleigh's and get dinner, and she hoped he had something more than sausages left. They might be off the ration but they contained less and less meat each time she bought them. Speculation about the content of Mr. Whorleigh's sausages stopped dead the instant she saw Gryffyth Pendragon leaning against the school gatepost.

Heaven help her! The man had come-hither oozing out of every pore of his body. He saw her and smiled and her throat went dry. Other parts didn't. Quite the reverse in fact. This was nonsense. It was also disastrous. Just when she'd convinced herself speculation would soon die a natural death, here he was, all with his glorious self. And she had to curl her toes inside her sensible teacher shoes to stop herself racing across the playground and into his arms.

It was terrible.

Saturday, she'd half blamed it on the beer. This afternoon she had no such excuse and was only too aware that every flicker of an eyelid and every breath she took was being monitored by the mothers gossiping at the gate.

Shifting her bag on her shoulder, Mary fetched her bicycle, dumped her papers and bag into the basket and, grasping the handlebars with a grip that threatened to twist metal, wheeled it toward the school gate and Gryffyth Pendragon.

She had a good fifteen yards to compose herself.

Fifteen miles wouldn't have been anywhere near enough.

"Miss LaPrioux," he said, a glint in his eyes and a definite air of expectation, "how do you do?"

She had absolutely no idea. She was using every atom of brain space to remind herself she had witnesses.

"How do you do, Mr. Pendragon? Chilly afternoon, isn't it?"

"I hadn't noticed."

Come to that, she wasn't the least bit cold.

"Heading home?" he asked.

Was she? Yes, eventually. "I've got to stop by Whorleigh's. Gloria's teaching a first-aid class tonight and I promised to make supper."

"Mind if I walk with you?"

A sensible Water Nymph would tell him no. Even a sensible human would. If she had her head screwed on right, she'd politely wish him good afternoon, mount her bicycle and ride off.

Obviously she had several loose screws in her head. She was smiling back. "By all means. It's a bit of a detour though."

"You can always give me a ride on the back of your bicycle."

Not after all her lectures to herself about decorum and sensible behavior.

They set off down the lane, side by side. Not talking, much to Mary's relief, since every word would be registered and reported and go twice around the village long before *Children's Hour* started.

And then, as suddenly as a shift in the air or a gust of wind blowing dead leaves across the path, Mary realized she didn't care a fig what anyone said.

She might in the morning, but for now all she cared about was the man walking beside her. "Have they roped you into joining anything in the village yet?" she asked.

"To do my bit for the war effort?" he asked, a hint of irony in his voice.

"I think you've already done that, and more. I was thinking more on the lines of 'Do your bit for Brytewood.'" He gave her an odd look. Had she offended him? But dammit, he had done his bit: losing a leg. How touchy was he about it? She'd have to fumble and feel her way there. "I got roped into Mrs. Burrows's knitting circle."

"Knitting what?"

"Comforts for the troops: gloves, balaclava helmets, socks." And the occasional baby blanket or jacket that no one mentioned because wool was scarce and there was even talk it would soon be rationed, along with clothing.

"Knit me a comfort, would you?"

"What sort of comfort would you have in mind?" Didn't sound as if he was asking for a pair of gloves.

He grinned. Wicked, sexy, and definitely enticing.

She grinned back. "Like a nice pair of socks, would you?" Damn! The minute she said it, she wanted to bite the words back. "Sorry."

"Don't be. I still wear socks. I just don't have to change my right one very often."

Interesting. "Of course you have to be careful the colors match."

"Never thought of that! Do they?" He paused and hitched up his trouser legs.

"For heaven's sake!" Lord alone knew what the mums, twenty yards behind, would make of that and really, she didn't care to find out. "Put your trousers down!" As the words left her lips, her face burned as her mind registered what exactly she'd said.

"You really mean that, Miss LaPrioux?" he enquired. That he kept his voice so steady was monstrously unfair.

"Nice socks," was the best she could manage.

This was not going any way it should. No doubt he thought because she'd asked him to dance, something no nice, respectable mainland girl would do—or any nice, respectable Guernsey girl for that matter—that she was his for the taking. She wasn't. Not this afternoon, anyway.

"Happy now?" he asked as they walked on, his trousers now covering his socks.

"I'm always happy when school's over for the day and I can catch my breath."

"Hard job?"

"Not really. Not compared with many people's. But it's hard on the children at times. They get terribly homesick. Don't ever let anyone tell you children don't worry. They darn well do: about the war, what's happening to their families, their homes. The villagers have been welcoming, on the whole, but you can't avoid friction at times. Too many people in close quarters and just about everyone worried constantly."

He went quiet a minute as they turned the corner by the church and headed for the village. Why had she jabbered on about school trivia when he had so much more to cope with?

He slowed his pace but didn't ask her to. Being all manly, she supposed, but she slowed to keep level with him as they crossed the green and headed for the row of shops and the post office.

"Tell you what," he said. "Mind if I sit a bit? You nip into the shops and I'll get off my pins for a while. I'll wait and walk you home," he added. "Just as I promised."

Had it been a promise? Not that she remembered, but wasn't about to argue. In his company she felt happy, when she wasn't berating herself over tactless gaffes. "I'll go on. There shouldn't be too long a queue this time of day." Mainly because there wouldn't be much left to queue for. "Can I get you anything?"

Gryffyth thought a minute. "Any chance of a bottle of Tizer?"

"Haven't seen any for over a year. I can offer a cup of tea later. If you like."

"I would like," he replied, watching as she mounted her bicycle and rode the few yards down to Whorleigh's.

He stared at the ducks on the pond and creased his

forehead in thought. What was he doing and what did he want? He knew what he wanted but he was dealing with a nice woman here, a schoolteacher, not a girl hanging around the barrack gates. Trouble was, he couldn't quite make up his mind about Mary LaPrioux. Attractive, yes. Lovely, really, and . . . damn, might as well think it. He had been ever since he first set eyes on her. She was sexy. Sexy with a strange, unselfconscious grace. She wasn't shy. Heck, she seemed quite happy to go after what she wanted. She even seemed to fancy him, but the way she'd walked out on him on Saturday night still rankled. He didn't own her, of course—not that he'd mind a bit if he did. But she disappeared just when he wanted to see more of her.

He'd wondered if she'd thought better of it, but now she was sending the opposite signals. She hadn't minded walking through the village with him, even though she must know that news was halfway to Dorking by now.

He pulled his coat around him and he hoped she wouldn't be long. He rather fancied a cup of tea with Mary LaPrioux and he wouldn't complain about a little extra to keep the cold out.

The shop was empty. Unbelievable. Probably meant there was nothing left and everyone else in the village already knew it.

"Afternoon, Miss LaPrioux," Mr. Whorleigh said, with his customary unctuous smile. Even if she didn't know about his under-the-counter activities, she wouldn't trust him two inches. Her reason and instincts might falter on some things but not in this.

"Afternoon, Mr. Whorleigh. I need something for supper tonight. Any chance of a couple of pork chops?" Slim chance, she knew, but it never hurt to ask.

He shook his head. "No pork except sausages. I had some nice stewing steak but it's all gone, I'm afraid. Sure you wouldn't like a couple of nice sausages?"

She smiled at his choice of adjective. How often, these days, she hankered for the fat juicy sausages her Uncle Walt used to make and sell in Town. "No thanks." But what else was there? The glass-fronted cabinet was bare except for the despised sausages and a couple of . . . "What about those marrow bones?" she asked, pointing at two fat ones pushed to the corner.

"Making soup, are you?"

Why not? They had plenty of vegetables, both from their own rather meager vegetable patch and regular gifts to Gloria from her patients. "It's that sort of day, isn't it? How about some lentils to go with them?"

He was handing her the wrapped bones and a small package of pearl barley (he was all out of lentils, he claimed) when the door jangled behind her.

It was a woman Mary knew by sight. "Afternoon," she said with a smile.

As Mary tucked her package under her arm and turned to leave, the woman asked, "Aren't you that new, young schoolteacher?"

The emphasis on 'young' rather irked, but Mary ignored it and smiled. "Yes. I was evacuated from Guernsey."

"You're the one danced all night with the young amputee who just came back?"

Was it the inflation by gossip, or the anonymous tag the woman put on Gryffyth that annoyed the most? Miserable old biddy! Mary smiled. Not very sweetly. "You mean Gryffyth Pendragon, the war hero and guest of honor? Wonderful party, wasn't it? I had a fantastic time." Until she fled in embarrassment that was. But she wasn't running now, she was angry. She gave another saccharine smile, slapped their ration books and money on the counter, thanked Mr. Whorleigh for the soup bones, and marched out. As the door closed behind her, Mary caught a querulous voice saying, "I wanted soup bones, Mr. Whorleigh."

Mr. Whorleigh was welcome to her. Serve him right for selling contraband off the ration. Mary was so wound up, she almost forgot her bicycle propped outside. She tossed their dinner in the basket and rode hard back to where Gryffyth was still contemplating the dying bullrushes by the edge of the village pond.

"Something the matter?" he asked, the minute she dismounted.

"Not really," she lied. "I just get annoyed that by the time I get off work, there's precious little left in the shop."

"Things are that bad, are they?"

She nodded. "It depends. At least there's just the two of us. Some people have families to feed."

"It's funny," he said, as they set off toward her cottage, "when you're out there getting shot at, or feeling sorry for yourself in hospital, you tend to forget how difficult things are for everyone." He glanced back at the ruin of the rectory. "When did that happen?"

"Back in September. Before I came. I heard about it, though. The vicar's wife was badly hurt and died, and there were several children, evacuees, trapped in the building."

"God! They got out?"

"Yes, from what I heard, after a rather spectacular rescue by Peter Watson. He risked his life to go down in the cellar and get two boys trapped there."

He went quiet a minute, shaking his head. "It's everywhere, the war. You can't get away from it."

No point in replying. The answer was obvious, from the

ruins at the end of the green, the overcrowded classrooms, the empty shelves in the shops, the Air Raid Precautions post in the hut next to the village hall, to the painted-out signposts at the crossroads.

Would life ever be back to normal?

She wasn't getting maudlin. She had food for their supper. The sun was shining, even if a bit weakly, and the sexiest man she'd ever encountered walked beside her.

She just wished she had cakes or biscuits to offer him for tea. She bet he was as sick of dripping toast as she was.

Dr. Alice Watson, nee Doyle, wasn't satisfied. She'd used petrol to drive to Guildford to see the coroner's office but realised she wasn't going to learn any more.

"It's clear from the post mortem: she collapsed and a few hours later, died. Looked like heart failure. No reason for an inquest. Nothing to suggest foul play. She was how old?" the coroner's assistant asked.

He knew that as well as she did. "Eighty-five, but no history of heart trouble." Alice knew the conclusions were reasonable. Old Mother Longhurst might well have died of heart failure brought on by exertion. She'd ridden all the way over to Bringham and half the way back, and at her age a collapse wasn't unreasonable. Even if she had been found while she lay in the ditch, there was no saying she'd have survived. Trouble was, Alice didn't quite believe it. Not with all the other things going on at the time. But she could hardly say, "Mother Longhurst was a witch and in excellent health for her age. Could she have been killed by a Vampire, do you think?"

They'd have her in the nearest padded cell in minutes.

Convinced there was more to it, Alice had tried, without success, to discover who Mother Longhurst had visited in

Bringham. It appeared no one had seen the old woman, spoken to her, or had any idea whom she'd visited, other than, most probably, another witch. Trouble was, you just can't ask your average resident *Is there, by any chance, a practicing witch in your village?*

"Thanks," she said to the increasingly impatient assistant. "It's just a shock. She was in such good health for her age." Blooming good health, actually. Had to be on account of the herbal remedies Alice had scoffed at for so long.

"Dr. Baynes noted it in his report. Wish I could help you more, but . . ."

Yes, she knew. There was a war on, and no one had time to waste on idle speculation. Old Mother Longhurst now rested in Brytewood churchyard with generations of Longhursts, and the knowledge of the whereabouts of her magic knife was buried with her. Still, if she'd been right, and Alice had no reason to doubt it, it was no longer of use anyway.

Alice thanked the man again and went out into the street. Dark was falling. At least the promised drizzle hadn't materialized as she headed for her car parked in a side street, down by the ambulance post.

Must be a change of shift. Several men and women stood smoking outside the post and a couple of others were going in and out. A young man stepped out and Alice did a double take. He rushed past, not even looking in her direction. But it was enough. Or was it?

The wild, Pixie part of her knew where she'd seen that man before. (If indeed he was even human, which she strongly doubted.) She'd found him, badly injured and barely conscious, in Fletcher's Woods, taken him back to her surgery, called an ambulance, and he'd disappeared before it arrived. The rational scientist inside her wanted to brush that off. But couldn't. He'd disappeared fast this time. At Vampire speed? She wanted, needed to know. Not that she could actually ask point-blank.

She opened the door to the small building.

"Evening, Dr. Watson," the supervisor said as he looked up from his mug of tea. "Off home are you? Or planning to hang around and see if we can use you tonight?"

"I've got to get back, I'm afraid. I've a call to make on the way home. Thanks for keeping an eye on my car."

"Glad to do it. Terrible nowadays, it is. Stealing tires and petrol like I don't know what. As if Jerry isn't more than enough to worry about. Any time, Doctor, any time."

"Thank you so much. By the way, the young man who left as I came in. I think I know him. Possibly once been a patient?" Of a sort.

"Might be, Doctor. I dunno. He's not local. Came down to stay with cousins when he got bombed out in London, I think."

"You know his name?"

"Paul Smith. Nice lad. Been here since September. We'll miss him. We need every pair of hands we can get."

Interesting that. He'd given his name as Smith when she found him. Had to be the same man. Or same whatever-he-was. "He's leaving?"

"Yeah, got a job and is moving."

Drat, to find him and lose him again. And no one seemed to know where he was going. All she got was the name and address of his current landlady, a Mrs. Thomas. No phone number. Not too surprising. No phone laid on, most likely. What now?

Either let it drop or go prying.

She stopped at a pub nearby and got directions to a narrow street of terrace houses at the bottom of the town. Halfway down, on the left, was a gaping hole where a bomb had taken out a house, leaving the two neighbors in ruins. The house she was headed for was down at the bottom on the left.

There was no reply to her knock. No sign of a light, but that could just mean an effective blackout. Except the torn curtains weren't drawn and a cautious flash of her torch showed a small sitting room with a bedraggled fern in the window.

"You looking for Mr. Thomas?" a voice behind her asked.

Mr. Thomas. That was interesting, she'd been distinctly told landlady. "Mrs. Thomas, actually. I'm a doctor," she added. That always helped allay suspicion.

"I'm surprised you haven't heard then," the man replied. "She died last week. And then yesterday, her son, young Steve."

"Dead too?"

"That's right. The next-door neighbor found him after she noticed he hadn't taken the milk and papers in. Put his head in the gas oven, he had." The man shook his head. "He was real close to his mother. Must have unhinged him."

Maybe or maybe not. Had he put his head in the oven or *had* it put in? Was she imagining trouble?

No! Didn't Gran say to trust her Pixie instincts? And every one of them was screaming *trouble.*

"How terrible! What about his nephew, or cousin I think it was, who lived with them?"

"You mean young Paul? He left yesterday. Taking a new job he said. Dunno where."

"No forwarding address?"

"Maybe he told Steve. Won't do anyone much use now, will it?"

No, it wouldn't. And rather handy if the mysteriously disappearing Paul Smith had wanted to cover his tracks.

Alice bade the man good evening and left. She was, for a few seconds, tempted to use her medical position to ask the police if there were any bite marks on the body, but on reflection, decided against it. No point in getting a reputation as an eccentric lady doctor.

But her mind whirled over the myriad implications and possibilities, all the way home.

Chapter Seven

"Without a doubt, something's going on," Gran said, as Alice retold the events of the afternoon over dinner. "And if another of those Vampires is involved, it can't be good."

"If the Vampires are involved, you stay out of it," Peter said, not having any hope either of the women would listen. A man worried knowing his wife could, and had, dispatched a Vampire, and Helen Burrows was no better. Always in the thick of things.

"Young man," his grandmother-in-law said, "do you really think we'd sit by and let those nasty Vampires do the Jerries' work for them?"

No point in answering that. "Do you blame me for worrying about Alice?"

"Certainly not, Peter. We all worry, but better not waste too much time worrying if we have work to do."

He didn't even try to hold back the sigh. She was right. Not that it made him any happier. "You really think we have another one to deal with?" he asked Alice.

She nodded. "I'd take an oath that the man I glimpsed in the ambulance depot, was one and the same that I found injured up in Fletcher's Woods."

"You think he recognized you?" Heaven forbid! What if the creature came looking for Alice? Damn, he'd take him on with bare hands. Or bare hands and oak staves rubbed with mistletoe. He knew that worked. Not that Alice wouldn't want to take the thing on herself. He'd already seen her dispose of one, and was no doubt preparing for a repeat performance.

Alice shrugged. "I recognized him. I'd rather work on the assumption he recognized me than pretend he didn't and have a nasty encounter somewhere along the line."

Seemed a nasty encounter was inevitable, but Peter kept that to himself. "What should we do, Gran?" he asked Helen Burrows.

It wasn't just tact that had him deferring to his grandmother-in-law. Since he'd arrived in Brytewood three months ago, he'd learned a lot about Pixies.

"I think," she replied after a few moments, "that we should talk this over with Howell and Gloria. At least we can be prepared this time."

Good point. The last two had rather taken them unawares. "Think we should include Andrew?"

Alice, his love, his wife, let out a chuckle. "He'd be as easy to keep out as you'd be."

"I'm glad you understand how things are."

She grinned at him. Made him want to take her by the hand and run her upstairs with him. But Mrs. Burrows had other plans.

"Alice, you give Gloria and Howell a call and ask them to come up here as soon as they can. I'll see what I can get ready. Peter, be a love and nip out and bring me in some apples from the shed. I think I'll have time to make some tarts. And I'll check the pantry."

Peter went out, shaking his head. How could they both be so unflustered over this? Alice just ambled off to the phone and Mrs. Burrows was more worried about whether she had tarts or cake to offer when the guests arrived, than facing another Vampire.

And if there was one more, why not half a dozen? That prospect made him shudder. Once upon a time, he'd thought Brytewood was a sleepy little backwater. Most people still did. They had no idea of the existence of Pixies or Dragons or Shapeshifters. But he did, and often wondered what else was living in their midst. And if it was for, or against, them.

"Not thinking of going anywhere, are you?" Gryffyth asked, as Mary tried to ease out from under his arm.

"The stove needs making up. I ought to go out and get some coke."

"I'll keep you warm," he replied. "Wouldn't you rather sit here with me, than go out into the damp and dark?"

The note on the table when she got home, told her Gloria was spending the evening with Andrew Barron, her intended, so what was there to do? Nothing but sit here with Gryffyth and act in a thoroughly forward manner.

She was truly enjoying herself and he didn't seem to mind in the least that she was acting like a fast woman. "Stay," he whispered into her hair. "Forget the boiler."

He stroked her chin, tilting her face up to his, and brushed the pad of his finger over her lips. Her breath caught. Her heart gave a little skip of anticipation. How many times had he kissed her since he'd walked her home? She'd lost count but knew she wanted more. He bent his head to oblige.

His lips were warm—no, hot! Burning with the same heat that roared inside her, no doubt destroying brain cells, but as his lips pressed on hers, Mary had no need for brain or reason. She parted her lips and brushed the tip of his tongue with hers.

A wild need and longing raced through her, as she caressed his tongue and he pressed closer, cupping the back of her head with his hand as he kissed back. Deep.

She sensed his passion like a wild flood of pent-up desire. But was it his? Or hers? Nothing had ever felt like this. Caught in the circle of his arms, she opened herself to him, soaking in the sensations of his touch and the sheer wonder of his kisses. She grabbed him, holding him to her as she curled closer, pressing her body against his and wantonly wrapping her leg over his. He kissed even deeper, pressing his tongue against hers until she felt a building need curling in her belly as she kissed him again.

Finally she pulled away, gasping for air but none too sure she even needed to breathe. Kissing Gryffyth seemed far, far more vital than breathing. She grinned at him as he caught his breath.

"Whee."

She'd have agreed but was still gasping. She settled for leaning against his chest and luxuriating in the strength of the arm that enveloped her. "Mary, my sweet love, it was my lucky day when you crossed that hall and asked me to dance."

Hers too. "I was of two minds whether to go or not, but had promised to help."

"Dad practically had to drag me."

"I'm so glad he did."

"So'm I." They paused for a while as she leaned into him, resting the flat of her hand against his chest to feel the steady rise and fall beneath her fingers. "Tell me one thing, Mary."

She turned her head to look up at him. "What?"

"Why did you walk out on me?"

Talk about ruining the moment. Mary pulled away and sat up. The conventional prevarications like *What do you mean?* or *I don't know what you're talking about* stayed unsaid. She gave a little sigh. They were so close in the big armchair that they were side-by-side and thigh-to-thigh. Somehow his nearness and his wonderfulness demanded the unvarnished, unadjusted truth.

"I ran away."

"From me?" He looked perplexed, and worried.

"Oh, no!"

"Why then? I looked everywhere for you after that ridiculous speech by Sir Gregory and couldn't find you. I thought old Tom had walked off with you but he was busy chatting up one of the farm girls. Where the hell did you go?"

She had enough human in her to like the thought he'd searched for her, but . . . "It'll sound so silly." She repeated the woman's comments.

"You were embarrassed by her? Silly old cow!"

Embarrassed! "Good Lord, no! I was so angry. Angry at her for even thinking, much less saying that. I wondered if everyone thought I was taking pity on a poor little cripple. Then I wondered if you believed that too. That was when I ran. I couldn't bear the thought that you thought that too. I spent all say Sunday fuming. Poor Gloria went out with Andrew, partly, I think, to get away from the tension. She asked me what was wrong and if something was bothering me. I darn well wasn't telling her the truth, in case she felt that way too. Then, when I saw you waiting by the playground gate I knew it wasn't like that."

He went quiet a minute, pulling her close so she ended up curled over his lap. "I was afraid," he said, at last, whispering, "that you'd thought better of it and decided you didn't want to waltz with a cripple."

"No!" She sat up fast. "I never thought or said that and never would!"

"Well, I am, you know. A cripple." He tapped his leg below the knee. "Hear that? It's not flesh and blood."

"So what?"

"So, why did you come up to me then?"

Was he fishing for compliments? Reassurance? A bit of both? She knew from her brothers how easily men's egos got bruised. Blow it all! The truth had served so far. Might as well stay on that track. "I looked around the hall, and through a gap in the crowd, I saw you and thought . . ." Maybe this was going too far.

"Thought what?" He gave her a kiss on the forehead.

Might as well go for broke. "I thought you were the most interesting man I'd ever seen and I wanted to hear your voice."

"Interesting?" He gave her a little dig in the ribs.

"Interesting and full of sex appeal."

His laugh only added to the sex appeal. "Did my voice come up to expectations?"

"Oh! No." She paused and sighed but had a hard time not smiling. "It far exceeded, curled my toes and made me feel warm inside." Exactly where inside she was not sharing right now. Truth only carried one so far.

"I thought I was dreaming," he said after her words had faded in the quiet and the only sounds were the clock on the mantelpiece and the occasional shift of a coal in the fire. "I saw this smashing looking woman. You were gorgeous. When you came toward me, I was sure you were looking for someone else. When you stopped in front of me, I thought you were going to ask me if I'd seen Tom Longhurst."

She tried to ignore the twinge of guilt, or was it annoyance? "Why would I ask for Tom Longhurst?"

He chuckled, tightening his arm around her shoulders. "You mean you haven't met our village heartthrob? He gets all the girls. Always did. Even the sensible ones like Alice Doyle—Alice Watson as she is now. They all fall for him—hook, line, and sinker—and now, with so many men away, he reels them in." He smiled. "But you came and spoke to me."

"Naturally. Tom Longhurst isn't my sort." Too damn full of himself for a start.

"You know him?"

"I went out with him. Once. Decided not to repeat the experience."

Gryffyth's shoulders stiffened and his voice took on an edge. "He hurt you? He bothered you?"

Dear heaven, he sounded ready to meet Longhurst at dawn. "No, he didn't. I went to the flicks with him once and that was it. Just don't fancy him. He's not my sort."

Gryffyth let out a belly laugh that made his chest rumble against her ear. "You mean to say, I cut in on Tom Longhurst?"

She pulled back, sat up and looked him in the eye. "Not really. He wasn't ever in the running, although he might have thought he was."

"Glad you picked me."

"I'm glad you were there to pick."

"Right!" He didn't waste any more words, just yanked her into him, and kissed her. Several times. Kissed her with the loveliest lips she'd ever tasted. Kissed her with a wild, burning ardor that left her wanting more. Much more. And judging by the pressure against her thigh, he felt the same.

She needed more. Longed to be naked with him. To feel his warm skin against hers and his hands on her bare skin.

She'd better get herself in hand or she'd be ripping his clothes off here and now, in Gloria's kitchen.

Still, one more kiss wouldn't hurt. She leaned into him, tunneling her fingers through his hair and angling her body against his, and pressed her lips on his. Amazing that each kiss was wonderful and each one magically different: a wild sweetness, coupled with raw heat and need. His hand on her breast almost did her in. She wanted him, skin to skin. She'd be a wild, brainless fool to go that fast this soon. She barely knew him, but didn't much care. She parted her legs, draping one around him, and kissed deeper. His hand pressed her breast—then, with a swift movement, was inside her cardigan, under her blouse and stroking her breast through her bra. Then, he was inside the bra, the tips of his fingers caressing her breast, stroking her nipple, and her body went wild. A fire roared inside, burning deep in her core, firing up a wild need and ache that ground into her. Body and mind. She was made for this. So was he. To have wild sex in front of Gloria's kitchen fire.

Whoa! Not here! Upstairs. Could he manage them? Damn, she'd help him up if needed.

"Shit!" That was Gryffyth—she swore, but never that. "Damn!" He looked up as she became aware of the phone ringing in the hall. She'd been so far gone she hadn't even heard it. "Ignore it," he suggested.

She was sorely tempted. "I'd better answer it. It might be something urgent for Gloria." Not that she was here. If some villager had urgent need of the district nurse they were going to be unlucky.

Mary wobbled to her feet. So, it was true about legs going like jelly. "I won't be long." She made it into the unheated hall, realized her blouse was hanging open and pulled her cardigan together as she picked up the receiver.

"Hello, Nurse Prewitt's house."

"Oh, Mary. Is Gloria there? It's Sergeant Pendragon."

Her faced burned as she replied. "Hello, Sergeant. Gloria's not here." But I am, and half naked with your son.

"I wanted to get hold of her. Know where she might be?"

"She left a note saying she was spending the evening with Andrew."

"He doesn't have a phone in that billet of his, does he?"

She squashed the instinct to offer to ride down and carry the message. Especially as she realized Gryffyth stood nearby.

"My dad?" he mouthed.

Mary nodded. Covering the mouthpiece with her hand, she mouthed back, "Wants Gloria."

"Never mind," Pendragon went on. "If you see her, would you give her a message? Tell her I called and Mrs. Burrows needs to talk to her."

"Not ill, is she?" Silly question—if she were sick, she had Alice right there in the house.

"Oh, no. Nothing of that sort. Just needed her help. Please tell her."

"I'll be sure to. Good evening." As she hung up, Gryffyth cocked his head to one side. "Checking up on me, was he?"

"No, looking for Gloria."

"That's a mercy. I was afraid he'd had reports you'd lured me here and were keeping me prisoner."

She had to smile. "Yes, I'm such a rapacious female. These schoolteachers have to be watched."

"I intend to watch you, Mary LaPrioux. Watch you very closely. Will you come out to the flicks with me tomorrow night?"

"Alright. What's on?"

"Who cares. I want to be with you."

She felt the same. It was insane, against all good judgment and reason, but just saying goodnight to him hurt. She did not want him to leave.

He didn't either, but they both knew if he didn't go now, he'd be there until morning, and that would set village tongues wagging.

She came to the gate with him and kissed him goodnight, after lending him a spare torch.

The night was pitch dark, no moon and few stars. Just as well. She didn't want anyone but her noticing the erection he walked home with.

Chapter Eight

Hans Weiss got off the bus a mile or so outside Brytewood and ran the rest of the way across disgustingly muddy fields. But a surreptitious entry was called for. He was not about to announce his arrival until the occasion arose. A prosperous village under his thrall held definite appeal. Unfortunately, with the invasion postponed until spring, that had to wait. There was, however, the bothersome and annoying fact that somewhere in the village, lurked an entity that was lethal to Vampires.

Whoever, or whatever, it had to be eliminated first.

Weiss paused as he reached the churchyard. Using what he'd learned from Eiche and Bloch's reports and the mostly accurate maps he'd studied back in the German headquarters in Adlerroost, he took his bearings. Vampire sight being a distinct advantage in the blackout the puny mortals affected.

To the west, beyond the curve in the lane and the flint walls, lay the commercial heart of the village, and Bloch's ill-fated bakery establishment. Across the lane, twenty meters or so from the ruins of a bombed-out building, sat the one-time residence of Miss Jane Waite, nee Claudia Heitz, from the city of Aachen and loyal spy of the Third Reich. She'd died unexpectedly, shortly after her arrest. Whatever their masters might insist, there was no way in creation that Weiss would have risked her revealing his presence to her interrogators.

A pity about that. She would have been a handy contact in the village and a useful source of sustenance. But humans were in good supply.

He set off toward the village at an almost mortal pace. Listening, watching, alert to the sounds behind blacked-out windows. He paused a few meters from the pub. Stupid names these Inselaffen gave their hostelries: The Pig and Whistle indeed. There was even a painted replica of a pig standing on hind legs and playing a tin whistle on the board swinging from the eaves. For the benefit of illiterate peasants perhaps.

Keeping to the shadows, Weiss made his way into the village center—a green with a duckpond—and a little further on, several cottages and shops clustered around a crossroads, a post office, a grocer and butcher, and the newsagent that appeared to sell vegetables and knitting wool as well. Intriguing combination, not that he was really interested.

Across the road and a few meters further on, was Bloch's shuttered and abandoned bakery. Finding out what had happened to his fellow spy and brother Vampire was a matter of supreme interest. He could, of course, venture into the pub and ask around, but he'd always found women easier to tap for information. How best to approach? As a worried cousin or relative of the sadly departed Bloch? A casual friend who'd heard he was living in Brytewood? The more tenuous the connection the safer.

Who knew what malignant force lurked between the hedgerows?

A noise caught his attention. A lone mortal stepped into the road from a side lane and walked on ahead of Weiss. Some peasant trundling on home to his hovel no doubt. How opportune. Might be worth a little entertainment and it had been a good two days since he'd enjoyed warm blood.

Weiss followed the mortal until he turned off the main street and headed up a lane bordered by hedges on both sides. Nicely private from any wandering villagers. The creature limped, favoring his right leg. Some sort of cripple, no doubt, but his blood was as good as anyone's.

Weiss closed the distance between them. When he was two or three meters away, the human turned and had the effrontery to glare and mutter, "What the hell?"

Hell, indeed. Weiss stepped forward, his hands gripping the mortal's shoulders.

The man dared to struggle. For that he'd break his neck. Later. Living blood tasted richer. Living blood from a terrified human was the finest. Weiss flared his eyes and drew back his lips to reveal descended fangs, a sight destined to make strong men quail and wet themselves.

The mortal wrenched himself from Weiss's grip. An impossibility. Weiss grabbed him again; there was a clatter as the mortal's stick fell to the ground. Now, he had him! With a roar that stunned Weiss momentarily, the creature reared back, breaking Weiss's hold a second time. With a sound like rending cloth, claws raked across Weiss's face.

Claws! What creature was this?

Fast as only a Vampire could move, Weiss attacked, fangs at the ready, leaping forward into a burst of flame.

His scream echoed in his ears as pain tore through him.

This had to be the destroyer! Whatever infernal creature it was, he'd discover later—for now, with a screech of agony, Weiss fled, knowing he had to find shelter, and fast.

He buried himself in the first patch of turned ground he found. As the healing earth and dark soothed his pain, he swore vengeance.

Once he had enough strength to restore himself and identify his attacker.

Once the adrenaline rush from the part change faded, Gryffyth Pendragon found himself sitting in a heap in the lane. Fumbling around, he touched broken glass. So much for a torch to help him get home. And where the hell was his stick? To say nothing of what in hades had attacked him? What now? Could he stand without his stick? He couldn't walk without it. Unless he had Mary to support him. Thinking of her brought a smile to his lips, but didn't help his current predicament. And on top of it, the sleeves of his shirt and new jacket were in tatters.

Shit! Should he hope someone would come by on their way back from the Pig? It was hours until closing time.

The narrow beam of a shaded bicycle lamp appeared in the distance.

Help, thank the heavens, but how to explain his condition? Convince them he was drunk this early?

"Hello," he called.

"Son?"

Crikey, if wasn't his father! "Dad?"

The bicycle stopped just a couple of feet away as his father leaped off, letting it fall, and crouched over him. "What the flaming hell happened to you, son? You tripped? You shouldn't be walking home in the dark."

"Dad! There's a thing loose in the village." He'd probably think he'd been drinking, but . . . "It grabbed me and had fangs."

"Not another one? Damn! Let me help you up." He grabbed him by the armpits and steadied him to his feet.

"What do you mean *not another one*?"

"Let's get you home first. Remember I said I had things to

talk about?" Gryffyth had imagined it meant a catch-up on village gossip. "Well, unless I'm mistaken, you just encountered one of those things. Where's your stick?"

"I dropped it." What was the old man talking about?

"Hang on a tick. Here, hold on to the handlebars." His father stooped and retrieved his fallen bicycle. "That'll steady you. Now, let's see if I can find your stick." He pulled a torch from his coat pocket and shone the beam over the ground. First thing he found was the broken torch. "This yours, son?" he asked, bending down to pick it up.

"No, Mary lent it to me."

"Mary Chivers?"

"Lord, no, Dad. Mary LaPrioux. The girl I danced with on Saturday night."

"Oh." Amazing how much meaning and speculation the old man could pack into one syllable. "She lent it to you."

"Yes, Dad, she did!" And right now he was not in the mood to share the circumstances. "I'll buy her another to replace it."

"You might have a hard time finding one, son, but never mind that right now." He'd happily change the subject too. "Hang on, let's see if I can find your stick."

Less than a minute later, Gryffyth had his stick secure in his hand. "Right, son, let's get back home and get you cleaned up."

In the light of the kitchen, Gryff looked a proper fright: his hair on end, and his jacket and shirt ripped to the elbow.

"Haven't I always told you to roll up your sleeves before you shift your hands?"

"There wasn't time. And what the hell was it that came after me? You know, don't you?"

"Yes, son. I do. I should have told you before, but I wanted you to get settled, and honestly never thought it would happen like this."

"Like what, Dad? And what the bloody hell was it?"

"Don't you start swearing at me, son. You get a move on and clean yourself up and put on a new shirt. I need to call Helen Burrows and tell her I'll be a bit late, and you're coming up there with me now you're home."

"Up where, Dad?" He was in no mood for a social call.

"Up to the Council of War." He avoided more questions by going out of the kitchen and picking up the phone.

Gryffyth took off his jacket and shirt and went over to the kitchen sink to wash up.

Dad reappeared minutes later carrying a clean shirt and a knitted pullover. "Here you are, son. Put them on. At least you'll look presentable. We'll see what we can do about mending your jacket in the morning. For now, let me tell you a few things."

"Alright, Dad, but first—what do you mean by *Council of War*?"

"Just that, son. We've been under attack. And I don't just mean the Blitz or the invasion." He shook his head. "I should have told you the whole business, but things have been quiet since the last one, and I wanted you to relax a bit. My mistake."

"What *last one*?"

"There's been two of them, maybe three."

"Three what?"

"Vampires, son. Vampires."

"Spare me, Dad. Vampires don't exist." Stress of the war had addled his father's wits. "They're a figment of Bram Stoker's imagination and a scary thrill for filmmakers."

"Now look here, Gryffyth. They do exist. You just faced one. You can't deny it. Wish you hadn't had to meet it unprepared, but that's done now. And before you start on about

Vampires being fiction, remember there's a lot of people would say Dragons don't exist."

"But we're real, Dad."

"So's what you met in the lane a little while back. What did you see? Feel?"

What had he? Gryffyth shuddered, thinking back. "I felt menace, violence, and I saw a twisted face in the dark and . . . fangs."

"We've got another one to deal with. Make no mistake about it."

This barely made sense. "Dad."

He held up his hand. "Hold on, Gryff. Wait until we all get together and we'll fill you in. Alice is on her way to pick you up. I told them I was bringing you, as you have news. Bad news."

Minutes later, there was a knock on the kitchen door, and Andrew Barron, the director of the new hush-hush munitions plant, stuck his head around the door. "Evening, everyone. Alice is outside. She stopped and picked Gloria and me up first. Everything alright?"

Apart from wondering what the blazes was really going on. "Smashing."

"We're ready," Howell Pendragon said, reaching for his coat.

Gryffyth put his back on, glad the army had had the foresight to go for stout construction that held up even under a Dragon's change, and grabbing his stick, went out and down the path. Alice was driving and Gloria Prewitt, the district nurse, was sitting in the back. They all piled in and Alice headed up the hill.

"Feeling totally lost and at sea?" she asked.

"Without map or compass," Gryffyth replied.

"I understand," Andrew said, from the back seat. "It's rather complicated."

That, Gryffyth was more than ready to believe, but why they seemed to be making a party out of all this was a bit beyond him.

He hoped he was going to find out.

Seated around the kitchen table in The Gallop, Alice's home, where she lived with her grandmother and new husband, Gryffyth felt even more at sea. Mrs. Burrows, Alice's gran, bustled around pouring cups of tea and offering apple tarts and Marmite sandwiches as if they were here to plan a village fete. But instead, unless his dad had completely lost his marbles, they were holding a Council of War about Vampires.

He needed something stronger than a mug of tea.

"Well, then," Mrs. Burrows said, as she sat down. "We're later starting than we planned but it's wonderful to know we have Gryffyth with us."

Gryffyth let the nods, smiles and "Hello, Gryffyth" greetings subside. "I can hardly be with you if I've no idea what's going on."

"Howell," Mrs. Burrows said, with a look of surprise. "I thought you'd explained."

"I told him we were dealing with Vampires, that's all. And he met one in the lane awhile back. That's what delayed me."

Dad's announcement certainly livened up the meeting. Gryffyth watched shock, horror, and amazement flicker over the faces around the table.

"Damn," Peter Watson muttered. "Sorry, Gran," he added, to Mrs. Burrows. "Just slipped out, but is there no end to them?"

"Seemingly not," Gloria replied. "But don't you think we should fill Gryffyth in with what's happened? Must add," she said, with a smile in his direction, "it's marvelous to have another Dragon on our side."

At that, Gryffyth almost doused himself with tea. Dad had revealed what he was to them! After having sworn him to secrecy. What the heck was going on here? And why were they all so matter-of-fact about Vampires and Dragons?

"Just a minute," Dad said, guessing no doubt the questions his confused son was about to throw at him. "Let me start. Son, we've been under attack from a series of Vampires. They appear to come singly, which is a mercy. First one, we didn't recognize at the time—but we have a few suspicions now—he disappeared on his own. Second came and lived in the village. Caused a bit of bother, but once we worked out what we were dealing with, Alice and Peter took care of him." He'd like to know how the hell they did that but didn't interrupt. "The third one, Nurse Prewitt here did in for us, with a bit of help from Andrew. And this one, seems he just announced his arrival to you. So see what I mean about a Council of War?"

Maybe. "Alright, Dad, but assuming these are Vampires—and I'll admit I encountered something not quite right and it had fangs—but how, please, with all due respect, did Alice and Gloria kill them? Aren't Vampires supposed to be immortal?" And nonexistent, but that he'd keep to himself.

"I think, Gryffyth, we need to explain a few things," Mrs. Burrows said. "You look confused."

"Understandably," Andrew Barron said. He shot Gryffyth a look of solidarity and sympathy. "I was for a long time. I think first, you should all tell him what you are."

"Good idea." That came from Gloria. "We know you're a Dragon, like your father, but you don't know what we are."

Other than confusing him totally, no, he didn't.

"Very well, then," Andrew said, looking at Alice. "Why don't you start, my dear?"

Chapter Nine

It was well and truly dark when Paul Schmidt walked up the curving drive of Wharton Lacey and approached the tradesman's entrance. He was not feeling well-disposed to the world around him. The "lift" that Weiss had arranged for him was in a farm lorry smelling of pigs. The old codger driving it, a shriveled specimen of humanity scarcely worth biting, refused point-blank to take Schmidt up the winding drive. "I was told to drop you here," he insisted as he pulled up at the gates. "That's what I was paid for. I'm not going up to the house."

Schmidt shoved aside the temptation to rip out the man's throat for his impertinence. Unfortunately that might draw too much attention to his arrival, and anonymity was a necessary precaution. He cursed the old fool and set off walking.

And walking. The first sight of the house, as he reached a bend in the drive, was favorable. He might just arrange to keep it as his headquarters when the time came. He ran on in the dark, heading for the back door as he'd been directed.

If he hadn't been a Vampire, he'd never have found it. The night was pitch dark and the drive bordered with shrubs, but he found his way around the house, pausing by a window to overhear a boring conversation about the quality of wartime cheese. Foolish mortals, death was about to rain on them and they worried about cheese!

He made his way around the side of the house and knocked on the kitchen door.

It opened a crack and a man's voice asked, "Who is it?"

"Paul Smith," Schmidt replied. "I'm the replacement gardener. Miss Aubin is expecting me."

"Come on in then." The door was opened just enough to let Schmidt slip in sideways. "Miss Aubin!" the man called as he led the way down a tiled passage and into a vast, warm kitchen.

And there, standing by the scrubbed table in the middle of the room, was their suborned ally.

"You got here alright then," she said, looking up from rolling out pastry.

Obviously, since he was standing a few meters from her. Stupid cow! "Yes, I'm here, and with my things." He indicated the cheap, cardboard suitcase Weiss had insisted he use.

"I don't suppose you need to eat, do you?" she asked.

He was tempted to say yes, he needed fresh warm blood, but it was a little too early to break his cover. Once his job was done there would be time enough to feast. "Not right now, no."

"Jacob, here, will show you your room."

The man led him back out of the door and across the courtyard and opened the door to a stable block. He paused to light a hurricane lamp.

"Up there." He indicated a flight of uncarpeted stairs. "You'll need the lamp. There's a row of rooms, used to be for the stable lads, when we had them. Miss Aubin had the one at this end cleaned out and the bed done up for you. It's the biggest and the roof there doesn't leak. You can come into the scullery to wash. There's a tap out in the yard, but water will be warm in the scullery." He handed the lamp to Schmidt. "Anything you need?"

Plenty, but it could wait. "No, I have what I need."

"Good. See you in the morning. Servants' breakfast is at six. Gets it out of the way before the family eat. 'Night then." Without another word the man walked back to the house, leaving Schmidt holding the flickering lantern.

Damn and double damn! He was to sleep with the horses! One day someone was going to regret treating Paul Schmidt this way. Meanwhile he'd bide his time, and out here he'd be conveniently unobserved. There were two horses below if hunger became too bothersome and he could even set up his radio if he felt so inclined. How would these fools of Britishers know what he was doing?

As long as he didn't hanker for creature comforts, it was close to perfect.

Gryffyth Pendragon looked across the table at Gloria. She smiled—well, it was almost a smile. Nervous grimace might be more accurate. "I'm a Shifter," she said. "I don't become a Dragon like you and your father." Of course, she wouldn't. She was English. "At full moon and sometimes in between, I turn into a fox."

"Saved my bacon twice," Andrew said, giving her a smile. And some smile it was. He almost devoured her with his eyes. Gryffyth understood the feeling. If only Mary were here too. "She raised the alarm back in September when the first one tried to sabotage my plant, and then last month when we ran into the second one."

"You helped, Andrew. You had the stakes."

"You ripped its throat and heart out."

"You killed it, just like that?" Gryffyth asked. Seemed odd to be talking about ripping out throats and hearts, sitting at the same kitchen table where he used to do jigsaw puzzles with Alice's younger brothers when it was too wet to play outside.

"It would have killed me. Tried to kill Andrew. You've been in battle, Gryffyth. So have we."

Pretty to the point, that. Still seemed beyond reason that little Nurse Prewitt would take on a Vampire and dispatch it to wherever Vampires went. But then if she'd faced it as a vulpine Shifter, that made all the difference. "Yes. I've been in battle and seems I've come home to another one."

"The war is everywhere, son," Dad replied. "You never get away from it."

Except he hadn't faced Vampires in Norway. At least to his knowledge. "What about the rest of you?" he asked.

"I'm Pixie," Mrs. Burrows said, going on and ignoring Gryffyth's dropped jaw. "A Devon Pixie. So is Alice. Not a fact we broadcast any more than you do your Other nature, but there you are."

"What about you?" Gryffyth asked Andrew.

"Me?" The man gave a shrug and a grin. "I'm a human hanger-on. Got caught up in all this through Gloria."

"Me too," Peter Watson added. "I got involved via Alice. Nothing special about me. I'm a conscientious objector, actually."

Interesting. And he didn't sound ashamed of it.

"No false modesty, now, Peter," Gryffyth's dad said. "We all know the truth, apart from Gryffyth here." He looked sideways at his son. "There's two lads cutting up and growing to be men up in London because Peter got them out when they were trapped in the cellar when the vicarage got bombed."

Interesting, and obviously embarrassing to Peter. "I didn't do it alone," he said.

"No, lad, you didn't. But you did it, and we all know why my part of it had to be kept under wraps." Definitely a story here. He'd have a few questions when they got home, but meanwhile . . .

"Let me get this straight." Saying it aloud might help sort things out. "Dad and I are not the only Others in the village: we have two Pixies and a Shifter. Anyone else?"

"There's another," Mrs. Burrows said, "who has refused to join us."

"We managed without him, Gran," Alice said.

"That's not the point. He has skills and gifts. But is unwilling to help."

Reminded Gryffyth of the time she'd scolded him and Alice's brother, Michael, for climbing on the roof of the garage to pick fruit off the high branches of the apple tree.

"There was another, too," Alice said. "Mother Longhurst."

Gryffyth stared at her. "The old witch?"

Alice nodded. "I used to scoff at her and her magic and herbs but she really helped. She knew more than any of us about Vampires."

"Won't she still help us?" She had been a solitary, independent old biddy, but . . .

"She's dead," Alice said. "Died in rather odd circumstances."

"Killed?"

"Who knows. I think the circumstances were odd. The police who found her, and the medical officer who did the death certificate, don't."

He'd like to get the whole story about that too. "So it's us," he said, "against Vampires. How many of them and what are they doing?"

"As for how many," Alice said, "we don't know for sure. We've dispatched two, another Gran and I saw. I found him injured, but he disappeared. Seems Gryffyth encountered another."

"Or maybe the same one," Peter suggested. "Alice knows what that first one looked like."

"I saw him too," Dad added. "Helped get him into the surgery from the car. He was in a bad way. Or appeared to be. He could barely stand and had a nasty wound in his side."

"But," Peter added, his voice grim, "by the time the ambulance arrived, a couple of hours later, he'd disappeared."

"After killing Alice's dog," Mrs. Burrows said.

"And no one saw him again?" Gryffyth asked. It was only a very tenuous thread of understanding, but he was slowly coming to grips with this.

"Until this afternoon," Alice said. She went on to explain the events of the afternoon in Guildford.

"Tall, blond, and youthful," Gryffyth said, almost to himself. "And you think he's come back?"

"If he has, there's three of us will recognize him on sight," Mrs. Burrows said.

"The one I saw wasn't as tall as I am and dark haired. Didn't get a feel for age, but he was strong. Not as strong as I am. Thank heaven."

"Then there's two we have to worry about," Andrew said. "Blimey, are they never going to stop?"

"Where are they coming from might be a better question," Peter said, and nodded across the table at Gryffyth. "We ought to tell you the story from the beginning."

"Or as much as we know," Alice said, with a smile at her husband. "Go on."

"Me? Alright then. The rest of you interrupt if I miss something. First thing was, as the sergeant said, Alice finds this injured person, brings him back and he disappears. Next one appears in the village, claiming to be a nephew of a villager. (Who, incidentally, was arrested as a German spy a little while later.) There's an odd incident up at Andrew's munitions camp. Guards collapse. A couple of days later, Gloria raises the alarm again and the place is found to be ringed with explosives. We get help from Old Mother Longhurst. She gave Alice a magic knife and told us what to do to get rid of him. It worked." He gave a shudder as if the memory wasn't one to be revisited more than absolutely necessary.

In the pause, Andrew took up the story. "The second one came and set up as a baker. Until . . . well, to cut it short, we twigged him. He tried some nasty tricks with Alice." Gryffyth noticed Peter squeezing Alice's hand. "The long and short of it is Gloria did him in."

"Alright," Gryffyth asked, "aren't Vampires supposed to be immortal?"

"But not indestructible," Alice said. "A magic druid knife and mistletoe work best, with stakes as backup." She shrugged. "It's not easy."

He'd worked that much out for himself. "Where do they come from and why Brytewood?"

That earned him a good minute's silence. "At a guess," Mrs. Burrows said, getting up to fetch the teapot and refill everyone's cup, "they come from the Jerries. Who else would want to sabotage an essential munitions camp?"

Very good point. Gryffyth took another tart from the plate Andrew handed him. Mrs. Burrows's cooking was the utter best. Even in these times. "So, you think this thing that went for me is another Vampire?"

"Seems like it, son." He stared at his father. This was really too much.

"So what now?"

"Now we all finish our tea and go home, I think," said Mrs. Burrows. "It's getting late, and we all need a good night's sleep if we have to deal with Vampires in the morning."

"I thought they couldn't come out in daylight?" Gryffyth said.

"That's a myth," Dad replied. "Made up by the talkies. This lot seem to wander about as they darn well please."

No one contradicted him. "Anything else I need to know?" Crikey! He'd thought Norway was tough. Seems there was trouble as bad lurking in the Surrey hills. "Have these Vampires killed, apart from your dog, Alice?" He remembered old Susie, who used to race across the fields with them.

The silence and nods answered that one.

"Now then." Mrs. Burrows stood up. "That's enough for one night. It's late. Gryffyth knows what's going on here. What we all have to do now is keep our eyes and ears open."

Gryffyth felt frankly lost as Alice dropped them at the gate and he hobbled up to the front door.

"You alright, son?" Dad asked. "No harm felt from the attack?"

"I think I did more harm to him . . . it."

"Maybe you did, son, but nothing seems to stop them for good."

"Except Alice and Gloria."

"Yes. Good girls they are. Strong in magic, both of them."

"Pity we don't have more on our side."

Dad opened the door. "There's another, son."

"The person Mrs. Burrows mentioned?"

"Not him," Dad replied, taking off his coat and giving Gryffyth a hand with his. "That's Whorleigh, a self-serving, no-use creature if ever there was one. There's someone else, son." He gave a smile. "You've met 'em and you'll work out who it is by the time we need 'em. They'll help us beat the Boches."

"What in heaven does that mean, Dad?"

"Think about it. Want a mug of cocoa before we turn in?"

Cocoa? How could Dad talk about Vampires, German spies, undiscovered Others and cocoa at the same time? And come to that, what was it with Whorleigh, the grocer?

And he'd thought it would be quiet, maybe even a bit dull back home. Shows what he knew.

As he undressed and got into his pajamas, Gryffyth wondered briefly who this mysterious, not Whorleigh, Other was. But what he really wondered was what Mary was doing. Undressing too, he hoped. He liked the thought of Mary with her clothes off. If her whole body was as smooth and warm as her breasts under his fingers . . .

He'd better watch it or he'd never be able to sleep on his stomach.

Chapter Ten

Bela woke. Gela was calling her. Not out loud, but by the mind link they shared. Quietly, so as not to rouse the others, Bela crept over to her sister's side. She was flushed and her forehead clammy. At her sister's touch, Gela opened her eyes. They were cloudy with fever but the voice in her mind was clear.

"You must go, Bela."

"I'm not leaving you."

"Soon, that will not be a consideration."

"No!" She spoke aloud, but no one seemed to stir. Careful to keep her words just between their minds, Bela went on. "No, sister. I will see you get well."

"You took me out of that hell, that was enough. I will not die there. That, sister, is a gift."

"You will get well."

Gela shook her head. "I'm dying, Bela. Maybe not tonight or tomorrow, but I'm dying. Joining Mama and Papa and our brothers. So you must go."

"I'll never leave you."

Gela gave a great sigh, her chest heaving with the effort. "You must. You have to tell the world what's happening. Remember Onkel Franz and Tante Elise? They will believe you."

Onkel Franz and Tante Elise. Bela remembered them. Friends of her parents. Human friends. He was a doctor of economics at the University of St. Gallen. And might as well be on the moon for all her hope of getting there. Gela's mind was wandering. "Hush. Go back to sleep."

"Promise me you will leave. It isn't safe for you here."

It wasn't safe for any of them. Another partisan group had been flushed out just a week or so ago, but it was safer than wandering the mountains in winter. "We'll talk about it in the spring. Meanwhile, rest."

"Promise me," Gela insisted, grabbing Bela's arm with a strength that belied her weakened body.

"I promise." That seemed to satisfy her. Gela shut her eyes and in a short while her breathing slowed.

"She's alright?" It was Rachel.

"Yes." Bela sat back on her heels, watching her sister. "She was restless but is sleeping now." Or was she?

"Get some rest yourself. You do more than the men when you're awake."

She could, she was Fairy and needed little sleep. The vile Nazis had imprisoned her, and let those filthy Vampires assault her, but they'd fed her well, and she'd been warm. If they hadn't, she'd be sick and weak like Gela. She could never leave her sister.

"She's not well, is she?" Rachel whispered.

"They starved her, what do you expect?"

"They are animals. They make me ashamed to be German. We have to beat them. How do people sit by and let these things go on?"

"Maybe they don't know?"

Rachel shook her head, her face set and hard. "We know. They must. Don't they notice neighbors disappearing? My best friend's family was taken. I told my parents we had to hide, or leave. They wouldn't listen. Even when the SS took my eldest brother, my parents still refused to leave their home, my father's shop. I fled. I left them, Bela. Sometimes I ask myself if I was a coward to run, but if I'd stayed . . ."

"They would have taken you too. This way you fight them. A few railway lines, a few stolen guns at a time."

"I worry about about my family. Seeing you and Gela, I dream about rescuing them, but how could I get them all out?" Rachel shook her head, blinking back tears. "I don't even know where they are. How did you know where to find Gela?"

"They boasted to me." True as far as it went. No way in creation could she tell Rachel the truth.

"But how did you get her out?"

She repeated the answer she'd given weeks back when they first joined the partisans. "I had help. But I gave my word never to tell who it was." Rachel wanted reassurance that she, too, would find and rescue her family. It was a vain hope. "No mere mortal, alone, could get anyone out of those hells."

Rachel nodded and settled back to sleep with a sigh. Bela lay awake a long time, worrying and thinking, until finally sleep overtook her.

"Hey, wake up!" It was Angela. Bela blinked the sleep out of her eyes and propped herself up.

"What is it?"

"Your sister's dead!"

"What!" Bela was out of her blankets and across the hut in seconds. Forgetting caution, she moved fast as only a Fairy could, and knelt by her sister's side. It was true. She didn't need to touch Gela's cold hand or breathless body to know. There was no life force in her sister, no energy. She was gone. Just as she said she would be.

"At least she won't be eating our food anymore."

"Be quiet, Angela," Rolf snapped. "Haven't we all had dead to mourn?"

"You seem really glad she's dead," Rachel said. "I wonder if you helped her along."

"No!" It was a cruel and unfair accusation, and besides, Bela was not having an argument over Gela's corpse. "She didn't!"

"What makes you so sure?" Rachel persisted.

"Look at her," Bela replied. "She died at peace. See her face." She was smiling. Gela had given up on life. "I want to bury her."

"In this weather?" Even now, Angela didn't stop. "You can't dig this frozen ground."

"I can and will. Rolf, may I use the spade?"

When it came to the point, Rolf and Hans helped. It was hard digging the frozen earth, but between them they managed, and the men helped her carry Gela out into the cold. They didn't use a sheet or blanket to cover her. They needed them for the living. Besides, once in the ground, Gela would return to dust faster than a human would. Fairies didn't decay, just melted back into the earth that sustained them in life.

It began snowing as they shoveled the earth back. By the time they started back toward the hideout, it was coming down in great flakes.

"Bad weather for those escapees to be crossing the woods," Rolf said, brushing the snow out of his eyes.

"Covers their tracks, though," Hans replied.

All this talk about the two escaped prisoners of war, but they never arrived. They'd no doubt been killed or recaptured. But if they did come, Bela was ready. There was nothing to keep her here. Not anymore.

Chapter Eleven

Mary was sitting by the kitchen fire, sipping cocoa and thinking about Gryffyth Pendragon's hand stroking her breast. On the radio, Lord Haw-Haw hectored on about the failure of the British government to protect its cities, and the inevitable capitulation of the British Empire, but it pretty much went over her head. One lone, derisory voice from Berlin hadn't a hope of distracting her.

She let him blether on, until the door opened and Gloria came in, looking tired. "Turn that thing off, please. I can't cope with him tonight."

Unlike her, Gloria usually answered the radio back, giving cheeky, even rude responses to his pronouncements, but tonight she looked downright drawn as she hung up her coat.

"Want some cocoa?" Mary asked. "There's enough milk." Gloria nodded and Mary jumped up. "I'll make it for you. Have a seat, you look done in." Gloria usually came back glowing from an evening in her fiancé's company. "Something wrong?"

Gloria hesitated a minute, as if sorting out her thoughts, or deciding what to say. "I'm just tired. This war's getting me down. I'm beginning to wonder if it will ever end." Mary understood that feeling. Gloria gave a weak smile. "Sorry, I shouldn't be moaning to you, should I? I've got a roof over my head. I'm safe in my own home—or as safe as anyone is these days, and I'm a proper Millie Moaner."

"Best let it out. It's getting me down too." Or had been until this afternoon. "Are you hungry? I stopped by Whorleigh's on my way home. I didn't realize you'd be out until I saw your note." Drat! That sounded like a complaint. Not what she'd intended. "It'll be good tomorrow. It's soup."

"You made soup?"

"Beef and barley and veg. Or rather, barley, beef and veg. All Whorleigh had was marrow bones."

"I bet he had more. If you'd been Mrs. Chivers or Miss Wallington, he'd have found a couple of nice pork chops."

"They're willing to pay the extra."

"Well, I won't, on principle. Makes me cross that he's raking in the money hand over fist while most of us keep the rules."

Mary agreed, but . . . "Doubt he gives a hoot about what we think. And there was a good bit of meat left on the bones."

"His mistake, no doubt."

Gloria really did have it in for him. Right now Mary was far too ecstatic, her mind too full of Gryffyth to get wound up over local black-market rackets. "Forget Whorleigh, let me make you a mug of cocoa. Sure you don't want any soup? There's lots."

"Let's keep it for tomorrow. Cocoa's perfect. Thank you, Mary, you're a love."

Something was up. No doubt about it. It wasn't like Gloria to collapse into a chair like that.

Cocoa ready, Mary handed her the mug. "Something the matter?" she asked, as she sat down opposite Gloria.

Gloria looked down at the mug between her hands. After what seemed like an age, she shook her head, "No." Her entire body said yes. "Just tired, but tell me." Her smile looked as if it took a good deal of effort. "Village gossip has Gryffyth Pendragon walking you home from school."

Heat flared from the base of Mary's neck to the roots of her hair. Her throat all but closed up but by dint of hard swallowing, she managed to say, "Oh, yes. I saw him when I came out, so we chatted a bit. I asked him in for a cup of tea." Might as well add that. Someone had no doubt timed to the second how long he was in her house.

"Just a cup of tea?" Gloria asked with a grin, the drawn look fading from her eyes. "You didn't offer him anything else? A little more hospitality?"

"Well, yes. But we stopped short of wild sex on the kitchen table." It was so good to hear Gloria laugh. Whatever bothered her had gone.

"I don't recommend the table, far too uncomfortable. I much prefer the sofa in the parlor. You'll need to light the fire first though. Passion only heats you up so much." She took a sip of cocoa. "So," she said, going thoughtful. "You like him?"

"Yes."

"Glad to hear it. After the way you gave Tom the brush-off, I was beginning to worry about you."

"Gryffyth Pendragon and Tom Longhurst are hardly comparable. Gryffyth hasn't run around sleeping with half the county."

"I don't think 'sleeping' is the operative word. On the other hand, Gryffyth hasn't carried on with every female in the village under ninety."

"Hasn't he?"

Gloria took a long drink of cocoa, no doubt to drag this out. "No," she replied, at long last. "Not as far as I know. Mind you, I've not lived here as long as Alice. She'd know."

No doubt, but Mary wasn't quite up to asking the doctor for intimate details of Gryffyth's past.

Gloria finished her cocoa and rinsed out the mug. "We

might as well both go to bed." Best way to keep warm. "You know," she said, as she reached for the tea towel and dried the mug, "people are going to talk. You ask him to dance and then he picks you up from school."

"So they gossip, Gloria. I'm used to village life. And what's to talk about? We're not going to have sex on the village green."

"But you are going to have sex?"

"I sincerely hope so!"

Lying in bed, the covers pulled up to her nose to keep warm, Mary wondered at her bluntness. She liked and trusted Gloria, but why had she been so shamefully honest? Because it was darn well true. She had a bad case of Gryffyth Pendragon, and she hoped she never recovered. He was a damn good kisser. He'd surely be fantastic once they got their clothes off.

As the sun rose, Sam Whorleigh pedaled his bicycle up past the church. He enjoyed being out and about while most people were still getting up or eating breakfast. Mind you, after that nasty shock a few weeks back, when he'd found the doctor's car in a ditch and her unconscious inside, he avoided the shortcut through the allotments. There'd been something downright wrong about it all.

He took the road these days.

Passing the winter-bare churchyard, he glanced at the tower, where the bells hadn't sounded in over a year. He glanced at the bombed-out rectory. Stared and clutched the handlebars in a knuckle-whitening hold. The earth over by the ruined tennis court was shifting, as if a giant mole were raising a molehill. Like a fool, Whorleigh stopped. Staring as the earth opened and, in a spray of wet earth and tufts of grass, a creature emerged. A creature that emanated the same menace as that baker had. The thing spied him and shot toward him, eyes blazing and fangs gleaming.

Leaping off his cycle and letting it fall to the ground, Whorleigh ran. Fast as only an elf can move, he leapt onto the church roof—the lychgate he'd used once before being far too close for safety—and lay panting on the leads, his fingers grasping the stonework until the thing ran off with a snarl and a quite unnecessary kick at the discarded bicycle.

Whorleigh jumped down, on the far side from the lane. No point in risking an early riser seeing him. One look at the twisted front wheel and fork of his bicycle and it was obvious he'd be walking to work from now on. Damnation! He couldn't even wheel it. He propped it against the churchyard wall and walked on up into the village center, his mind whirling.

There was no denying that he'd seen something. Just as there was no denying, no matter how hard he tried, the strange incident with the baker who'd so mysteriously disappeared last month.

What sort of Others were these, invading his bailiwick? And why him? And what were they after?

The memory of a challenge old Mrs. Burrows had thrown at him still burned. He wanted to keep himself to himself and put away for a rainy day. Looked as though a tempest was about to break.

When he reached the village center, he walked right on past his shop and headed up the hill toward The Gallop. Much as it went against the grain, perhaps he needed to talk to the doctor's grandmother after all.

Mary LaPrioux lay awake, looking at the ceiling and summoning the courage to get out from under the warm covers into the unheated bedroom. She'd have to get up soon; it was her turn to take the damper off the boiler and make tea. But five more minutes . . .

Forty-five wouldn't be enough to sort out her thoughts. Maybe she needed another nocturnal trip out to the hammer-pond to hope the water would clear her head. Was it possible, rational, or sane to fall in love like this? Maybe not, but it had happened. She burned for Gryffyth Pendragon's touch, longed for him to wrap his arms around her, and ached deep inside at the thought of another kiss. Or twenty. Or a thousand. Or a lifetime of them.

Whoa there!

She put a foot out from under the covers. Maybe the chilly morning air would cool her ardor.

It just cooled her foot.

What was wrong, or maybe right, with her? She was pretty much prepared to offer to bear Gryffyth Pendragon's children and she had no idea if he was even interested.

Alright. He was interested. She'd noticed that much even when they were dancing. She'd bet the next month's butter and sugar rations that it wasn't part of his wooden leg she'd felt as he held her close. And as for when they'd snuggled up and shared the big armchair by the fire: He'd been very interested.

Question was, was he interested in the same way?

One way to find out was to ask, but brazen as she was feeling right now, that was a bit overmuch. He'd probably run a mile.

She smiled. Wrong word. Running was something Gryffyth wasn't likely to be doing.

Oh! Darn it! Life had been so nice and calm and settled. Or at least as nice and calm and settled as was possible in the middle of a war, with her home invaded by the blasted Jerries.

On the other hand, if there hadn't been a war, and Guernsey

invaded, she wouldn't have evacuated, wouldn't be here in Brytewood, and would never have met Gryffyth.

She sort of owed nasty old Adolf a thank you.

She also owed Gloria a cup of tea.

Bracing herself for the cold air, Mary grabbed her dressing gown off the foot of the bed and pulled it on, then swung her legs out from under the covers and felt around for her slippers. Feet in and cozy, she got the rest of herself out of bed, stood up, tied the sash of her dressing gown and pattered downstairs.

The boiler had gone out.

At least they'd fetched in coke, last thing. She didn't have to go outside and freeze the marrow of her bones. It was so cold here in England. How she longed for a nice damp, rainy island winter. None of these awful heavy frosts. The children might be excited at the prospect of snow. She was less enthusiastic.

She riddled the boiler hard, tucked in a few twists of paper and a handful of kindling, tipped in a little coke and reached for the matches on the mantelpiece. Her hand froze in midair at the sound of a scream of utter terror.

Chapter Twelve

"Gloria!" Mary yelled, fumbling with the bolts on the back door before grabbing her coat and pulling it on as she ran down the garden path in her slippers.

The postman was staggering to his feet. His bicycle lay on its side, wheels still spinning and the contents of his mail-bag scattered across the lane. Mary grabbed his arm and helped him up. He was shaking, ashen-faced and gasping. Had to be shock.

"What is it?" Gloria had her coat on over her nightgown but her feet were bare.

"I don't know. Something happened to him," Mary replied. "And you need to put something on your feet."

"A monster, I swear it was," the postman muttered, and started shaking even more.

"Come on inside," Gloria said. "I'm Nurse Prewitt. I'll look at you and we'll call the doctor if we need to."

"I know who you are, Nurse. Deliver your post, don't I?" He gave a weak effort at a smile. "Hell, the post! Sorry, ladies," he added.

"Don't worry about that," Mary said. "I'll pick it up. Gloria, you get him inside."

Didn't take long. Mail bags were sturdy and held together. Those convicts did a good job on them. Mary gathered up the scattered letters, including a few that ended up across the lane. She hitched the bag on her shoulders and picked up the bicycle, wheeling up the path, and went back into the cottage.

By now she was freezing.

The cold kitchen didn't help but the fire had at least caught. Mary filled the kettle. "We'll have you a cup of tea," she promised. "The place should warm up soon." To hasten that along, she lit the gas oven and left the door wide open. Might not be considered as conserving all possible fuel, but shock victims needed warmth. "A nice cup of tea will pick you up."

He didn't look as if it would, though. Still sickly pale, he sat shuddering in a chair while Gloria put a blanket around his shoulders.

"Sorry to be such a pest, Nurse," he muttered, "but it were awful."

"What was?" Gloria asked, looking at a nasty bump on his forehead and a graze across his cheek.

"It. The thing!" he whispered. "Honest, I'm not making this up."

"I'm sure you're not, Mr. . . ." She paused.

"Bowles," he replied. "Harry Bowles at your service, Nurse."

"Don't worry, Mr. Bowles, as soon as that kettle boils we'll have you a cup of tea, and once I have some warm water, we'll clean up those cuts. You hit the road hard."

"I'm not surprised, Nurse. Scared the willies out of me, it did. Never seen anything like that in my entire life. And let me tell you, I saw some bad things back in the trenches."

"What did you see?" Gloria asked.

He shuddered again. "Beats me. It were fast, nasty, and I felt scared out of my wits as it passed."

"Did you see it?" she went on.

"I felt it, that were more than enough, Nurse. It came over me all dark and nasty like. Moved too fast to see." He paused. "You think it was some sort of weird weather: one of those there tornados like they have in America?"

"I've heard they're terrifying," Gloria agreed.

There was something not quite right here, though Mary had no idea exactly what. Perhaps it was Gloria's utter calm and acceptance of the bizarre story. Just then, the kettle started boiling. Mary reached for it, put a little hot water in a bowl, added cold from the tap, and handed it to Gloria. After she fetched Dettol and a cloth, Mary reached for the teapot. She darn well needed a cup.

She'd never heard anything like that scream in her life. Postman Bowles had been utterly terrified. By what?

"What do you think it was?" Mary asked Gloria after Mr. Bowles had gone, saying he couldn't hang around, he had the morning post to deliver.

"I don't know," Gloria said as she looked at the letters he'd left them. "This one looks a bit the worse for wear." She held up a beige envelope.

"It must have been one of those that ended up in the road." It wasn't like Gloria to be this casual over an injury. Was she unconcerned or distracted?

"What do you think it was?" Mary repeated.

Gloria shrugged and tore open the envelope. "I really don't know."

"But a tornado?" Aside from the fact she doubted one had ever been seen in Surrey, this was too much like the Wizard of Oz. Only poor Mr. Bowles hadn't gone any further than the road beneath him.

"Really, Mary. Odd things happen in wartime. He was fine when he left."

If Gloria wasn't actually lying, she was hiding something. Mary had looked too many short liars in the face not to recognize one her own size. But why? There had been something out there. As she ran down toward the gate, Mary had felt vestiges of a horror, like cobwebs dissipating in a breeze. But there'd been no breeze, no cobwebs, just one scared-out-of-his-wits postman and a woman Mary thought her friend, lying.

"It was a bit odd, don't you think?" Mary persisted. "Should we let the police know?"

"What could they do? Postman falls off his bicycle, it's hardly criminal or a national emergency, is it? You really think it was something we should report?"

It was on the tip of her tongue to say *Yes, I do. It was something out of the normal run. I know. I'm one of those somethings.* But she bit it back. How could she explain to sensible, down-to-earth Nurse Gloria about Water Sprites?

"Want some toast?" Mary asked instead. "Since we're both wide awake, we might as well have breakfast while the water warms up."

It was only after Mary got to school and settled her class, that she paused to think, and then remembered Gloria's cut and grazed feet. She hadn't treated them. Oh, well, she was the nurse after all, and maybe they weren't as grazed as Mary remembered. It had been a rather chaotic incident after all.

* * *

"So, Sam Whorleigh, you're scared and so you need my help." Not very charitable a greeting, but Helen Burrows forgave herself. The shopkeeper wasn't her favorite person at the best of times, and he'd been quick enough to refuse to help when she'd asked.

"Lord alone knows if anyone can help, but you . . ."—he hesitated as if searching for the right words—"intimated you understood about these things. So I came to you. You believe I saw that thing?"

"Oh yes, you saw something," she replied.

"A Vampire," Alice said.

Whorleigh's face was a picture. If he'd been scared before, now he was positively petrified. A nice woman wouldn't smile at his obvious terror. Helen Burrows accepted she wasn't truly nice.

"Alice is right," Peter added.

They'd both come downstairs to her summons and now they all sat around the kitchen table. She'd made a pot of tea, for Alice and Peter really, not Sam Whorleigh, but she'd offered him one (he'd had a shock after all) and he was now on his second cup.

"You're kidding me," he replied, with obvious scorn. "Vampires! Phooey!"

Little did the man (or whatever he was) know.

"If not a Vampire, what do you think you saw, Mr. Whorleigh?" Peter asked.

"I dunno, but it couldn't be a Vampire. They don't exist."

Alice stood. "We know otherwise, Mr. Whorleigh. I'd stay and explain but I have calls to make and had better get dressed. You don't seem permanently injured. Thanks for the tea, Gran."

"You need something to eat," Mrs. Burrows said.

"I'll grab some toast on my way out. I must get going, I've

two calls up on Ranmore. Peter," she said, and smiled as her husband looked up at her, "be a love and explain things to Mr. Whorleigh, or at least as much as you think he can stand."

Sam Whorleigh scowled as she went out. Damn it. He'd never liked her. She'd been a know-it-all child, and hadn't improved. One reason why he was darn glad he never needed a doctor. The last one he'd want treating him was stuck-up Alice Doyle-now-Watson.

"What is going on?" he asked, looking at Peter Watson. Maybe he'd get it straight from a man.

"As to what's actually going on, we're not certain, but as to what you saw, I believe Alice was right. We suspected there was another Vampire in the village last night and seems it must have gone to earth in the vicarage ruins. I think you've been very lucky, Mr. Whorleigh." He paused to take a mouthful of tea. "How did you happen to get away from it so easily?"

"Easily?" he echoed with as much scorn as he could muster while shuddering inside. Had to be the casual mention of *another* Vampire that gave him the heebie jeebies. Was this one the same as Block?

"Yes, easily," the man repeated. "They move awfully fast. Faster than humans can."

"What exactly are you implying?"

"You know exactly what he means, Sam Whorleigh. How did you get away unscathed? And don't pretend you don't understand me!"

Damn Mrs. Burrows, the woman never let up. "I got up on the church roof, so there!" Let her chew on that one!

She just nodded. "Good. You're not my favorite person, Mr. Whorleigh, but I'd hate to think he'd caught you."

So did he, but that he wasn't admitting out loud. "Right." That was a lie if ever he'd uttered one. Nothing seemed right, and coming here had been a mistake. Or had it? At least they believed him. Anyone else would have believed he'd started drinking before breakfast. "What's to be done?" He had to ask even if he wasn't sure he wanted to know.

"What would you be willing to do, Mr. Whorleigh?" Peter Watson asked. "Are you willing to take a few risks? Stick your neck out a bit?"

"What do you mean?"

"Well . . ." The man was too damn relaxed for Whorleigh's idea of comfort. "Let me explain. Another cup of tea please, Gran?" There was a pause while Mrs. Burrows poured tea and Whorleigh gritted his teeth. Damn the man. He was doing this on purpose. "You accept what you saw was a Vampire?"

Did he? "There's some would say they don't exist."

"Don't let's waste time, Mr. Whorleigh. You saw one. I've seen more than one. They exist. Just as you do. Trust me."

What did he mean by *just as you do*? And besides, "Why should I trust you?"

Mrs. Burrows put the teapot down with a clink. "For goodness sake, stop this, Sam Whorleigh! You came in here white as a bleached sheet and scared out of your wits after an encounter with a Vampire. Now, with a couple of cups of tea inside you, your tune has changed. Vampires exist. Just as you and I exist and you'd better get used to the idea. If you're here to join us and help get rid of these pests, fine and good. If not, you can just go back down that hill and open your shop." She scowled at him. Probably casting some curse or other. "And by the way, what are you?"

Nosy old bat. "What are you?"

"I'm Pixie. And you?"

"A Pixie?"

"Oh, come off it. Are you going to say they don't exist either?"

"No." Not much point and who'd make it up? Pixies indeed!

"Well, then?"

The woman never gave up. "I'm an Elf." And he'd damn well deny it to his dying breath if anyone said a word about it beyond these walls.

"An Elf." She smiled. "Wonderful! Are there any more of you around?"

Did the questions never end? "If there are, I've never met one."

"You came into your powers on your own?"

Was it any business of hers? But since she'd asked and this seemed to be a morning to tell all, "I had a grandmother. She taught me most of it. My dad died in the trenches and I never knew who my mum was. I heard she scarpered off when I was born. My grandmother died ten years or so back. That was when I moved here and took over the shop."

"Well, Mr. Whorleigh, I don't see why Elves and Pixies can't work together."

What at? Vampire hunting? That prospect sent a lump like cold lead into his gut. "We'll see. Tell me. You're Pixie. That means the doctor is, right?"

"That knowledge is for you and you alone, Sam Whorleigh."

He wasn't barmy. "Fair enough. I wouldn't want my Other nature bandied about the village any more than you would, but . . ." He turned to Peter Watson. "You're a Pixie too?"

"Good lord, no." He shook his head. "No such luck. Just married to one. I'm a conscientious objector."

That's right. There'd been that nasty incident in the Pig and Whistle back when he first arrived. "So, what next? Is that thing going to come after me again?"

"If he does, I think you can cope, Mr. Whorleigh," Peter

Watson said. "If you move faster than a Vampire, you've got a head start on the rest of us."

"Maybe, but what if he finds out where I am? I'm not exactly hidden, am I?"

"None of us is, Mr. Whorleigh, but we've beaten two of them. We'll get this one."

"How do you beat them?" Did he really want to know? Moving far away seemed a good idea, but where could he go? He had a nice, tidy business here.

"A combination of magic, knowledge, brute force and luck," Peter told him.

"We'll have to have a meeting. With everyone," Mrs. Burrows said. "Tonight's out—I've a committee meeting about the children's Christmas party." Committee meetings when they had a Vampire on the loose, Whorleigh thought. Honestly! "How about tomorrow? Wednesday?"

It was the night he played cards, but this was more important than winning a few bob. Or was it? "Why are we meeting?"

"For you to meet the rest of us and so we can set up a plan to find out where this one is lurking, what he's up to and how to get rid of him."

That was all? Why not just take on the whole bloody German war machine while they were at it? But he was intrigued. Especially at the mention of the others. Who the hell were they? Knowledge was always useful. "I'll be here Wednesday. What time?"

"Eight o'clock," she replied.

He'd stay in the shop and walk on up. If he couldn't cadge another bicycle before then. "I'll come."

"Good," she replied, looking unnervingly self-satisfied.

"It's good to have one more on our side," Peter Watson said, holding out his hand.

Whorleigh took it and was about to ask who else was

involved, when the door opened and the doctor put her head around the door. "I'm off, Gran. Might as well get an early start. Mr. Whorleigh, would you like a lift down into the village?"

"Thank you, Doctor, I would." Beat walking.

Peter kissed Alice goodbye and watched them drive off. He'd better get going. He was due up at the clinic at the munitions plant at eight. "Odd chap, isn't he, Gran?"

"Very," his grandmother-in-law replied. "I'm none too sure about him."

"But you pretty much press-ganged him into joining us."

"Better have him on our side and close enough to watch than starting trouble out there. And he was truly scared. He might not be much use—they say Elves are flighty at the best of times. But one never knows. He's got nerve enough to break the law. I wonder how he gets away with it so blatantly."

"Perhaps it's part of being an Elf?" Ouch, that was a bit flippant.

Didn't seem to bother her. "I wish I knew more about them. There's so much I don't know about Others."

"We've two Pixies, two Dragons, a Were-fox and now an Elf. Anyone else around, do you think?"

"I think so," she replied.

Peter wondered about that as he pedaled his bicycle up the hill toward the heath. Who else might be Other?

Chapter Thirteen

"Well, son. Got any plans for today?" Howell Pendragon asked, as he handed Gryffyth a bowl of porridge.

Gryffyth paused, spoon in hand, and swallowed to ease the lump in his throat. This was his father he was talking to, not the Reverend Roundhill! Why the stupid rush of nervousness? "I'm meeting Mary after school and we're going to the flicks. Thought we'd have dinner out, too."

His father stared, his hand paused in midair on the way to the teapot. "Like that is it, son?"

Gryffyth took a taste. Porridge was bland without sugar, but he'd rather put his sugar ration in his tea. Swallowing a mouthful or two gave him time to think. Didn't help. "Like what, Dad?"

Howell picked up the teapot and poured. "Don't give me that, Gryff. I've never known you to take a girl out unless you were smitten. She seems a nice girl. Like her, do you?"

Gryffyth took the cup his father handed him. Might as well go for broke. "Dad, I want to marry her."

His father's familiar face broke into a grin and his eyes sparkled. "And how does she feel about that idea?"

"Give me a chance. I haven't asked her yet."

"It's customary to, you know, son."

"I've only known her three days."

"So what? You're sure, right?"

He'd expected his father to laugh, be shocked, astounded, horrified even, but he was acting as if it was the most commonplace announcement in the world. "Yes, I'm sure."

"Most likely she is, then."

What a stupendous thought, but . . . "Dad, would a girl like Mary want a husband with half a leg?"

"Why not? Women don't pick husbands for their legs. Most consider other parts more important."

"Dad!" Talk about shocked over breakfast. "Honestly!"

"Oh, son!" He smiled and shook his head. "Elevate your mind a little. I was thinking brains and heart, but . . ." He took a sip of tea. "Since you brought up the subject. Everything is alright in that department?"

"As far as I can tell, Dad, yes." And that was as much detail as he was giving.

"That's a mercy. I was a bit worried about that. Saw some horrid injuries in the last one." He shook his head.

God. So had he in this one. Sometimes one needed reminding that losing a leg wasn't that bad after all. "Think she'll have me, Dad? Tin leg and all?"

"Holy smoke! How should I know? Ask her yourself. It's the only way to find out."

"But, Dad, it's a bit fast."

"Not so sure about that. I asked your mother to marry me the night I met her."

Gryffyth all but choked on a mouthful of porridge. "Dad?" He'd never thought about his parents meeting or courting. They had just always been married.

"I met her at a dance, son." His father's eyes went misty as if looking back to a warm and pleasant past. "She was the most beautiful thing I'd ever set eyes on. Looking back, I don't know how I got the guts up to ask her to dance, but I did. We had two dances, then went and sat out. I offered to get her a glass of lemonade and she said she'd rather have beer. Took me back a bit, that did, but I fetched two beers, we drank each other's health and then I asked her to marry me."

Gryff'd never have imagined it like that in his wildest dreams. "What did she say?"

"That she'd think about it. And she did. Two days later, when I met her at the factory gate, she said yes." He paused, as if remembering, and Gryffyth waited. "We decided to keep it a secret. I agreed to ask her father the coming Christmas. We started saving. Thought we'd marry the June twelvemonth when we'd have a little nest egg to start out with. I even took on extra hours to have more to squirrel away. Then, the war came. I knew I had to sign up. So we got married right away. Two months before I was posted to France. She was already pregnant but we didn't know it then.

"By the time I heard you'd arrived, you were five weeks old. When I got back you were running around the place like a little steam engine." He went quiet. "Always regretted missing those years. Bron and I wanted more, so I'd have the fun of a baby to keep me up at night, she used to tease. But it never happened. Still . . ." He smiled. "Seems I'll have grandbabies instead."

"Hang on a mo', Dad. I haven't asked her yet."

"What are you waiting for? If you want her, get your word in before some other lad pips you to the post. I know young Longhurst has looked in her direction."

"Tom Longhurst isn't even in the running."

"She told you that, did she?"

"Well, yes."

Dad threw back his head and let out a great laugh. "Well,

I'll be blowed! She'd hardly be likely to tell you that if she wanted you to take a running jump, now would she?"

Well, no, but . . . "Damn it all, Dad. How can I be sure?"

"You can't. Just go ahead and ask her and find out. Life's a risk. You don't need me to tell you that. You learned that at Trondheim. If she says yes, you plan a wedding. If she says no, you come home and drown your sorrows. If she says maybe, you'll have to hang on and hold yourself together the way I did. Almost did me in." He muttered the last bit as if to himself. He looked around the kitchen. "Hope she says yes. This place would do nicely for you, starting out. We've got the bathroom we put in a few years back. Kitchen could do with a little sprucing up, but that'll have to wait until after the war. You've got the nice front bedroom, and a couple of others for your babies." He looked downright thrilled at the prospect.

"Wait a minute! If and when she says yes." If only. "And if and when we get married, we're not turfing you out of your own house."

He shook his head. "I might not be needing it much longer." What the hell? Was he ill? "I've been thinking about matrimony myself."

Gaped wasn't the word for what his jaw did at that. "You? Dad?"

"Don't look so scandalized. I'm not quite tipping my toes up yet."

That was blooming obvious. "Who?" He raised an eyebrow and treated him to a smug grin. Gryffyth thought a minute. He just couldn't see Dad going for any of the obvious widows or spinsters of the parish, but . . . "It's Alice's grandmother, isn't it? Mrs. Burrows!"

His father grinned. "Right first time."

"You asked her?"

"No. Been thinking it over, though."

"Dad, you get on at me to propose to a girl I've known three days, and you're *thinking it over* and you've known her fifteen years. Longer, in fact."

"Maybe I have, but I had you to bring up, and she had Alice and her brothers. It wasn't the time for us."

"What about now? You're itching to get me hitched. Alice is married, her brothers grown." And—please, God—would be coming home. "What are you hanging around for? Want her to ask you?"

"'Course not! I plan on asking her. But I'm not going to do it with an audience, and with all that's going on, it's hard to get time together."

"I see." Gryffyth scraped up the last bit of porridge and washed it down by draining his tea mug. "Right you are then, Dad," he announced, putting his empty mug down on the table. "I'll ask Mary LaPrioux tonight, if you'll ask Mrs. Burrows at the same time. We can come back and celebrate or drown our sorrows together."

"Eh?"

Wasn't often he left his father speechless. Better savor the moment. "That's the deal, Dad. Take it or or leave it."

"Nothing like having your own flesh and blood turn on you!" From his tone, Gryffyth knew Dad wasn't really upset. Just astounded perhaps? That made two of them. "Is it a deal, Dad? Better get your word in before someone pips you to the post. Sam Whorleigh might fancy her."

Dad laughed at that. "She can't stand him!"

"Told you, did she?"

"She didn't need to. I've eyes and ears in my head. Besides, he's a funk and a crook. Feathering his own nest at others' expense. He's no competition."

"Reverend Roundhill's a widower now. Mrs. Burrows would make a fantastic vicar's wife."

"Get along with you, Gryff! I'll ask her. Might as well, since you'll be gone. But you'd better not chicken out."

No, he'd better not, but he had all day to get his courage up. "Well, that's settled then."

His father stood and started to gather the dirty plates and mugs and head for the sink. "Here, let me do that, Dad. I can't sit around while you do all the work."

Howell hesitated a moment, then handed over the dish mop. "Thanks, son. Will give me a chance to shave. You are coming down to join the Home Guard this morning?"

"Of course, I'll sign up. Might as well do my bit."

"We're delighted to have you with us, young Pendragon," Sir James Gregory said, as the meeting broke up. Not before time. With a bit of help from the ARP volunteers, they'd managed to terrify half the village, testing and installing the newly arrived air raid sirens.

"I'm glad to do my bit, sir," Gryffyth replied.

"You've done that, and more, already, young man, but you're needed here as much as you were overseas. We're not going to win this one by sitting it out."

Howell nodded. Pity that slacker Whorleigh wasn't around to hear that. "Gryff'll be an asset to the Home Guard," he said. "I'll work him into the roster, sir."

"Good man." Sir Gregory nodded. "Now, best be off, Lady Gregory has plans for luncheon, but let me give you a lift back. Better save that leg for the home front."

At the gate to their home, Howell said, "Go on in, son, and put the kettle on. There's something I need to ask Sir Gregory."

"What's the matter, man?" Sir Gregory asked, as Gryffyth walked off.

Sir Gregory reminded Howell so much of his old

commanding officer, he almost flubbed out, but yanked up his courage. "I've a favor to ask, sir. A big one. I heard you'd kept some camellias in your greenhouse."

"I did. Some of them, at any rate. Might not be what Lord Woolaton wants, but I couldn't bear to part with them all."

"Well, sir." Holy smoke, he was scared to ask, but for Helen, he'd do it. Damn. "It's like this, sir. I'm planning on proposing marriage to Helen Burrows this evening, and I thought a nice camellia might . . ."

He didn't get to finish. "Bolster up your suit, eh?" Sir Gregory said, with a grin. "By all means. Come on up now and I'll cut you some. Hop in, better bring your bicycle or you'll have a long walk back."

Howell all but flew into the house to tell Gryffyth he had to pop up to Wharton Lacey with Sir Gregory. Grabbed his bicycle, tossed it in the vast boot, and nipped in the passenger seat. Seemed a bit odd to be riding while Sir Gregory drove, but he drove himself these days, his chauffeur having joined up back in September '39.

Sir Gregory was as good as his word, insisting on cutting four beautiful branches. "Would give you more, but we're expecting guests and Lady Gregory will spiflicate me if we don't have enough for the dinner table."

"These are beautiful, sir." Beautiful wasn't the word, they were exquisite. He just hoped he got them home without mishap.

"Good luck then, man. I proposed to Lady Gregory on her uncle's yacht during Cowes Week. Different times then, weren't they?"

"They were indeed, sir," Howell agreed. Never having been to Cowes in his life. "And thank you again."

"Can't think of a better use for them. Tell her to slit the

ends of the stalks, and they like a little aspirin or a couple of pennies dropped in the flower water."

Howell had them in hand as the hothouse door opened and a young man walked in. Then backed out fast. Howell just caught a glimpse but there was something vaguely familiar about him. "Got a new gardener, I see." He wondered who it was. Most of the able-bodied young men left in the village worked up at the munitions plant.

"Yes, we have. Lucky break it was. Our cook put us on to him. A heart murmur kept him out of the army and he wanted to work out of doors so we got him. Makes a difference having him. Old Jacob can't cope with it all on his own. We used to have hands come up from the Home Farm to help, but they're really needed there."

Howell thanked Sir Gregory again, tucked the bouquet in his bicycle basket, covering them with his cape to keep them safe, and set off home.

As he headed down toward the village, he wondered why the barely glimpsed young man seemed so familiar.

Chapter Fourteen

Through the staff-room window, Mary saw Gryffyth waiting for her at the school gate.

So did everyone else.

"Young Pendragon is out there again, I see," Mrs. Winslow, the head mistress, said, with a little smile.

"Oh, yes." Casual and unexcited was the best bet. If she could manage it with racing heart and fluttering in her stomach—and lower. It was Mary's turn to wash up the teacups so that gave her a reason to get busy and leave the room with a loaded tray.

As she came back ten minutes later, a conspicuous silence descended on the room. Either angels were busy carrying everyone's last words to heaven, or they'd been chewing over her and Gryffyth. Maybe both. Mary crossed the room, arranged the cups and saucers, ready for the morning, and filled the kettle. "We're getting a bit low on tea," she said, hoping to break the silence.

"I'll mention it at the staff meeting tomorrow," Mrs. Winslow said. "If we all bring in a couple of spoonfuls, we'll be set for a while."

"We could see what Mr. Whorleigh has," suggested Mrs. Brown, who taught the infants.

"Certainly not, Mrs. Brown. What an idea!" Mrs. Winslow left the entire room in no uncertainty where she stood on that subject. "We are not encouraging his underground commerce."

"Beats me, how he gets away with it," Miss Groves, the other evacuee teacher, said. "You'd think they'd put a stop to it."

"If they wanted to, they would," Mrs. Winslow said.

"Maybe they're trying to catch him red-handed," Mary said, not wanting to think either of the two village policemen were capable of condoning, or at the very least ignoring, such a scofflaw. "I think everything's ready for the morning." When it was someone else's turn to make tea. "I'll be off."

"You run along, Miss LaPrioux," Mrs. Winslow said with a knowing smile.

"Better not keep him waiting," June Groves said, with a grin.

Mary nipped off before anyone else could add to her embarrassment. On the other hand, what on earth was embarrassing about having a gorgeous man like Gryffyth Pendragon waiting for her? Knowing half the village was watching and the other half would hear about it before the kettles boiled for tea, was a bit off-putting. But only a wee, tiny bit. Nothing could really put her off Gryffyth.

It took all she had not to run across the playground and into his arms. But she didn't. After taking her bicycle from the rack, wheeling it sedately across the expanse of tarmac and calling a warning to two boys balancing precariously on the wall, she walked up to Gryffyth. "Good afternoon, Mr. Pendragon," she said, stopping just far enough away not to be able to touch him. She wanted to, so darn much it hurt.

"Good afternoon, Miss LaPrioux. Had a good day?"

"Not bad at all," she replied, as he took her bicycle and, balancing his stick on the handlebars, wheeled it for her as he walked beside her. "I had playground duty, broke up one fight, applied witch hazel to a bumped forehead, and took care of a couple of grazed knees." Dear God, he was beautiful, handsome, and bedworthy.

"No major crises then?"

Only her not being able to concentrate all day. Times tables and subjects and predicates had not been engrossing enough to keep her mind off his kisses and the touch of his hand under her blouse. "We had one. Two boys in the top form were found guilty of soaking the blackboard chalk in water so it wouldn't write."

He threw back his head, his eyes took on a dark sparkle and sexy laughter echoed from deep in his rather magnificent chest. "Still play that old trick, do they? I remember Jim Barrett and I got the ruler across our hands from Mr. Carver—he was head back in our day."

"You shouldn't have done it."

"Maybe not, but he acted as if we were headed for Borstal and a life of crime. Old misery-guts, he was." He paused. "Hope you didn't have to wallop those two."

"Wasn't my responsibility. Mrs. Winslow took care if it with guilt. Went on at length about sailors dying to bring ships across the Atlantic. She had them half in tears."

"Rotten old teachers," he said, with a grin that crinkled the edges of his eyes. "Don't change much, do you?"

"You came down here to tell me that?"

"No. I came down to remind you of your promise to go to the pictures with me."

"I didn't need reminding."

"*Gone with the Wind* is playing in Leatherhead. Thought you might like it."

"I'd love to. I really would, but I'll need to take my bicycle home and leave a note for Gloria."

"We can do that, then nip down into the village and get the bus."

He wasn't going to let her refuse. Not that she had the slightest intention of doing so. She was halfway tempted to make him wait while she changed out of work clothes but she had precious few clothes anyway, might as well keep on what she had. The skirt was warm and who knew if the cinema would be heated properly.

Once home, she scribbled a note to Gloria, who'd give her a thorough quizzing when she returned, but who cared? Being with Gryffyth was what really mattered.

It certainly mattered to the crowd at the bus stop. Mary felt they were counting the hairs on her head and the buttons on her coat and would be checking her fingernails if she hadn't put her gloves on. Gryffyth received even closer scrutiny, if possible.

He carried it off with aplomb. "Evening," he said to the crowd as they pretended not to stare.

"Evening, Mr. Pendragon," Constable Parlett responded as the others made similar murmurs.

"Off for the evening, are you?" Mrs. Parlett asked.

"Going to see *Gone with the Wind*," Mary replied, determined to match Gryffyth for casual and unconcerned if it finished her off.

"Oh, it's wonderful!" she replied. "We saw it in Dorking last week. That Rhett Butler. I had dreams about him."

Mary felt a pang of sympathy for Constable Parlett, whose sandy hair and pink nose rather lacked the allure of Clark Gable.

"Nice to see you back home, Mr. Pendragon," Constable Parlett said, obviously trying to turn the conversation from his wife's heartthrob.

"It's good to be back. Very good," he said, with a glance at Mary.

She couldn't help grinning back. The entire village would be talking about them anyway, so why worry about it?

"That were a nasty business up in Norway," a man Gloria had seen around the village said.

"It's all nasty," Gryffyth replied. "Some of us are lucky and come back alive. I've too many friends who didn't."

There were murmurs of agreement but the bus pulled up before anyone came up with a reply to that.

The bus was packed. There was a sticky moment, when Constable Parlett, still very much the policeman, even in mufti, asked the entire bus, "Surely there's someone can give up a seat to a lad who fought for us at Trondheim?"

To Gryffyth's outright embarrassment, three or four people stood up. One was a schoolgirl.

"I'm not sitting down while Mary stands," he muttered to Parlett.

"It's no bother," Mary said, hesitating to add she had two good legs, even if her feet did ache after a day spent standing.

"'Course not," Parlett added, with confidence.

They ended up sitting side by side while two young men, workers from the munitions plant, Mary guessed, stood.

"Back on leave?" one of them asked Gryffyth.

"Back for good," he replied. "Lost a bit of my leg. I'm not much use to the army now. I'll have to find something to do here."

"You could come up to the plant with us. Pay's not bad and there's more girls there than in your wildest dreams."

Gryffyth shook his head. "I've the only girl I'll ever need right here, but might think about it. I met Andrew Barron the other evening."

"You know the boss?"

"Just met him. I've only been back a week."

Mary couldn't miss the change in their manner. Just like that, Gryffyth had slipped from a good lad to pal of the boss.

"He's good," the second one said, "and we've a decent

plant manager now. The old one was a proper bastard. Sorry, miss," he added to Mary, with a shake of his head. "But he were a hard one to get on with. Proper spiteful to the girls, he was."

"He left?" Mary asked, surprised she hadn't heard mention of him.

"They took him away. Some sort of breakdown. I don't wish no harm to anyone—except old Adolf and his lot—but that customer hasn't been missed."

The bus stopped. The two lads moved along, to let people behind get off.

Gryffyth took the opportunity to cover her hand with his. The smile he gave her set her on a reckless path. "You meant what you said?"

"About joining the Home Guard?" he asked, with a chuckle. "Yeah! Dad roped me in this morning."

"No, not about the Home Guard. About your choice of female companionship."

"Why do you think I'm here and you're beside me?"

"Perhaps you don't like going to the flicks alone?"

"Yes, that's it! I'm scared some stranger will come up to me and offer me sweets."

"If he does, I'll punch him one, after I confiscate the sweets of course."

He squeezed even closer. "You'd resort to violence to protect me, Miss LaPrioux?"

"Any time you want," she replied, resting her head on his shoulder and smiling up at him. For a second or two, as their eyes met, there was no one else in the world but the two of them.

Until she remembered they were on a bus packed with interested locals.

She sat up straight but squeezed his hand. "Alright,

Clark Gable," she whispered, as she pressed her knee against his.

The night air chilled as they left the cinema, hand in hand.

Clark Gable had a presence and oodles of sex appeal, Mary would grant that much, but really, he wasn't a patch on Gryffyth. Dear Lord, he was wonderful. Sex on legs wasn't far off the mark. Alright, sex on one leg!

"You're smiling," Gryffyth said.

The man didn't miss much. And she was not about to voice her last thought. "Just thinking about Clark Gable."

"Really?" Was it her imagination or was there a note of pique in his voice?

"Yes, really. I was thinking how the sorts of men people get sloppy over on the screen aren't a patch on the ones you meet in real life."

"I was afraid you were going to ask me to whisk you up in my arms and carry you up a wide, sweeping staircase."

They were halfway down the High Street, almost at the crossroads. "Wouldn't do that," Mary said, giving his hand a squeeze and stepping a little closer to him. "I don't think there's one like that in the whole of Brytewood."

"I bet there's one up at Wharton Lacey."

"The big house?" She chuckled. "I don't need carrying anywhere, Gryffyth."

"I think that's why I love you," he replied.

She stopped dead and looked at him. Had she dreamed that? Had to have!

"You heard right the first time," he said with a sexy little smile. "I love you, Mary."

"Gryffyth." It took an effort to get anything out, her throat was so tight and her blood was throbbing in her ears. "You've only known me three days."

"Why does that matter? I fell in love when you crossed the village hall to ask me to dance." He put a finger under her chin and tilted her face up. "I love you, Mary, truly I do. I love you and I want to marry you."

"A bit sudden, isn't this? We barely know each other."

"What else do you want to know? I'm twenty-six years old, minus a chunk of my right leg, currently unemployed and living on an army pension. Cripes." He broke off, shaking his head. "Makes me sound like a miserable prospect, doesn't it?"

Her heart clenched for him. She stood on tiptoes and kissed his chin. "Gryffyth. I think you are a wonderful prospect."

He eyes gleamed in the dark. "You're accepting?"

Oh, dear. "Not exactly. I really don't know you well enough, but I like everything I've seen so far." Now was not the moment to mention her rather lurid, if thoroughly delightful, nighttime fantasies. "But it's so sudden—for all I know you go out to the pub and get drunk and gamble and drown kittens."

"I've been to the Pig and Whistle once since I've been back but soon decided drinking more than one beer, before walking home on a tin leg, was a lousy idea. The only gambling I've ever done was playing rummy for penny points and buying a ticket in the Grand National Sweepstakes and I've never drowned a kitten. Good enough for you?"

Lord, yes. He was the answer to her dreams, but still she hesitated. "I think I love you too, Gryffyth."

He wrapped his arm around her shoulders, so her face rubbed against the heavy woolen cloth of his army greatcoat. "But you're still not sure about signing up for life?"

"I wish I were." It was the utter truth.

"I wish you were too, but how about this: you'll marry me unless you discover I've a hideous secret life that repulses you."

She had to laugh. "Gryffyth, be serious."

He held her shoulders in both hands, turning her to face him. "I am, Mary, totally serious. I want you as my wife, in my bed, and for the rest of my life."

Her chest went tight, as her heart raced. In his bed! Dear heaven, that was a prospect. "Give me a couple of weeks." Why delay? She wanted him, but darn it, she had to think this over.

"Two weeks, it's a bargain," he replied. "I'm tempted to say, 'Let's go to the station, get a train up to Town and see if we can find an empty table at the Savoy,' but I think that will have to wait until you say yes."

"Sounds like a good plan. Hungry?"

"Hungry for you, my love." He pulled her close, oblivious to the stragglers from the cinema who headed toward the bus stop, wrapped his arms around her and kissed her, lifting her off her feet as he pressed his mouth on hers. With a little gasp, she parted her lips and welcomed him, their tongues brushed and caressed as he held her against him and kissed deeper. He was incredible, wonderful, and he wanted her. That was obvious as he held her inside his coat. Dammit, she wanted him too, but for now a wild, insane kiss would have to do. Her pulse raced as her thoughts shimmered into a glorious fog of sensation, and she softened into his embrace and kissed on.

She whimpered with disappointment as he broke the kiss and set her back on her feet. "I love you," he repeated.

"I love you, too." How could she doubt it? He was her dear heart, her hopes and her other self, but caution, uncertainty, and the unease of the times—and knowledge of her nature—held her back. How, as much as she wanted to, could she marry this nice man when he was unsuspecting of her Other nature?

Should she go ahead and tell him? And watch him recoil in shock? Or laugh it off in disbelief? Either would cut her to the quick. What if he was that one human in a million who didn't ridicule or recoil at her nature? Who might even, wonder of wonders, accept what she was? Even then, could she make a life-changing decision on the basis of knowing him three days?

A nagging voice reminded her that she'd made the decision to evacuate with her pupils in a matter of hours.

That was different. Well, sort of.

"Come on, love. Since I can't take you to the Savoy or the Ritz, a British restaurant will have to do."

Much more suited to their pockets too. She took his hand and together they crossed the road and headed up toward the church hall.

Chapter Fifteen

Schmidt declined supper and retired to his meager quarters, climbing up onto the roof to survey his future domain and ponder the nagging disquiet about the man who'd accompanied Sir Gregory into the greenhouse that morning. Something about him tweaked his memory. Schmidt hadn't recognized him. He'd had a good look at him through the branches of one of the orange trees, but there was something about him, his voice perhaps, that was so familiar. But if so, why did he not recognize the human? Vampires didn't forget. Not much at least. But he'd take an oath, he hadn't seen that man's face this time in England.

His previous visit had been back in 1640. He'd crossed the Channel to avoid the turmoil of the Thirty Years War, being too young a Vampire then to truly appreciate the conveniences of battles. He'd learned that fast, though, when England descended into civil war two years later.

This was no time for nostalgia. The here and now needed his attention. Or rather the human he'd recognized. Could it have been around three centuries earlier? Was he some sort of immortal? And if so, had he destroyed Eiche and Bloch?

Schmidt sat immobile for several minutes, pondering that.

What now? Share the news with Weiss? Without proof, Weiss's ridicule was more likely than his praise. Better find out more.

What did he know already? The man was tall, broad shouldered and appeared strong. From the overheard conversation, it was apparent he was part of the local Home Guard, and about to propose marriage to some fellow human. Not much to go on. He presumably lived nearby. Trouble was, Schmidt didn't dare venture into the village to ask. Their trusted party member, Miss Waite, was no longer there to shelter him. And there was the risk of being recognized. He'd been so weak and failing when that doctor woman rescued him, that he didn't know who had, and had not, seen him.

He should have stayed in the kitchen for supper, in hopes of picking up something from the servants' gossip, but the trouble with ingesting mortal food was the bother of regurgitating it, since his body no longer assimilated nourishment from solid food. It might be worth the inconvenience, if he learned what he needed.

Finding, and eliminating, the thing that had destroyed his fellow Vampires would be a delightful coup.

Howell Pendragon dismounted his bicycle and paused to catch his breath. The years were gaining on him. His heart never used to race like this going up the hill out of the village, but he'd never before ridden up it planning to propose matrimony.

He propped his cycle against the hedge that bordered the kitchen garden, and waited another few seconds to let his heartbeat settle.

It didn't. If anything, his pulse sped up as he took the bunch of camellias from his basket and eyed the kitchen door.

He hoped he'd timed it right. Alice should be busy with patients in her surgery now. Peter would still be at work, and Helen Burrows should be pausing for a cup of tea before starting to cook dinner.

He'd better get a move on.

He was scared witless.

Only one way to go. He crossed the gravel to the brick path that led up to the back door and gave it a firm knock.

Too firm. He heard it resounding over the sounds of *Music While You Work* on the wireless from the other side of the door. Then the wireless went off, he heard footsteps on the flagstone floor, and the doorknob turned.

Helen's face lit with recognition. "Why, Howell. How nice to see you, come on in." With a smile that bolstered his confidence, she opened the door and stepped back for him to cross the threshold, then closed the door behind him. "Getting a bit brisk out there, isn't it? Did you want to see Alice? She should be finished in half an hour or so."

"I don't need to see the doctor. I came to see you, Helen."

"That's nice. Come in and have a seat and I'll pop the kettle on."

He was too damn anxious to move from where he stood. As she filled the kettle, he looked at the flowers clutched in his right hand. He'd wrapped them in newspaper; it had protected the blooms but wasn't anywhere like the shiny paper florists used before the war. Still, it was the best he could do, and she'd know that.

"Don't stand there, Howell, take off your coat and have a seat." She put the kettle on the stove. "I made an apple tart. Would you like a slice with your tea?"

"Yes, thank you." His throat was closing up on him. He had to get this said.

She took cups off the dresser and looked at him, rooted to the same spot. "Something wrong, Howell?"

"No! No, nothing wrong. It's just. These are for you." He held out the newspaper package.

"Thank you." She laid them on the table while she cut the string, close to the knot so as to be able to reuse it, and opened the newspaper.

And stared, open mouthed. "Camellias. Howell, where did you get them?" She picked up the stems, holding her other hand under the flower heads. "They are absolutely beautiful. Thank you, Howell, but where on earth did you get them these days?"

"Sir Gregory's greenhouse. He kept three bushes, said he couldn't bear to part with all of them."

"He gave them to you?"

Did sound incredible, didn't it? No wonder she gave him a searching look. "I asked him for them." She almost dropped them at that.

He stepped forward and put his hand under the blooms. "Said I had something special I needed them for and could he spare just one. He gave me a whole bunch of them." He'd gone this far, better finish the job. He took a deep breath while she stared in total bewilderment. "I wanted to bring you something beautiful, like you, Helen. I wanted to show you what I think of you and ask you, if you might, possibly . . . I mean, I want to ask you if you'd consider marrying me."

She landed in the nearby chair with a thump. "Howell?"

"I mean it, Helen. From the bottom of my heart." He was in full flow now. Determined to leave nothing undone, he went down on his knee by her seat, and looked up at her face. She was smiling so he went right on. "Marry me. I love you. Have loved you ever since you first came to Brytewood. Please, would you? Could you marry me? You are the most wonderful woman in the world. I'd give anything to win you. Get you anything. Do whatever you ask. Just please, say yes."

"Howell." She appeared composed, although he was still shaking. "You're asking me to marry you?"

"Yes!" Hadn't he been clear enough? He wasn't too sure what he'd said as his mind was whirling so fast. "Please, would you? I know you could have your pick of the men in all of England, but I love you."

In the pause as he caught his breath, she smiled. "Yes, Howell."

The room spun around him as he grabbed her hands. "You mean it?"

"I'd hardly be saying yes if I meant no, now would I?" Neither would she be smiling at him as if he'd just offered her the entire universe. "Here, get up."

He managed that with her help. It was no joke getting up off a stone floor at his age, and he stood looking at her. Grinning like an old fool in love, no doubt, but that's exactly what he was. "I love you, Helen."

"I'm so glad to hear it," she replied.

"Dear heaven, Helen, you don't know how happy you've made me."

"I think I do," she said, and wrapped her arms around him and kissed him. Hard.

He kissed back. Almost drowning in the wonder of it. Lost in her glorious woman's warmth and the wild passion of her kiss. His head swam, his heart raced. He could die from the beauty of her touch and could think of no better way to go. Only he wanted to live, for her.

They broke the kiss together; her face was flushed and her eyes bright with desire. He knew exactly how she felt.

"I think," she said, smiling up at him, "this merits something more than a cup of tea."

"I'd have brought Champagne if I thought I could have found any at the Pig."

"How about a glass of sherry? There's a bottle in the dining room sideboard. You go and get it while I put these beautiful camellias in water."

By the time he got back with the sherry and a couple of glasses, she was slitting the last stem and arranging them in a vase. "There," she said. "How kind of him to give them to you. Beautiful, aren't they?"

"Not a patch on you, Helen."

God! She was so wonderful and when she laughed like that, she was downright fantastic. "Here's the sherry. Want me to pour it?"

"Please." He handed her a glass and they sat down, side by side. "To us," she said, raising her glass and beaming at him.

"To us," he replied, clinking his glass against hers.

"Think we should go talk to Reverend Roundhill about putting up the banns?" he asked, after a lovely companionable moment of silence.

"Yes." Certain about that she was. "How about tomorrow?"

"Tomorrow it is. After I take you shopping for a ring."

"Think we'll be able to get one? Everything's so scarce these days."

"I'm sure we can. Remember the jeweler in Leatherhead, the one up at the top of the High Street, by the Duke's Head? He's been buying up jewelry since the war started. Lots of people are selling. I bet he has an Aladdin's Cave there. What do you fancy?"

She pondered that a moment or two. "Something red. Red as dragon fire. Garnet, carnelian, ruby. Let's see what he has."

"I'll give him a ring in the morning, ask him to look some out for us. Whatever you want. It's yours."

That kiss went on even longer, and by the time they broke

the embrace, his body was very happy too. "We could go away for a weekend somewhere close and celebrate," he suggested.

"We could indeed. Dorking isn't far."

"Might shock our families."

"They'll get used to the idea." They were going to have to. "Let's have another sherry," she said, handing him her empty glass. "I don't know what else I'm keeping it for."

"Our wedding?" he suggested, giving her a gentle nudge with his elbow.

"I'll want Champagne at that!"

She was grinning, so he might as well niggle her a bit. "I'll have a word with Sam Whorleigh. Bet he can manage a case or two."

"I don't doubt it, but it would taste sour. And, talking about Sam Whorleigh, let me tell you what happened this morning."

Howell listened. "Think he was serious?"

"He couldn't be drunk that early in the morning, could he? Besides, he was sober as a judge and scared out of his wits. No, he wasn't making it up. But at least we now know what he is, and he's joining us—for whatever good he'll be."

"Don't be too hard on him, Helen. Who knows, he might just have the skills we need."

"So far his only skills seem to be moving fast and running rackets."

"Don't forget last month, he stepped in and saved Alice from what could have been an awkward predicament."

She conceded the point. "I can think of better things to do than talk about Sam Whorleigh."

So could he.

They spent the next half hour exploring them. Until Howell, reluctantly, decided he'd better head home before it got dark. Not that he worried about Gryff. With a bit of luck, he'd be very late home, but there'd been a cyclist killed over in Headly a few days back, in the blackout. Getting run over was not in his plans for the near future.

Howell took a very tender farewell of his fiancée, and, after promising to pick her up at nine the next morning, set off down the hill. Singing out loud.

He had news for Gryff when he got back.

Chapter Sixteen

Paul Schmidt looked up and frowned. How the hell did Weiss move like that? Appearing in an instant in the middle of the room.

"What do you want?" Schmidt asked.

"A report on your progress," Weiss replied, walking noiselessly across the bare boards to stand over Schmidt.

Well, he wasn't getting up. Let Weiss loom over him, if he wanted to. Schmidt wasn't that easily intimidated. "Have a seat. The chair by the door isn't too rickety."

Weiss brought it to the middle of the room, turned it around and sat astride it. "Comfortable accommodation?"

If Weiss wanted complaints, he was going to be disappointed. "It's private and I have sustenance right below me, or just a short run across the grounds. I've had worse."

"Haven't we all?"

Schmidt wasn't disposed to discuss his accommodation. He wanted to run across the night fields to the Home Farm and feast off a nice milch cow. He planned on reserving the horse for emergencies and bad weather. "You wanted a report on my progress?" Now Weiss was at eye level, Schmidt noticed the shiny mark of healing skin. What had happened to his esteemed leader?

Weiss nodded. "What have you learned?"

In not quite twenty-four hours? If Weiss anticipated a negative response, he was doomed to disappointment. "First: very important guests expected this weekend. Who exactly, I do not know, but Cook has been complaining about the extra work, and a shortage of butter."

"Find out who it is. If it's Churchill, no playing games. Kill him. As messy as you like."

"With pleasure." So, Weiss wasn't going to do the dirty work himself. He should have expected that. "Also, I may have identified the killer of Eiche and Bloch."

Not even a raised eyebrow. Damn Weiss. "You think so?"

"He is Other, but what he is, I've no idea. He's part of their pathetic Home Guard. An old man."

"An old man with the strength and power to annihilate two Vampires?"

"I said he is Other. He must possess inhuman strength. He lives in the village. His voice was familiar, took me awhile to remember where I'd heard him. He helped that doctor carry me into her house."

"He's a Vampire killer and let you live, in your weakened state?"

"Maybe he failed to recognize what I am."

Weiss had a particularly nasty laugh. "I think not, my friend, because I encountered the killer last night." That explained the healing flesh. "He's something I've never encountered before; he breathes fire."

"What sort of creature breathes fire? A Chimera? The Khalkotauroi? A Dragon?"

Weiss dismissed those suggestions with a flick of his hand.

"We deal with reality here, my dear Schmidt. Not myths and legends."

Schmidt forbore mentioning that most humans considered Vampires myths. "What do you think he is?"

"A young man. Strong." Not the old codger then. "He's some sort of Other. He breathes flame and carried no weapon. The fire came from him and in an instant." Interesting, but Schmidt was not about to discount the old man he'd seen in the greenhouse. "This one is dangerous." Obviously, if he'd killed two already. "We must target him. Find where he lives and dispose of him."

"Before Churchill?"

"Most definitely. Once their Winnie is dead, we will have more important things to do than dispose of peasants."

Made sense, Schmidt supposed. Not that he'd argue with Weiss if it didn't. But for his money he was going to keep his eyes and ears wide open for any trace of the old codger from the Home Guard. Schmidt granted that the chance of two Others living in the same village was slight. Surely one would long ago have disposed of the competition. But there were other hamlets and villages around.

"There is another matter," Weiss went on, "that I will investigate since you are reluctant to go into the village."

Reluctant to expose himself to recognition was the gist of the matter. But he kept that to himself too. "What's that?"

"There is another Other there. I plan to identify him and, if we cannot suborn him, eliminate him."

This was beginning to sound like a comic opera or a farce. A deadly farce, but still ludicrous. "Yes?" Something seemed required in the silence.

Weiss repeated the incident of the morning. "He disappeared. What sort of creature moves faster than one of us? A Fairy perhaps? There was a mention in one of Bloch's reports of a village shopkeeper who had evaded him in a similar fashion."

"So you know where to find him. How many shops are there in that village?"

"Five, six counting the defunct bakery. I will find this creature easily enough. Your job is to find somewhere that we can hold him captive while we use him."

"There's plenty of space up here. It's a bit close to the house, but no one ever comes up here. There's the two horses below, but Sir James and his wife groom them and I get to muck out the stalls." A task that infuriated him.

Weiss looked around the barren, uncarpeted room. "Let me see the rest of the place."

He inspected every room. He tried doors and judged the height of the tiny windows. "Not perfect, but it will suffice. You can keep an eye on him, and I can approach from the woods at night. We could work on him unobserved."

"When do we take him?"

"On Saturday. No one will miss him until Monday, and we can enjoy a most entertaining Sunday."

The poor bugger had no idea what was in store for him.

Mary smiled at Gryffyth across the long trestle table. Irish stew and cabbage followed by prunes and custard wasn't the sort of dinner to celebrate a marriage proposal. She'd once imagined linen tablecloths and nice glasses, but the gorgeous company was what really mattered, and his more than made up for the cracked oilcloth and the heavy, white china mugs of tea.

"To us," Gryffyth said, raising his mug.

She raised hers in reply. "To us."

"So, you agree there is an us?"

Dear heaven, she hoped so. She wanted Gryffyth Pendragon in the worst, or was it best, possible way. "Before we go any further, Gryffyth, there's something you must know about me." Where had that come from? Not her brain. Her tongue had a mind of its own, it seemed. And she had to tell him.

"What? Don't tell me you're already married?"

"Good heavens, no." It was much worse than that, and would no doubt send him running, or calling for a padded van, but she couldn't let him keep thinking she was just a nice, normal, human schoolteacher. "Gryffyth." She glanced around to be sure someone wasn't sitting behind them. "Please listen—and I'm not losing my mind." Deep breath. "You think I'm a schoolteacher. A normal woman evacuated to Brytewood. I'm not. My family is different from most people." So far so good, he was still listening.

"The women in our family are not quite human. We look and act and appear human but we're Sprites. We take sustenance and strength from being in and near water." There! She'd done it.

He picked up his tea and took a long drink. What now? Was he going to call her loony? Walk away in horror and disbelief? In telling him, she'd gone against everything her mother and aunts had drilled into her, but she couldn't keep it from him.

"So," he said, "you're Other and a Water Sprite. We're landlocked here in Surrey, unless you count the rivers. Must be hard for you."

"It's not been easy but I found water. Not the sea, but it does."

"Where?"

"There's a hammerpond up on the heath. It's a long walk but I cut through the woods."

"You mean up on the Longhurst farm? I'd rather you didn't go there."

He accepted it, even if it stirred his jealousy. "It's either that or the village pond, and frankly, Gryffyth, I'm not bathing naked there, even to keep you happy."

"No," he agreed. "Not with every drunk from the Pig staggering past at closing time. Tell me," he went on. "How often do you go?"

"Always at full moon, and in between when I get itchy and anxious."

"I'm coming with you next time."

"I swim naked."

He had a wicked grin. "Good."

"It's cold up there this time of year."

"We'll keep each other warm."

They really had better get engaged then, except . . . "Wait a minute. You said I was 'Other.' What did you mean by that?"

"Other is the term my father uses to describe anyone who's more than human, who has another nature, or uses or can control magic of some sort."

"You're not a Sprite. You can't be. Only women are."

"Right, I'm not a Sprite."

"What are you then?" She'd started this but where was it going?

"Finish dinner and I'll take you outside and show you."

She really wasn't hungry any longer, but after all her exhortations to schoolchildren about wasting food, she finished her prunes.

Gryffyth took her hand in his. "Let's go down by the river."

Seemed romantic enough, apart from the chill night air, but he had a reason other than romance to go down to the dark at the bottom of Bridge Street. She could see fairly well, despite the blackout, and he appeared to have no trouble at all finding his way. At the bottom of the hill, by the bridge, was a pub, shuttered and blacked out, but the sounds were unmistakable.

Gryffyth turned off the road to the left and they walked across a stretch of land and into an area of woods.

They were alone in the dark and quiet of the winter night.

"This should be far enough away from everyone," he said. "How well can you see in the dark?"

"Well enough to see you just pushed up your coat sleeves and undid your cuffs."

"Good, I did. Learned the hard way to unbutton them first. Now, just a tick." He pulled off his coat and draped it over her shoulders. "Be a love and hold that for me. I bet the ground is muddy this time of year." He pushed up his jacket sleeves. "I don't want to frighten you."

"Really? You lure me down to a deserted riverbank in the dead of night and then tell me you don't want to frighten me?"

"Good," he chuckled. "I knew you weren't the sort of girl to scare easily. I'm going to show you what I am, at least partly. You'll understand. I hope."

So did she. So far things were about as clear as the duration of the war. "What are you doing?"

"Look at my hands."

Mary stared. She no doubt gaped, but she couldn't take her eyes off his hands. They changed, grew larger, his wrists thickened and his fingers curled. His nails turned into claws that he sheathed like a cat, and his skin darkened. A glance up at his face showed he was still her Gryffyth.

She reached out and stroked the back of his hand. The skin was smooth and rippled, like a . . . she'd no idea what. She took his hand between hers and felt his palm. It was harder than the back of his hand and now his fingers were half their usual length, but as she watched he extended and drew back his massive claws.

She should be scared, running like all possessed, except when she looked at his face, saw the same beautiful dark eyes and his wondrously sexy smile, she knew this was all the man she loved.

"What are you?"

"A Dragon."

Of course, with a name like his she should have guessed. But how could she? Never dreaming Dragons walked the Earth. "Your father too?"

He nodded. "Yes, but don't tell anyone."

"As if I would." If she didn't love him so much, she'd be insulted at the suggestion.

"It doesn't repulse you?"

"If you can accept I swim naked in Tom Longhurst's pond, I can cope with you growing claws."

"Not sure about you going up to Tom Longhurst's pond."

"There is nowhere else. Trust me. I scoured the maps. The river isn't deep enough. That pond is the only place within walking distance that is secluded."

"I'll just have to come with you then."

"I said you could." The more she thought about it, the more she fancied the idea. They could dry each other off and keep each other warm. A Dragon should be good for that. "Can all of you change?"

"Of course, in fact it's easier than just part, but I'm twice as big when I shift completely and would ruin my best clothes."

"Let me see you change completely one day."

"You'll have to see me naked to do that."

"Smashing." It was fun being shameless and forward with Gryffyth.

"I'll show you one thing now." He stepped away from her and faced the dark, open expanse of the river. "Watch this."

She gasped as a great tongue of flame shot out in the dark. Dragons really did breathe fire.

"Hey, you, down there. Douse that light!"

"What the blazes is going on down there?"

"Shit," Gryffyth muttered. "Damn air raid wardens."

He grabbed her hand in his, the skin still rough and hard, and hobbled away at surprising speed, dragging her along. One hand was in his, the other clutching his coat around her shoulders until the shouts faded and they were alone, miles from anywhere it seemed.

"You alright, Mary?"

"Yes," she replied, handing him back his coat. "So, Dragons really do breathe fire."

"Only when absolutely necessary."

"Like when convincing someone to marry you?"

"You are a comedienne, Miss LaPrioux. How about it then? Want to be Mrs. Pendragon?"

It did have a rather lovely ring to it. "My answer's the same as before. Give me a little time. It's a big decision."

"Maybe this will persuade you." She expected the kiss. She opened her lips and a great wildness seized her as their tongues touched. Only it didn't stop there. Their tongues mated with each other, stroking, caressing, and teasing while he continued to whirl her around until she was giddy with the motion, the sensation and sheer and wondrous delight of his kiss.

By the time he broke the kiss, she was too giddy to stand, and clutched onto him as the world around them still turned.

"I love you, Mary," he said, not the slightest bit breathless. Lucky him, having Dragon lungs.

"I love you, too."

"I'll settle for that. For now," he said.

"Talking about settling. Do you have any idea where we are other than a long way from the town?"

"I know where we are. Sort of. If we head away from the river, we should come out somewhere near the parish church."

They did, after a bit of trespass on a couple of private gardens and a privet hedge. She rather wondered how they looked. Disheveled, and a bit rumpled, no doubt. But Mary really didn't worry too much.

She had far more important things on her mind.

Chapter Seventeen

"Evening, son. Fancy a beer?"

There were three bottles and a glass tankard on the kitchen table. Gryffyth couldn't help noticing his father already had a half-empty glass. Celebrating? Or drowning his disappointment?

"Thanks, Dad, I will." He snapped off the cap with the bottle opener and picked up the spare tankard. "Well, Dad," he said as he tilted the tankard and poured the beer slowly to avoid too thick a head. "How did things go?"

"Let's put it this way, Gryff. I'm taking Helen shopping in Leatherhead tomorrow. She wants a ring with a red stone."

Gryffyth grinned. Couldn't help it. He might be in limbo but his father's joy was written all over his face. He left the beer and mug on the table as he shook his father's hand and gave him a filial thump on the back. "Oh, Dad! That's smashing. She said yes!"

"She did indeed, son. You're looking at a very happy man." He raised an eyebrow. "Any luck?"

"Sort of. She didn't refuse. Just asked for time to think about it."

"Can't blame the girl for that, son. You did rather leap in there. But she left you hopeful?"

Hopeful? He'd say he was. "The thing is . . . hold on a minute, Dad. I've stuff to tell you." Gryffyth grabbed his beer and sat down opposite his father. Felt good to be by the fire. "It's like this . . ."

Dad was a good listener. Always had been. He sat silent, nodding and giving his own particular smile as Gryffyth told him about Mary.

"Capital!" Dad said, as he finished. "A Water Sprite, eh?" He sounded pleased with himself. "Who'd have guessed it? And the poor girl stuck in landlocked Surrey."

"She goes up to the hammerpond on Tom Longhurst's land." There was absolutely no justification for that bellow of ribald laughter. "You may think it's hilarious, Dad. What if that old lecher sees her?"

"He's not that old, son, only a couple of years older than you."

"That's the whole point. How would you feel if the woman you love went nude swimming in someone else's pond?"

That left his dad bereft of speech for a good fifteen seconds. "Hell, son, I'd go swimming with her!"

That's what he'd planned, but on second thoughts . . . "She'll see me, Dad. My stump."

"She will when you marry her, son, if not before. Might as well get used to you."

He really hated it when is father was so completely right.

"What the blazes am I going to do, Dad?"

"About what? Your Mary?"

He liked the sound of that. His Mary! "She's not mine yet."

"That's up to you, isn't it? Look here, son. She fancies you, made that pretty clear Saturday night in front of the entire village, and let me tell you she's a sensible girl. Yes, she went out with young Longhurst once, maybe twice, but she soon gave him the shove. She picked you, lad. Count your blessings there. And, according to you, she didn't turn green, faint, or run screaming at the knowledge that you grow wings, turn scaly, and breathe fire when the mood takes you.

"If that girl—sorry, Sprite—can cope with that news, I don't think your missing a chunk of leg is going to cause her to even blink." He paused to tip his tankard and drain it. "She loves you, Gryff. You've nothing to worry about. Not there."

Seeing the empty tankard in his father's hand, Gryffyth fetched and opened another bottle for him.

"Thanks, son. So," Dad went on, as he poured the beer with a well-practiced wrist, "you told her about the get-together tomorrow night?"

"No, Dad! I didn't! You can't want her caught up in all that." He knew better than go against that look on his father's face. But damn it. "Dad, she could get hurt. She's not from here. She's worries enough of her own without getting caught up with our problems."

"Ask her, Gryff. Give her the choice. She understands about war and knows more about invasion than either of us."

Smashing! He could just see Mary hobnobbing with Alice and Gloria and sharpening stakes. If Peter and Andrew were willing to let their women risk getting killed, that was their affair. He wasn't taking any risks with Mary. "I'll think about it, Dad."

"You do that, son, and while you're at it, see what you can find out about Sprites. Don't know much about them myself. I thought she was some sort of Fairy."

"How did you know she was Other?"

"After a while you notice it. Knew Nurse Prewitt was, long before she admitted it. Come to that, you knew about your Mary."

"Dad, I didn't."

He wasn't about to budge. Stubborn old man. "Yes, you did, son. That was part of the attraction. Same for her no doubt. Why do you think she picked you out of a roomful of people? Your Otherness called to her, even if she didn't realize it at the time."

"If that's true, Dad, how do you explain Alice and Gloria falling for plain, common, or garden humans?"

"Can't, really," he replied, with a twinkle in his eye. "Just know it was Otherness drew you two together. Be a good lad and mention tomorrow night to her. She might be just what we need."

Quite possibly, but they'd manage without her. If there were Vampires lurking around, he was keeping Mary right away from them or his name wasn't Gryffyth Pendragon.

Gloria picked up the mail from the front door mat: a thick, buff envelope full of even more government forms for her, and a letter for Mary. Interesting—Mary seldom got any post. Not that it was any business of hers who did or did not write to Mary.

"One for you," she said, passing the white envelope to Mary across the kitchen table. After she'd noticed the local postmark.

"Thank you." Even the little crease between her eyes didn't dull the glow on Mary's face. She must have had a really nice time last night.

"How did things go with Gryffyth?" Nosy, but maybe it sounded friendly and interested.

Beaming might be a good word to describe the look on her face. "Gryffyth Pendragon asked me to marry him."

"Jeepers!" That sounded rude. "What did you say?"

"I told him I wanted a little time to think about it."

"Don't blame you. He's a fast worker. Talk about jumping the gun a bit."

"It seemed too soon to say yes."

Gloria picked up her cup, drank, and wondered if they didn't both need something stronger than PG Tips, but they did both have to go to work. "You wanted to?" And she thought she and Andrew had moved fast.

"Yes, to be honest. Part of me fell in love with him the minute I saw him Saturday night. The more I see of him, the more convinced I am we belong together and I'll never find anyone else who suits me so well. The sane, rational side of me says you can't possibly fall in love and decide to marry a man in four days."

"I dunno about that."

"You and Andrew?"

"Me and Andrew?" That was ungrammatical, but thinking about him scrambled her syntax. "Don't take us as an example of how to choose a life partner. I think we broke all the rules."

"Didn't know there were rules," Mary said. "Might be easier if there were, wouldn't it?"

"You're uncertain?"

"No. I'm dead certain I want him but I'm stuck here, the Channel and the German Army between me and my family. I don't know when, or even if, I'll ever get to go home again. Who knows what's going to happen in the next few months or years, and where I'll end up?"

She had several good points, but . . . "Come to that, do any of us? We're all just one bomb away from never having to worry about food shortages or blackout curtains ever again. If Gryffyth Pendragon is who you want, grab him."

"You're right."

"You sound much less certain than you did five minutes ago." And there was the sticky question of Gryffyth being a

Dragon. Or did Mary know about that? If she didn't, it was his job, not hers, to break the news.

"It's just . . ." Mary paused, chewed a mouthful of toast and Marmite very slowly, then went on. "I love him, Gloria. We've more in common than I ever dreamed of, but I have this awful feeling that bad things are about to happen and I don't want to drag him into them."

"Do you imagine for one minute that you could keep him out?"

She chuckled. "Good point. I so want to say yes to him, but something is holding me back."

Who was she to give anyone advice? At least Mary didn't have to worry about going furry once a month. "Never mind. If he's who you're meant to have, you'll end up together." She remembered her old mentor saying that. About just about everything. "Why not look at your post? Want another cup?"

Mary shook her head. There'd be a cup waiting at school. Which reminded her, she needed to bring in a spoonful to donate to the communal tea caddy. Meanwhile, she picked up the envelope. Who was writing to her? Gryffyth? Looked too precise for his manly handwriting. Not that she'd actually seen his handwriting, but imagined well-formed letters and strong flourishes.

Only one way to find out. She slit open the envelope with her knife and pulled out the single sheet. "Good heavens!" She looked up at Gloria's obvious curiosity. "This is a turnup for the books. It's from Miss Aubin. The cook at Wharton Lacey I met the other day. She's inviting me to tea."

"You are honored."

Mary wasn't so sure. "Perhaps. She says she'd like to make the acquaintance of a fellow islander."

"Seems reasonable enough. You don't think so?"

"Yes, it's just . . ." How could she give a history of centuries of rivalry in sixty seconds? "There's this thing between the islands. We call them crapauds: toads. They call us Guernsey donkeys. If my old grandfather were here he'd say to have nothing to do with her. She'd be devious and untrustworthy. But we're two exiles and I bet she gets as homesick as I do."

"When's she inviting you?"

"This afternoon, if it's convenient, as she has Wednesday afternoons free. If not, next week I think I'll go." Might help get her mind off Gryffyth. Not that she really wanted to.

Chapter Eighteen

Leatherhead

"Like that one?" Howell asked as Helen slipped the ring over her knuckle.

She looked down at the simple, oval garnet in a Victorian gold setting. "Yes," she replied, "it's perfect." She glanced up at him; by the look on his face, he agreed.

"We'll take it."

"Excellent, sir," the little man behind the counter replied. "If I may say so, a beautiful choice. You don't see workmanship like that anymore. Anything else?" he asked. "I have some fine wedding rings."

Helen looked at her old wedding ring, lying on the strip of black velvet. The slim band of gold Paul gave her decades ago. She picked it up and slipped it into her handbag. She'd loved him since her girlhood, but life moved on. "Another day," she said. "I want to enjoy wearing this one for a while first."

"Later," Howell agreed. "We'll come back another day. All set, Helen?"

"Yes." She hadn't thought she could be happier than she

was last night, but walking down Leatherhead High Street beside Howell Pendragon, she realized she'd been mistaken.

"Let's not go back yet," she said. "I feel like being frivolous."

He glanced at his watch. "Pubs are open. How about we celebrate?"

Since there was one just across the road, they crossed over and found a seat in the corner of the lounge bar. Helen settled for Guinness when the landlord claimed he had no gin.

"To us," she said, raising her glass.

"To us, and our families," he replied, clinking his glass against hers. "May we not shock them too much."

"I doubt we will and if we do, they've got a lot more to worry about right now than what we're doing. How did things go with Gryffyth?" She wasn't sure whether to ask, but he had mentioned it last night.

"He hasn't had my luck. She's making him wait while she decides."

"Can't blame her. He was pretty fast in asking. I hope she says yes though. She's a nice girl and I think they'd do well together." She took a sip of Guinness. "She's Other, isn't she?"

Howell nodded. "Don't miss much, do you, Helen?"

"I try not to. Gryffyth knows?"

"Yep. I told him, if he wanted to marry her he'd better come clean. You can't keep that sort of thing from a future wife. If it's going to make her do a runner, best find that out before they sign their marriage lines. Seems he was all set to tell her but she pipped him to the post and told him her news first. Between us now, she's a Sprite."

"Well, I never! Know anything about Sprites, do you?"

"Not a dicky bird."

"I suppose we'll all find out. He can bring her up to The Gallop for supper tonight. Will be a good time for everyone to get to know about her."

"You're right it would be, but . . ." He let out an exasperated sound. "Gryffyth's gone all protective. Says he doesn't want her put in any sort of danger. Doesn't want her to know what's been going on. I tried to talk sense into him but you know how young men are."

Having helped bring up Alice's two brothers, yes, she did. But seemed a bit curt to agree wholeheartedly. "One can understand why he wants to keep her safe, but doesn't he realize she's caught up in it? As is everyone in the village, whether they know it or not. And that those of us with powers need to use them for the good of the country?"

"He does, deep inside, but I'm not about to lecture him about sacrificing for England."

Good point. "Fair enough. Anyway, if she's half as alert and astute as she appears, once she's been around the pair of you for a little while, to say nothing of living under the same roof as Gloria, she'll no doubt cotton on to things." Helen just hoped it wasn't too late.

"And he might just get it through his thick head that there's not much point thinking he can keep a woman from doing anything these days. I think he only half believes what your Alice and Gloria did to those two bloodsuckers."

"If Mary's half the girl I think she is, she'll show him."

"Will be fun to watch, eh, Helen?"

She chuckled, half to herself, as she lifted her glass and sipped. "Just as long as you don't start getting ideas about keeping me out of things."

He shook his head. "Helen, I'm not a man to beat my head against a brick wall. Mind you, anything you do, I do. We're in this together."

"For better or for worse, eh?"

"Let's go for the better, my darling. Once this war's over," he added.

"Amen to that."

They sat a few moments in silence. She longed to ask what he was thinking, but bit back her curiosity. If he wanted to tell her, he would. No point in prying.

"I was thinking," he began, putting down his beer. "How about we go and have lunch to celebrate? According to Gryff the British Restaurant up in the parish church hall does a decent enough meal."

Why not? She drained her glass and smiled at her husband-to-be. "What a good idea. Can't be too late though. I have to get back and take care of supper tonight, if we're still holding our Council of War." And it would be fun to see how long it took everyone to notice her ring.

"I'll get you back in time, Helen, don't you worry. I'll even help peel potatoes if you like."

Wharton Lacey was a house and a half. After a long pull up the twisting drive, Mary paused on the crest and admired the view. It was like something off a calendar or a chocolate box: a lovely, old, pale yellow stucco house surrounded by rolling fields and winter-bare trees. She headed on down and looked around for an entrance. She doubted the wide front door was appropriate for tea with the cook. Dismounting, Mary wheeled her cycle around the side of the house, looking for a back door.

Instead she found a man she immediately recognized as Sir James Gregory, talking to a younger man in corduroy trousers who carried a spade over his shoulder. A gardener?

"Excuse me," she said.

Sir James smiled. "It's the new schoolteacher, isn't it? Forgive me, my dear, if I don't remember your name."

"Mary LaPrioux," she replied. "I came to see Miss Aubin and can't find the door."

"Ah, a get-together of the Islanders," he said.

"Sort of," she replied, uncomfortably aware that the gardener was staring at her. Something about him bothered her. A good deal. "Which way should I go?"

"Cut through the drawing room," he said. "Cross the hall and head for the baize-covered door that leads to the kitchen. That's her domain."

"Thank you."

She was unreasonably relieved to get inside and away from the disturbing young man. She found the door, slowing just as much as she dared, to get a good look at the drawing room. The windows had been taped, just like every house in the village, but the blackout curtains were disguised under green satin striped ones. Nice.

"You came in that way," Miss Aubin said, sounding a mite disapproving.

"I got lost and ran into Sir James Gregory. He told me to come this way."

"Fair enough. He's a good employer. Can't help being rich." She led the way into a small, cozy parlor, leaving Mary by the fire while she fetched the tea.

And it was some tea.

Mary couldn't decide and felt it rude to ask, if they always ate like this at Wharton Lacey or if Miss Aubin had put on a special spread for her. Cozy wasn't the word for sitting by a roaring fire in Miss Aubin's snug sitting room, eating a slice of jam sponge and that was after all but stuffing herself on ham and salmon sandwiches made with real butter.

"Another cup?" Miss Aubin asked.

"Please." Mary passed over her cup and saucer. "It's been a delicious tea."

That was a definitely sly smile. "We don't go short of anything here, that's the truth. I'll pack up the leftover sandwiches and cake and you can take them home with you. I'll bet you and Nurse Prewitt can eat them up between you."

After two days of marrowbone soup it would seem like a feast. "Oh, we could. It's kind of you."

"Just sharing it around. We've plenty. The government gets some of the production from the Home Farm, but we seem to keep the lion's share. We get a lot of visitors down here. Which means extra mouths to feed, but they won't miss a few sandwiches and a bit of ham." She handed the cup back to Mary. "Ever get news from home?"

A bit of a switch. "I get those Red Cross letters from time to time. But there's not much you can say in twenty-nine words. I did get a letter sent via a friend in Switzerland, but that had so many bits blacked out. I couldn't help wondering which end did that. Or maybe both."

"They're all still on the island?"

Mary nodded. "All of them. Can't help but worry about them. Your family?"

"Still there. Apart from my brother's wife who left to go back to her family in Devon." She took a taste of tea and seemed to find it too hot. "Do you know anything of what's happening on Jersey? About people getting taken to France? Or worse?"

"I don't know much about what's happening on Guernsey, much less Jersey. But we set up a sort of code, in case things got really bad. So far no bad news. You haven't heard anything?"

"Seldom. My family isn't much for writing." The expression in her eyes matched the worried tone in her voice. If it had been someone her own age, Mary would have hugged her, but Miss Aubin was the age of her mother, and she held back.

"It's awful. Some days I wonder if this hideous war will ever end."

"Or if anyone will be alive to see it." Miss Aubin shook her head. "Sorry, my dear, dumping my worries on you."

"They're my worries too."

"If you ever hear news of Jersey, or deportations, you'll let me know."

"Of course." Although her family were unlikely to use their limited words on news of the crapauds. "Something is really worrying you?"

Miss Aubin shook her head as if to deny it but let out a long sigh. "Yes. I've heard bad things. That everyone is in danger and people are getting taken away. I was hoping you might have heard something."

"Only that the place is overrun by Germans, which I'd worked out for myself. And they make everyone keep their boats in the harbor in St. Peter Port." One look at Miss Aubin and she longed to reassure her that everything was fine, her family was well and there was nothing to worry about, but Mary wasn't that big a liar. "It's been a lovely tea but it's getting on." She'd have a long ride in the dark as it was.

"I know. Let me wrap up everything for you."

As well as the packets of sandwiches and a good three quarters of the jam sponge, Miss Aubin produced a long loaf wrapped in paper. "It's a Guernsey gauche, dear. Thought you'd enjoy it."

Mary almost gasped. She knew just how much butter and eggs it took to make one, to say nothing of the dried fruit. "Thank you, but . . ."

"No buts, my dear. As I said, we don't go short here. I just got a shipment of dried fruit to make a Christmas cake. A little peel and raisins won't be missed. Hope I got it right. I've tasted it, but never made one before."

Not surprising. Mary doubted many Jersey cooks made a practice of cooking Guernsey specialties. "It will be wonderful." And it was a darn good thing she had a big basket on her bicycle. "Thank you so much," Mary said again, as she put on her coat and dug her gloves out of her pocket.

"My pleasure, dear. We must do it again. You don't know how much better I feel after our chat."

"You must visit us too. We can initiate Gloria into Island history. Remind her that we conquered England." It was an old claim and brought a smile to Miss Aubin's face.

"A bit of history never hurts, does it?" she replied as she led Mary to the back door.

Her bicycle stood where she'd left it, over by the stables. How had she missed the door? Looking back, Mary noticed it was hidden by a tall hedge. Next time she'd know.

She loaded her lovely loot into her basket. "Thank you again," she called and then stopped still, as she felt the hairs on her neck itch. Turning, she saw that the young gardener stood by the stable entrance. She wasn't sure why he gave her the willies, but he did.

"There you are, Paul," Miss Aubin said. "I wondered where you got to."

"Talking to Sir James about the brussels sprouts," he replied.

"Now you're back, I need you to bring in some coal for the dining room fire."

"Be along in a minute," he said, as he gave Mary an odd look and walked toward the stables.

His voice carried a tinge of insubordination but that wasn't Mary's concern. He was. The man oozed menace and danger in a way she'd never encountered in her life. Once Miss Aubin shut the door, she leapt on her bicycle and pedaled along the drive just as fast as she knew how.

Until the gardener reappeared in front of her, fifty yards or so from the gates.

She braked, and he had hold of the handlebars.

Every instinct she possessed was on the alert. Danger and

threat seeped out of his pores. He smelled strange. One would expect a gardener to smell of outdoors and fresh air. Not like a butcher shop. Odd. Maybe he'd been killing chickens or something.

He smiled. "From Jersey, too, are you then?" he asked. "Relatives back there?"

"No," she replied. "I'm not." And was not in the mood for conversation.

"Oh, really? I distinctly heard Sir James say you were."

"He said 'Islanders.' There's more than one island."

"Which one are you from then?"

"What about you? Are you from these parts?" Might as well turn the questions back on him.

"Lord, no! Wouldn't be here if I didn't have to. You were evacuated?"

He wasn't giving up, and she wasn't telling. She didn't want this unpleasant young man to know anything more about her if she could help it. And darn it, she would help it.

The gates were in sight. Or at least the gateposts were. The iron gates were gone; no doubt that was Wharton Lacey's contribution to the war effort. Just ahead was a low bridge over a stream. One more curve and she'd be out in the lane and riding away as fast as she could.

"Good afternoon," she said. "I need to get on home. Would you mind getting out of my way?"

Seemed he did. He didn't let go but he did move to stand beside her, not directly in front. "Just a minute," he said, leaning toward her and grabbing her shoulder.

Mary gave him a shove with her bicycle but he didn't budge. Just shoved back so she fell off it.

She scrambled up and grabbed her bicycle. He let go of it, but before she could remount, grabbed her and stared into her eyes.

Unease washed over her. There was something really nasty

about him. She let go of her bicycle and ran, taking several steps before he threw the bicycle down and advanced on her. He was snarling. No other word for it. Panic surged inside her. What was he? It happened so fast, faster than she could think, but as he grabbed her, mouth wide, teeth gleaming and eyes flashing, she sensed water.

She was on the low bridge. She was safe. Drawing on the power under her, she shoved him sideways, pushing him off the bridge. The water was deep with November rain and he let out an unearthly scream as he splashed in.

Mary ran back and grabbed her bicycle, then pedaled as fast as she could, letting the downhill momentum add speed. As his wails faded in the distance, she wondered if he could swim. So what? It couldn't be that deep, after all, and cold water might cool him off.

It was only after a mile or so of frantic pedaling that she felt safe from pursuit and slowed a little. Not that her heart rate eased. What had happened? He'd attacked her. No other word for it. Why? For rape? She shuddered. If so, it was an odd spot to pick, but she hadn't sensed that sort of sexual menace. It was as if he'd wanted to take something else from her. And those nasty teeth. The funny look he'd given her disturbed her too. Boring into her eyeballs sounded fanciful but that was just how it felt.

Damn! That gardener was some sort of Other. What now? Better talk it over with Gryffyth. He might know.

Paul Schmidt hauled himself out of the stinking stream, still shaking and swearing revenge. How dare that insolent female throw him into water? And how in the name of hades had she managed that? What the hell was she? She'd not succumbed to his compulsion. Of course he had been on the bridge, and running water weakened him, but even so.

He trudged up the drive. Who or what was she? The first he'd get from the cook, when he brought in the coal she wanted. She wouldn't dare evade his questions like this one had. But what? Was she the killer? Seemed the whole damn village was populated with possible suspects. But if it was this one, he'd had a lucky escape. But how could that puny little creature slay two full-strength vampires? It defied reason.

He'd meet her again and enjoy himself next time. Schmidt smiled at the prospect. And shivered with the cold. He need warm blood tonight. Fresh warm blood was what he needed to counteract the pain of his immersion and there was a mare waiting for him in the stables.

Chapter Nineteen

Mary rode away as if the devil were at her heels. She wasn't too sure he wasn't. Going downhill a good bit of the way only added to her speed, the wind was cold on her face but she scarcely noticed it. Putting distance between herself and the glimpse of nightmare had occupied her totally. The feeling of panic and urgency lasted until she descended into the village. Once back there, she felt strangely safe. As if she were home again and away from the nasty creature lurking up at Wharton Lacey. As she calmed, she began to worry about Miss Aubin and the people up there. Should she warn them? Would they think she was insane, or drunk?

She'd worry about that later. Right now all she wanted was to go straight to Gryffyth and the safety of his strong arms. She didn't even stop at her cottage but raced on past, heading for the Pendragons'.

At the gate, she rammed her brakes too hard and almost skidded, but steadied herself and dismounted. Pushing open the gate, she wheeled her bicycle up the path and hesitated. Shyness seldom bothered her but suddenly she wasn't too sure of herself. Was she intruding? Sergeant Pendragon had aways been friendly and courteous but never invited her to his house.

On the other hand, his son had just asked her to marry him, so surely she wasn't intruding. Darn it! She wanted Gryffyth. She propped her cycle against a dustbin and knocked on the door.

His father opened it. "Who's there?" he said, from the other side of the blackout curtain. "Alice? You're early."

"It's Mary LaPrioux."

"This is a turnup for the books." He pulled the curtain aside and grabbed her hand. "Come on in." He pulled her into the warmth of the kitchen and shut the door. "Now, my dear. What can I do for you?"

For several long seconds, she had no idea, her throat still tight from fear as she stood there, panting, chest heaving from the exertion. She looked around at the comfort and coziness of the warm kitchen and, to her utter embarrassment, burst into tears.

Through her sobs, she heard him call, "Gryff, come on down!" as he led her over to the fireplace and sat her down in an easy chair. "Now there, my dear," he said, "don't worry. Whatever happened, it's alright now. Gryff's coming."

She felt a fool, but couldn't stop sobbing.

"Mary!" She looked up through her tears and there he was. Her love. Her Gryffyth. She stood, all but pushed past the sergeant and rushed into her lover's arms. "What the hell happened?" he asked over her head, as he drew her close.

"Beats me, son. She knocked on the door, came in, and burst into tears. Something happened to upset her."

"I can see that, Dad!"

She had to get hold of herself. "It's alright. I'm alright now. It was just so . . ." She couldn't hold back the shudder.

"Here, love." Gryffyth pushed a neatly ironed handkerchief into her hand. "Dry your eyes, and tell me what happened."

"You take care of her, son," the sergeant said. "Don't you worry, my dear," he went on. "You just sit down with Gryff.

I'll get you a nice cup of tea and when you calm down you can tell us what happened."

She blew her nose and took a deep breath and noticed Gryffyth was in his dressing gown. She wouldn't think about what he did or did not have on underneath, and made herself not look at his leg. At least the proximity of Gryffyth déshabillé went a long way to settle her nerves. Or rather tweak them in another direction entirely.

"Here you are." Sergeant Pendragon put a heavy mug in her hand. "It's very sweet. You drink it up. Best thing for shock."

Sweet wasn't the word—by the taste of it, he'd put in half their combined sugar ration. The sheer kindness almost had her sniveling again, but she held it back and drank.

"Mary . . ." Gryffyth began.

"Give her a minute, son. She'll tell us what happened. You drink that up, my dear. Do you the world of good."

She was halfway through the mugful. When she looked around her, at the warm, welcoming kitchen, it was so settled, so normal, it made her encounter up at Wharton Lacey seem like a wild figment of her imagination. Maybe that creature had just made a pass at her. Improper, but not the horror she remembered. No, it had been awful. She had not imagined one second of it. She glanced at Gryffyth, sitting so close his warmth seeped into her bones, and at his father, standing by the table, looking worried, and reminded herself she was talking to a pair of Dragons here. They understood about these things. She looked at the sergeant. "Did Gryffyth tell you what I am?"

He nodded. "That he did."

That made one less explanation. "Then hopefully you won't think I'm loony."

"I doubt I would have anyway," the sergeant replied. "Tell us what happened."

She told them.

"I'll blast him to smithereens!" Gryffyth said—no, more like yelled. "I'll fry his hide and incinerate him."

Knowing he had the ability to do that—literally—added an extra edge to his threat.

"Hang on a minute, son. Time enough for that later." Sergeant Pendragon pulled a chair from the table and sat in front of her. "Mary, can you tell us what he looked like? Height, hair, age. All that."

"Yes. Tallish, about as tall as Gryffyth but slender in build. Sandy hair, sort of blond gone dark, if you know what I mean."

He nodded. "How old do you think?"

"Twenties? Thirties? Not middle-aged."

"Not dark haired? You're sure? Couldn't have been dark, almost as dark as Gryff's?"

"Oh no, definitely not. Unless it changes, like his eyes. They seemed normal at first, sort of gray blue, but then they almost blazed at me. And his teeth . . ." She shuddered.

"So much for the new gardener," Sergeant Pendragon said. "I sensed there was something Other about him. Now he's shown his colors. I wonder if he's one of them."

"Christ, Dad!" Gryffyth said, as he held her closer. "Just thinking about one of those creatures having a go at you, Mary, drives me batty."

"What creatures?" It was good to know her instincts had served her right, one did need to know what one was dealing with.

"Vampires."

"Vampires?" If it had been anyone but Gryffyth, she'd have laughed at the idea. "They exist?"

Both men nodded.

"They do indeed, Mary," Sergeant Pendragon said. "And for some reason best known to themselves, they're closing in on Brytewood. In the last couple of months we've had two move in. One after the other. Now it seems we have a couple more of them to deal with. Bloody nuisance they are too." He paused and let out a tsk of exasperation. "Sorry about that, my dear. Just came out."

"Don't apologize. If they're Vampires, it's the right adjective."

Gryffyth chuckled, pulled her close and pecked her on her cheek. "See what I said, Dad, isn't she the one for me?"

Mary couldn't miss the broad smile on his father's face. "Better work on convincing Mary you're the one for her then, son." He stood up. "Now, seems to me you'd best get your trousers on. Alice'll be here in ten minutes and Mary, I'll get you another cup of tea and then you'd best come with us."

"Come where?"

"Up to The Gallop," Gryffyth replied. "As long as you don't mind the rest of them knowing what you are."

"Now hang on a minute, Gryffyth. I told you. You told your father. Fair enough, but I'm not announcing my nature to the entire village."

"Good heavens, no. That wouldn't do at all!" the sergeant said. "Just a few of us are getting together. Others, like you and us, they have secrets of their own, and have had to deal with Vampires."

Oh, my! "More Others?"

He nodded.

"If you're feeling stunned, my love, join the club. I just learned all this Sunday night. There's more to sleepy little Brytewood than meets the eye." If it was the haunt of Vampires, he was dead right. Wrong expression, that. He stood. "Be back in a jiffy, Mary. I wanted to keep you safe from all this, but in light of what just happened, you're coming with us."

He wasn't exactly asking. "Are you sure it won't be an imposition?" An extra plate to fill was a hardship these days.

"You'll be a welcome addition," the sergeant said. "You've

repelled a Vampire. That's an ability will come in handy. We need you with us."

"You'll just listen and learn what's been going on," Gryffyth said. "You won't have to do anything."

"Now come on, Gryffyth. If there's a Vampire containment project going on in Brytewood,"—had she really actually said that?—"I'm in with everyone else. I'm not a passenger."

"We'll see about that," he replied.

She fancied she heard his father chuckle as Gryffyth went out.

The evening was an eye opener. From Alice Watson's first surprised "Mary?" as she came in the Pendragons' back door, and the sergeant's, "She's joining us, Doctor. Meet our one and only Water Sprite," things just got more confusing. But more reassuring.

To find there were so many Others in the village wasn't quite the same as being home on Guernsey with her aunts and cousins, but the closest she was likely to encounter on the mainland.

After explaining to everyone what she knew and didn't know about being a Sprite, and trying to understand the varied natures of the rest of the group, they sat down to a dinner that featured a hand of roast pork.

Mary wasn't the only one salivating at the aroma as Mrs. Burrows placed the roast on the table and invited Peter to do the honors of the carving knife.

As plates were passed down the table, and dishes of potatoes, carrots and brussels sprouts handed around, Alice said, "In case you're all thinking Gran has gone against her principles and bought it under the counter, I brought it home. They killed a pig up on Ranmore and offered me a joint. I thanked them profusely and raced it home to Gran."

"We've one at school," Mary said. "I think some of the London children will go through trauma when it's slaughtered. I don't think they quite get the link between a pig and sausages."

"They'll soon get it when they taste some," Sergeant Pendragon said. "Are you having it cured?"

"I'm not sure. I wish I'd arrived early enough to buy a share in it though. A nice ham would have been a treat for Christmas." Come to that, peace would be nice for Christmas but that seemed a long way off.

"Mrs. Burrows," Gloria said, as she reached for a plate. "Your ring!"

"Yes, my love," she replied with a wide smile, "Howell and I went shopping this morning."

That brought on a wave of congratulations, general good wishes for the future and regrets at the shortage of Champagne in these war-torn days.

And earned Mary some pointed sidelong glances from Gryffyth. "What do you think?" he whispered.

"That I'll let you know." He was not bulldozing her into a decision. She had enough on her plate already with Vampires, and Pixies, and a Shifter right on top of learning about Dragons.

"Now," the sergeant said, once the excitement settled and the gravy boat resumed its way around the table. "Time to get back to business. Mary learned something today."

Mary had learned a vast amount in the past twenty-four hours, but knew which specific new knowledge he was referring to. She repeated her nasty experience by the stream at Wharton Lacey.

"Can you describe, as exactly as you can, what he looks

like?" Alice asked. Mary obliged and wished her classes were half as attentive as the group around the table.

"I think it's him," Alice said once Mary had finished. She looked straight at Mary. "The others know this. I've seen him twice. Once, when I found him injured up in Fletcher's Woods, and on Friday night, in Guildford. Seems he's been working as an emergency fireman, but left suddenly. He went by the name of Paul Smith."

"Miss Aubin called him Smith," Mary said. Of course, it wasn't exactly an unusual name.

"I knew there was something about him," Howell Pendragon said. "Should have had a better look at him. He was lurking at the back of Sir James's greenhouse."

"I wonder what he's doing up there," Peter said. "Aside from scaring Mary, that is."

"I have an idea," Mary said. "Miss Aubin mentioned they have a number of government people visiting. There's even a party coming soon. He could be there to glean information."

"Or worse," Andrew Barron said.

Gloria picked up on that. "Assassination, you mean?"

The thought was terrible.

"Why not?" Andrew went on. "Disposing of key people in the government would be a blow to the country."

"And a good move for the enemy," Gryffyth added. "So, we know where he is and what he's most likely up to. What now? We cook his goose for him?"

"It's not quite that easy," Gloria pointed out. "They take a lot of killing and it's messy." She sounded quite grim.

"But he backed off from Mary when she drew on her power," Gryffyth said.

"Repelling one and actually exterminating are two different matters entirely," Alice said. "Trust us, Gryffyth. Gloria and I both know, so do Peter and Andrew. Besides, if this is a

Vampire, and it seems quite certain that he's up to no good, we can't just toddle on up to Wharton Lacey and stake him. Aside from any legal repercussions, it would draw too much attention to ourselves."

"Shouldn't we tell the police if these Vampires are spies of some sort?" Mary asked.

"Think about it, Mary," Gloria said. "Imagine the reaction if one of us went up to Sergeant Jones and told him we suspected Vampire spies in the vicinity."

She had a point. They'd be laughed out of the village.

"We don't know for certain," Mrs. Burrows said. "But everything points to that. The first one was supposedly the nephew of a woman who was arrested as a spy. She had a radio hidden in her attic."

"And later died in rather odd circumstances before they could take her up to London for questioning," Alice added. "The second one set up shop as a baker, had access to all the gossip and goings on. We do know that they are strong, ruthless, don't mind who they hurt or injure. And are up to no good."

"And were rather fond of attempting sabotage to my munitions plant," Andrew added.

"And now there's more of them," Gryffyth said. "At least two."

"What makes you think that?" Peter asked.

"I encountered one Monday night. It didn't match Mary's description. He was dark-haired and almost swarthy and about my height, and the one up at Wharton Lacey is definitely light-haired."

"So, unless they can shift appearance too, we've a couple poaching here." No one disagreed with Peter.

"Could they shift?" Gloria asked. "I can, and the Pendragons can, but we change completely. It's not like changing your skin tone or hair color."

"I don't think that's it," Mrs. Burrows replied. "Seems to me the one Gryffyth repelled is the selfsame one as scared the living daylights out of Mr. Whorleigh."

Mary let out a gasp. "The grocer!"

"What happened to Sam Whorleigh?" Gryffyth asked, saving Mary the need to ask one more question.

Mrs. Burrows told them.

Peter nodded. "Sounds like the same one. The scarring and redness on the face could have been a figment of Whorleigh's terror, but more likely the result of Gryffyth's attack the night before."

"Wish I'd done him in for good," Gryffyth muttered, "but he moved so darn fast. He was gone in a flash."

"I think that makes the whole point," Peter said. "We're up against creatures that move like the wind, recover fast and are not easy to corner."

"And we have two to deal with," Alice said. "There's six of us Others, plus two believing mundanes." The last she said with a grin at Peter and Andrew. "If we can't manage with the numbers in our favor, we're not exerting ourselves."

"Would be better with Whorleigh adding his bit," Mrs. Burrows said. "Drat the man, comes here scared and begging for help, but when I ask him to join us and actually contribute something, he funks out."

"He missed a nicer piece of pork than he's ever had in his shop," Andrew said. "I wonder what he's doing?"

"It's of little interest to me," Mrs. Burrows said, "although I intend to give him a piece of my mind tomorrow morning."

Sam Whorleigh was propping up the bar of the Pig and Whistle and ordering a second pint. He was in dire need of Dutch courage to venture out into the night and walk home, his bicycle unfit to ride. He'd had to invent a story of theft to explain why Constable Parlett found it bent and twisted near the church. Bicycles weren't that hard to get hold of, not with his contacts, but it would take a couple of days and a bit of haggling. Meanwhile he faced a walk home.

He was reluctant to pass the bombed-out vicarage again and hadn't used the shortcut across the allotments since the morning he'd found Doctor Watson, drunk and surrounded by a miasma of trouble and danger.

And thinking about the lot up at The Gallop, Mrs. Burrows had as good as commanded his attendance this evening. The old biddy could sing for it. He wanted nothing to do with her. Even if it meant missing a free meal. There was something wrong in the village. He'd sensed it long before this morning, and she was probably causing it. The old bat as much as intimated that she knew what was going on.

"You look worried, Sam," Fred Wise, the landlord, said. "Trouble in the shop?"

"Not that. Got my bicycle pinched."

"Rotten luck! Bet you'll come across another."

He resented the implication. Or was it admiration? "Right, I will. But meanwhile I've got to walk home."

"That's one thing I don't ever have to worry about," the landlord replied with a bit of a chuckle. "Draw you another pint, can I?"

Why not? But better stop at three. He wanted to get home.

Whorleigh sensed the distant presence as he walked down the lane. He cursed that third pint that dulled his Other senses, but not enough to slow him down if he needed to move fast.

He quickened his pace, opting to take the shortcut by the allotments. Everywhere was pitch black these days, and a stroll past the old rectory was just too much for his nerves right now. Not that he'd admit that aloud, but in these days caution made good sense.

He walked fast, almost running, bumping into fences and gateposts, but the sense of menace followed him every inch of the way. Once home, he locked the door behind him and stood panting, back against the door. He was safe. Whatever was out there had passed him by.

Chapter Twenty

"Tell," Gloria said as they closed the door behind them. "Spill the beans. Blab. What's going on between you and our sexy soldier, returned from the wars?"

"You mean Gryffyth?"

Mary wanted to play thick, did she? "Can you name another man you've danced with and paraded through the village? And tonight you could barely keep your eyes off him. So don't try to convince me you're not interested. How are things?"

"He asked me to marry him."

Gloria paused, her coat half off her shoulders, but she managed to close her mouth. "Oh my! This needs more than a cup of cocoa. I'm going to get out the Garibaldi biscuits I was saving for Christmas and you're going to tell me everything."

"Don't open them. I've got masses of stuff Miss Aubin gave me. Sandwiches, almost a whole cake, and a gauche she made for me and . . . oh, damn!"

"What?"

"They're in my bicycle basket."

Gloria shrugged her coat back on. "I'll pop out and get them, save you putting your coat back on—and what's a gauche?"

olutely most delicious fruit bread you can imagine, my bicycle up at the Pendragons'."

oria didn't even worry about gaping or goggling. Talk out blasé and unconcerned. She was seeing a new side to Mary. "You left it there, outside Gryffyth's front door?"

"His back door, actually. I rode straight there after seeing that Vampire thing. Then Alice arrived and drove us up to her house. She brought us all back and I clean forgot about it."

"Holy smoke! Definitely biscuits needed. You do realize," Gloria said, as she hung up her coat, "that the whole village will know by breakfast that your bicycle sat outside Gryffyth's back door all night. You'll have to marry him now."

"What utter rot! Especially since we'd have had a chaperone all night."

She sounded more wistful than annoyed.

"So," Gloria said, pouring milk into a saucepan. "He proposed."

"Yes."

She was going to have to dig it out of her. Didn't altogether make sense. Seeing them together, you could feel the attraction between them, but now Mary was acting as if she got marriage proposals twice a week. "Pass me the matches, please. They're on the mantelpiece."

Gas lit, milk warming, Gloria reached for a couple of mugs.

"Let me do it," Mary said. "You made it last night."

Might as well let her. Gloria dug into the dresser for the biscuits, opened the package and put them in an empty tin. So, Mary had clammed up. Not for long, if Gloria had any say in the matter. She stoked up the boiler. Might as well keep the place warm if they were going to sit up and talk, and they *were* going to sit up and talk.

Mary brought over the mugs, handed one to Gloria, took

a biscuit. "I used to love these as a child. We called the squashed fly biscuits."

"You and your brothers?" Being an only child, she envied Mary having a family.

Mary nodded. "Clarence tried to convince me they really were dead flies. I almost believed him before I realized if they were, no one would eat them." She took a bite, chewed, then took a sip of cocoa and said, "So, you want to know about Gryffyth and me?"

Gloria nodded. Smiled, in a way she hoped was encouraging, sipped her cocoa and sat back.

"I'm in love, Gloria. It's insane, impossible, and beyond fantastic, but I took one look and fell for him, hook, line and sinker. He says he loves me and wants to marry me, as ludicrous as it seems after knowing him," she glanced at the clock on the mantelpiece, "four days and three hours. You think I've a few tiles loose in the top story, don't you?"

"No. I'd always fancied Andrew, knew him for ages, but he was always so frightfully professional. Then he knocked me off my bicycle and . . ."

"It was all straightforward after that?"

"Good heavens, no! Once he made it clear he really fancied me, that's when the soul-searching started. Here he was a nice, ordinary, or rather extraordinary, man, but a normal, mundane human. How the hell was I going to tell him I turn furry at intervals? And what if got my nerve up to tell him and he was repulsed? Or worse, told people. Can you imagine me keeping my job? War or not, they'd probably strip me of my nurse's certificate. I used to lie awake worrying about it."

"But it worked out, Andrew loves you the way you are."

"True, but I think the fact we'd both be mangled corpses pushing up daisies if I hadn't shifted when we encountered that mean with sex." Her face was a picture of

Dragons and Sprites aren't meant to mate?"

ught more in that direction than Gloria ever

a good point. "You're worried things won't

een you in bed?"

ll. Yes."

want to, right, you really, really want to sleep

h."

s!"

easily taken care of. We'll arrange for me to be

ening, you ask him in for a nice cup of coffee and

e him. Easy as pie."

ever seduced anyone before. It was rather the other

nd."

n't think you'll have any problem. You fancy him. He

you. Now, when are you next going out?"

eel bad about tossing you out of your own house."

on't. Have you noticed how late I come in some nights?

am about waking up in the morning beside Andrew, but,

r heaven, would that give the gossips something to wag

ir tongues over!"

"Instead it will be me slandered over my darn bicycle. I'll

et dubbed a loose woman and I haven't any of the benefits."

"Don't worry, Mary. We'll make sure you reap every benefit of your sexy soldier."

"So," Weiss said, seated across the room on the same rickety chair in Schmidt's quarters. Why these mortals couldn't provide better for their servants, he'd never know. "We know where
this shopkeeper lives. We will take him and interrogate him and
if he is the Vampire killer, he will die. Very, very slowly."

Vampire, had a

And if a human

"Oh, it's not th

I've ever dreamed

men with Sprite bloo

of them."

"Wouldn't they be Sp

Mary laughed. "Oh no.

trait but only girl babies g

become men. What about W

"There are male ones. My n

But how it's passed on, I don't

about it. Doesn't seem to bother

sure we can have children."

"I hadn't even thought that far. W

"Dragons who like to swim?"

"Only our daughters."

"So you are going to marry him." Mary

at her mug with a solemn look on her fac

other squashed-fly biscuit." Mary took one

end. "What's bothering you? You love him

You're both Other and accept your differences.

"Yes, but . . ."

"But what?"

Mary's brow creased. "I'm afraid I'll shock you."

"Mary, I'm a district nurse. I did my training in L

I've seen and heard things you'd scarce credit. I'm unsh

able." At least as far as anything Mary could possibly say

Another chew of the biscuit appeared to bolster Mary

courage. "It's like this. We've kissed and been very friendly

and we mesh together wonderfully, but, well, I can't marry, or

even promise to marry someone without being sure we're

well-matched. I

anxiety. "What i

Mary had th

had. Still, it w

work out betw

"In a nutsh

"But you

with Gryffy

"Lord, y

"That's

out one e

you sedu

"I've

way aro

"I d

fancie

"I

"D

I dr

dea

the

"And what about the other one?" Schmidt asked. "The female. Aren't we taking her too? She has power."

So he claimed, thought Weiss. Schmidt wasn't going to forget his dunking in a hurry. "Identify her. The cook must know who she is."

"And we'll take her too, like the grocer?"

Schmidt was ripe for revenge. An admirable trait. "One at a time. We start with the shopkeeper. Let us peel what he knows from him. Taking two at once might be a mistake, since we don't know what we're dealing with. What if they grow stronger together? We can't take the risk. We take the grocer creature. Take him Saturday after the shop closes, that way he won't be missed in the village until Monday, and keep the woman in reserve. After you find out who she is and where she lives . . ." He paused for added effect. "One more thing. Find out who is coming to Wharton Lacey next week. We're not wasting effort on a couple of replaceable cabinet ministers, or the chairman of one of their committees. We have one target and one only. Take out Churchill and we will have the mortals in the Wehrmacht eating out of our hands and baring their necks for us."

Schmidt sat thinking after Weiss left. His not-so-revered leader hadn't faced the power of that female one. Whatever she was, she needed eliminating. No doubt about it and, as far as he was concerned, the sooner the better.

Come morning, he'd weasel the information out of Miss Aubin. If she balked, and threats to her nearest and dearest failed, there was always force.

"Dad, we've got to do something about Mary's bicycle. She'll need it in the morning."

"She will," Howell agreed, trying not to smile. The lad's pride was a bit touchy at times. Understandable, really. Must rankle a bit to know your father pipped you to the post when it came to getting that all important Yes.

"Could we take it over, do you think, Dad? I'd go on my own but I don't want her thinking I'm knocking on her door late for other reasons."

"She might not mind, son. She's a decent girl, but doesn't strike me as the shy type." At least as far as Gryff was concerned. That was the wrong thing to say. Poor old Gryff went the next best thing to purple.

"Dad!"

"Don't look so shocked, son. The girl fancies you so hard it's written all over her face. A tender night together might help to convince her you're the very man for her."

Gryff couldn't go any darker in the face but his eyes looked ready to pop. "Really, Dad!"

"Why not? If you want to marry her use all your powers of persuasion, and don't start on about your damn leg. She knows what you are and what you have and don't have. Believe me, son, a man's legs aren't what matters when you're getting snug and cozy." Wasn't often he'd managed to leave Gryff speechless in the last few years. "Anyroad, son. As far as her bicycle goes, you're right. Let's take it back, and afterwards I think we should have a stroll around the village. See what's going on. As long as your leg holds up."

"My leg's fine, Dad." Gryffyth paused, thinking about Mary, Howell hoped. "You think these Vampire creatures might be about?"

"I've no idea, son, but night is when they're strongest we've been told, and it never hurts to have a look-see. And if we do encounter one, I think between us we could take care of it."

"And if we do, Mary won't embark on some tomfool project with Alice and Gloria. I'm game, Dad."

* * *

They left a little after midnight. No one was likely to be about with the Pig closed. And if they were, they were up to no good.

Howell walked slowly; no point in tiring the lad if they were facing an encounter. They retrieved Mary's bicycle and left it propped against her house. Howell was a bit curious about the contents of the basket, but it wasn't any of his business. He hoped it didn't rain overnight. They could have put it away in the shed, where he guessed Gloria kept hers, but decided it might be overlooked in the morning. No point in having her walk to school when her cycle was sitting waiting for her.

"Now, son," Howell said, "let's do a walkabout."

Walking pretty much in silence, they made it through the village center down to the church and past the ruined rectory and the ARP post. There wasn't a sound inside there, no doubt they were enjoying a quiet night.

"Isn't that where Whorleigh claimed to have seen the Vampire thing?" Gryff asked as they stood looking at the dark outline of what was left of the rectory.

"Yes, and don't doubt he saw one. Sam Whorleigh isn't the imaginative sort." The cowardly, self-serving sort more like.

"Plenty of space there for someone to hide," Gryff said. "Undisturbed too. Although I bet the kids play there in daylight."

"They're not supposed to. That side wall might go any time."

"Think we should take a closer look?"

"Why not?"

They circled the ruin, treading carefully. "It's empty," Gryff whispered. "No heartbeats."

"There won't be."

"Crikey, you're right, Dad. How do you know if they're there?"

"That one you met, what did you sense?"

"Nastiness, evil, like a great sticky black miasma."

As good a description as any. "That's what we're on the lookout for."

They crossed the abandoned tennis court and the ankle-deep, yellowed lawn and headed back to the lane, across the vegetable garden. Pity the last cabbages and brussels sprouts hadn't been harvested. Howell made a mental note to mention it to the vicar. Someone in the village would be glad of them.

Then Gryff stopped, tapping the ground with his good foot. "Dad, over here. What do you think?"

"Ground's been disturbed."

"Is it true they sleep underground?"

"Dunno for sure, son, but could be. Also I've learned there's more than one sort of Vampire. Maybe he hid here after you got him, then in the morning scared the willies out of Sam Whorleigh."

"So he might come back here."

"He might but we can hardly keep watch just on the off chance."

They headed back. Verifying Whorleigh's story was satisfying but hardly helped anything. There weren't any Vampires about. Tonight at least.

They made it back to the center of the village and were about to turn up Bell Lane toward home, when Gryff stopped and grabbed his father's arm.

"Dad," he whispered.

Howell stopped. A sick, cloying sense of unease passed them and was gone.

"That was it," Gryff said, "but faint, weak, as if it were a distance away. But there's no mistaking it. It was here in the village but it's gone."

"Gone how far, and what was it doing?"

Questions neither of them could answer.

Chapter Twenty-One

"Tomorrow," Rolf said, "I go to meet the escapees. I want you to come with us, Bela."

She looked up from shoveling the heavy wet earth into Gela's grave. Even with Rolf and Hans's help it had been an arduous task in the bitter cold. "How far is it?"

"A good day's travel, but you never have trouble keeping up."

The strength from that last Vampire's death was fading slowly, but she still had to slow her pace to keep level with the men.

"Will you come? You'll be able to talk to them, make them understand."

"Of course." Why not? With Gela dead she had no roots or ties left anywhere, except her link to the woods and the earth. "I'll come."

They left before dawn, Bela wearing Angela's boots and skis. Not loaned willingly, but Rachel's boots were too large.

"You cadge and scrounge everything from us," Angela griped.

"I'll bring them back safely, don't worry."

"And when will that be?"

"As soon as they can," Rachel replied for all of them. "The

escapees will slow them down. I doubt they're used to the woods and mountains as we are."

Rachel stood in the cave opening, waving them on their way. Angela, no doubt, was muttering on about the loss of her boots and skis and the burden of two extra mouths to feed.

The going was fair. Three times they had to carry their skis and clamber over rocks and what looked to have been a small landslide. They seldom spoke, aware that sound carried in the clear air. Just as dark was falling, they were met by two wild-eyed partisans in dire need of a shave. And a wash, Bela noticed as they settled by the fire in their lean-to.

There was no sign of the escapees. Just two Communist partisans.

"What happened?" Bela whispered to Rolf as they settled to sleep on the ground.

"They'll be here tomorrow," he replied. "The Frenchman has difficulty walking. Slows them down."

It was late afternoon the next day before they arrived, footsore and weary, the Frenchman limping. Even a thick-headed mortal could see the man needed to rest before going on.

"Sorry about being late," the Englishman said, in atrocious German. "Jules had a rough time of it."

They were sitting huddled in the back of the lean-to, eating cold, baked parsnips and sharing a couple of tins of bully beef the Englishman carried with him. He and a resistance worker, a bearded Dutchman called Piet, whom Bela had met before, hauled a large sack of supplies with them. Piet left almost immediately to return to his camp before dark and the Communists delved into the sack.

"Where did they get all this?" one of them asked.

The Englishman shrugged and looked at Bela. "Tell him I haven't the foggiest idea," he replied. "They gave it to me to carry and I said, 'Thank you.'"

"I told them," she replied, "but I think they wanted explosives, not food."

He grinned at her in the dark. "Didn't realize they'd put in an order."

She laughed, much to the obvious disgust of the two Communists. They'd never volunteered their names, but Rolf had warned her they were mistrustful of everyone, even their allies. "Have you been free long?" she asked the Englishman.

"Six weeks," he replied. "We should have been on our way before this, but Jules got sick and needed to rest. He's still in a bad way."

"We're only a day's travel away. Our place is bigger, and deeper in the mountains. I'd be mistrustful and uneasy, too, if we were this close to the farms."

He held out his gloved hand. "I'm Simon."

"Bela. I won't share the others' names. We have to be careful."

"Fair enough, Bela. So we spend the night here then move on?" She nodded. "Leave first thing, if we can."

At least she hoped so. After the scowls and sidelong looks from this pair, Angela would seem welcoming and friendly.

Food shared, they took it in turns to go outside, Rolf and Simon helping Jules, who still had trouble walking. Then they settled into shared blankets and bed rolls. They were cramped, but they'd be gone at first light.

In the morning, it was clear to everyone that the Frenchman was too weak to travel. But the prospect of feeding all five of them until he recovered, was unacceptable to their stingy hosts. In the end it was decided the Rolf would stay and help take care of Jules. Hans, Bela and Simon would go ahead, and Rolf would follow with Jules in a day or two.

They left right after a breakfast of hard black bread and

more parsnips. "Can that Englishman ski?" one of the Communists asked.

He could. "Not awfully well," he told Bela. "But I can keep upright most of the time," he added with a lopsided smile.

A hundred meters after they left, it was obvious that he could do more than stay upright. "You've skied before?" she said.

"A few times. My parents took my brother and my sister and me to Switzerland a couple of times. It's been a while. Beats walking though."

They continued in cautious silence for hours. That was why Bela heard the first gunshots and the baying of the dogs ahead.

"Into the trees," Hans said in a hoarse whisper. Shouldering their skis, they fled into the shelter of the trees and hunkered down together among a cluster of dark pines.

No point in asking what was happening—gunshots meant only one thing. "Let me go and see," Bela said.

Hans nodded.

"What's going on?" Simon asked. She told him and he as good as exploded. "You can't go on alone. You're a woman."

He still harbored the illusions of his comfortable life before the war. "I can move fast. I'm used to the woods and I know my way. You stay with Hans. I'll be back."

Bela unslung her gun. "I assume you know how to use this?"

"Yes, but . . ."

"Take it. Without it, I'm a peasant gathering wood. With it, I'm a partisan."

He wasn't happy but Hans got the gist of their conversation, even before she translated. "Go," he said, "find out what's happening."

"I will." She knew what it cost him to stay, knowing Angela and Rachel were in danger. "I'll be as fast as I can."

Pausing only to gather a bundle of wood to strap on her

back, she set off, fast as only a Fairy could travel. The cold hampered her a little but she covered the distance in a fraction of the time a mortal would.

She smelled cordite and blood from a distance and slowed, moving from tree to tree with a Fairy's skill. She tamped back the fear that the German soldiers were looking for her and Gela. That they'd developed some means of tracking her spirit. Unlikely. Attacks on partisans were more commonplace than hunts for Fairies.

Hidden in the trees she waited until the last of the soldiers left and the quiet descended once again.

She made her stealthy way forward. Their camp was wrecked and burning. Foolish mortals—even in winter a fire could spread. Did they care? She didn't care much, either. Then she saw Angela, face down in a bank of red snow. Bela blinked back her tears. Angela had been no friend of hers but she'd been a brave fighter and hated the Nazis as much as Bela did. Now she was gone. Her life snuffed out just as Gela's had been.

Of Rachel there was no trace.

Once she was certain no mortal remained within scent or earshot, Bela stepped forward. Their camp was truly wrecked. They'd smashed and broken everything in sight, even ripped open sacks of beans and flour and pissed over them to render them inedible. Only a few stores remained intact. There was precious little they could salvage.

That must wait.

By the time she returned to Hans and Simon, it was close to dark.

"You're sure Angela is dead?" Hans asked. They were cousins.

"They blew off the back of her head at close range. We must warn the others."

"Let me think." It took Hans only a couple of minutes.

"I'm going back to warn the others. We have to spread the word. Thank God there's a moon tonight. You go ahead, with the Englishman. You'll need these." He dug a compass and folded map in a waterproof envelope out of his inside pocket. He unfolded the map. "Here's the camp," he said, stubbing a gloved finger on the map. "Head for Axel's group. They need to be warned. It's the next stage in the escape route. Get there as soon as you can."

"I will." But not as soon as she could on her own. Simon looked downright perplexed. Bela explained what she'd found. He paled visibly.

"Poor woman," he said, shaking his head.

She was more worried about Rachel being taken prisoner. How long could she hold out? "It's a risk we all take."

"So," he went on. "We go ahead."

"Yes, it's a steep path. Our skis will be useless. We'll have to walk most of the way."

In the end, they left their skis where Hans could find them later. He retraced their path to go warn the others. She and Simon went on.

As Bela passed within a hundred meters of Gela's grave, she bade her sister a silent farewell. She would not be coming back. "Wait here," she said to Simon. "I'm going to get what I can from the camp. There's not much left, but I might find something we can use. We've a journey ahead of us."

"How about I come with you?"

She shook her head. "I can go faster on my own, but give me your rucksack. I'll be back." His trust impressed her, but maybe he realized he had no option. If the Nazis caught him, out of uniform, no doubt they'd shoot him out of vindictiveness.

She ran even faster this time, her senses alert to scent or sound of humans. Nothing. The cave was even colder, but she found Angela's secret storeroom. Not so secret from Fairies.

Gela had noticed and told Bela. Inside were chocolate bars, packets of rusks and biscuits, foil-sealed cheese and cans of evaporated milk. No can opener, though, and she didn't have time to search the debris for one. She did find a packet of tea. Might be handy for trading or bargaining. She stuffed the lot into Simon's pack and then, by a wonderful chance, noticed a large package stuffed high on a ledge. Yanking it down, she discovered she had two sleeping bags. She tied the entire bundle to the rucksack and made her way back to Simon.

"Quite a haul," he said, as she showed what she had. "Sure no one saw you?"

"If they had, I wouldn't be here. Let's split up this load and get going. It's some distance." She wasn't about to tell him how far. He looked worn out already, but insisted on carrying most of the load, aside from what she stuffed into pockets and inside her jacket. The roll of sleeping bags, when they opened it to take one each, also contained a length of good rope. He immediately put that over one shoulder and across his body.

"You're a climber?"

He nodded. "With my brother. Before the war."

Might be easier than she thought to get him up to Axel's camp. At least there was a moon and it seemed Simon had little trouble keeping up.

After an hour, she purposely sped up. He hesitated only a few moments then matched his pace to hers and kept up all the way. She stopped a little after midnight, a short distance from where she guessed lookouts would be posted.

"What now?" he asked.

"What now is we announce our arrival and ask for help."

Chapter Twenty-Two

The new, so-called gardener walked into her kitchen and Edith Aubin wanted to slam his hand in a drawer. That would wipe the nasty smirk off his face. Might just bring retribution on her family, though. Mind you, talking to Mary yesterday had lifted her hopes. Perhaps things weren't as bad as feared back home. Except Jersey wasn't Guernsey and never would be. But still . . .

The arrogant fool had the nerve to walk into her kitchen in muddy boots. "Take them off, and leave them outside," Edith snapped. "I won't have boots like that over my clean floor."

He actually looked as if he were about to refuse but with Molly, the one remaining housemaid, as witness, it seemed even Paul Smith had his limits.

"Sorry," he mumbled, not sounding the least apologetic, and backed out to reappear moments later in stockinged feet.

"Come for breakfast?" Edith asked. "Kitchen meal is over. Molly just got back from taking up the house breakfast." Strange chap. He hadn't eaten one meal in the kitchen since he arrived three days ago. Just grabbed sandwiches or toast and took it back to his room. Odd, but it spared them his company.

"Never mind. I wouldn't mind a slice or two of bread."

"How about a couple of slices of toast?" Molly asked.

Edith delved into a drawer to hide her smile as Molly retrieved the two slices she'd scraped and then rejected as too burned for the house breakfast.

"Thanks," he replied with a nasty smirk. Edith longed to point her finger and denounce him for a spy. Why had she let her fear for her family drag her into this? She'd convinced herself it was the only thing to do, but in her heart she knew better.

After Molly left to take care of the bedrooms, Paul Smith (Honestly, what a name! Weiss could have picked something more original) came over to where Edith stood, measuring out flour to make a pie.

"Who," he asked in his nasty, arrogant voice, "are these expected visitors?"

"As if they'd tell me," she replied. "Six extra, is what they told me, and six is what I'm cooking for."

"I heard it was Churchill coming."

"You did, did you? If you know that for sure, why are you asking me?"

"If I ask, you tell me. Who was the woman here yesterday?"

Did he never stop? "A friend of mine." Who did not need to have to cope with the likes of him. "And in case you're interested, she doesn't work for the government, isn't a cabinet minister and can't tell you any state secrets."

"Her name?"

He was not getting Mary's name from her. "Guinevere Pettigrew. If it's any business of yours."

"Woman, watch yourself," he hissed, as he kicked the table and sent everything wobbling.

"You watch out for that bottle of milk. This floor was washed yesterday." His face was sour enough to curdle the milk. "You'd better get to work. And if you want lunch, come on time. The kitchen eats at eleven-thirty."

He snarled. It gave her the willies and she couldn't suppress a shudder. Whoever he was, he was nasty. As he slammed the door behind him, she wondered at her temerity. Could have been the lovely chat with a fellow islander yesterday, but really it was the letter in her apron pocket. It came in the morning post from her married niece in Plymouth. Yes, there had been some inked-out lines. No doubt about bombing or food shortages, but the important news was that everyone was well at home, even to the point of her sister having had a new daughter.

Rather reinforced what Mary told her. Things were sticky but so far no deportations or mass arrests. Smith, and the other one who called himself White, had lied. It had worked, hadn't it? She'd been ready to do anything to save Beryl and Julia and the rest of her family. So ready, she'd sunk to treason. The word sent icy shivers across her skin. How had she come to this? And what was she going to do now?

"What the bloody hell am I going to do?" Andrew Barron forgave himself for swearing. He felt more than justified. He reread the letter, just to make sure he hadn't skipped words and misunderstood.

He hadn't.

Because of security problems (and he couldn't deny they had had their difficulties), the plant was closing and he'd be transferred to a vast plant now under construction in the north of England. Damn, he didn't want to leave Brytewood. He was getting married, settling here with Gloria, planning a life together.

Bang went all their plans. Like thousands of other couples torn apart by the bloody war.

He balled up the paper in disgust and tossed it across the room. The childish act made him feel better for all of ten seconds. Then he had to get up and retrieve it before smoothing it out on his desk. He had no choice. There was a war on and he was a government employee.

He might have to leave but he wasn't going to leave a single man.

Gloria said she didn't want a big wedding. She'd get her wish. It would just be a little sooner than they'd planned.

He glanced at his watch. No point trying to give her a call, she'd be out and about by now. Except, hadn't she said something about checking on the Watson twins for Alice? And the Watson farm was one of the few with a phone.

He picked up his and asked the operator for the number.

"Something up?" old Mrs. Watson said when he asked her to give Gloria a message.

He stifled the impulse to say his life was in shreds. "Just something came up. Ask her to give me a call when she gets there, please?"

He hung up, hoping Gloria wasn't making the Watson farm the last stop of her afternoon.

She called twenty minutes later. Twenty minutes he'd spent planning how to salvage his life.

"Andrew? Something wrong?"

Everything. "I need to have a quick word with you and not over the phone. Can you meet me?"

"I suppose so. What's happened?" He had to tell her face-to-face. Holding her hand, with his arm around her.

He wouldn't say *don't panic*, or *don't worry*. Those words were pretty much certain to guarantee the opposite. "I need to speak to you. Can I meet you? Soon?"

"Where?"

"I'll borrow a lorry." Invent some lie or other. "And meet you on the road by Fletcher's Woods. Can you ride down there and wait for me?"

"I suppose so. After I finish my visit here."

"I'll wait."

He hung up before he blurted out the lousy news. Now, time to beg, borrow, or steal a government vehicle for personal use.

Gloria was direly tempted to call Andrew back and demand an explanation but Melanie Watson's curious, "Something wrong, Nurse?" brought her back to her responsibilities.

"Just needed to check something. Now let's see how those bonny boys are doing. Big boys for almost three months, aren't they? Let me wash my hands and we'll have a look at them." She left a threepenny piece by the phone to pay for the call and headed for the kitchen to wash her hands in the sink. Her mind was reeling with a hundred possibilities but the Watson twins came first. A fine lusty cry the elder one had too.

"Alright," Gloria said, as Andrew jumped down from the cab and hoisted her bicycle into the back of a lorry big enough to carry half the army. "What's going on?"

"Hop in," he replied, "and I'll tell you."

Sitting side by side in the warmth of the cab, he told her.

"Oh, my God!" she said, fighting back tears. "When?" She'd only just found him, how could they be parted so soon? But they would be, and she had to stiffen her spine and cope, like thousands of other women all over the country.

"They didn't say. I keep thinking I'll get another government communication tomorrow telling me I need to report on Monday."

"But Yorkshire?" She was whining. And needed to stop.

"This is between us, understand? I shouldn't even have told you."

"I know. Foxes can be really quiet when they want to be." At least that got a smile from him. "What now?" She was glad he'd told her right away but she did need to get back to work. So did he, come to that.

"Right now?" He almost grinned. What did he have up his sleeve? "We skive off together and go over to Epsom and get a marriage license. If we pay the extra, we can get married in three days. No banns, no waiting. We go back on Saturday, sign our marriage lines and whatever happens, we're together."

Even if they were several hundred miles apart.

Gloria let out a long sigh and realized he was watching her anxiously. That was an understatement. He was pretty much shaking with worry. Did he think she'd refuse? "Let's get a move on. I do have patients to see today."

He let out a great whoop of laughter, crashed gears and headed down the hill.

They were getting married! Gloria's throat went dry as her body melted inside. Married. She'd wanted a small, quiet wedding. She was getting one. She reached over and put her hand over Andrew's on the steering wheel. "I love you."

"Good," he replied with a grin. A lovely, sexy grin. "I thought you did."

He deserved a jab in the ribs for that, but he was driving, and crashing the lorry would delay getting there.

Married. And to Andrew. She had to tell Alice and Mary. This was going to work out so well. She'd spend Saturday night—and every night thereafter until he moved—with Andrew in his cottage, and if Mary played her cards right, she had a chance to have her wicked way with Gryffyth.

It was going to be a satisfying weekend all around.

"What are you chuckling over?" Andrew asked.

Had she been? Most likely. "Life is truly wonderful," she replied.

Chapter Twenty-Three

"What are you?" Bela asked Simon, as they sat together in the main hut in the center of Axel's camp.

"I'm a first lieutenant in the King's Royal Surrey Regiment."

This was not going to be easy but she had to know and trusted that no one else around understood English. "I know that but you're more. A human couldn't have covered the ground you did yesterday at the speed we did." She'd set the pace out of desperation and as he kept up with her, went even faster. He never lagged behind but kept even with her. He was something more than an escaped soldier.

That earned her a sidelong glance and a pregnant silence. "I'm not doing this to pry," she went on, "but I know. I'm a Fairy. That's why I'm fleeing the Nazis too. They took me prisoner and used me. They use Others. You have to be extra careful. You have to hide what you are."

The silence continued but now it was a thoughtful silence. Just when she was about to get up and remove herself from this awkwardness, he said. "My mother was a Pixie."

The words hung in the air between them as he turned and looked her in the face. She let out her breath, not realizing she'd held it. She'd been right! "Then," she replied, picking her words carefully, "I think it is very important we get away as soon as possible. We can ask them for help." She angled her head at the partisans talking together. "I hope the escape route isn't compromised, but we need to get far away."

"Why the urgency?"

"First, if Rachel breaks, she could reveal where this camp is. Second, you're out of uniform; they'll treat you like a spy or one of the partisans. Third, although it's winter, we're stronger and faster than humans. And fourth, I will not be taken again and if they got any hint of what you are, they'd find a way to use you. Trust me, I know. They are gathering in and using anyone with Powers, every sort of Other they can find. You don't want to be taken."

He didn't argue. Wise man.

"What happened?"

"The Nazis told me if I worked for them, my family would be safe. They lied. My parents and my two younger brothers died in their hellhole in Flossenbürg. My sister I rescued, but she died a few days ago. She was too weakened even for the woods to heal her."

"What do you plan?"

She took out the map Rolf had given her. "We're here," she pointed. "Your route was via safe houses to Switzerland. We can't guess how safe they will be now, but if they give us contact to the first one, we can get clothes and papers, then make our own way to Switzerland. We'll do best traveling at night and sleeping by day. Nights are long this time of year. For humans it would take weeks, maybe months, for us much less."

"And to cross the frontier without support? It's bound to be guarded."

"The roads and railways will be, but they can't watch every meter of the mountains, and who in their right mind would try to cross the Alps in winter? Once across the frontier, I have an aunt and uncle in St. Gallen."

He was even quieter now. She could almost hear his mind turning over her proposal. "Pity we left those skis behind."

She smiled. He was with her. "Rolf and Hans will need them. And your sick friend. We have good boots and we can swap some of our tinned goods for lighter stuff. We'll need money to buy food on the way. There's not much we can live off from the land this time of year, but cabbages and potatoes."

"When do we tell this lot?"

"The sooner the better. They'll be glad to see us gone."

"I hate to go ahead and leave poor old Jules behind."

They both knew they already had. The Frenchman's chances of survival were slim indeed. Bela shuddered inside. So many dead and dying and the end was nowhere in sight.

No one at the camp begged them to stay, but they did offer help. Two days later, Bela and Simon left, with directions to a farm a day's walk away, and a password to gain the occupant's trust.

Chapter Twenty-Four

"Gran, have you heard the news?" Alice burst through the door and stopped in her tracks. Gran and Sergeant Pendragon were sitting either side of the kitchen fireplace, newspaper spread on the floor between them, sharpening stakes.

Just in time, she bit back the suggestion that they were both far too old to go Vampire hunting. Gran would slay her with a look, and the sergeant, well, he could incinerate with one.

"What news, my love?" Gran asked, looking up and smiling.

She closed the door behind her, still a little unnerved at the sight in front of her. "Andrew and Gloria. Andrew's getting posted somewhere up north so they're getting married this Saturday."

"Holy smoke!" Gran said. "How wonderful. That they're finally getting married, I mean. Shame about him getting moved."

"That's the war for you, Helen," the sergeant said. "We'll miss him. Good lad, he is."

Gran stood, brushing the wood shavings from her apron onto the newspaper. "Don't get up, Howell," she said, but he ignored her and stood with her. "We need to see what she needs. Perhaps we could have everyone up here afterwards. We've more space than either of their cottages."

"Hang on a minute, Gran." She was about to plan the wedding and their next ten years. "It's all taken care of. Andrew told Peter who told me. They're getting married at ten-thirty, at the registry office in Epsom. After, we're all invited to lunch at the Spread Eagle. It's going to be really small, just the few of us. They asked Peter and me to be witnesses and Mary's to be bridesmaid." She glanced at her watch. "She might not know that yet but she will once she gets out of school."

Gran smiled and looked at Sergeant Pendragon.

"How about it, Helen?" he asked. "Want to make it a double wedding?"

"Certainly not! You know we've talked about this. I'm not poaching on Gloria's day and besides, we're waiting until Mary and Gryffyth are all set. You're not pipping him to the post again."

"He'd best get a move on then. They might have forever to make up their minds but we don't, at our age."

No one did. But Alice wasn't saying aloud what every one of them already knew. Life was too darn uncertain these days to count on anything.

"What can we do for her, my love?" Gran asked. "And would you like a quick cup? It's fresh in the pot."

"Can't stop, Gran. I have to go into Dorking and pick up some supplies. But there is one thing. Do you think Sir James Gregory would be persuaded to part with a few more camellias? They'd make a lovely bouquet for Gloria."

"Perfect!" Pendragon replied. "Just what we need: a good reason to go up to Wharton Lacey."

"Yes," Gran said, nodding at the pile of sharpened stakes.

"Hold on a tick!" Maybe she did need that cup of tea.

"What exactly have you two concocted?" Damn. She knew, but had to hear it to be sure.

"It's simple. Howell and I want to have a good look at that new gardener. The one who tried his nasty tricks on Mary. Howell sensed something Other about him but we waited until we were sure he was up to no good. After all, he could have been like that nice Mr. Clarendon, quite benign."

Nice Mr. Clarendon was a Vampire, doing to the Germans what these Vamps were trying to do to them. Alice hoped he wasn't about to be set upon by a pair of French sexagenarians—alright, a Pixie and a fire-breathing Dragon. "What are you going to do? Attack?"

"I think we have to, Alice," the sergeant said. "As long as he sat up there and did no harm, it was live and let live, or rather let live until we learned otherwise, but this attack on Mary last night . . ." He shook his head. "We can't have that."

"And the one who went for Whorleigh," Alice added. "What about that one? Going after him too?"

"We're not sure where he's lurking, so one at a time."

"So you need a reason to hie up to Wharton Lacey and do the deed?" She went cold. "For heaven's sake, be careful. It's not like open country, or even like our drive, hidden by the hedge. What if someone sees you?" Dear heaven! Dispatching Vampires had become so commonplace it was being observed by a passerby that worried her!

"We'll be careful," Howell Pendragon said.

"You can't really walk in there, say thank you for the flowers and then stake the gardener." Alice shook her head. This was supposed to have been a five-minute pop-in. Supplies were going to have to wait. "Gran, I think I'll have that cup of tea, after all." She went over to the table. "You want another? Sergeant, how about you?"

They both said yes. So Alice topped up their cups, poured

one for herself and thought fast as she refilled the milk jug. "How about," she said, as she handed Gran a cup, "I give Sir James a call? If he can spare more camellias, I'll drive up there after dark. Easier to hide stakes in the car." Although what she was going to do about the mess afterwards, Lord alone knew.

"You are not going up there alone, Alice! Both times it took two to best the nasty things. Solo won't work."

Gran was right. Alice handed Howell Pendragon his cup. "If it's not going to seem too much like an expedition, I was thinking the three of us." That way Peter would be safely out of it. He'd helped last time but this wasn't work for humans. Others needed to be the ones who coped with Vampires.

They both took to that idea with relish.

"Would be better, my love," Gran said, sipping her tea. "We'll arrive fresh and ready instead of worn out and legs aching from the pull up Newcome Hill."

"I'll give him a call." She stood. "Won't be a jiffy."

Alice's hand shook as she picked up the receiver. She was about to call the local gentry, or at least the closest Brytewood had to gentry—Sir James Gregory, Colonel of the Home Guard and entertainer of politicians—and arrange to stake his new gardener. Assuming he did turn out to be the missing Vampire, that is.

"Number, please," came the voice on the line.

"Brytewood three-nine-five."

"Calling Wharton Lacey, Doctor? It's Mildred."

The perennial gossip. "Hello, Mildred, everything well? How are your mother's chilblains?"

"Not too bad, Doctor, but the bad weather hasn't really started yet, has it?"

Alice agreed it hadn't, and she, too, hoped it wouldn't be as bad as last winter. "Can you connect me?"

"Yes, you're in luck. Line's been busy today, but here

you are." There was a click and then the familiar ring on the other end.

Miss Aubin, the cook, answered and a minute or so later Sir James came on the line. Alice grasped the receiver with a sweaty hand.

"Of course," he said, as she explained her request. "But no need for you to drive up here. Save your petrol for your patients. I'll send Proudfoot or one of the farm hands down with half a dozen, all fresh cut Friday evening. How about I have him take them straight to Nurse Prewitt? Will be a nice surprise for her."

She could hardly refuse and insist on driving up there, on the off chance his new gardener needed staking.

"Give the happy couple our best wishes," Sir James continued. "You know what camellias stand for? Admiration. Perfection."

She hadn't. "How lovely. Perfect for a bride. Thank you, Sir James."

She hung up and went back to the kitchen to break the news to Gran and Howell Pendragon.

"Drat," Gran said. "We had it all worked out."

"Never mind, Helen, gives us more time to prepare. Maybe this weekend, after the wedding, we'll have a chance."

"Why not sharpen a few more stakes while you're at it?" Alice said. It would keep them both safely at The Gallop.

After she heard Sir James hang up the phone, Edith Aubin took a deep breath. She was going to do what was right and face the consequences. She took off her apron and crossed the hall to the study. Opening the door before she lost her nerve, she walked in. "Excuse me, Sir James, but I need to speak to you."

Chapter Twenty-Five

Sir James paid her the courtesy of listening without interruption. When Edith finished, he sat silent a good two minutes, no doubt trying to decide whether to call in the army or the police.

"And this chap arrived when?"

"Last week, sir."

"And it took you this long to decide someone needed to know about him?"

She deserved that. "No, sir. I knew all along I should report it to someone but they threatened my family. I was terrified for them."

"And what made you change your mind?"

"I spoke to Mary LaPrioux. The young teacher evacuated from Guernsey," she added as she doubted he had any idea who Mary was. "She's had news from home, and all seems well. Then I heard from my married niece in Devon. They preyed on my fears for my family."

"Did this Smith give any indication what he was doing here?"

She shook her head. "No, sir, but I assumed it was to report on visitors. Given as we have so many important ones."

"It's a good thing the house party this weekend has been postponed." He gave her a searching look.

"Indeed, sir."

"We just heard this morning. Postponed, not canceled, but it gives us time to think. What can you tell me about this chap? According to Baines he's a fast worker but likes to work on his own. Doesn't care for company."

"He keeps to himself. Not used to this sort of work, I'd say, sir."

"Why?"

"He's not got much idea how a house like this runs. He comes in and eats at odd hours, cadges sandwiches and eats back in his rooms. He seldom exchanges two words with anyone and those he does are curt and offhand."

"And he lives over the stable, all on his own?"

"Yes, sir. I put him there, seemed best. And it's where the single lads slept, before the war."

"I'll have a word with him. Have a closer look, then make the calls I need to, and Miss Aubin . . ."

"Yes, sir."

"Not a word to anyone."

"Of course not, sir."

Back in her kitchen, waves of doubt hit her from all directions. What was Sir James going to do? Was she in trouble? Of course she was! She'd helped harbor an enemy agent. And just because a letter this morning told her her family members were safe a week ago, didn't mean they were now, or would be tomorrow.

Was anybody?

It was war. She'd done what was right at last, she'd have to pay the price. Whatever it was. She hoped her family didn't as well.

With no house party to prepare for, she was at a bit of a

loose end. No point in cooking quantities if there was only the household to eat it. In the end, she burned up some of her anxiety by going through the linen cupboards and looking for sheets to turn sides to middle.

It was halfway through the afternoon, lunch long over, and she and Molly were enjoying a cup of tea, when the summons came.

Molly answered the front door, and came back saying Sir James wanted Miss Aubin in the drawing room.

Edith took off her apron, smoothed her hair and went out to face whatever awaited the other side of the drawing room door.

"Ah, Miss Aubin, this is Inspector Wallis, he'd like a few words with you." There were two other men, plainclothes policemen by the look of them. They were not introduced.

"Of course."

"If you would come with me, Miss Aubin?" Inspector Wallis said.

Dear heaven! They were arresting her. "Let me get my coat and hat." Would they let her pack her toothbrush? Spare reading glasses? "Should I get anything else?"

"No need, Miss Aubin, we'll just drive around a bit and talk. Shouldn't take us too long."

She took his word for it. Not that she had much alternative.

Once settled in the back of the car, Edith turned to the inspector sitting beside her. "What do you want to know?"

"Everything, Miss Aubin." He tapped on the glass panel separating them from the driver. "Up to Box Hill and back, I think, Jarvis. If we need longer, I'll let you know."

"So." The inspector gave his attention back to her. "Tell me all you know about this young man, how you met him and why you introduced him into the household."

Throat dry and her hands sweaty inside her gloves, she told him all she knew. He was a good listener, no doubt trained to take confessions every day. He asked few questions, just let her talk herself out.

"I see," he said after a long silence. "How did they contact you?"

"I was in Guildford, looking for enamel saucepans, since we donated many of the aluminum ones for the metal drive. It was back in September. I could look up the exact date, as I have the bills from the hardware shop."

"That would be helpful. Could you find it easily when we get back?"

So, they were taking her back. That was a relief. "Of course."

He nodded for her to go on.

"This man came up to me. Tall, dark, rather swarthy. He knew my name, knew where I worked, and said he could give me news of my family back home. Have to be honest, I hadn't heard anything since the invasion and I was worried. He offered to buy me a cup of tea. So we went into that tearoom in the High Street, and he presented an ultimatum. He would keep my family safe and sound, if I agreed to sponsor a young man as gardener and claim him as my nephew." Her voice faded with shame. She'd known all along what was involved. She'd lied to herself.

Lying was over.

"What do you think he wants?"

"I imagine to watch who comes to the house. Maybe eavesdrop?"

"Could be. Does he have access to the house?"

"He's not supposed to. Just the kitchen for meals."

"But, short staffed as you are, could he get in?"

She nodded. "From the French doors into the drawing room, or the side door, or even the door by the back stairs. Yes, it's possible."

"If he's left any listening devices, the two lads I left in the house will take care of that." Listening devices? This was more like a spy story by the hour. But wasn't that exactly what she'd abetted? "Now, Miss Aubin, you have a choice. You can work for us, watch this Smith chap with hawk eyes and report everything back to us, or we can arrest you. Which is it?"

"Where's the cook?"

Molly looked up at the new gardener and then down at his boots. "You're lucky she's not here. She'd tear a strip off you for coming into her kitchen in boots. What do you want?"

"Just wanted to know where she was. I thought I saw her drive off in a motor car."

"She's doing something for Sir James. She didn't tell me. Not my business and it certainly isn't yours." Sweet Jesus! He gave her the creeps, with his nasty, cold blue eyes. "Look, if you want to ask something, I'll give her the message when she gets back."

"When will that be?"

Some people never gave up. "Hell if I know. Before kitchen supper, I hope, or you and me will both be hungry." She stood up and carried her tray into the scullery. "I'll tell her," she called through the open door.

Although what she was supposed to tell Miss Aubin, she had no idea. She was a bit curious herself.

Something was happening. Paul Schmidt knew it deep in his bones. Why else would an official black car, complete with uniformed chauffeur, pick up Miss Aubin and drive off? Did they suspect her? Had she blabbed? If so, she was dead. He was in the mood for a human feed. He was getting tired of horses and cattle. Pity how the mind link with the Fairy had broken, she'd have been able to contact Weiss—or would she? The connection with the Fairy had been odd. He'd felt her in his mind but never quite understood what she was doing. Didn't miss her either. Her blood and struggles had been sweet, but having her poke into his head made him uneasy.

No point in thinking about that. It was either give Weiss a phone call, which meant going into the house, asking permission and risking being overheard, or hang on until he appeared. Which would be Saturday. Unless Weiss had changed his plan of kidnapping the village grocer.

Damn. He should have stayed in Guildford, with his steady supply of injured humans for sustenance, as well as his host and that whingeing mother of his on tap whenever he wanted. He'd been safe and cozy there, but now he risked exposure from the tattletale cook, and on top of it all, the house party, the whole point of his coming here, was canceled. He'd overheard that.

It was a bad sign, too.

He was sorely tempted to walk off and let Weiss get on with it on his own.

Trouble was, without papers and identity card, he'd be reduced to hiding in bombed-out ruins and sleeping rough, and he liked walking about, planning how he'd rule his little fief when the time came.

He'd just sit tight and bide his time. They'd have some fun this weekend after all.

"Here," Mary said, placing a small bronze coin on the table. "Not exactly a silver sixpence for your shoe. It's two Guernsey doubles, but it might bring you luck."

"Thanks, I'll put it in one shoe and a silver sixpence in the other," Gloria said.

Alice had dropped by on her way home, and the three of them were sitting around Gloria's kitchen table, eating up the last of Miss Aubin's gauche and talking weddings. "That reminds me," Alice said, "brought you these." She pulled a pair of silk stockings from her pocket. "Not new, I wore them for mine, but somehow a wedding needs the real thing."

"Thank you," Gloria said. "That will be my something borrowed."

"Take care you don't get a ladder in them, then you can pass them on to Mary when she needs them."

Mary decided to let that go. "Do you believe the old rhyme?"

"Not sure I do, but never hurts to keep it. It's fun anyway. I've no difficulty getting something old. And I bought a new pair of gloves in Woolworth's in Dorking."

"So you just need something blue," Mary said.

"I can cover that," Alice said. "I've a pair of blue crepe de chine French knickers you can borrow. Perfect for the unveiling."

Gloria blushed. "Please!"

"If you don't want them, I'll borrow them," Mary said. "I'm planning my own event for Saturday night."

"Oh, I want them," Gloria replied. "Thank you, Alice. With a bit of luck, I won't be wearing them long anyway."

"So," Alice said, grinning as she turned to Mary, "you're planning on seducing our war hero?"

"Yes."

"She's giving him an ultimatum," Gloria said. "If you want to marry me, you have to roger me first."

"I'm not being that blunt!" Was she? "I'll just invite him in for a cup of tea after the wedding." And try her luck.

Alice had a wonderful laugh. "Seems to me it's going to be one wild weekend. I'll have to plan a long conversation with Peter myself. And by the way, Mary, I have a pair of red satin French knickers with rather fetching black lace. Want to borrow those? Gloria really gets first dibs on the blue ones."

"Where," Gloria asked," did you acquire this collection of sexy knickers?"

"All over the place. Some in Paris, before the war. Some up in Town, in a rather nice place in Bond Street. Can't get them now, so I keep them for high days and holidays and special friends," she added with a smile. "I'll drop them off tomorrow."

"I've a better idea," Gloria said. "Andrew and Peter and Gryffyth are off to the Pig for the evening tomorrow. Why don't you come here? I'll try to get a bottle of wine and we'll have our own version of a stag party."

"A hen party?" Mary suggested.

"I'll be here," Alice said. "And I'll bring an apple pie or a tart for pudding."

This was so wonderful, Mary thought to herself. She still missed her family and home, but she'd been here barely two weeks and had good women friends who were Other, and she no longer had to hide her nature.

A nature which, even now, yearned for water. Cold or not, she was going up to the hammerpond very soon. "I think I'll go up to the hammerpond tonight," she announced, "but it's going to be darn cold."

"There's always the swimming baths in Dorking," Gloria pointed out.

It was just not the same and she bet Gloria knew it. "Would you want to shift, and run circuits inside the village hall?"

Gloria smiled. "No, not really. Mind you, isn't it wonderful to be able to talk about it and not hide what you are all the time?"

"I didn't have to at home," Mary said. Maybe that sounded too wistful, but it was the truth.

Alice chuckled. "Gran rather shoved it down my throat. I was the one didn't want to know. Funny really, but we all listened to her stories. My brothers claimed to believe them. I always thought they did it to humor her, and be contrary to me." She shrugged. "Who knows."

"Going out tonight then, Mary?" Gloria asked.

"Yes." Winter weather or not, she need the caress and sustenance of water.

"Maybe you should invited Gryffyth along," Alice suggested.

She ignored that.

"If you're out, I'll nip down and see Andrew. My last chance before Saturday."

"I'll be off then, and let you two indulge yourselves," Alice said. "But before I leave, come out to the car with me. I've a bundle of stakes Gran and Sergeant Pendragon insisted I bring. They think we all need to be armed."

Chapter Twenty-Six

"So, you're here?" Schmidt scowled at Weiss. Intruding into his room was one thing, sprawling on his bed as if he owned the place was another. And what would stringy old Miss Aubin have to say if she saw his shoes on the blanket?

"Of course," Weiss replied, making no effort to even nod, much less smile. "We have a busy weekend ahead and need to prepare."

"Not as busy as you think. They postponed the house party."

That got his attention. He even sat up. "Why?"

"Hell if I know! They neglected to share that detail with the gardener. All I know is Miss Aubin was fussing about wasted cooking." He could mention about Miss Aubin's temporary disappearance, but would keep mum until he knew exactly what was going on.

"I see." Weiss scowled a minute. "No matter. We can devote the entire weekend to that killer shopkeeper. Once he's out of the way, there'll be no one to hinder us."

Assuming the grocer was the murderer. Either way it would be fresh blood.

Since Weiss had appropriated the bed, Schmidt pulled the straight-backed chair from the corner and made himself as comfortable as one could on a sagging cane seat. "So, we spend the weekend enjoying the grocer."

"Yes. We take him tonight."

"He'll be missed."

"So what? Let these peasants go without their eggs and bread for a weekend. It's going to be easy enough. I've been watching him. He shuts up shop punctually at five-thirty. His assistant sweeps up and then leaves. Whorleigh lingers about twenty minutes more, to close the cash register, count his money, and do whatever country shopkeepers do at the end of the day. Then he goes home. He found a replacement bicycle very easily, but that won't help him. We'll wait for him in the narrow lane behind his shop. We take him, render him unconscious, and bring him here. You do have the room ready?"

"As ready as I can with only a bed frame. I stole some rope from the potting shed. He can have my chamber pot. I have no use for it."

"And food? No point in having him expire before we finish with him."

Schmidt indicated the stack of wrapped packages on the narrow table. "Over there. I've been accumulating from the kitchen. I can bring more as we need it. The cook daren't refuse me. We can get water from the tap downstairs."

"Ah yes, the cook. And how cooperative is she?"

Damn, why go into that? Might as well tell, even though Weiss was bound to blame him. "Cooperative enough, but . . ." He almost enjoyed passing on the events of the afternoon.

Weiss's eyebrows almost met between his eyes. "So, she has betrayed us!"

"I didn't say that. Unusual, yes, but she came back with two crates of wine, and a hamper of food. Part of it was a large cheese, I overheard later. Could well have been a little illegal food transfer. It happens a lot round here. You should hear the talk about Whorleigh."

"I have no desire to," Weiss snapped. "I care nothing for how these humans get their food supplies. You've stayed away from the village?"

Did Weiss think he was simpleminded? "Of course! I'm not an idiot." He did not care for the expression on Weiss's face but he let it go. No point in mentioning the old man who'd seemed oddly familiar, either. But he did have something useful after his talk with that Proudfoot person. Stupid names these Inselaffen had. "Have you given any thought to how we'll bring him back here?"

"If we can't carry him between us we can hardly call ourselves Vampire."

"And risk being seen as we traverse fields?"

"You have a superior alternative?"

Oh yes, he did. "I believe so. One of the farm workers was told to deliver a bunch of flowers to a house in the village, late tomorrow. He wants to leave early for London, his mother-in-law was bombed out and they're going to help. He asked if I'd run the flowers down for him."

"Have you no sense? Go into that village where you might be recognized?"

"Won't be like that. He's lending me one of the farm lorries and I'll go after dark. All I have to do is deliver the bouquet and come back. With Whorleigh in the back of the lorry."

Even Weiss couldn't disagree. "Much easier. Why ask you?"

"He doesn't want anyone on the farm to know he's leaving early. He told me where he'll leave the lorry, with the keys. I said I'd do it as a favor. He was so grateful, he gave me a packet of cigarettes."

Weiss laughed. "We can use them on the grocer. Humans squirm amusingly when burned. Makes them talk too. We need some worked iron. Remember how it weakened that Fairy? Let's hope it works as well with this creature. He can move fast. We have to be ready for that."

Damn! Now he had to scrounge for stray chains. Did Weiss have any idea how hard that would be? Any extra metal had been collected to help the pathetic Inselaffen war efforts. "I'll see what I can do."

Schmidt managed. Mainly by stealing a length of chain from the barn over at the Home Farm, and snapping the handles off two hoes after deciding the loops might make passable wrist restraints. Pity he hadn't been able to accost one of the village policemen and steal a pair of handcuffs.

It was going to be an entertaining weekend. He left his cache of iron in his room, almost snarling at the sight of Weiss stretched out on the bed, and went back down to rake the leaves off the lower lawn and cut back the dying plants in the herbaceous border, just like a hardworking and industrious worker.

Humans were so easily duped.

"This is what you have to deliver?" Weiss all but snarled at the basket sitting on the seat between them.

"That's it." Why complain? The lucky coincidence of access to a lorry was simplifying abducting the grocer.

"What is it? Love offering to some wench he wants as a mistress?"

"Could be, he doesn't part with his camellias often." Apart from that old man that Schmidt still couldn't quite place. Not that he was wasting time or effort on that now.

They parked up the narrow track, fifty meters or so from the main street. And waited, Weiss saying nothing and Schmidt wondering how Weiss knew his way around so well. Had to have been scouting out, or maybe just snooping.

It was a short wait.

Weiss led, taking them through the trees, carrying the chain wrapped around his waist to keep it from clanking, and Schmidt had a hoe blade in each pocket. Honestly, the things he did for Germany. Traipsing through mud in the dark, carrying broken garden tools. Damn good thing this was all going to turn to his advantage very soon. He was damn well earning it.

They took up position behind a rickety storage shed behind the grocer's shop. It was a full twenty minutes of sitting in the damp before Weiss moved. Without a word, or even looking back to see if Schmidt followed, Weiss walked closer to the back of the shop where Whorleigh's bicycle was propped against the wall.

Weiss climbed the back of the building and found a perch on the window ledge; Schmidt decided to go for the narrow porch over the back door. So poised, they waited. Listening intently for sounds inside: drawers opening and closing, the sound of money being counted, the smell of a cigarette as Whorleigh wound up business for the day. Footsteps approached the back door, there was a pause, the sound of bolts being drawn back— and then it opened.

They leapt together, landing one each side of him, blocking him in. There was a delightful shriek of terror and he ran, faster than any human could move, and leapt upwards. They'd have lost him, but Weiss, moving at Vampire speed, whipped off the chain and swung it, narrowly missing Schmidt but catching Whorleigh neatly around his knees and felling him.

There was another shriek, this one muffled, as Schmidt jumped on him and closed his hands around Whorleigh's neck until he passed out.

"Enough! He's no use dead," Weiss snapped.

Nothing like gratitude for silencing a dangerous Other, and the possible eliminator of Eiche and Bloch. "He's not dead." Yet. And even dead, he still had blood in him.

Grabbing the inert form, they ran down the muddy track to their hidden lorry.

They dumped him in the open back, leaving the chain around him, and tossed a tarpaulin on top. Then Weiss sent Schmidt back for the bicycle. "That way it'll seem he went home as usual. Leave it there someone would notice." Absolutely true, but it didn't make Schmidt very happy.

He tossed it into the back, under the tarpaulin.

"I'll drive now," Weiss said, jumping up into the driver's seat before Schmidt thought to object. "Now where is it you go to complete your flower delivery?"

No reason to make it sound as if he were making lace, or tatting. He was working undercover for the Fatherland and Weiss had better not forget it. "He drew me a map." He brought out the paper; he'd even marked the row of shops and the village green. Make it easy enough.

"Not far," Weiss said, tracing his finger on the paper. "Right here then, that one on the left. Be there soon enough." He started the engine, turned right and stopped a short distance further on. "Here you are, Schmidt."

"Here? I'm not getting out here."

"Yes, you are. It's a narrow lane, easier for foot traffic. Look at the map, it's only a little way up. You go take your flowers to the lady, and I'll get our Fairy creature to safety. Better not wait around. Too much of a risk." As Schmidt hesitated, he added, "Get out, I can't sit here idling the engine, someone will notice."

Short of a stand-up fight, he had no choice. Hefting the basket, Schmidt stepped out of the cab. As the lorry drove off and the engine faded into the distance, he hoofed it up the narrow lane. Honeysuckle Cottage was on the left. Should be easy enough to find. Hell, there weren't that many cottages up here and he could read, even in the dark.

Chapter Twenty-Seven

"All ready, Gran?" Alice asked. It was later than she'd hoped but somehow this Friday had produced a bumper crop of patients.

"Just about, my love. Peter, you help me load this lot into the car. Alice, don't forget the corkscrew, just in case Gloria doesn't have one. And Peter, leave the cake, that's a surprise. We'll bring it tomorrow."

"You women are doing yourselves nicely," he said as he hefted the hamper and made for the door. "I'm beginning to think we should join you."

"No need. No need," Gran replied. "Howell has a chicken in the oven for you lot before you repair to the Pig and Whistle."

"How did you manage the cake?"

"Ways and means, Peter. We have eggs, I'd been saving up sugar for Christmas, and I shamed Sam Whorleigh into parting with some dried fruit. It's little enough by all accounts considering what he could be doing to help. Now don't forget the stakes."

"Gran, we all have stakes. I took a batch to Gloria last night and there's a bundle in the car."

"Can't be too careful, especially after dark, my love."

"What's this?" Peter asked as he picked up a carrier bag and looked inside. "You're taking lingerie with you?"

"Something blue and borrowed for Gloria."

"And red?"

Trust him to poke. She grabbed the bag and shoved everything back in. So much for ironing and folding them.

"Red and borrowed?"

He wasn't going to give up. "For Mary, and don't ask. It's a woman thing."

Especially since Gran chuckled behind her. "Taking the initiative, is she? Good for her."

Poor Peter looked downright confused. Just as well. She didn't quite trust him not to let on to Gryffyth.

"Be a love and get those two bottles," Gran said. "It's elderflower Champagne Alice's father made before the war. Should be nice and ready by now."

They loaded it all in, along with the carefully wrapped wedding presents they'd rushed into Dorking to buy earlier that afternoon. Alice dropped Peter at the Pendragons' house and headed for Gloria's. Funny how the sexes split up before a wedding. No doubt went back to prehistoric days when men went hunting for brides and women stayed home and tended the fires.

They'd do more than tend fires tonight.

It was a meal and half, Mary decided. Not just the food, although how Mrs. Burrows managed she'd never know. Must be Pixie magic. It was the company of friends and watching Gloria's happiness that made the evening.

"This is incredible," Gloria said, her face flushed with excitement with her first glass of Champagne as they insisted she sit while they put the food out. "It's lovely. Thank you all so much."

"It's my pleasure, my love," Mrs. Burrows replied. "If the men are off enjoying themselves, why shouldn't we do the same? No point in Alice and me eating alone up in that big kitchen. Besides, I do love a wedding and this seems to be the year for them."

Was that smile aimed at her? Mary suspected so. "What about yours?" Mary asked. Then wondered if she'd been too forward.

Seemed not. Mrs. Burrows laughed. "All in good time, my love. All in good time. He kept me waiting to ask me. He can hang on a bit. I told him I'd marry him after we've taken care of all these dratted Vampires."

"How many are there?"

"And how," Alice asked, "will you ever know if we've got them all? You could keep the poor man waiting until doomsday."

"I don't think so," Gran replied. "It'll all be taken care of before Christmas, you mark my words."

No one called her optimistic or asked for clarification, so Mary didn't either. "Are we ready for the pie?" she asked. A steak and kidney one was keeping warm in the oven.

"Good idea, my love. I think we're ready."

Alice was stooping to take it out of the oven when there was a knock on the door.

"I wonder who that is?" Gloria said, getting up to open the door.

"A surprise," Mrs. Burrows said.

"A present from Sir James Gregory," Alice said, with a big grin.

"Sir James?" Gloria echoed. "Why?"

"Not some of *droit du seigneur*, is it?" Mary asked.

Mrs. Burrows let out a laugh. "No, my love, not that." There was another rap on the door. "Better let him in."

Gloria lifted the blackout curtain and opened the door. "Yes?"

"Miss Prewitt? I was asked to deliver this." He held out a basket.

"Come in." Gloria lifted the curtain and a young man stepped inside.

"Here," he said, handing her a basket of camellias.

They were lovely, but Alice and Mrs. Burrows were staring at the man.

"You!" Alice said.

He turned and stared at her.

It all happened so fast. He snarled, leapt at Alice, claws extended, then lurched back, staggering. Gloria dropped the basket and turned to grab a stake from the pile by the dresser.

Mary was closer and faster. She grabbed one and leapt across the kitchen and drove it deep into his chest.

The snarl became an ungodly shriek that echoed in the low-ceilinged room. He staggered backward, hands tugging at the stake. Seemed all of them had stakes in their hands by now, but it was Gloria who got him from behind. He staggered forward, knocking dishes off the table and overturning chairs until he collapsed on the floor with a hideous gurgle.

All four stood, horrified. Staring as he twitched and kicked and then went still.

"So that's a Vampire?" Mary said, in a voice much higher than usual.

"Yes," Gloria and Alice replied, almost in unison.

"Was a Vampire," Mrs. Burrows said.

Then the stench came, in a great cloying cloud of foulness.

"Open the door," Mary said.

"Can't." Gloria said. "What about the blackout?"

"Turn off the lights, grab a torch." Trust Mrs. Burrows to think fast.

Mary grabbed the torch off the dresser. Gloria doused the light and opened the back door.

"How long do we stand out here?" Mary asked. "You've killed them before, I haven't."

"It was out of doors," Gloria said. "I noticed the smell but it wasn't as bad as this."

"Best leave the door wide open. We should have brought out some chairs," Alice said. "Got any deck chairs in the shed, Gloria?"

"Only one, and it needs new canvas. Sorry." She gave a groan. "Here I was, anticipating a lovely dinner, and instead we're standing in the flipping cold while the men are snug and warm."

"Maybe we should join them?" Alice suggested.

"Why not?" Gloria asked. "It would be rather fun to troop in there, and when they ask what we're doing, tell them my kitchen is out of bounds because it's been stinked up by a Vampire."

Mary capped it when she added, "I can just see it, years down the road, Gloria, when you have children at your knee and some little treasure looks at you and asks, *What did you do in the war, Mummy*?"

That set them all off. Alice felt tears running down her cheeks. Mary and Gloria were hugging each other for support and Gran was laughing so hard, Alice feared she'd have an attack.

"Pipe down," she said. "At this rate we'll have people coming out of their houses to see what happened."

They calmed at last, laughed out and weary.

"Best laugh I've had in years," Gran said, "but we need to go back and clean up. He should have dissolved by now."

"Is that what happens?" Mary asked.

"Yes," Alice replied. "It's a bit disgusting. It was hard enough to get off the drive. I dread to think what it's done to the floor."

"Best get in and take care of it," Gran said. "Before someone reports us as drunk and disorderly."

"Oh, my," Gloria said. "If Constable Parlett comes along and wants to know what's going on, what could we say?"

"Sorry, Constable. We've just done in a Vampire. We won't do it again," Alice suggested.

Gloria let out another laugh.

"I hope I don't have to," Mary said. "It was nasty."

No one disagreed.

And Gran had been right about the mess on the floor. There was a heap of foul-smelling black sludge right by the sink, half oozed over one of the upended chairs. Broken china and spilled food seemed minor by comparison.

Alice looked at the mess. It had been hard enough cleaning up outside. This was going to be ten times worse.

"Let's get going then," Gran said. "It's a nasty mess, but nothing four women with mops and buckets can't manage. Now. Gloria, we need a shovel and a mop, and where's your bucket?"

Under the sink, and Mary fetched another from the bathroom. Using the coal shovel and a chamber pot, they scooped and filled both buckets. There was still a good deal left.

"What on earth do I do with it?" Gloria asked. "Think it will work on the compost heap?"

Chapter Twenty-Eight

Bela jerked as the rush of power hit her.

"Are you alright?" Simon asked. When she bumped him, he slopped stew over himself and on the ground.

"Yes. Just jumped, sorry I knocked you."

"Not to worry, as long as I can get a second helping."

Jurgen, who seemed to be chief cook and forager, refilled Simon's dish from the communal cooking pot. "Don't spill this," he said. "Supplies aren't limitless."

"I'll be careful." Simon seemed stung by the comment, but Bela understood. Food was always scarce up in the mountains, doubly so this time of year, and the group had skinned and stewed two rabbits in their honor. Two extra mouths to feed was a burden. They couldn't stay much longer.

Seemed Willi, the leader of the group, felt exactly the same.

"We have the first two stops arranged," he said, later that evening. "After that they will give you contacts as you go. No one knows much, it's safer that way."

"What about papers for Bela?" Simon asked. "I've my fake set but she has nothing."

It had been so long since anyone had even thought, much

less worried, about her safety or danger, she almost gasped. "I can manage," she said.

"Not if we go anywhere near a town or even most villages. Once they stop you and you don't have papers, it's all over."

No one argued. He was right. "What if we keep cross country?"

"There's bound to be times we need to go into a village, if only for food. And you're not planning to walk all the way to Switzerland, are you?"

She had been, but "It might be the safest," was all she said.

"Not in this weather," Jurgen said. "Use the safe houses."

"How safe is anywhere?" Simon asked. That she didn't translate.

"How soon can we start?" she asked instead. They'd been undisturbed in the new hideout for almost two days but it was only a matter of time. Rachel might break, or they'd recapture the Frenchman. To say nothing of Rolf and Hans.

Every hour was a danger.

"Tomorrow, at dawn," Willi said. I'll show you the way. Pity you don't have skis."

"We'll manage." With the power surging inside, she could carry Simon, if needed.

"What happened back during dinner?" Simon asked, as they walked back toward the camp after their nightly stroll to the latrine pits.

"It's complicated."

"More complicated than both our natures?"

"Linked to them." They were speaking in English, with little danger of being overheard and considerably less of being understood, and if he didn't mind standing out in the cold, this was as good a time as any. "Let's walk a bit more."

They walked for almost an hour before they headed back.

"Good God!" he muttered from time to time, interspersed with the occasional "Blimey!" but he listened, and it was a strange sort of joy to speak of the fantastic and to be believed.

"So three are dead?" he said, when she finished. "That leaves one more."

"I think he will fail too. The English must have a spell-caster or a powerful witch working for them."

He was too much of a gentleman to argue, but the thought of the War Office conscripting witches and wizards almost had him laughing. What a thought! If they existed—but given that Bela and he existed, and so, apparently, did Vampires—who was he to offer a differing opinion? Old Mother Longhurst back home had been reputed to be a witch, but he couldn't see her being anyone's secret weapon.

There was one thing bothered him though. "When you had the mind link thingy with them, did you ever know where they were?" He wasn't sure he wanted to know the answer, but damn it, a man couldn't help worrying.

"Seldom. I was in their thoughts, that was all. I caught thoughts of London and Churchill more than once." To be expected, if they were out to aid the invasion of England. "And they used to meet at one place. Where the leader, Weiss, lived. A place I'd never heard of before. Geelford."

"God, no! Guildford?"

"That might be it. You know this place?"

Like the damn back of his hand. "It's near my home. A big market town."

In the silence of the woods, he heard her sigh. "You are worried. You have family, relatives there?"

"My sister, my grandmother. Our parents are dead."

"I am sorry. Just the two of them?"

"I've a younger brother. He's in the navy. Hope he's alright." Couldn't think "safe." How could he be, out on the high seas?

"But you worry for your sister and grandmother."

"With Vampires tramping over the countryside, you bet."

"But only one Vampire. Someone is killing them. I know when they die."

He didn't think a Vampire could die. Wasn't the whole point that they were already dead? But Bela seemed so certain, and seeing the four monsters had as good as raped her, she was the expert here. "Maybe they've been on a killing spree?"

"No!"

"You sound very certain."

"I am. Of that much. When I entered Weiss's mind once, he was berating Eiche for killing, said it would draw unwanted attention."

And if three Vampires were goners, maybe it had. "Still can't help worrying. Think of the bombing."

"There's bombing here too," she pointed out, "but I understand. I still worry about my family and they are all dead. All but Onkle Kurt and Tante Elise."

He reached out for her hand. "We'll get there."

"I know. How can we fail together? My parents spoke of Elves and Sprites, but never Pixies. Now that we have formed an alliance, we will escape. I'm strong and will be stronger when the last Vampire dies."

Couldn't come too soon as far as he was concerned. "Do you know how they die?"

She shook her head. "I just know when they are dead. It must be the link the Germans forced us to forge. I take in their anima, their life force. I am very glad you English have this great spell-caster at your service."

The thought of some Merlin-type figure traipsing over

the North Downs and zapping Vampires was a bit hard to swallow. He chuckled.

"You laugh?" she asked. "Why?"

He told her.

"Someone must have great magic," she insisted. "If not a spell-caster, then perhaps a strong Other. Your grandmother or perhaps your sister?"

This time he laughed aloud. The idea of Gran abandoning jam making and knitting to chase after Vampires, or brainy Alice—who'd told him as a child that Gran's stories were just that: stories—taking up Vampire hunting, was just too much for words. "I don't think so but I hope whoever it is, they take care of the last bloodsucker."

"Why should they fail with one when they've conquered three?"

Good point, but a man couldn't help worrying at the thought of Vampires running rampant over his home. "Think we'd better go back before they send out search parties for us?"

"I don't think they will. If we die of cold, they won't weep over our graves."

Maybe not, but they were greeted by what had to be ribald comments when they got back. Poor Bela blushed. Damn! "Put a sock in it!" he said, not having much hope they'd understand. Suddenly remembering a phrase learned from a German pupil at his school, he snapped, "Halt die Schnauze."

"Ah. She kip you varm, Englander!" Jurgen snickered, as Simon reached for his sleeping bag.

But he did make a point of lying next to Bela. Just to make sure no one bothered her.

Chapter Twenty-Nine

Weiss felt like humming as he drove away. He had the grocer creature captive and the satisfaction of putting Schmidt in his place. He was getting a far too inflated notion of his worth. Let him deliver those flowers and get back by his own feet. Or he could fly, if he had enough reserves of energy.

Driving carefully, no point in inviting the inconvenience of being stopped by the local constabulary, Weiss drove back to Wharton Lacey, pulling the lorry up close to the stables. Hoisting the creature, who moaned rather pathetically, over his shoulder, he mounted the rickety steps to the loft and dumped his prisoner in the last room. It was dark, cold and dingy—so what? He wasn't entertaining a valued ally but a creature he wanted to investigate. A creature who'd bested him once and, if reports were right, had evaded Bloch's embrace and maybe even killed him. Although the idea of this pathetic specimen destroying a Vampire was beyond reason.

"What are you?" Weiss asked, looking at the cringing figure whimpering at his feet. Whorleigh had the effrontery to sneer. A good kick and a sharp jerk on the chain to tighten it took care of that. Still, he might recover, or be desperate enough to uncoil the chain.

Weiss lifted him onto the bed frame, looping the end of the chain through the wire springs and testing to be sure they'd last a few minutes. Foraging downstairs he found a chunk of concrete, used no doubt to prop open doors, but perfect for anchoring the two ends of the chain. Just in case the thing got its voice back, he gagged him with Schmidt's spare shirt. Then he tore the creature's trouser at the crotch and bit him in the groin. Just to let him know what was in store. He made laudable efforts to resist but didn't have a hope against the power of a Vampire.

"Next time, there will be two of us," Weiss promised, as he paused in the doorway, "and we will feast off you together. Enjoy the anticipation and terror until we return. I will."

Weiss moved the lorry down the drive until it was out of sight of the house, and left. Schmidt could take it back to the farm when he returned.

He ran back up to the stable and stretched out on Schmidt's bed.

That way he'd know immediately when he returned.

It would be fun working the creature over together. Fear made blood so much sweeter.

Chapter Thirty

The milkman first noticed the parked lorry blocking the drive up to Wharton Lacey. Since his horse was placidly inclined, he maneuvered past and up to the house. With the household still asleep, he left the milk, and the papers he always brought as a service to the Whartons, then took his horse and cart back down the drive, repeating the tricky maneuver. Muttering that some mothers did have 'em, he went on to the cluster of cottages at the bottom of the hill and then into Brytewood village.

Frank Woolgar, the manager of the Home Farm, was the first to notice the farm lorry missing. Cussing under his breath at the laziness of some people, he sent Gracie, one of the land girls, off to Jim Proudfoot's cottage. If Jim hadn't left yet, he told her, he was to drive the lorry back himself, as he should have last night. If he'd already left, that gave him two whole days to re-hearse what he'd say when tearing Jim off a strip. Having the weekend off to help out his wife's sister, who'd been bombed out in Croydon, was one thing. Neglecting to return the lorry was another matter entirely. For one hideous moment, he wondered if the Proudfoots had taken the lorry with them. If so, that was a firing matter.

The lorry was nowhere in sight. Gracie thumped on the door for several minutes, and only succeeded in rousing the two little evacuees who lived next door.

"You're making too much noise," the taller boy said. "You'll wake the baby and he's been up half the night."

"Sorry," Gracie said. "I was looking for the Proudfoots."

"They're gone."

"Left yesterday," the younger one added. "Right after lunch. They took the bus into Dorking to go to the station."

"The bus? You're sure? They didn't drive a lorry?"

They both shook their heads.

At least the lorry wasn't in Croydon, by the sound of things.

"They went to help Mrs. Proudfoot's sister," the elder one said. Gracie searched her brains for their names but with no luck. "She got bombed out."

"Think they'll be back?" the other one asked. "Mum went off to help Gran after her house got hit and then got bombed herself."

Poor little blighters. Gracie remembered the talk a month or so ago. "Sorry about your mum." What else could she say? "You two had best get indoors before you catch your death of cold."

Mr. Woolgar was none too happy at the news. "Where the hell's the damn lorry then? Sure it wasn't there?"

In the Proudfoots' tiny garden there wasn't space to hide a wheelbarrow, much less a farm lorry. "Not a sign, and the boys were quite certain they left on the bus. I asked particularly if they'd taken the lorry."

"If he left after lunch, what the blazes happened to the flowers Sir James wanted delivered? Did they get where they were going, I'd like to know? And where's the dratted lorry?"

* * *

Lady Gregory answered that one. Returning from her morning ride across the fields, she took a detour around by the cottages and up the lane toward home. The sight of a farm lorry parked askew in the drive struck her as odd.

Back in the house and settled over her toast and coffee, she asked her spouse, "What's a farm lorry doing parked in the drive? I know we're not expecting company this weekend, but if anyone does try to come up, they'll never get past it."

"Eh?" Sir James looked up from the *Times*. "In the drive you say? What's it doing there?"

"That was what I was asking, dear. It ought to be moved."

"Proudfoot had it last. I sent him down to the village with camellias for that Nurse Prewitt. She's getting married today to the chap from over at the munitions plant."

Interesting, but since the district nurse wasn't a tenant or employee, a wedding present wasn't called for. "It still needs to be moved. Won't they need it today?"

"I'll have Smith, the new gardener, drive it over. Can't think what got into Proudfoot."

"One more thing!" Edith Aubin muttered at the latest request from the dining room. And, of course, Smith hadn't yet put in an appearance in the kitchen. No doubt waiting to want toast after they'd finished with both breakfasts.

"What's the matter?" Molly asked, hands in the sink as she washed up.

"Seems someone left a farm lorry down in the drive. Sir James wants Smith to move it and of course, is he anywhere to be seen? Still lolling in bed, I'll be bound."

"If he's not over here by the time I get these done, I'll go and give him a yell," Molly offered.

Fifteen minutes later, Molly pulled on her coat to nip across to the stable yard. She wasn't in the best of moods. She'd been up since 6:30 and here was this layabout still snoozing. It was a less-than-friendly voice that called up the stairs. "Mr. Smith? Sir James needs you, so look sharp!"

Getting no response didn't improve her mood. If he was still snoring away while she'd been up working for hours, she was going to tear him off a strip, even if it wasn't her place to.

She climbed the open steps that led up above the stables. She wouldn't normally venture into a man's room, but she was cross enough not to care. His room was the second one along and the door was closed. She gave it a sharp rap and called out, "Wakey wakey, Sir James needs you, better get going." When he didn't respond she rapped harder and longer, and called his name.

Having no luck there, she opened the door a few inches and peered in. She had a straight line view of the bed, and saw at once the bedspread was crushed, as if someone had slept on it, but not bothered to get inside. She opened the door wider and surveyed the empty room.

Where the blazes was he?

She closed the door, and it was her especial good fortune that she'd not been curious enough to look behind it. Weiss clung to the wall, ready to pounce if she'd seen him. As she left, he looked for alternative exits. The window was the only one possible.

Outside, Molly hesitated, wondering if Smith were in one of the other rooms. She walked down, calling his name and peering in the unfurnished rooms. In the last room she heard a noise, like a groan or gasp. She pushed open the door, and at the sight of a half-naked man chained to the bare springs of the bedstead, screamed.

Weiss snatched the moment and leapt through the window, hoping her screams would mask the sounds of splintering wood and breaking glass.

He was bleeding; time would heal that. Not hesitating a second, he headed across the parkland and toward the fields, racing in the direction of his previous resting place in the ruins of the rectory tennis court.

Poor Molly gasped, took a deep breath, and crossed the room.

"My God! It's Mr. Whorleigh! What happened?"

He gave a weak gurgle as if it hurt to speak and rasped out, "Get this off me. Please."

It took all her strength to shift the chunk of cement and she wondered how on earth anyone had got it up here. Once free, he struggled to sit up and stand.

He grabbed her shoulder for support. "Thank you," he croaked. "Where am I?"

He didn't smell of drink and seemed more weak than intoxicated. "Where am I?" he repeated. "And where are they? He said they'd come back."

"You're over the stables at Wharton Lacey, and who put you here?"

"They . . ." he began, but broke off, shuddering. "Help me." He grabbed at her coat, digging his fingernails into the cloth.

"I am helping you." Realizing she'd snapped, she lowered her voice. "Look, Mr. Whorleigh. I've got to get help. I can't get you down on my own."

He clung to her even more tightly. "Please. Don't leave me!"

"Alright, listen. I'll help you to the top of the stairs, then you wait there while I get Miss Aubin to help. If she tried by herself, she'd end up breaking her leg and then bang would go her day off.

He wasn't happy about it, but waited at the top, crawling into a corner and shaking while she climbed down as fast as she could and ran across the yard to the kitchen door to call out for help.

"What's going on?" Miss Aubin said. "What's the fuss? And where is that Paul Smith? I'm about give him a piece of my mind."

"He's not there, but Mr. Whorleigh is. He was tied to one of the beds."

It took Edith Aubin all of thirty seconds to decide Molly had to be telling the truth. It was too impossible to make up. "Where is he now?"

"At the top of the steps. He can hardly stand, and I didn't think I could get him down without help."

"I'll help."

Together they got the shivering man down and safely into the kitchen and wrapped him in a blanket. While Molly made him a cup of sweet tea, Miss Aubin went to relay the news to the dining room.

Molly poured the tea, thinking the poor blighter needed a shot of brandy as well as extra sugar, but it wasn't her place to help herself to spirits, even if they hadn't been locked up. "Here you are, Mr. Whorleigh," she said, pulling up a straight-backed chair beside his. "A nice cup of tea. Just what you need. Do you the world of good, it will." Looked as though she'd be late leaving, but would she have a tale to tell when she did get home!

"Really, Miss Aubin, what on earth is going on out there?"

"As to that, sir, I can't rightly tell you. I haven't searched the stables myself, but Molly found no trace of Smith, but she did find Mr. Whorleigh, the grocer from Brytewood. He was chained to one of the spare beds, wearing nothing but his torn-up trousers and minus one shoe." Now she came to say it aloud, it did sound preposterous. "I'm thinking we should call the doctor for Mr. Whorleigh. He's not in a good way."

"Call Dr. Watson," Lady Gregory said. "And I think the police too. If that man was chained up in the stable loft without any blanket or covers, he'd have died if Mòlly hadn't had the foresight to look."

Miss Aubin called, but half an hour earlier, Alice Watson had redirected her calls to the locum in Leatherhead. She was not missing Gloria's wedding for anything short of pestilence or air raid.

The locum agreed to come out as soon as he could get there.

She then called down to the police and disturbed Sergeant Jones enjoying a late breakfast with his family. He agreed to come up right away.

Once he heard the ring on the line indicating she'd finished, Sir James Gregory called the office in Whitehall he'd spoken to yesterday. "Parish," he said, when the line picked up the other end. "I need to speak to Parish. It's James Gregory. It's urgent."

"Just a minute, please, Sir James," the young man at the other end said. "He's home right now, I'll connect you through." He waited while the line clicked and buzzed.

"Hello," Peter Parish said. "What's happened?"

"Seems the bird has flown but left an injured cuckoo behind."

"This line's secure, or as secure as any of them are. Tell me what's happened."

Sir James Gregory told him.

"We'll be there in two hours, and whatever you do, keep that grocer person there. He must be caught up in this somehow."

Chapter Thirty-One

The men had gone ahead on the bus. Alice and Gran picked up Mary and Gloria, a definitely beautiful bride, complete with bouquet. (A couple of the camellias had been squashed in the melee last night but who was complaining?) As they headed out of the village, the crowd outside Whorleigh's caught Alice's eye.

"What's going on there?" she asked. "Looks like a queue for the London sales."

"Stop a minute, my love," Gran said, "and I'll have a word with someone."

"Please, Gran. Whatever it is can wait, surely?"

"I suppose so, my love. I just think if something is going on, we need to know about it."

Having learned the hard way to trust Gran's hunches, Alice pulled up in front of the shop and wound down her window. "What's the matter?"

"Hello, Doctor. Shop's not open," someone said, "and Marion here don't have the key."

"That's right," Marion, one of Whorleigh's numerous assistants, said. "He always has it open by the time I get here."

"Rum do, if you ask me," a voice in the crowd muttered.

Alice's conscience twinged. She should see if anyone was

hurt, but it would delay them all. Then Constable Parlett emerged from the newsagent and post office next door, and announced he was cycling over to Whorleigh's house to see what was happening.

He could take care of things.

Alice thanked him and drove on.

Even Gran seemed relieved they hadn't stopped, but she said very quietly, "Something's wrong, my love. He always opens on time." And came in early to boot, something Alice once had reason to be profoundly grateful for. "Still, there's not much we can do, I think," Gran went on. "Not now. This is Gloria's day." It was indeed, and they'd taken care of one of the Vampires yesterday.

The wedding was brief and businesslike but no amount of bureaucratic briskness could quell the joy and happiness in the little room, or the glorious look of love on Gloria's face. Mary pushed aside a pang of envy at the sight of Gloria and Andrew walking hand in hand down the street toward the Spread Eagle where they were all lunching.

She didn't doubt she loved Gryffyth. She knew why she hesitated and, darn it, she was taking care of that tonight. She'd have the cottage to herself. She'd even made up her bed with clean sheets that very morning. Was that being presumptuous?

No, she decided. Optimistic.

"You've gone very quiet," Gryffyth said, walking in step beside her.

"Just happy for Gloria, and a little worried on her account. Who knows when Andrew will get the word to go?"

"It's hard on them," he agreed, "but I doubt either is worrying about that right now. I envy him," Gryffyth went on. "The woman he loves, didn't turn him down."

"Oh, for heaven's sake! I haven't turned you down."

"No, even worse. You're keeping me dangling."

If he wasn't careful, she'd give him a firm answer and it wouldn't be the one he hoped for. "I'm making up my mind. If you want to try convincing me, come over to our house this evening. I'll be all alone."

That left him speechless for several seconds. But only seconds. "What do you mean?"

As if he didn't know! And if he really didn't, she was darn well not spelling it out in words of one syllable. "Seven-thirty, and bring your own beer, we don't have any." His face was a picture to behold. Time to toss her last match on the possible conflagration. "You can make it later, if you like. I was thinking of going up to the hammerpond and it sometimes takes me a little while to get back."

"You're not going up to the pond on Longhurst's land."

Oh, no? "Where else can I go? Gryffyth, you have to understand, I need to be in deep water. Salt water for preference, but that hammerpond is the best I can do in Surrey. You shift and breathe fire. I need to feel water flowing over my skin. All my skin," she added. Just for the sake of making her point.

She succeeded.

"You're not swimming naked in Tom Longhurst's pond!" She'd never heard that exact tone of voice in her life and it sent a little shiver of excitement down her spine. She'd certainly piqued his interest. Maybe a wee bit too much. "If you go, I'm coming with you!"

Mary didn't bother to respond, since they were about to cross the road. Didn't need to. Her heart raced behind her ribs. Tonight was the night.

She so hoped.

They had a big, round table in a small, private room and in the place of honor was Mrs. Burrows's cake, which had ridden down with them, hidden under a blanket in the back of the shooting brake. How it miraculously appeared from there to sit on the silver cake stand was a mystery, but weren't more than half the company Other? Only Peter and Andrew were full human. Must have been a bit of Pixie magic. Or perhaps Dragon magic?

No, she hoped all the Dragon magic was waiting for her tonight.

They were between courses and had the room to themselves (thank heaven) when Mrs. Burrows said, "Thank you, Howell, my love, for getting everyone here on time."

"Doubted me, didn't you, Helen? Thought we'd all be too hung over to get here."

"I did not. Not really. I just know how enticing Fred Wise's beer can be."

"We got here, Helen, all safe and sound, and with clear heads."

"And what were you women doing? Didn't go over to the Stepping Stones in Westhumble, did you?" Andrew asked.

"We spent the evening at Gloria's," Alice said. "Nice quiet evening it was, until Mary staked the Vampire."

"You did *what*?" Gryffyth all but shrieked. Mary had never realized eyebrows really could disappear into the hairline like that.

"I staked a Vampire: the one Alice remembered finding hurt, weeks back. She recognized him." Mary held back the grin. Surprising your man was one thing. Infuriating him beyond measure was a bit much.

"Christ almighty!" Peter announced.

Gryffyth wasn't the slightest bit interested in supplications to heaven. He had his arm around her and turned her to face him. "You staked him. Just like that?"

"Not 'just like that.' Alice recognized him and he grabbed

for her, hissing and fangs snarling. She did something that made him reel back and I grabbed a stake and got him in the chest. Took a lot of effort to shove it in, by the way. It's nowhere near as easy as it sounds. He stumbled around wailing and shrieking and I worried the neighbors might hear. Then Gloria grabbed another stake and got him from behind. That finished him off."

Andrew got the first word out. "You weren't hurt, were you, Gloria?"

"Not this time. Mary bore the brunt of it, that and Alice's *stay away and begone* bit. That was impressive."

"I've seen it," Peter said. "You're right."

"But no one was hurt," the sergeant said. "That's the main thing."

"The kitchen was a bit of a mess," Alice said. "Gloria really needs new lino for the bit by the sink."

"Now hang on a minute!" Gryffyth finally got his voice back. "You could have been hurt, killed, injured, sucked dry, bitten . . ." He grabbed her tighter, as he ran out of alternatives.

"But I wasn't." Mary shrugged. "I was scared out of my wits but we're safe. No harm done, apart from the damage to the kitchen and a few plates, and he's finished."

"I can *not* believe this! You women dispose of a Vampire and act as if you were shelling peas!"

"Better get used to it, mate," Peter said. "They make a habit of it. They just initiated Mary into the Nemesis of Vampires club."

If Gryffyth got any closer to her, he'd be sitting on her lap. "What happened?"

"Pretty much as Alice said. The chap knocked on the door. Alice recognized him, and did something that sort of threw him back. After all the talk about Vampires and you and your father equipping us with stakes, I grabbed one and that was that."

"What happened afterwards? After you'd finished pincushioning him, I mean?"

That was the bit she'd rather not remember but he seemed intent on knowing every last detail. "We had a nasty, smelly mess on the floor and had to clean it up."

Gryffyth wasn't sure whether to hold her close and never let her out of his sight as long as she lived, or to shake her. The latter might not go down too well and looking around the table, none of the others appeared to share his horror. Even his father, whom he'd always thought sensible and sane, seemed to be regarding Mary with a cross between admiration and delight.

"No one hurt," his dad said. "That's what matters, and now, thanks to Mary and Gloria, we can all rest more easily in our beds."

"Not too easy on Andrew's part, I hope," Peter said with a dirty laugh.

"You behave yourself," Alice told him with an elbow in the ribs.

"Just wishing a pal good luck."

"How about we cut the cake and wish them both good health?" Mrs. Burrows suggested.

No one argued with that. After toasts and Howell Pendragon's speech and Andrew's rather humorous one, Andrew and Gloria cut the cake, and they all had another drink and then the pair of them stood and Gloria tossed her camellias at Mary. She inhaled the scent of the clustered flowers and met Gryffyth's eyes. Yes, tonight should be just as she planned.

When she looked back at Gloria, she was grinning. She might have mouthed *good luck*. Certainly looked like it.

Andrew and Gloria thanked everyone for coming and then they were gone. Upstairs no doubt.

Anticlimax descended on the room, until Mrs. Burrows started giving the staff instructions to pack up the rest of the cake. "We ought to send some up to Wharton Lacey as a thank you, and I'm sure Gloria has people she wants to send pieces to."

Gryffyth had never quite worked out the thing of passing around slices of wedding cake, but he was more worried about Mary than slabs of cake.

"Think we can all pile in the car?" Peter asked, as they wandered out into the chill of twilight. "It's a bit nippy to be hanging around for a bus."

"If someone doesn't mind sitting on the floor in the back," Alice said.

"I will," Mary offered. "I'll hold the cake."

"I'll hold it with you," Gryffyth offered and glared at his father's chuckle. "We've got a couple of sharp hills and bends. I don't want to see it get squashed."

Quite a brilliant move, he decided after he settled beside Mary. There was plenty of space. Less would have been better. Mary held the box on her lap tightly with both hands. Just to make sure it didn't shift. Gryffyth put his arm around her and held the cake with his free hand, or rather held her hand holding the box.

He was perfectly content, until she rested her head on his shoulder, and he about went into orbit. Damn! He wanted her so much it hurt. Quite literally. Had she been serious about asking him over for the evening? Why not? They were almost engaged, after all. Even more to the point was her talk about swimming in Tom Longhurst's damn pond.

How could she? How could she not, if that was her nature?

"I'm coming with you tonight, if you insist on going up to that dratted hammerpond."

"Alright," she said. "No need to bring a bathing suit. I never bother, but it is cold afterwards."

He was too damn hot to worry about winter chills.

Chapter Thirty-Two

Mary did her best to feign casual and relaxed as her mind whirled. He'd agreed to go up to the hammerpond. No, he'd pretty much invited himself, but right now she had a need that superseded water. Still, it had worked. He was going to latch onto her like a burr on a sheep and that was just peachy.

She needed Gryffyth. His arm around her was very nice but she wanted more. Lots more than a nice hug and a shoulder to lean on. She wanted him naked. She wanted to be naked and damn it, it was going to happen. They'd be undisturbed until she had to get to school Monday morning.

Should be enough time.

"Come home with me," she whispered.

"I thought we'd already settled that. You're not going anywhere without me."

"Good," she replied. For now, she'd keep to herself the news that she was skipping the hammerpond. She had better ideas of how to spend a Saturday night.

Might as well start by nestling closer and kissing his cheek.

At least that was what she planned.

As if anticipating her, he turned so her lips brushed his

mouth. Brushed them and stayed, opening to his touch as he held the back of her head and kissed her.

Blimey! What a kiss! His tongue stroked hers, gently at first, then with a wild insistence and sheer and delightful verve, as he pressed his mouth on hers and sent her reason into a spin. She kissed back, leaning into him, wrapping her arms around him and pressing her body into his.

Until the cake slid off her lap and landed on its side.

"Damn," he muttered under his breath as he scooped it up. There were a few cracks in the hard icing but it wasn't too badly battered, aside from the little celluloid groom having a bent top hat. "Sorry," Gryffyth said.

"I think Gloria will forgive us," Mary said. In exchange for full and complete details, no doubt, but Gryffyth didn't need to know that.

"Not too badly bashed up, I think," he said.

Mary wedged the cake against the side of the car. "Should be safe there," she said. "Could we continue our conversation?" To be sure he got her meaning, she molded her body into his, or as well as she could through her winter coat and his old army greatcoat. Kissing hard and furious. Willing him to want her. To need her and to come home with her.

Layers of clothes came between them but he took care of the top few layers, unbuttoning her coat and easing his hand inside to cup her breast. She felt every finger tip through her jumper, blouse, petticoat and bra. Damn, she even had an extra vest on too. Might keep out the cold, but didn't keep out his touch. What was it about Gryffyth that she responded to so intensely?

She was in love. Had to be.

She was half giddy with elation when he broke the kiss. "I love you, Mary LaPrioux," he said, "and you're not going anywhere near Tom Longhurst's land without me."

She grinned. The hammerpond could wait. "Alright. If you insist."

Wasn't much more to say, really. She nestled close and tried to imagine how much better she'd feel if his hand was inside her blouse. Seemed he had the same idea.

One by one, he unbuttoned the tiny pearl buttons. He caressed the skin above her bra and she almost cried out with pleasure.

She bit her lip to keep quiet. Before, she'd responded to him with fire in her veins. Now her whole being hurt with needing. Her heart raced and she burned for him. Inside and out. Especially inside. How much further was it to get home? Better concentrate on not ripping the trousers off him right here in the back of Alice's car. For a few wild moments, she'd forgotten they weren't alone.

That, or something equally unnerving, seemed to have hit Gryffyth. He gave a sigh and looked down at her. "Not much longer," he said. "We're just beyond Leatherhead."

How could he tell? Dragon sight in the dark? Or complete familiarity with the road? He'd been here all his life and for her it had been what? Just over two weeks.

Two weeks. Evacuation to Sheffield was a lifetime away and home, that was another world. To quell the spate of homesickness, she snuggled even closer to him. Within the circle of his arms, her head against his beating Dragon heart, for the space of a few minutes she could forget the horrors and upheaval around them.

He'd been right about the distance. Ten, fifteen minutes later, Alice pulled up beside Gloria's cottage.

"Here you are."

"Thanks ever so, Alice."

"Yes, ta, Alice," Gryffyth added, as he thoughtfully checked Mary to make sure all her buttons were done up.

He finished just in time as Peter opened the back of the shooting break. "Need a hand down, Mary?"

"I'll help her," Gryffyth said, getting out first and steadying himself, then holding her by the waist as she eased her feet to the ground.

"All set then?" Peter asked.

"Perfect," Gryffyth replied. "I'll see her safely home. Good night, everyone," he called over the back seat. "See you later, Dad. Thanks again for the lift, Alice. 'Night, Mrs. Burrows."

Mary added her good-byes. Peter closed the door and climbed back into the car.

Gryffyth took her hand and reached into his pocket for a torch. "This should get us home safely. Sorry I broke yours."

"We hardly need it tonight." The moon was rising in the sky. It was a beautiful, clear night. Unfortunately clear skies meant bombing. But she was in Brytewood, not in the middle of Sheffield. "Come on in," she said. "I'll make you a cup of coffee. We have a packet we keep for special occasions."

That was interesting, Peter thought to himself as they drove away. What exactly were the odds that Gryffyth would be walking home? Pretty damn slight to verging on the highly unlikely. Couldn't blame him, or Mary. Anyone with half an eye could see they were mutually smitten. He wondered what Gran and Sergeant Pendragon thought about it, but darn it, these days were too bloody uncertain to not grab what happiness you could.

Not five minutes later, Alice pulled up in front of the Pendragon house.

There was an odd pause as the engine idled and the sergeant seemed to hesitate. Then he jumped out and made his way around the car to open the passenger door. "All set, Helen?" he asked.

"Gran," Alice began, before sealing her lips. Peter just kept quiet.

"Just stopping to have a drink with Howell. Don't wait up for me."

While Howell Pendragon opened the gate for his fiancée, Alice sat open-mouthed. "What on earth . . ." she began, and shook her head.

Wasn't often his wife was bereft of words. Peter wished them luck. Age shouldn't exclude anyone from grabbing happiness.

"They had it planned," Alice said as she let off the brake and headed the car toward home. "They must have cooked it up between them."

"They couldn't have known they'd have the house to themselves, could they? Gryffyth might have gone home."

She gave a laugh. "Mary was hell bent and determined to take Gryffyth home with her tonight."

"She told you that?"

"Yes, dear, between killing off that Vampire. I lent her a pair of red French knickers to help things along."

"I thought you lent a blue pair to Gloria."

She nodded. "Yes."

"Stone the crows, Alice. Do you have any knickers left for you?"

"Better find out when we get home, hadn't you? After all, if everyone else was getting friendly tonight we might as well too."

He wasn't about to argue with that. "And we have the house to ourselves. We can make love in every room."

"Only the ones with beds and warmth," she replied. "Passion only heats you up so far."

"Want to stop by the Pig for a nightcap?"

She considered that a moment or two. "Better get on home. Gran might have forgotten the chickens in her ardor, but I haven't, and it's dark already. Don't want to lose them to a fox."

"Don't worry, Gloria's not here tonight."

That earned him a jab from her elbow. "She'd never raid a henhouse. I'm certain of that but," Alice went on, "I wonder if she does hunt when on all fours. I must ask her."

"Not tonight, you won't."

"No?"

"No," he echoed. "I can offer you a much better way to spend the evening."

"Yes," she replied, "I know that. I'm so glad I'm married to you, Peter."

The feeling was mutual. Talk about a fellow having the luck. "Marriage is in the air, it seems. Us. Now Andrew and Gloria and your gran and the sergeant."

"And Mary and Gryffyth, unless I'm very much mistaken. You know he asked her to marry him?"

"Eh? She told you that too?"

"Yes, dear, she did."

"They're engaged too?"

"Not yet, she's making up her mind."

Seemed to him, she already had. He wished them both the joy he'd discovered. Damn, he wished the whole world joy.

Chapter Thirty-Three

Mary was so darn nervous, she almost dropped her key, but Gryffyth caught it in his strong hand and unlocked the door, standing back to let her in first.

The house was freezing cold. Darn! In the rush and fuss that morning, neither she nor Gloria had thought to make up the boiler.

"Drat. I'd offer to take your coat," she said as they pulled the curtains over the windows, "but I think we'd better keep them on for a while."

"Boiler gone out?" She nodded. Brilliant start to a grand seduction. "Hand me the hod, I'll fill it up. Where's the coal bunker?"

"Just to the right of the back door. First one is coke. We're saving the good coal in case we ever want a fire in the sitting room."

"I'll get it."

As the door closed behind him, she ran upstairs and plugged in the electric fire in her bedroom and put up the blackout curtains. Hopefully they'd be too engrossed in other things to remember it later. Yes, definitely anticipating, but why not? She didn't think he'd come in just for a cup of coffee.

Downstairs, a filled hod stood by the stove and, bless him, he had a bundle of kindling in his hand.

"Hope you don't mind, but I went looking in the shed. Thought you'd need this to get it going."

Nothing like a man who knew how to light a fire. "Wonderful. I'll get some newspapers."

There was something deliciously, and almost worryingly, domestic about sitting side by side, twisting pages of newspaper into firelighters. Gryffyth knotted his after rolling up the page. She'd aways folded them over and over, making a tight plait, the same way her mother and grandmother did. His way was faster, his strong hands twisting and knotting two or three in the time it took her to fold one.

"Heavens, you're fast!"

He looked up, met her eyes and gave her a wicked grin. "Not always. I can be very slow when needed."

When her heart settled from that flip, she smiled back. "Let's hope this stove lights, or we're going to freeze." To say nothing of having to boil kettles or wash in cold water.

"If the matches won't take, there's always Dragonfire."

"Works, does it?"

"Always."

Dear heaven! How could a single word send great thrills of anticipation down her spine? "Let's get it going then."

"Right you are, Miss LaPrioux."

And God bless him, he riddled the grate and took out the ashpan to empty it as she dropped kindling, firelighters and a few handfuls of coke into the belly of the stove. The kindling caught right away. It would take a while to warm the kitchen but at least they'd come down to a warm room and have hot water in the morning.

She rather fancied sharing the bath with him.

She had to boil a kettle for them both to wash off the coal

dust. Standing side by side at the sink, she was utterly aware of his presence, and what she was about to do. She wanted him so desperately it was like a wild burning deep inside. Dragonfire perhaps?

"You're happy," Gryffyth said.

"Of course. I've just come from the wedding of my best friend here in Brytewood and now I'm with the man I love. Can't ask for much more, can I?"

"You love me, Mary?"

She nodded. "Yes." Saying it aloud gave her the jitters inside. But they were darn good jitters.

He stepped close, stroking the side of her face with his still damp hand. "Then marry me."

"I've never said 'no,' Gryffyth. I just need time. It's not the sort of thing you jump into."

"Why not, when you're sure? I love you. I want to marry you. You love me. Why the hesitation?"

"Some would call it being cautious, careful, and wanting to be certain."

"They might," he agreed. "They might also call it dilly dallying and keeping a chap hanging."

She took a step back—more than one was impossible with the sink at her back—and looked at him. "They might. Do you?"

Her mouth went dry as she waited for his reply. "No," he said, after what seemed like an endless pause. "I don't, Mary. Beats me, really, why you didn't sock me one for moving so fast."

"I think you know why." Let him mull on that a minute or two. "I'll put the kettle back on."

He stepped back just enough to let her turn and grab the kettle. When she moved to the oven, he had the gas already lit. "Really, honest to goodness coffee?" he asked.

"Yes, it's in Gloria's secret cache. But I doubt she'd mind

us digging into it. Some things will keep to celebrate peace, but coffee won't."

The aroma was already fading, she noticed, as she opened the tin. Never mind, she'd add an extra spoonful for taste. It was in a good cause after all.

She warmed the jug, measured out the coffee and poured on the near-boiling water, covering the jug with a saucer to keep it hot. "Would you like toast? Are you hungry? I've some eggs Alice gave me, but I thought we could save those for breakfast."

Dear lord! That just came out.

He didn't seem upset, though. Just gave a quizzical look. "Are you inviting me to stay for breakfast, Miss LaPrioux?"

Why be coy? She knew what she wanted and so did he. "Yes."

"You do realize," he said, "how much scandal that will cause."

She grinned. "I think your reputation is safe. Once word gets out about Gloria and Andrew's wedding, the rest of the weekend will fade into the background."

He shook his head, but his eyes weren't telling her no. "I hope you realize, I walked all this way and back with your bicycle to preserve your reputation the other night."

"Now's your chance to destroy it. What do you think?"

"I think, Mary, that your nice, demure schoolteacher image is downright misleading."

Demure? She had to laugh. "Gryffyth, demure women don't ask men to dance. Besides, I'm not a human woman. I'm a Water Sprite who swims naked when the mood takes her."

"That's right, you do, don't you?" He was back close now, their knees almost touching. "Are you going to get naked up on the heath tonight?"

"I don't think so. We could get naked here." Oh! God! Had

she really said that? Heat burned her face and neck. "Coffee should be ready by now." Why was she on such a seesaw? She wanted him. He was not averse to the idea, but here she was, fussing over stirring in a tablespoon of cold water to settle the grounds. She had no idea if Gloria even had a coffee strainer, so she grabbed the tea strainer. And she'd forgotten to warm up the milk.

"Here." She handed him a cup. "Do you want sugar?"

"You know what I really want?" he said as he took the cup.

"Sugar? We have a little."

"Forget sugar. Let's go back to what you said about getting naked." He gave a wondrously sexy smile. "What I really want is you."

Something leapt inside her. "I'm so glad."

"So'm I. Come on, let's sit down."

They squeezed close in the big armchair. There was actually warmth coming from the stove by now. "Good coffee," he said, as he took a sip.

"Thanks."

They sat in silence a few minutes. Was his mind as scrambled as hers? Was he having second thoughts? Worried about what people would say?

"Mary," he said, looking away from her, his attention fixed on a point somewhere across the room. "Don't think I don't love you and don't think I don't want you, because, dammit, I've been dreaming about you every night since I met you, but you seem to forget. I'm missing pieces."

"You're missing a leg, Gryffyth." Dear God! It sounded so harsh said like that, but was that what make him hesitate? "If you can stand it, don't you think I can?" Wrong word, that.

He didn't seem to notice. "It looks pretty awful."

"Oh, Gryffyth," she said, "as if it makes a blind bit of difference to me. I love you, you great lummock! I fancy you.

Dammit, I'm asking you to spend the night with me. I'm not going to beg you to stay."

"You won't need to," he replied, taking her mug out of her hand and putting both hers and his by the fender.

Then he wrapped his arms around her and kissed her.

Hard.

With a wild heat and passion that left her in no doubt as to his intentions. Just to add to the assurance, he pulled her against him and his erection made his interest totally clear. She was gasping for breath then he let her go. Only just long enough to pull her coat off her shoulders. "Stand up," he said. "We've both got too many clothes on. Besides, it's getting warm in here now."

Warm? She was burning with need as he took her coat and spread it on the floor, then put his own beside it.

"Here?" she asked.

"I bet it's warmer than upstairs."

Didn't seem the moment to mention she'd plugged in her bedroom fire. "Yes," she replied, pulling her knitted jumper over her head as she kicked off her shoes. "Am I the only one getting undressed?" she asked as she started unbuttoning her blouse.

"I like watching," he replied, "but better still, I like helping." He undid the buttons on her blouse, and eased her petticoat straps off her shoulders, pulling it down to her waist to reveal her most unromantic liberty bodice. Then he undid those buttons and pushed the lot off her shoulders.

She should be cold, standing there in her bra.

She wasn't. "My turn."

She took off his jacket and unknotted his tie. Then, unbuttoned his shirt, she was startlingly aware of the tension is his body. In a flash, she understood. Gently she brushed the shirt off his shoulders and and saw the leather straps and webbing over his shoulders.

She looked up at him and marked the strain etched in every muscle. Did he really think this would put her off? She smiled, almost to herself. If Gryffyth Pendragon thought that, he was about to learn otherwise. She stood on tiptoe and kissed him. She brushed her lips over his. Then ran her hands over his chest and arms, stroking and caressing as she rubbed her face against his chest. She let her hand rest on the strap over his shoulder. "I may need some help with this."

"Darling, we'll both need a bit of help."

"Do you keep it on? I mean in bed?"

He shook his head. "I take it off at night, but what to do at times like this, we'll have to work out between us. I haven't met many girls since I came back."

"Damn good thing too!" She grinned at his shock at her swearing. "You're mine, Gryffyth Pendragon, and don't you ever forget it."

"Think I'm ever likely to want to?"

"I hope not!" She also hoped he could manage in spite of that contraption.

Just to help things along, she started unbuckling his belt.

"Hold on," he said. "If my trousers drop too fast, I'll trip over them."

"I'll catch you if you trip."

"No need, just let me hold your shoulder to steady myself."

Easy enough to do. Stepping out of the second leg wasn't the most graceful action in the world, but it definitely showed he was up and ready. She so wanted reach out and touch him. She hesitated, for a couple of seconds, before resting her hand over his erection. It was hard and glorious through the soft cotton.

The straps and supports and the metal leg didn't matter, but, "Yellow? It's yellow?"

He shrugged. "I said the same thing, wondered if they'd made a mistake and given me a Chinaman's leg, but no, they're all yellow. They claim it looks more natural, I think they had a job lot of yellow paint."

"I think you're wonderful."

He looked suddenly serious. "I want to make it wonderful, Mary. I want to be your lover."

She looked from him to their spread coats. "Let's go upstairs. It's got to be easier on the bed than on the floor." The room would have the chill off it by now. Hot water bottles would help but somehow they didn't sound sexy.

"You know, I think you're right. Upstairs."

The chill of the hall was downright icy but by comparison, her room seemed cozy. He grinned at the electric fire sitting in the middle of the room. "Don't tell me you left that on all day."

"'Course not, I nipped up and plugged it in while you were getting the coke in. I hoped you'd come on up."

"Here I am." He pulled her close, his mouth pressing on hers, his arms enfolding her as she molded her body into his. She thought of the power of his erection, the scent of leather, the strength in his arms and the glory of his kisses. She wanted him. Her very own Dragon.

"You could warm us up, I imagine."

He shook his head. "Too risky. Might end up burning the house down. That would be a nasty shock for Gloria to get back from her honeymoon to find her house a ruin. I think we can generate enough heat between us, without resorting to Dragonfire."

"Let's get off some of your superfluous clothes." Her skirt landed on the floor as she stepped out of it, her petticoat fell with it. Her bra went almost as quickly. Her French knickers got the reaction she'd hoped for. "Never knew schoolteachers wore stuff like that!"

"Undressed a lot of schoolteachers, have you?"

"No, but a bunch of us boys used to speculate what Mrs. Wallis wore underneath. She was younger then," he added.

"That's shocking!"

"Isn't it?" he agreed. "We were only lads then. Now I have much better taste."

She shivered, part chill, part anticipation. "Get in bed," he said, "we can get cozy under the covers."

"Do you need help," she asked, "with that contraption?"

He nodded. "Dad usually gives me a hand."

"Tell me what to do."

In the end it only took a couple of minutes. Then he was beside her, under the covers, his hands on her breasts and his mouth on hers. Like a wild thing she ran her hands over his chest and down, to stroke his erection. He let out a groan as she closed her hand over him.

"Shit!" he muttered.

She jumped back. "Sorry, Gryffyth."

"No!" He pulled her tight. "Not you, me. Thickheaded me! I've a packet of condoms snug in my trouser pocket. Damn! I got so carried away."

"Don't worry. I'll get them." She was out of bed in an instant and grabbing her dressing gown. "I'll be back." She needed them as much as he did.

He sat up. "No, Mary. You shouldn't be going down for them."

"Gryffyth. You stay there and imagine what you're going to do to me when I get back. Shan't be a jiffy."

She found them in his back pocket and smiled to herself as she palmed the little packet. So he'd planned in advance too. Good! Made her feel a little less brazen.

She took the stairs two at a time, then paused before opening her bedroom door. This was it!

Chapter Thirty-Four

Heart racing, hands clammy, Mary opened her bedroom door.

His smile almost undid her. He was sitting up in bed, the covers pulled up to his waist. Waiting. For her.

Her throat went dry. "I found them."

"Good."

Yes, it was. Almost as good as he was.

He patted the bed beside him. "Come on in. It's warmer under the covers."

She was warmer already.

She undid the sash, before slipping her dressing gown off her shoulders. A nice seduction move. She hoped. He watched as she walked toward him wearing only her borrowed French knickers. The chill air and goosebumps rather spoiled the effect but it took only seconds to slip under the covers beside him.

"Here you are." She held out the paper package.

"We'll need those later," he said, taking them from her and putting them on the bedside table. "Much later."

He pulled the covers up to their shoulders. As she slid

down beside him, his erection brushed her thigh. She reached out and stroked his hip. "You're naked."

"And you're not. That's a rather fetching garment you have on." His hand stroked over the silk that covered her belly.

He kissed her again. Hard. With an urgency that had her kissing back with a wild abandon as her hands wandered over his chest, and lower.

Dear heaven! She was turning into a sex maniac and it felt fantastic. She curled her leg over his as his hand slid up her leg and stroked the top of her thigh. She gave a little whimper and shifted to let him explore further.

His touch was magic. But then it really was, wasn't it? This is what had been lacking with her other beaux. They'd been simple humans and now she had a magnificent Other lover, whose hand was between her legs. Stupendous was too tame a word.

Her fingers stroked down his chest and belly, until she reached the tight nest of curls in his groin and her hand brushed his cock. She closed her hand around his erection, gently moving the foreskin as her thumb skimmed the smooth head.

"Easy, Mary," he gasped. "I want this to last. For both of us."

"I think it will."

"Not if you don't let go a minute, it won't. Have you any idea how much I want you?"

"Show me."

He took her up on the invitation.

He rained kisses on her face and neck, and across her breasts before taking her nipple in his mouth and suckling, as if to draw sustenance from her. She caressed his head, running her fingers through his hair, and closed her eyes to shut out the room, the night, the war, the cold. Everything except Gryffyth's touch.

As he kissed, his hands skimmed and stroked, and worked

their way over her belly and inside the elastic of her borrowed knickers.

"Let's get them off." He sounded hoarse and raspy as he tugged them down.

"Alright." She wiggled and shifted her hips to make it easier. "Be careful, don't tear them."

"Mary, my love, I want you so much it hurts, but I'm not so far gone as to rip the clothes off you."

"You could, you know. It might be exciting, but better not, since they're Alice's."

"I do wonder if she has any left to wear herself. She seems to have been lending sexy drawers all around the village."

"Well, everyone has to pitch in. There is a war on, you know." Oh, dear heaven, that was tactless! But he didn't seem to mind.

"Good point. What if they do bring in clothes rationing and women decide not to waste coupons on underthings? Could really spur on the war effort."

"If we don't all die of pneumonia first."

"I promise to keep you warm."

Just being close to him did that. She kissed him hard and deep, caressing his tongue with hers, until she gave a little sigh and realized his hand was between her legs.

The sigh became a gasp as he stroked her bush and gently opened her.

"Gryffyth." His finger came into her and the gasp became a full-scale cry.

"You're so wet," he whispered.

"Must be you! Doesn't happen when I'm at Mrs. Burrows's knitting evenings."

He let out a lovely Dragon roar of laughter. "I should hope not!" He looked into her eyes. "Keep your sexiness for me, promise?"

It wasn't hard to say, "Yes."

He kissed her again, as his hand played between her legs. She was panting now, gaspingly aware of her body's response and her growing need.

Seemed he was too. Awkwardly he moved between her legs. She held him by the waist to steady him as he stroked between her folds with his erection, nudging her nub with the tip until her body cried out for him. She needed him deep and hard and, as if he could read her mind—maybe he could; who knew what Dragons could do?—he paused a few moments to grab the tiny paper envelope with the condom, and he was inside her. Deep. As her body closed around him, she caressed him with her inner muscles.

"Gryffyth, please," she cried.

"Yes, love!" He started moving, with strong, certain thrusts, as he took her higher and higher. Mary was vaguely aware of little cries coming from her, and the burgeoning need that swelled like a vast echo deep in her core. Pleasure built, peaking again and again until she thought she would die from the pleasure of his cock. He leaned forward, capturing her mouth with his, and her mind spiraled out. She could no longer think, barely knew her name. It was no matter. Nothing mattered but Gryffyth Pendragon and what he did to her.

She felt the damp of his sweat against her skin. Or was it her sweat? Who cared? Who knew? She called his name. Screamed it, and then her body took over, wild surges of utter pleasure carried her higher and higher. She was flying with her Dragon and with a great scream of joy, she climaxed. He came too, and sagged on top of her.

She loved the weight of him, pressing her into the mattress, his cock still fluttering inside her as his erection faded.

She tightened around him. Not wanting to ever let him go. Knowing she couldn't.

They had found each other through war, loss and destruction and the magic of the ancients melded them together.

At some point, he slipped out of her, and turned for a moment to peel off the condom. There was no way he could get to the bathroom to dispose of it.

She reached into the drawer in her bedside table and handed him a handkerchief. "We can get rid of it in the morning."

"Yes," he replied, as he dropped it on the floor. "In the morning. There's two more in the packet, remember."

As if she'd forget. "I want to wake in your arms."

He gave her a gentle kiss on her cheek. "Mary, if I have my way, you're never going to wake anywhere else."

She was too sated, satisfied and joyous to even think about arguing. "I love you," she said, and snuggled into him.

It must have been ten, fifteen minutes later as they lay in the glorious intimacy of the aftermath of lovemaking that the siren wailed. They sat up, clutching each other in the dark.

"Damn!" Mary muttered. "Gryffyth, we've got to get downstairs."

"You have a shelter?"

"Yes, but it's cold and miserable this time of year. Gloria uses the cupboard under the stairs."

He sat up, swinging his leg and stump over the side of the bed. "Can you give me a hand?"

She helped him back onto his leg and pulled on her dressing gown and grabbed her slippers. "You go on down. I'll bring the bed clothes. Gloria put an old inflatable mattress in there but didn't have spare blankets."

They got down, Gryffyth retrieving both their coats from the kitchen floor. "A bit crumpled, I'm afraid," he said as he pulled his on over his nakedness. It was a pity to spoil the view but he had to be freezing.

"They'd be more crumpled if we'd slept on them."

"I wasn't thinking of sleeping on them actually."

She hadn't been either.

As it turned out, they were glad of the coats. The inflatable mattress had deflated since the last air raid. They spread her coat out and squeezed inside the cupboard, covering themselves with the blankets.

"I say, this is pretty cozy," Gryffyth said, snuggling deliberately close.

"We'll keep each other warm."

"I think you're already warm," he replied, stroking her breast. "Should we try to keep our minds off what's happening overhead?"

Right now, not much was, but who knew? She'd never forget the hideous nights in Sheffield.

"Scared?" he asked.

"Yes." She'd be lying to say anything else.

"Let me distract you," he said, sliding his hand down inside her dressing gown to stroke between her legs.

This was utterly insane: making love in the cupboard under the stairs when bombs could be dropping any minute. On the other hand, if they did get one overhead, what better way to spend their possible last moments? "I love you, Gryffyth Pendragon," she said, kissing him hard as she opened her legs to his caress.

"This is going to be tricky," he said.

"We'll manage."

They did. Rather nicely in fact.

"Damnation!!" Howell Pendragon muttered at the first wail of the warning. "Just when I finally get you all alone, Jerry comes calling."

"We should have expected it," Helen replied. "First clear

night for days, and with a new moon." Thing was they never did. Two or three undisturbed nights and you imagined it was over for the winter. "Where do we go?"

"Down in the cellar. As long as you don't mind sharing a mattress?"

"Might as well get used to it, my love. What shall we take down with us? Got a torch? And let's take the cocoa. How about some biscuits?"

"How about we scarper and get under cover? Come on, Helen, give me those mugs and you turn on the light."

They took the stairs to the cellar. He had made it snug and, she noticed, there were two mattresses against the wall. "The other one's Gryff's," Howell explained. "This one's mine."

"He won't be using it, will he?"

"Woman," he said, obviously fighting a smile that threatened to crack wide open. "You belong on my mattress. Come over here. Let's practice being married."

Since that was what she'd had in mind from the start, why argue?

They settled side by side, backs against the wall, and drew the covers over them. Odd blankets and with a strange smell. "A bit strong, aren't they? When did you last air them?"

"Never, Helen. They're old horse blankets."

He was lucky she didn't douse him with cocoa. "Horse blankets? Where did you find them?"

"The Home Guard. Sir James donated them after he closed the stable. Thought they'd come in handy in an emergency. Then the Women's Voluntary Service gave us a nice stack of pieced blankets they made from tailor's swatches. Nice wool, they were, and clean. They were going to chuck these out and I took them home. Better than nothing. It gets cold down here."

Helen shook her head. "Well, Howell, you really know how

to court a woman. Come and stay the night with me and we'll spend it on the floor of the cellar, under old horse blankets."

"But you came, didn't you? And stayed."

"You're the only man in the world I'd do it for."

"Glad to hear that," he said, and kissed her.

She smiled. Kissing was good, but she fancied a whole lot more. "I had been hoping for smooth sheets and warm covers with soft pillows."

"I'll see about that next time. Here," he said, reaching to a ledge behind him. "Want an Osborne Biscuit? I might even have a couple of Lincoln Creams in here." He put the tin on his lap and took off the lid. "Help yourself."

Cocoa and Osborne Biscuits wasn't exactly Champagne and caviar, but given the time and the circumstances, nothing to be sneezed at. "Thank you, my love. There's many worse places to be than safe here next to you."

"Think you could sleep? I'll grab Gryff's pillow if you like."

"Sleep? While I'm listening to hear if anything drops? No, let's talk."

"Suits me. What do we talk about? When we set the date?"

"Maybe if you . . ." she broke off, her senses alert. "They're coming, Howell." She grabbed his hand.

He put his arm around her shoulders and held her free hand in his. He didn't ask how she knew. She was Other. If she said the damn Luftwaffe was heading their way, he believed her.

"Bloody hell," Alice muttered, as the sound of the siren cut into the delicious, after-loving drowsiness.

"Swearing, dear wife?" Peter asked.

"Yes! No one's here to tell except you. So . . . bloody, bloody hell." She sat up and reached for the bedside lamp. "If Gran were here, we'd know if we should get out of bed or not."

"Might as well. It's safer downstairs."

"While we're at it, might as well get dressed. If there's a raid, we'll both need to go out."

They pulled on clothes and went downstairs, Alice grabbing their pillows, and Peter the eiderdown.

Once in the kitchen, Alice put the kettle on and they settled under the kitchen table. More comfortable than the earth-floored cellar, and they'd decided it was the safest place. Nothing short of a direct hit would destroy the six-inch-thick oak table top.

Once the kettle boiled, Alice made two mugs of Bovril. They sat side by side, the eiderdown wrapped around them, and waited for the sound of engines overhead.

They'd barely settled when the first wave droned overhead and faded into the distance.

"Wonder where they're headed?" Peter said.

Seemed selfish to wish they were headed anywhere but Brytewood. Wherever they were going, people would die. Alice grabbed Peter's hand. She knew he'd never quite get over the nightmare of bombing in London when he'd been a CO locked in his cell in Pentonville. "You're here now, darling. With me."

He kissed her. "I can't believe what happened. That I get sent here and meet you and you love me."

"Believe it, Peter, I do." A second and then a third wave passed overhead. Alice realized she was holding her breath and made herself breathe deeply. Seemed they might be lucky this time, but neither of them would relax, or sleep, until the all clear.

A fourth wave came and went. London was really getting it tonight, or were they headed for Croydon and the airdrome? Or the barracks in Guildford? It could be any one of a dozen, a hundred places, including the munitions plant. Anywhere was a target.

The next wave sounded smaller, but they seemed lower. Then came the barrage of explosions, loud, clear and terrifying.

Somewhere close, maybe several places, had been hit.

Alice didn't wait for the all clear. Peter was even faster.

"Where?" he asked.

"Let's head for the ARP post. They'll know what's happening."

Stopping only to put on coats and to grab their bags, they headed for the car.

Chapter Thirty-Five

The third explosion was so close it deafened Mary and sent plaster dust raining down on them as Gryffyth held her close. There was an awful sound of glass shattering, a great screaming thud that seemed to go on forever, followed by a series of bangs and thumps and the wall at their back shifted and settled back. After interminable minutes and even more plaster. Who knew so much could fall in a cupboard? There was quiet and the smell of dust and dirt.

The lull didn't last long.

There was a string of loud thumps and a couple of smaller explosions but the house didn't move any more.

"Shit," Gryffyth muttered. "Sorry, love," he added.

"Don't apologize. I echo that sentiment. Shouldn't we try to get out?"

"Let me find the ruddy torch first. See what it's like in here."

He found it. It looked bad, at least what she could see in the beam of light did. They were both covered with plaster and the eiderdown would never be the same.

"At least it wasn't a direct hit," Mary said. They were still alive. She couldn't help but worry about who wasn't. Somewhere nearby had been hit. "It was close though. I think we should try to get out. If we can."

"I agree, love. Except we seem to be safe in here. Says something for the builder. They did a nice solid job back in those days."

Before she could reply there was another great thud, like a chimney or chunk of wall falling.

They looked at each other in the gloom and burst out laughing.

"Good old quality building!" Mary said, through her giggles.

It was nothing to laugh over. The house might collapse over their heads any minute, but she'd just had the most perfect sex of her life and she was with the man she loved. There were far worse ways to die.

Except, damn it, she wanted to live, to have a life with Gryffyth and bear his children. "Still want to marry me?"

"Eh?" Alright, he was entitled to look dazed.

"You asked me to, remember?"

"Of course! You're the one kept me dangling."

"No, I didn't. Not dangling. I just wanted to think about it and I have. I've made up my mind. Yes!"

She heard his intake of breath, his sexy little gasp and then he let out a great whoop and hugged her. "You will?"

"Of course."

"Then let's get the hell out of here." He crawled over her and reached for the door knob. It turned and the door gave about an inch. "Drat," he shook his head, kissed her and said. "Something's blocking it. Won't budge."

A wave of panic engulfed her. Were they trapped here for good? Of course not. The air raid wardens would be out and searching. Assuming a bomb hadn't hit the ARP post. The thought turned her cold. Were they trapped here forever? What if the house collapsed completely, burying them alive?

"Mary," he said, "you're shaking. It's alright. I'm here."

His arms engulfed her as she leaned into him. "Sorry," she said. "I'm such a ninny." She could not let herself panic. They were safe. Well, marginally so. The house didn't seem to be collapsing anymore, and she must not let herself get all het up. Panic was useless and pointless.

"You're not a ninny. You're my love," Gryffyth said. "I'm scared witless too, but we'll get out of here. Tell me about Guernsey. We're going to go there after the war. I'll ask your father's permission to marry you."

"Nice thought, Gryffyth, but I don't want to wait that long. Also, he's dead. Died when I was ten. Drowned. He was a fisherman and the boat went down. Took my uncle and cousin too."

"Oh! My God, Mary, how awful!"

"It was, but we managed. My aunt was a teacher, and my mother ran a stall in the fishmarket. I used to help her during the holidays. I think that's what made me decide to be a teacher. Selling fish is cold, wet work."

"They were all Sprites?"

"Of course. We were female. My aunt had two younger sons. Fisherman too. They stayed, although what they're doing now, I don't know. Seems the Germans don't let them take the boats out."

"You know, love, we've got to win this war."

"Well, I struck a blow against them last night." Or was it the night before, now?

"I hope you don't make a habit of it, because I hate the thought of you being in danger."

"Gryffyth, we're in danger right now. Not much we can do about that, and if I see another Vampire, you can count on me doing the same again, if I get half a chance. I'd have known something was wrong with him, even if Alice hadn't recognized him right away. He was just not right." Very scientific, that.

"He's taken care of now."

"But Mrs. Burrows thinks there's another."

"Dad and I'll take care of him."

They went silent for a while, listening, but at least there were no more planes overhead. "Tell me," Mary said, "if we have children, the girls will be Sprites and, I suppose, the boys Dragons."

"There are female Dragons too."

Now that was a thought. "Aquatic Dragons?"

"We'll find out."

If they lived long enough. No, dammit. There was no *if* about it. They would live long enough.

"Blimey, I'm a fool!" he said. "You've had me distracted, Mary. I'm sitting here acting as if I'm a human. And drat it, I can get us out of here."

"What?"

"I'm a Dragon, darling. Let me stand up."

Not easy to do given his height, his artificial leg, and the low ceiling, but he managed. "Get back as far as you can against the wall," he said. "It seems sturdy enough. I may end up taking some of the staircase down with me. And hold the torch for me."

He pressed against the door. Just as before, it moved barely enough to notice, then he steadied himself and put his shoulder to the door. It moved a little, accompanied by the sound of splintering wood. "Let's have another go," he said, and shoved.

The door shattered, and with an awful noise fell out of its frame, and he went with it.

"Gryffyth!" she screamed. He picked himself up and reached out his hand. "Come on."

She didn't need a second bidding. She stepped forward and

grabbed him, remembered to shove the torch in her dressing gown pocket, and climbed over the ruins of the door.

They were standing in a heap of rubble. Part of the ceiling sat on top of the smashed case of Gloria's grandfather clock.

And that was just the beginning. The chill around them wasn't the night cold of an unheated house. It was the damp of the night outside. Seemed Gloria no longer had a parlor.

"We'd better get out," Gryffyth said.

She wasn't about to argue. The kitchen was relatively unscathed, apart from the blown-in windows. The tape on the glass held but the frame was in pieces.

Gryffyth rescued her coat from the dust and mess on the cupboard floor and put it over her shoulders. "That's thicker than your dressing gown." Even wearing both, she wasn't exactly warm. "I wish I could find my shoes," he added.

"What about your stick?"

"I don't need it, if you'll give me your arm."

"Of course." He could have any part of her he wanted.

"We should get out of here. Who knows if another bit won't go?"

They made their way through the kitchen by torchlight, and found the door still bolted, although the window, three feet away, was blown into the sink.

Just as they stepped outside, and Mary realized how thin her slipper soles were—and Gryffyth didn't even have slippers—the all clear sounded.

"Can you walk?" he asked.

"Yes, but it's damn cold." In the circumstances, she felt justified in swearing.

He didn't even seem to notice. "If we head for the ARP hut, they'll have blankets and something warm to drink."

A stop by the Pig sounded an even better idea but it was

well after hours. They set off, Gryffyth's hand on her arm. At least the moonlight would help them find the way.

And it also showed that the front half of the cottage was a shambles, the lane was strewn with rubble and the row of four cottages across the lane was gone.

"Bloody hell!" Gryffyth stood and stared. "They got a direct hit. We caught the fringe of it." He looked back at the house. "Damn good thing we went downstairs, look at your bedroom."

She didn't want to, but couldn't help it. Not that there was much to look at. Her bedroom just wasn't there. They'd be dead if they'd stayed upstairs.

Her legs crumpled under her and she grabbed on to him. Needing his strength, at least for a few minutes. "Let's get out of here."

"You know we're certifiably loony, driving through an air raid," Peter said.

"I bet you did it enough times as a driver."

"That was different."

Alice wasn't going to waste breath arguing. "Same war. Same Luftwaffe." Wasn't much he could say to that. "Think we should pick up Gran and the sergeant?"

"Best wait until the all clear. I can go and get them later if you want."

Made sense.

At the ARP headquarters, in the old church hall, everyone was on the alert.

"Glad to see you, Doctor, and you, sir," Mr. Black said with a nod to Peter. "Looks bad. We've sent a couple of runners out to see what got 'hit. Sounded as though a couple landed."

Alice's stomach clenched. They'd been luckier here than

many places, but she'd never forget the night the vicarage got a hit. "Any idea which direction?"

"One was out over toward the common. With a bit of luck it hit open ground. The other was closer. We'll know soon."

The other worker, a man Alice didn't know, answered the field phone. "All clear," he said, and reached for the crank. They were almost deafened by the siren but the long, single note was a welcome sound.

Minutes later one of the runners appeared on his bicycle, panting from pedaling hard. Followed closely by Gran and the sergeant, he on his bicycle, she riding sideways on the crossbar.

The runner called out, "Down on Bell Lane! Those cottages copped it. All of them."

"No!" It was out of Alice's mouth before she could stop it. A chill like frozen mercury plummeted inside her. Gloria's house was on Bell Lane. What about Mary and Gryffyth? She should have asked them up to The Gallop. Damn, the house was big enough for all of them.

"The nurse's cottage?" Peter asked.

"They got the edge of it. The row the other side of the road got a direct hit."

She heard them as if muffled through a thick fog. "Come along, dear." Gran shook Alice. "There's bound to be work to do. You get set up. Peter, you take the car and drive everyone down there. The sooner you get there, the sooner people get help. I'll put on the kettle."

Gran was right. Alice opened her bag and took out her instruments. Everyone else reached for tools and first-aid boxes and piled into the car. "Better call for an ambulance, we'll need it either way," Mr. Black called.

True. A direct hit meant few, if any, survivors.

Gran was pouring the first round of tea for the two WVS

ladies who'd just arrived, when Peter returned. "Alice! Look who I found!"

Dear God! Alice wasn't sure whether to cry or smile as Mary and Gryffyth hobbled in. "Found them on the road tottering along. They need a bit of first aid. Must get back."

"Mary, you've a cut on your head and your feet!" Gran was right, her feet were bleeding through her slippers. And so were Gryffyth's, or one of them was. He wore one shoe.

"Couldn't you find the other one?" Silly, inconsequential question, but . . .

He shook his head. "Didn't look for it. I never take this one off. It's my tin leg."

The two good women of the parish didn't miss one little nuance of that, or how they arrived together, both thoroughly disheveled.

Too damn bad.

"Were you both in Nurse Prewitt's house?" one of the good women asked. Nosy old bison.

"Yes, madam," Gryffyth replied. "We had to climb our way out after the front half caved in." He also gave her a glare she totally ignored.

"Miss LaPrioux's billet too," the other one said.

Mary took care of that. "That's right. We might as well announce it. We're getting married soon and decided we'd better start practicing so as to have it perfect by the time we have a honeymoon."

If hot tea down the nose were fatal, they'd have had another casualty that night. As it was, the news would be all over the village by breakfast.

Not that Mary or Gryffyth seemed to care. He was grinning like a Cheshire cat and Mary was glowing. Seemed Gryffyth had made her happy in a way even the Luftwaffe couldn't quell.

"Let me have a look at both of you. Then I'll have Peter take you up to The Gallop." They'd been lucky, maybe part and parcel of their Otherness? Just grazes, a few cuts and their roughed up feet. If they were the worst injuries tonight, Brytewood had been spared.

They weren't. The ambulances took five bodies and two badly injured to Dorking.

It was Brytewood's worst night of casualties so far.

And they were still digging in the rubble the next day.

Chapter Thirty-Six

It had been an annoying twenty-four hours.

It was not Weiss's nature to flee at the approach of a mortal, but Schmidt's failure to appear was a matter of concern. Schmidt was sulking, Weiss had decided at first. But when Saturday morning came and there was still no sign of him, Weiss remembered how Schmidt had gone on about a woman with power. Did they, after all, have the wrong creature? Wrong one or not, he sustained himself from their captive. Quite delightful it had been as the man struggled and fought. The experience had been mildly reminiscent of feeding off that Fairy creature they'd all fed off in Adlerroost. Satisfied, he awaited Schmidt's return.

But instead of Schmidt returning for censure, a servant had appeared. Strategic withdrawal seemed wisest. He could have fed from her, but why reveal himself this early? Time enough to terrorize the household later.

Watching from his roost on the stable-block roof, he was none too pleased to see his prey taken into the house, a building he couldn't enter until Schmidt returned and invited him in.

And there was the stumbling block: Schmidt didn't return.

Mortals came, one in a car, and a fat policeman pedaling his bicycle. Later in the day, three more arrived, and scoured the stable lofts, but as Weiss listened on the roof, all he learned was that the fool mortals were perplexed and confused. Long may they stay that way. Early afternoon, he gave up his watch of the house and set off to the village to haul Schmidt back.

The house he'd delivered the flowers to last night was empty, and the big excitement in the village was the failure of the shopkeeper to open for business that morning.

Their annoyance and confusion were interesting, even a trifle delightful, but a potential distraction. What mattered was locating Schmidt.

And he was nowhere to be found.

Convinced that the cook knew something, Weiss returned to Wharton Lacey and waited. She didn't appear but the servant who'd disturbed him that morning did. She was wearing a coat and hat, and after fetching a bicycle from the stables, set off down the drive.

He pursued. Not exactly a challenge. He avoided stopping her on the bridge. Best to have solid earth under his feet, but once she was out of the gates, he leapt over the shrubbery and landed a meter or two in front of her.

Her shock and horror were quite rewarding.

"Who the dickens are you?" she asked, braking hard, a frown on her impudent face. "Gave me the shock of my life, you did!"

That was his intention. He stepped closer, smiled and grabbed her arm.

She struggled. Hard to do and maintain her hold on the bicycle. Only made his job easier. He grabbed her chin, forced her head up until he caught her eyes with his and compelled her.

It was disappointingly easy. Simpleminded, he supposed. "Who are you?"

"Molly Durbridge. I'm the parlormaid up at the big house. Who are you?"

That impudent question would go unanswered. "What happened to the man found in the stable loft?"

"Him? Gave me a right turn, that did. They called the doctor and had the copper from down the village in to talk to him."

"Is he dying?" Had he talked too much? One never quite knew with mortals.

"He thought so. Proper carry-on he made. But he don't sound like a dying man."

"Is he leaving?"

"You're asking me? I don't think so. Not for a while at least. I hear Sir James was calling in more policemen."

Mixed news. The man dying might have simplified things but now he needed to lie low. Weiss looked in her eyes and let a frisson of fear wash over her. He was tempted to feed but wasn't that hungry. For safety's sake, he held her head in both hands and wiped her memory clean of this meeting and of him. "Off you go, Molly Durbridge, and take your time coming back. No point in hurrying." He'd no idea where she was going, but her returning late would only add to the confusion up at the house.

Time to look for Schmidt and administer a little much-needed discipline.

Unfortunately, search the village and the estate as he might, there was no trace of Schmidt. Weiss even ran back to Schmidt's old lodgings to see if he'd returned there, and enquired at the ambulance post, but no one had seen him. What the hell had happened to Schmidt?

The bombing in the village that night was a mild source of amusement and entertainment, but didn't help to solve the pressing conundrum.

"Doctor, it's Edith Aubin up at Wharton Lacey."

"Yes?" Alice stifled the yawn. It was light already, she

noticed that coming downstairs to answer the phone, but after a very long night another hour of sleep would have been nice. "Something the matter?" Had to be. Why else would they be calling—she glanced at the clock on the wall—at eight on a Sunday morning?

"Sir James asked me to call you. It's about Mr. Whorleigh."

That took care of her drowsiness. "Mr. Whorleigh? What happened?"

Miss Aubin told her.

"And he's still up there?"

"In one of the spare rooms. The doctor who came yesterday said he needed rest. The man was in such a bad state it seemed best to keep him here, but now he's insisting on going home and I must admit he does seem better."

She bet he did. No doubt recovered fast. Like Gloria repairing a broken leg by shifting and changing back. But the whole kidnapping business sounded odd in the extreme. "I'll be up there right away. You said Constable Parlett spoke to him?"

"Yes. It's really odd. Molly heard someone leave the stable block but there's no trace of them."

Unlikely to be, if what she suspected was right. "Keep him there. Tell him I'm on my way and will drive him back home if he seems well enough."

"What's going on, darling?" Peter called from the top of the stairs. "Someone gone into labor?"

"No, not that." She told him.

"A rum do if ever there was one."

Definitely. "I'm on my way as soon as I get dressed, and I'll bring him back here. Can you tell Gran and get everyone up here? We're going to find out what's going on. Seems Sam Whorleigh's policy of noninvolvement has come forcibly to an end."

"And this all happened Friday night while you lot were

staking that Vampire? Think he took Whorleigh, then cashed in his chips with you lot?"

She shook her head. "Miss Aubin mentioned someone leaving the stables early Saturday morning. I'll find out. Be a love and make me a cup of tea while I get dressed."

He didn't just fix her tea, he made a sandwich with doorsteps of bread and a great hunk of cheese. "We skipped dinner last night, remember? You'll need something. Lord alone knows when you'll get back."

"Thanks, love. I'll be back as soon as I can, and I'll bring Whorleigh with me."

Sir James Gregory himself came out to greet her. "Ah, Doctor Watson, your patient is awake. Miss Aubin will show you up, but first may I have a word with you?"

She could hardly refuse, and it would be interesting to get a human perspective on these odd events.

"What happened?" she asked, after she'd refused, as graciously as she could, the sherry he pressed on her.

"Strange business." He shook his head. "Doctor, I know I can count on your discretion but this is rather difficult."

"Of course."

"We often have important visitors here. Government people," he added. Alice nodded. The whole village knew that, it wasn't exactly a state secret. When glossy black cars drove though the village, everyone knew where they were headed. "That's why it's so delicate. Wouldn't do to have this sort of thing happen with a house full of guests."

She agreed it wouldn't but since she didn't exactly know what had happened, she asked. "You found Mr. Whorleigh in your stables?"

He nodded. "Molly, the parlormaid, found him. He was missing clothes and chained to a bed frame in an unused room. He claims two men set on him as he was locking up Friday night and threw him in a lorry and brought him up here. We did discover one of the farm lorries blocking the drive early yesterday.

"Police have questioned him, including a couple of detectives from London. For security reasons, you understand. He seems very vague about what happened but was truly upset and in a bad way when we found him."

"But he isn't now?"

"He claims he's better. This whole business doesn't make sense though."

It did to her. Not that she was about to share that, even if Sir James did entertain cabinet ministers and senior civil servants. "Perhaps after I see him, I'll have something to add. Upstairs you said."

"Miss Aubin will show you."

Whorleigh was up in one of the now unused servants' rooms. He looked up and glared as the door opened. "Bringing me clothes are you, woman?"

"No, bringing the doctor." The look he gave Alice was less than welcoming. "Anything you need, Doctor?" Miss Aubin asked.

"I don't think so. I need to examine him. Please tell Sir James I'll be down in a while." She felt a pang of guilt at sending the older woman back down those two flights of stairs, but needed to be sure she was alone. What she had to say was not for anyone else's ears.

"Called you up here, did they? No point. I'm fit as a fiddle."

"More likely fit as an Elf who's just recovered from a bad shock. Let me get your blood pressure." More out of curiosity than anything else, she tightened the cuff around his arm and slipped her stethoscope inside.

"Don't waste my time, Doctor. I'm well enough."

She paused in inflating the cuff. "Then tell me what happened. All of it."

"Why?"

"Because then I'll tell Sir James that you are well enough to leave and offer to drive you back myself." Pressure check—much lower than a human's. Interesting. She let the cuff deflate as he pondered that prospect.

"Oh, alright then. If it'll get me out of here."

"You're lucky it was me Miss Aubin called this morning. The locum would have had a few questions about your sudden recovery."

"That's why I want to get home."

He was wearing what looked like borrowed pajamas. Alice deliberately pulled the neck open. "So he didn't bite you," she said.

"Yes, he did, but not there. And what do you know?" Gracious wasn't his middle name.

"About these creatures? More than you do, Mr. Whorleigh. Where did he bite you?"

She almost felt sorry for him then. But not quite. He was clearly embarrassed. "Top of my leg."

"Your groin?"

He nodded, obviously scared she'd ask to look. "Why don't you get dressed? I'll go and talk to Sir James."

"I don't have any clothes, do I? That woman took them all."

"I'll ask about them."

Heaven give her strength. He was a disagreeable man. Alright, a disagreeable Elf. Were they all like that? She hoped she never had occasion to find out, as she closed up her bag and headed downstairs.

"How is he, Doctor?" Miss Aubin was standing at the bottom of the stairs as Alice descended.

"Much better. Seems he has an iron constitution. I suggest he leaves with me. I can drive him back home."

"I think that would be for the best. You need to talk to Sir James and he's on the phone. Had a call just after you went upstairs. Would you like a cup of tea while you wait for him?"

Why not? "Yes, please. And could you get Mr. Whorleigh's clothes up to him?"

"I'll have Molly take them. They were in a bad state. We washed what we could and brushed down his trousers. Never did find his other shoe."

"Give him what you have. He'll be in the car after all."

"He'll need a shirt. His was in shreds. I'd ask the new gardener to lend him one but the man's disappeared." Forever, as it happened, but that Alice wasn't about to share. "I'll see if we can find him one."

While she bustled off to consult with the lady of the manor over one of Sir James's castoffs, Alice enjoyed a cup of tea in the kitchen with Molly Durbridge. She'd known Molly for years. She was the eldest of a vast family, and Alice had signed the papers for Molly to be exempt from call-up because of her asthma.

"So," Alice said as she sipped her tea and accepted a couple of flapjacks. (Where did Miss Aubin get golden syrup these days?) "You found him."

Molly nodded. "That's what they say."

"What do you mean?"

"It's the oddest thing. I don't remember. Really made that policeman from London cross, but honest, I don't. He and Lady Gregory and Miss Aubin all say I did, and screamed, but I don't remember. I had the day off yesterday, on account of no weekend guests. Miss Aubin said as how I could go home and see Mum. She's a bit poorly, you know." Alice did. Mrs. Durbridge was nearing term with her fifteenth child.

"So I went off. Spent the day at home. I was late back. Not sure why, but Miss Aubin covered for me. Tore me off a strip though, she did, but then I had to see those London policemen. I'm not sure they believed me not remembering, but I don't. I believe them when they say what happened though, but it must be delayed shock."

"Did you meet anyone going home?"

She shook her head. "No. I had to have been a bit dazed. Don't remember much about leaving the house, but I remember pedaling home from the end of the drive."

Odd. Stress and shock did things to the human mind but, given what else had happened, it just felt wrong. And if Gran was right about there being two Vampires . . . "Didn't the new gardener find him?"

"Him? He's done a runner. Went off Friday night and never came back. The coppers asked about him too, but he's disappeared into thin air." No, into a pile of sludge on Gloria's kitchen floor. "That's another thing as has them all het up." The nod of her head indicated the world the other side of the kitchen door. "And Miss Aubin too. She recommended him. He was some nephew of a friend of hers or something."

Interesting. "At least you got to see your mother this weekend. Next one might be busy."

"This week will be. We've people coming on Tuesday, so Miss Aubin says. So we start cooking today, Sunday or not."

"Yes, we do, Molly," Miss Aubin said, as she came in the door. "Time to stop gossiping and get on with the ironing, and Doctor, Sir James would like a brief word with you."

It was very brief, but just as well. She was dying to get Whorleigh to The Gallop.

"So, you're taking him off our hands, Doctor?"

"He's well enough to move and everyone rests better at

home. Besides, you've more pressing things to do than provide accommodation to stray villagers."

A bit snooty, that, but he nodded in total agreement. "We do indeed, Doctor. Not that I grudged it, you understand. He was in a bad way when we found him. A bad business, this. Very bad."

"Odd too. He told me he was kidnapped and brought here."

"As I said, a bad business, but seems the perpetrator has fled. Fortunately no lasting harm done."

She was not about to disabuse him on that point. After all, his erstwhile gardener wasn't going to cause any more harm.

Miss Aubin was waiting in the hall. "Doctor, could I come down and see you tomorrow?"

"Of course. Surgery hours are five to seven."

"May I come a few minutes early? I need to be back to serve dinner. Molly does well, but I should be there."

In ordinary circumstances Alice would have refused but she sensed it wasn't her health that Miss Aubin wanted to discuss. "Come about a quarter to? I should be home then. Unless I have an emergency call."

"Thank you."

Wondering what that was about, and consigning that concern to later, Alice drove Whorleigh home, down to Brytewood.

"You can drop me at home," he said. "And thank you for getting me out of there."

"Not so easy, Mr. Whorleigh. You're coming home with me. Gran wants a word with you."

Chapter Thirty-Seven

"Thank you, Doctor, but I need to get home. You do understand, don't you?"

Attention on the road, Alice found herself agreeing with Whorleigh. He was probably worn out, and needed rest. "Of course."

"Good of you to give me a lift. Much obliged I am."

"My pleasure." Not entirely true.

"I need a nice quiet afternoon on my own to recover. Would be best." Alice nodded, her attention on the bend ahead. "If you just turn off up Clandon Lane you could drop me off and avoid going through the village."

She had her mouth open to agree, when something snapped into place in her mind. "Mr. Whorleigh, what are you trying?"

"Damnation!" he muttered, half under his breath. "Why doesn't it work on you? You're just like your grandmother!"

"I take that as a compliment, Mr. Whorleigh, and on a point of interest, what were you doing?"

"Just talking, and I *am* weary."

"I'm sure you are, Mr. Whorleigh, but not too tired to tell us all you know. If this unpleasant incident hasn't shown you we have trouble right here in Brytewood, nothing will, and you deserve to be hauled off by Vampires for good!"

Definitely poor bedside manner, but she was tired too and worried into the bargain.

"Vampires." She could almost hear him gulp with horror. "That's what your grandmother said."

"Pity you didn't listen to her. Might have spared yourself a nasty experience."

He was quiet as she passed the end of Clandon Lane, obviously given up all thoughts of skiving off home. "I should have guessed."

"Their strength?"

"That and . . . oh, sweet Jesus! That one bit me, will that mean I turn into one?"

He was starting to shake. She pulled the car to a stop and grabbed his shoulders. "Calm down, Mr. Whorleigh, and no, I don't think so."

"How do you know? All the stories say . . ."

"There are also stories about Pixies and Elves. How much of all that is true?"

"How do you know it isn't true about Vampires? How do you know I won't turn into one of those things? You don't, do you?"

He looked petrified. "I can't swear to it, but listen. The two who took you, we have every reason to believe are German spies." That definitely got his full attention. "We also have Vampires on our side. Gran met one who's working in France with the resistance. He told us a good bit about Vampires, although they vary depending on what he called the blood line, but he was certain a single bite didn't turn a person. It takes more, but . . ." An idea struck her. "Feeding off a human does set up a sort of interdependency." It had with that weasly Jeff Williams, Andrew's old plant manager. That might be useful.

"I think, Mr. Whorleigh, you are entitled to revenge." That

cheered him up no end. "Want to join with us and try to kill this thing?"

"Don't have much choice, do I, Doctor? You're as good as abducting me as it is."

"You'd really rather I left you here by the side of the road for one of them to find you again?"

The look he gave her answered that. "I'm in with you, but what do you think you and your old grandmother can do against two of them?"

"It's not just the two of us, Mr. Whorleigh, and there's only one. Now."

"What do you mean?"

"They grabbed you from the shop then stopped and argued while one made the other get out?"

"That's right, he had something to deliver up Bell Lane."

"Yes. Flowers from Sir James Gregory to Nurse Prewitt. She got married on Saturday morning. You don't have to worry about that one. I recognized him from an earlier meeting and Gloria and Mary staked him."

"Mary who?"

He was going to know anyway. "Mary LaPrioux. The new schoolteacher, evacuated from Guernsey."

"I know who she is. She registered in my shop. But she's only a little thing."

"True, but short or not, she staked him. I helped, but she and Gloria did the deed. Just like you and me and Gran, there's more to Mary than anyone would guess. So, you're in with us? Want to make sure this one gets his chips?"

"Yes, Doctor. I'm with you lot. Whatever you all are."

She started the engine and headed for home. Amazing how a man couldn't stand thinking a girl could outdo him. "I'm glad you're joining us, Mr. Whorleigh. England needs all of us right now."

He said nothing else the rest of the way. Alice drove as fast as safety prescribed. No point in giving him time to get cold feet.

Good thing she'd asked Peter to light the fire in the drawing room, Helen Burrows thought to herself. It gave young Gryffyth and Mary a nice private place for their argument. Not that it was that private, the way Gryffyth was raising his voice, but at least they were together, and as long as she kept the kitchen door closed, she couldn't always hear what they were saying.

Peter came in from feeding the chickens, and looked toward the closed door. "Are they still at it?"

"That they are," the sergeant said, taking the pipe out of his mouth. "They'll settle it soon enough."

A particularly loud, male, "Will you listen to common sense?" reverberated through the door.

"Don't tell me what to do!" wasn't as loud, but the higher pitch carried even better.

"Dammit, Mary!" made up for it.

"Are you sure someone shouldn't intervene?" Peter asked. It sounded like Dunkirk all over again in there.

"Heavens, no," Helen Burrows replied. "It's just a lover's spat. You and Alice have had your share."

"Yes," he agreed, looking at his grandmother-in-law, "but I don't grow talons or breathe fire when I get irate."

Howell Pendragon gave a little chuckle. "Not to worry, Peter. My boy won't do a thing to her. He's too much in love with her, as you are with your Alice."

"What are they arguing about?"

Helen Burrows gave a sigh. "Where she's going to live. She insists she's going to camp out at Gloria's once they get the roof covered over and the windows repaired. He wants her to move in with him and Howell."

Peter let out a whistle. "She's a schoolteacher! Do you blame her? Around here tongues wag like flags in the breeze."

"Come off it, Peter. They can hardly say much with Howell living there as chaperone, and there's no way Gloria's house will be habitable for weeks."

"They will though."

"Not if they get married," Howell added. "That's really what the lad's bowling for."

And he thought he and Alice had moved fast. "Good luck to them both."

"They need to sort it out soon," Howell went on. "Alice is on her way back by now, I'll be bound."

With Whorleigh. "Do we really need him with us? If ever there's a scofflaw, it's Sam Whorleigh. How he gets away with it I don't know." He paused. "Still, I do owe him one. If he'd acted differently, lord knows what would have happened to Alice after that baker creature attacked her."

"Whorleigh did us a favor there. Maybe we'll get some sense out of him, now he's tasted trouble," Mrs. Burrows said.

"Well, if you ask me . . ."

They were destined to never hear the end of Howell Pendragon's words. A great crash and a cry of shock from the drawing room had their complete attention.

"Oh, dear, I do hope that's not the French clock on the mantelpiece. I was meaning to pack it away in case we got hit." Mrs. Burrows shook her head, and went on with her knitting.

"That should settle things," Howell added. "Shocked a bit of sense into them, I hope."

Things had gone quiet. A few minutes later, Mary and

Gryffyth appeared. She was red in the face and he looked as if he'd been running his hands through his hair.

"Excuse me, Mrs. Burrows," Mary said. "We've a confession. I'm really sorry, but . . ."

"We knocked off a vase and broke it. The blue one. Terribly sorry," Gryffyth added.

"The Wedgwood one, I'm afraid," Mary specified. "I'm so sorry."

"Didn't throw it at Gryff's head, did you?" Pendragon asked.

"Good Lord, no!"

"I knocked the table, to be honest," Gryffyth said.

"Best clean it up then, son. Ask Helen for the dustpan and brush."

Peter knew where it was kept. He grabbed it from the broom cupboard and handed it to Gryffyth and they both went out, Mary apologizing again as Helen Burrows waved her off.

"That should settle them," Pendragon said, sounding frightfully pleased with himself.

"Pity about that vase. It was a wedding present to Alice's parents, but better break a vase than a heart. You're sure they'll sort it out?" she asked Pendragon.

"Yeah, if not, I'll have Mrs. Chivers, as billeting officer, assign her to me. Even Mary won't argue with that."

Mrs. Chivers might. "Why not just say so from the beginning?" Peter asked. "You could have saved them a big argument."

Pendragon chuckled. "They needed that. Gryffyth had to learn Mary isn't the wet dishrag sort. She might be sweet and nice-mannered, but she's made of steel underneath. Just what he needs."

When Alice got back, Peter would repeat the whole incident to her. Maybe she could make sense of it.

But seemed his grandmother-in-law and Howell had been right. Mary and Gryffyth emerged smiling, and peace reigned in the kitchen as she and Mrs. Burrows got busy checking the pie and the vegetables, and Peter, Gryffyth and Howell were set to lay the table.

"I imagine that Sam Whorleigh will be in need of a good meal when he gets here. If we feed him well, even he'll be hard pressed to be awkward."

No one argued with Mrs. Burrows's words of wisdom.

Chapter Thirty-Eight

"Come in, Mr. Whorleigh. I told Alice to be sure to bring you back with her."

Peter suppressed a smile. The man looked ready to bolt. Pendragon must think so too, he'd taken up a post by the door. Ready to head him off if he tried to run?

"I think Gran's got lunch almost ready," Alice said, giving him a gentle nudge forward.

"It is, indeed, and Sam Whorleigh, you look as if you need a good, solid meal. It's been a nasty weekend so far for you."

Hadn't exactly been a picnic for the village either, but the man did look awful. The confident, blustering shopkeeper looked more like a cowed dog. Of course, facing a roomful of Others you're not sure are one-hundred-percent friendly could have that effect. Peter had been knocked off kelter more than once by this lot.

"If you're sure it's not too much trouble, Mrs. Burrows," he said. "I told the doctor, I'd be happy to go on home."

"I'm sure you did," Pendragon said, with a laugh. "Bet you tried your Elf persuasion on her too. Did you find it didn't work?"

Whorleigh was clearly not amused.

"Get that sour lemon expression off your face," Mrs. Burrows told him. "We all know what you are. If you'd just joined with us when first asked you might well have escaped a nasty experience, but you're here now. That's what's important. We've a lot to do."

"I didn't see much of them," Whorleigh volunteered. "And what are you going to do about them anyway?"

The man—sorry, Elf—was going to have a revelation in the next couple of hours.

"That can wait until after lunch I think, Mr. Whorleigh. We were just waiting for you and Alice to arrive."

Peter stared at the laden table with amazement. Honestly, Lord Woolaton should call on Helen Burrows for advice on stretching food rations. She'd made two enormous chicken pies from the hen Peter had helped her kill and pluck on Friday. The pies were stuffed with potatoes, onions, carrots and tinned peas as well, and the aroma had been making his mouth water for the past hour. They also had dishes of cabbage, carrots, brussels sprouts and masses of mashed potatoes, no doubt from one of the farmers who seemed to pay Alice in kind rather than coin of the realm.

Once they'd delved their way through that lot, she produced rice pudding and baked apples.

"Now," Helen Burrows said, after most of them had opted to have both and were busy spooning and chewing, "we might as well get started. I know Mr. Whorleigh has questions, but first we should let him know what's going on."

"First, I'd like to know why you think my business is yours?" Whorleigh said.

Staying long enough to eat his way through second helpings of everything, made his business theirs. Not that Peter was about to say that out loud. Instead he replied, "There's been a lot of trouble here since September, Mr. Whorleigh. We've been under attack. I'm sure Alice mentioned something."

"She said the ones who took me were Vampires." Didn't sound as if he believed that one hundred percent.

"You doubt our good doctor?" Pendragon asked. Almost sounded like a challenge.

"Not after what they did to me!" Whorleigh replied. He looked at Mary. "You took a stake to that one." Peter understood the man's skepticism. Looking at Mary, small, peaches and cream skin, and hair curled around her face, it was hard to imagine her shoving a stake into a Vampire.

"Yes, with Gloria's help. He's done for."

"Good!" He smiled. Not a nice smile but no one missed the meaning. "Thank you. Anything you need, just ask. Tell the nurse the same too. I'm much obliged."

"Mr. Whorleigh," Mary replied. "I appreciate the gesture, but it's not groceries and supplies we need most from you."

"Eh?"

"You're Other, Whorleigh," Howell Pendragon said. "We need your gifts and powers to help take down this last one." His tone brooked no arguments.

"What can I do?"

"That depends on you, Whorleigh." Gryffyth did not sound pleased. The slight to Mary's Vampire-slaying skills must have rubbed him wrong. "It's very simple. We have Vampires among us. We had four, now we're down to one. The police or the army can't take care of them, so it's up to us."

"Why us in particular?" His glance took in the whole table.

"We're Other," Gryffyth replied.

"What are you?"

"He's my son," Pendragon replied.

"And you are?" The man made no attempt to be nice. Did they really need him?

"I am the Pendragon," he replied, standing. He took off his jacket and rolled up his shirt-sleeves. Peter knew what to expect. Whorleigh had no idea.

Pendragon let out a roar, pressed his hands on the table and they all watched as his fingers turned to claws, his nails to talons, and his skin became nothing short of reptilian. No matter how many times one saw it, it was downright impressive.

Whorleigh looked ready to go into shock. "You're really a Dragon?"

"The Pendragon," he replied, as he slipped his jacket back on and sat down.

After that Pixies and Water Sprites seemed a bit tame, but Whorleigh seemed willing to give his respect to Vampire-killing Pixies and Sprites. "What about you?" he asked Peter.

"Me? I'm just plain common or garden-human, I'm afraid. I'm along for the ride."

"And to help kill Vampires when needed," Alice added, with a grin in his direction.

"Alright," Whorleigh said. Pendragon's demonstration seemed to have knocked the stuffing out of him a bit. It was an improvement. "So there's Vampires lurking about. Some are dead, but not all." They were all dead to be exact, but now wasn't the time to get pedantic. "What the heck are they doing here?"

"We've all asked the very same question," Alice replied. "We don't know for certain, but because of the first one's connection with Miss Waite, who was arrested as a spy, we suspect that's what they are. And as such, up to no good. There's been more than one attack on the munitions plant, and it doesn't take much imagination to know why they're interested in Wharton Lacey."

"The weekend visitors," Howell added.

"Sorry, I'm not with you there, Dad," Gryffyth said.

"Visitors. Quite a few of them and, by the look of the cars that go up there, they're army or government people," his father replied. "It's an open secret, like the munitions plant. Everyone knows about it, but knows they shouldn't talk about it, especially after finding out about Miss Waite."

"No wonder the Germans want a spy there," Gryffyth added.

"Maybe more than just watching," Mary said. Her clear teacher's voice got attention. "Wouldn't killing a few selected government people really tilt things in their favor?"

"I wish I could tell you what they were talking about," Whorleigh said, "but once they got that chain on me, I was dazed and everything went blurry and I was as good as deaf and dumb once they had me on that bed frame." He looked at them. "Worked iron does that to us."

"But they knew that," Mary said. "I wonder how?"

"Beats me," he replied. "They knew somehow. Kept calling me a *fee*."

"It's German for Fairy," Alice said. "They thought you were a Fairy of some sort."

"I'm darn well not! Frippery creatures, Fairies. Always hanging about in trees and playing in the woods."

"But they must be some sort of kin," Peter said. "Perhaps worked iron affects them the same way."

"How would I know?"

It hardly mattered right now.

"Best get back to the point." Pendragon was right there. "We have a rogue Vampire in the neighborhood. And we know very well from past experience, he's not here to admire the beauty of the Surrey hills. We need to get ourselves organized."

"Well and good, Dad," Gryffyth said. "But what can we do? We can hardly knock on the front door of Wharton Lacey and say, "Tell your visitors to be careful, there's a Vampire around full of evil intent. They'd lock us all up!"

"But we can't sit around and do nothing."

"We can't sit around and talk about it either," Alice said. "We need to find him and take care of him. Mr. Whorleigh, did you see the Vampire clearly enough to get a good look at him?"

He shook his head. "Wish I had. They grabbed me from behind and threw something over my head, like in the talkies. I heard them, until they got the iron on me. They were talking English. The only thing I am sure of, one of them, the one who carried me out of the lorry and bit me, smelled like the thing that went for me the other morning."

"Distinctive, was it?" Helen Burrows asked.

"They were both distinctive. Like most people," he replied. "Tell you something else. Remember that baker chap who disappeared suddenly? He was Other of some sort. He went for me as well, but I got away from him."

"Mr. Oak?" Alice asked. "He was a Vampire too, but not to worry about him. Gloria ripped his throat out."

Terrible of her, really, to throw it at him like that, but his face was a sight to behold.

"You mean Nurse Gloria? Nurse Prewitt?"

"That's right," Pendragon said, with a broad grin. "She's Other too. Pity she's not here right now, we could use her."

"We're not interrupting her honeymoon," Helen Burrows said. "We need to take care of this. Seems Wharton Lacey is where they hang out. Don't you think that's where this one will come back to? May even be lurking there as we speak?"

"We need a spy of our own," Gryffyth said.

"Right there, son, and we have a candidate," Pendragon said. "You!"

"Me?"

"Why not? You give Sir Gregory a call, tell him you're looking for a job and you heard he's lost his gardener. He'll take you on like a shot. Won't say no to an old soldier. You'll be right there on the spot, and we know they can't resist Dragonfire."

"Wouldn't mind having a go at him. He got away last time. Won't now."

"Wait a minute," Mary said. "It's dangerous."

"No more dangerous than shoving stakes in them." He looked around the table. "I'm game."

"It's always taken two before," Alice said.

"You didn't have a Dragon before."

"She's got a point, son," Pendragon said. "I just don't see how we can get two of us up there without it seeming fishy."

"I can make myself close to invisible," Whorleigh said. Then looked downright shocked at himself. "I could go up there after hours. Didn't you say night was when they're strongest and most dangerous?"

"It seems so," Alice replied. "What if I gave out that you were so weak from your ordeal you need a couple of days in bed? Your assistants could man the shop. Maybe work extra hours, and you could hang around Wharton Lacey and keep an eye on things."

"Marion can hold the fort and her Vernon comes in after school some days to lend a hand. Would be worth it. I'd like to see that thing get his comeuppance."

"Sounds like a plan," Mrs. Burrows said. "Anyone want another cup of tea?"

"Mind if I use your phone, Alice?" Gryffyth asked. "Might as well call up there now."

He came back not three minutes later. "That's done. The job's mine as long as I want it. We're in business." He looked almost elated at the prospect.

Mary didn't.

Chapter Thirty-Nine

"That's interesting," Sir James said as he walked back into the dining room where two dark-suited men sat around the remains of lunch. "Word spreads fast in a village."

They looked at him. "News got around that the gardener had skipped off and I already have a replacement."

"Seems a bit sudden," Parish, the taller one, said. "You know who he is? After this trouble we need to be careful."

"I've known him since he was a boy. Gryffyth Pendragon. His father's in the Home Guard."

"What's this lad doing hanging around the village? Wasn't he called up?" Baynes, Parish's superior, asked.

"Just got back. He was a sergeant. Invalided out. Lost a leg after Norway. Said he'd thought of going up to the munitions plant but with it closing decided an outdoors job might suit him better."

"Some returning amputees come back with resentment and a chip on their shoulders," Parish said. "He could be trouble."

Sir James knew better than to be certain. Not after the business with nice Miss Waite, and the carryings on this weekend. "I doubt it. He's a good man. And while he might be sour about the war and what it's done to him, he's hardly likely to aid and abet the Jerries who took his leg. I told him he had a job. If that Paul Smith ever turns up, he's fired."

"If he does, he'll be arrested," Baynes said. "Your cook admitted he was a plant."

"Talking about your cook," Parish said, pushing back from the table. "Why don't we have her bring in some coffee and have a little chat with her?"

It was inevitable, Edith Aubin supposed but the summons still came as a shock. With a leaden pit in her stomach, she took off her apron and nodded to Molly. "Not sure how long I'll be. Clear the dining room and do the washing up. Give yourself a break and if I'm not back, take the linen keys and check there are enough sheets in the airing cupboard to make up six extra beds. If you've still time, might as well get on with dinner for tonight. Soup's already simmering but you could start the vegetables. We'll have it with jacket potatoes and cheese." The house ate simply when there was no company.

"Think you'll be that long?"

"Who's to tell, Molly, but I might be."

"They're not staying for dinner?"

"I wasn't told they were." Most likely they'd leave right after they arrested her. "Just be sure to take a break, Molly. No point in wearing yourself ragged." Especially since she'd be single-handed tonight. Edith vaguely wondered who they'd get to replace her but shrugged it off. She had far more pressing worries than that.

She smoothed her hair, brushed down her dress and, picking up the coffee tray, headed for the drawing room.

"Ah, Miss Aubin, have a seat." If Sir James intended that to throw her off kelter, he'd succeeded. She might sit with Lady Wharton when they discussed menus or household business, but she'd never in her life sat at Sir James's invitation. "And would you please pour coffee, including one for yourself."

She sat down in the straight-backed chair by the tea table and poured coffee with a shaking hand. Asking about sugar and milk as if she poured coffee every day for people about to arrest her. Cups handed around, she put her own back on the tray for fear of spilling, and waited. The two men had not been introduced.

"Miss Aubin," the taller one began. "I want to remind you that you signed the Official Secrets Act yesterday."

As if she was likely to forget! "Yes, sir. I did."

He took a sip of coffee, looking at her as he put the cup back in the saucer. "We just read the report you made about this Paul Smith." Her confession in essence. She waited. "Could you please tell us exactly how you came to recommend this unknown man for employment?"

Her face burned with guilt and shame. Now came the reckoning. She'd explained this in detail, but no doubt they were checking for inconsistencies, errors on her part. "I was approached by this man. He said he had contacts in Germany and could take care of my family who were left on the island."

"Jersey?"

She nodded. "My family have lived there for generations. Things were lean between the wars, so I came over to the mainland to find work. I used to go back for a couple of weeks each spring. I missed the past two years because of the limits on travel. I hadn't heard any news since the invasion, then this man approached me. Told me things were bad on Jersey. Whole families being rounded up and taken to Germany.

"I was shocked. Scared for them, but he said he had friends as could ensure my family weren't deported. I just had to promise to do him a favor when needed."

She paused and thought back. "I knew what had to be involved. I won't lie and say I didn't, but I was terrified. My parents are old, my sisters have children and grandchildren. I felt

I had to do something. I heard nothing more until three weeks or so ago. He was waiting for me outside the post office. It was very simple. All I had to do was introduce this young man as a nephew and find him work up here."

They said nothing when she paused, so she went on. "He was quiet and kept to himself. I watched him carefully when he was in the house. Which wasn't often. He never ate with the rest of us in the kitchen. Used to take toast and sandwiches back to his room. Odd, that was. He obviously wasn't used to laboring, but he did his job and I watched him as best I could. Until . . ."

"Until what, Miss Aubin?" the other one prompted.

"Until I decided I couldn't let it go on anymore and told Sir James."

They passed glances between themselves as if sending some sort of facial semaphore. She let out a breath she'd barely realized she was holding. What now? She'd confessed. The man had run off, there wasn't much more to say. Would they give her a chance to say good-bye to Molly? Most likely not. Well, the girl could hold the fort tonight, but she'd need help if the expected visitors came.

"So, Miss Aubin, you just changed your mind like that? Remorse and guilt brought you to admit you'd abetted a possible spy?"

She stared at the speaker. The shorter one who'd not spoken much. "No." Dear God! She'd just said she didn't feel guilt or remorse, how would they take that? She was past worrying. She was done for after all. "No, not that. It was Mary LaPrioux."

"The new schoolteacher?" Sir James broke in. "She's in on this too?"

"No! No! She doesn't know anything about it. I met her at the party for that young man who came back after losing his leg." A look passed between Sir James and one of them. She ignored it and went on. "She's from Guernsey and I invited her up for tea. She and her family set up a sort of code to send news, and according to them, there was no rounding up of islanders there. Some of the beaches were requisitioned for the Germans and use of boats was restricted, but people were safe. Then I got a letter from my sister-in-law in Devon, telling me pretty much the same.

"I have to be honest. It was anger at being duped and fury at myself for believing his lies that led me to tell what I knew."

Mother had been right all those years ago. Getting it off your chest did feel better. Now came retribution and it was going to be far worse than a swat from a wooden spoon on the back of her legs.

For a good two minutes, the only sounds in the room were the ticking of the marble clock on the mantelpiece and the coals shifting in the grate.

She swallowed to moisten her dry throat and waited. It was all over.

"Miss Aubin." The first one spoke and made her jump. "The one who approached you. Would you recognize him if you saw him again?"

"Yes, of course."

"You're absolutely certain?"

"Yes. I saw him twice, it was broad daylight both times, and we were together for several minutes. I'd know him." Maybe they already had him and wanted her to identify him.

Another silence. Longer this time.

The other one spoke this time. Did they have this rehearsed? Was it a ploy to put her off balance? If it was, it was working very well. "You have a choice, Miss Aubin. You can either work with us and help catch these two men or we can arrest you for treason."

She must have looked like an imbecile staring at him, but she couldn't help it. There was an alternative?

"Well?" he snapped.

"Of course I'll help. I've no idea where to contact him. Each time he just appeared and then slipped off."

"We feel sure he'll be back," Sir James said. "They went to a lot of trouble to make a cover for this Smith chap. They wanted him here. Most likely to keep watch on comings and goings. These gentlemen also think they are linked to the sabotage attempts at the government installation on Brytewood Heath, and possibly connected to the spy arrested in the village back in September."

It was too much to digest on top of the earlier shock, but she did her best to appear less than inane. "I see." It was a lie but he seemed to expect her to say something.

"Good." That was the taller one again. "We'll supply you with a device." What sort of device? "A recorder. Wear it at all times. When you see him, turn it on. Keep it off otherwise, as we're short of batteries. It's winter time so it's easy enough to conceal under a cardigan or jacket. Record any conversations and we'll have him. You'll also be monitored and recorded if he approaches you near the house. It may take awhile but we think we'll get him."

"Both of them," the second, who wore a striped tie, added. "White and Smith."

Nice ordinary English names that wouldn't get a second consideration.

"Or Weiss und Schmidt," Sir James said.

She'd been such a fool. Convincing herself she was acting to protect her family when she'd been abetting the very people who'd overrun her home. But she was a free woman. She signed the paper they put in front of her, glancing at it first to make sure it wasn't a confession, and handed it back.

"Welcome to the Service, Miss Aubin," the shorter one, with the blue tie, said. "You do understand what signing that paper means."

"Yes, of course."

"Now, Miss Aubin, we want you to make sure the news leaks out that important guests are expected Tuesday. Can you do that?"

"Yes, mentioning it once in the village is as good as putting up a notice in the village hall. Word spreads."

"Good, now go about your business as if nothing has changed. We'll get you set up with our little device."

That took all of five minutes. It was light enough, but felt like a rock against her skin.

"Well, Miss Aubin, help us catch this chap and we'll drop every charge."

If only it were that easy.

"What do you think, Sir James?" Baynes asked after she left. "Can we trust her?"

"Time will tell. She's our best link to them."

"Our only link," Parish said.

Baynes raised an eyebrow but said nothing. "We'll leave a man here," he said to Sir Gregory. "You have the direct phone number?"

"I do."

"Then it's all up to your Miss Aubin. Let's see what she can do."

Chapter Forty

"What do you think?" Parish asked Baynes as their car pulled down the drive and headed for a certain government installation twenty miles away, in a secluded Sussex village.

"I think we have trouble. Maybe just the beginning, but all signs point to it. It was too much to hope, I suppose, that we'd be the only ones using Vampires."

"What makes you say that?"

"First we have the tip-off from J that they might be operating in the area. Then we have a sensible, practical woman. The sort who would normally go running to the nearest police station if she were approached by a strange man claiming connections in Germany. Instead she goes along with what he wants. Even things a three-year-old would see as fishy. Sounds like mind control, if you ask me.

"Add the maid: a sensible girl who initially gave the police a very clear account that the cook, Sir James, and Lady Gregory all corroborated, but when the girl gets back from her day off, she doesn't remember a thing. Mind control again? No doubt encountered one on her way home, or coming back. We need to enquire if she told her family anything or not.

"Then the disappearing man. Jumps out of a high window,

smashes the glass, leaves blood behind and appears to have just upped and walked away. Add the horses that seem to be ailing and it's all too much to be coincidence."

"Bloody hell," Parish replied. "So, do we call in J? He's back from France."

"Yes. I wonder how soon he can get here."

"We should be glad it's only Vampires we have to deal with. What if they start sending over Werewolves?"

Next morning Alice dropped Sam Whorleigh at the bottom of the drive at Wharton Lacey, since his presence was definitely clandestine, and drove up to the kitchen door to let Gryffyth get out.

"Thanks, Alice," he said. "You're a brick."

"No trouble. You'd better explain that your arrival time may vary a bit. And my pick-up times too."

"Wildo, hopefully this won't last long. I'm not sure gardening is my forte."

"Maybe they'll be so impressed they'll want to keep you on."

"God forbid! When we get this taken care of, I've a mind to marry Mary and disappear somewhere."

"Good luck! Can you see her abandoning her class?"

No, he couldn't. "Maybe not, but I'm sure as hell not planting radishes the rest of the war."

"Wrong time of year for radishes. You plant those in the spring. Good luck."

He'd need it. This was a bat-brained idea if ever he'd had one. On the other hand, if Mary could stake a Vampire and Gloria could rip out another one's throat, he ought to be able to do as much. He'd sent him running last time. This time he'd get him.

He couldn't see Whorleigh anywhere; no doubt he was still slogging it up the drive or lurking in the shrubbery. Then a flicker of a shadow by the stable caught his eyes. A swift movement, then it was gone. Whorleigh was here and doing his invisibility thing.

The back door was opened by a young woman about Mary's age. "Hello," she said. "You the new gardener?"

"Yes, I am."

"Come on in. Hope you last longer than the last one. Odd bloke he was."

She had no idea how odd.

"Ah, Mr. Pendragon," an older woman said as he stepped into the kitchen. "I'm Edith Aubin. Sir James wants a word with you."

More than a word, no doubt. He must be wondering why he'd been so eager to take the job.

He wasn't. Not the least. But he was curious how Gryffyth knew the former gardener had left. *Because my fiancée staked him* seemed a little too honest. "I heard word, Sir James. After Alice Watson came back from taking care of Sam Whorleigh. Was mentioned in the Pig last night too." Was bound to have been.

"But you called yesterday afternoon?"

"Yes, sir, after Alice mentioned he'd gone. She knew I was looking for something. I can't sit around and do nothing and I like the idea of working out of doors."

"There'll be odd jobs too, when the weather's bad. Miss Aubin will tell you what's needed. Would you mind helping in the house if we want you to?"

"Well, no. What sort of help?"

"Serving food when we have guests, helping Miss Aubin out."

What had he let himself in for? "No, sir, but I might need a bit of help with knowing what to do. And transport might be a bit tricky. Can't ride a bicycle yet. Alice Watson gave me a lift up here."

"Don't suppose you'd care to live in?"

Good God, no! "Thank you, sir, but I think Dad's counting on me being home awhile."

"Talk to Miss Aubin. She'll tell you what's needed." He held out his hand. Not the usual greeting for a gardener surely. "Glad to have you aboard. Hope you last longer than the last one."

That wouldn't be hard.

Thirty miles away, Jude Clarendon sat in a wingback chair and looked at Baynes and Parish, the two men his controller insisted were anxious to meet him. Maybe they were, but Jude had no interest in meeting them. Just home off a mission, all he wanted was to go to earth and restore himself. Instead he was being polite.

"We need your particular skills and knowledge," the one called Parish said.

Jude nodded. They always did.

"Recently we encountered a difficulty," Baynes said.

So had he, several of them, and nearly lost two good resistance workers to boot. "So I was led to understand." He knew he wasn't helping them along, but why should he? He was tired of humans who were afraid of him. Most were, and once this damn war was over, he'd fade into obscurity.

"We've a difficulty. Not far from here. A place called Brytewood."

Jude nodded and thanked Providence for a Vampire's control. How had the men in suits learned about Brytewood and its interesting inhabitants? What had they learned? "Tell me what you want." He wasn't feigning the tiredness. He was worn to his soul.

What they told him chilled what was left of his spirit. His brave friends and the delightful Mrs. Burrows were in imminent danger of discovery from their own side and attack from yet another Vampire. The third, wasn't it? Although he had every confidence in that little cluster of Others when it came to disposing of the enemy, they might not be so nimble in escaping the notice of the British Secret Service.

"So, you see," Parish wound up, "we're not the only side using Vampires."

"Using" being the operative word. When this was all over, there would be no medals for Vampires, no knighthoods, no honours. Just as well when you thought about it.

"J?" Parish asked.

Yes, he'd been woolgathering. He needed blood and rest and it looked as though he wasn't getting either in the near future. "You want me to find this one and eliminate him?"

"In a nutshell, yes," Baynes replied.

How nutshells came into it, Jude had no idea. "I will." But on his terms. Protecting the Other identities of his friends was as important as stopping this Vampire. "But it will be tricky. I have to go alone. No helpful humans getting in the way." They didn't like that but too damn bad. "What's the nearest station?" He knew, but let them think they could teach him something.

"Box Hill," Parish said.

"I want train times. And remember, I go in on my own. I can't be trying to save anyone who gets in the way."

"This is irregular," Parish started.

"I don't have company back in France. I don't need it here." Wasn't risking having Brytewood's secrets exposed.

"But . . ." The man didn't give up.

"You want this done? I go alone. I'll find him and eliminate him." Assuming it was a him, of course. The Jerries might just as well have sent in a Vampire Mata Hari. Now that was a thought. "He'll disappear off the face of the Earth."

That was what they wanted to hear. "I want a workingman's clothes and a violin case."

"Anything else?"

"Tell me everything you have learned about him."

It wasn't much. No doubt his redoubtable Mrs. Burrows could tell him more. But the kidnapping of a villager worried him. Still, he'd soon find out all there was to know. "I want to leave within a couple of hours."

"There is one difficulty," Baynes said. "There will be a meeting of cabinet members at Wharton Lacey Tuesday. Nothing must interfere with that."

"Cancel it, until I tell you it's safe."

"We can't. There's an important personage from overseas coming in," Parish said.

There would be. "Then I'll need everything within an hour," Jude said. Nothing like making things difficult, but he'd have some excellent allies.

"We will. Anything else you need?" Baynes asked.

Jude let himself smile, anticipating their reaction. "Yes, blood. Better stop by the nearest hospital."

Funny how mortals went pale like that.

Chapter Forty-One

Hans Weiss sat in the shabby easy chair beside the empty grate in this landlady's front room and glowered. He really wanted to break windows, rip the mantelpiece off the wall and toss furniture at the mottled glass chandelier.

Mayhem and destruction would have to wait.

The puerile mortals who dubbed themselves his masters evinced little concern over the disappearance and destruction of three Vampires. Not that Weiss was mourning their passing. But he was concerned that he discover the identity of the murderer or murderers before anything else. The masters in Adlerroost might think the assassination of Churchill was of prime importance. Weiss put his continued existence far above that of any mortal. No matter how esteemed, loathed, or feared he might be.

The prime minister of Great Britain was only mortal. Hans Weiss was Vampire. Someone, something, had been killing his brethren and he was on a mission to find out who.

When he did, he would enjoy himself.

Slowly.

He was doing now what he should have done right after Eiche's disappearance. Sifting very diligently through the clues and evidence, just like those English detective stories. If a fussy old woman like Miss Marple or a foppish Belgian refugee could do it, Hans Weiss had no doubt he could. It was just a matter of directing one's thoughts. And all thoughts led in one direction: the village of Brytewood.

Eiche had disappeared there shortly after the arrest of his contact. The word from Adlerroost was that the Fairy reported him dead. Most probably the truth. That nasty creature had been in and out of his head, and the others' too. She'd have known if there was suddenly no head to pry into.

Then Bloch. It had taken weeks to set up his cover, and what happened? He disappeared off the face of this accursed English soil. And now Schmidt. He'd been fine and active as long as he stayed at the estate. Venture into the village and he was gone.

Coincidence was beyond the bounds of reason.

He could eliminate the grocer, their first suspect. He'd been bound and helpless and under Weiss's scrutiny all night. There was another malevolent entity there. Lurking.

This danger had to be eliminated before the German forces arrived if the Vampires were to have complete security. He thought about reexamining the grocer, but he'd had nothing to tell, no matter what Weiss did to him. He was Other, yes, but a weak and puny Other. Weiss's prey was a strong and powerful magic user.

One might have perished by chance misfortune. Not three. It was tantamount to a declaration of war. This creature had to be annihilated.

He might as well start where he last saw Schmidt. Pity he hadn't kept the map to the cottage, but how many cottages could there be up a narrow country lane?

* * *

Fewer than on Friday.

It was midafternoon when he strolled up Bell Lane. A row of cottages on the righthand side was all but demolished. One cottage was half standing, the rest was a vast pile of rubble. Even the cottage across the road was boarded up in front with sheets of corrugated iron over a gap in the roof.

Damage was always good to see, but in this instance it was somewhat inconvenient. Annoying, really. He'd planned on knocking on doors to ask where Schmidt might have delivered the damned flowers, only to discover there were no doors to knock on. But there were Inselaffen. A half dozen of them. All busy as ants scurrying around a destroyed anthill.

"Good afternoon," Weiss said to the closest one, a tall, broad-shouldered man.

The man paused in shifting rubble and turned to fix Weiss with a confident eye. "Good to see you. Come to help?"

Not in the slightest. "I was looking for a friend. An acquaintance."

"Oh?" Weiss did not like the man's attitude. But he'd learn deference and servility in time. "Yes, he came to visit someone near here. On Friday."

"Then he's most likely a goner, mate, if he were up here," another man interrupted rudely. "The only ones we got out alive were Mr. and Mrs. Grant from the end cottage, and they're both in a bad way in hospital. Doubt we'll find anyone else alive."

Why bother digging then?

"He's right, I'm afraid," the first man said. "It was a bad raid. Two direct hits, one after the other. What are the odds of that?"

Weiss did not know and had little interest in the mathematics involved. Besides, he didn't think Schmidt would have accepted an invitation to stay the weekend. Not with a fat juicy grocer waiting in the stables. Had everyone perished, except the two taken to hospital? If so, had the killer expired too? There was always the chance Schmidt had been attacked by the fire monster and gone to earth, but he'd have healed by now.

"Want to lend a hand?" the first one asked.

Why not? It was beneath him, but peasants gossiped and he was curious to learn more about the house across the street that was still half standing. Why hadn't he looked at that damn map better, and learned if Schmidt's destination was on the right-or-left hand side of the street?

"How about it?" the impudent man went on, holding out a pickax.

"Ta. I will, can't stay long but might as well do my bit."

Howell was ready to jump up and down, wave his hands in the air and shout a few old Welsh battle cries. He didn't. Instead he kept his eye on the newcomer, while maintaining a safe distance.

Wasn't every day you had the Vampire you were looking for right under your nose. Had to be him. It could be a nice neutral or friendly Vampire: the pleasant and helpful Mr. Clarendon came to mind, but Howell did not think so. The creature was asking about cottages up here and a *friend* who'd come this way on Friday night. Too darn much of a coincidence.

This was the one they were looking for. But he couldn't stake it in front of half a dozen people.

Damn!

Jude Clarendon walked up from the station, his stake-filled violin case in hand. He had to ask the way to The Gallop but as he climbed the hill leading out of the village, he recognized the road and the house standing back from the street.

There was little question in his mind that the doughty Others of Brytewood could dispose of this last Vampire, or was it two? His personal mission was to make sure the eager beavers in the Security Service remained in ignorance about the cluster of Others in Brytewood.

If they chose to join the Service, well and good, but he didn't want them coerced into working for the government.

They were needed here.

As he walked between the brick pillars and up the gravel drive, he looked around for change. Not much. There was the sound of chickens somewhere. Mrs. Burrows must have taken up poultry keeping. Lines of laundry flapped in the breeze and the empty drive showed the doctor wasn't home.

Good. He wanted a quiet talk with Mrs. Burrows.

He went up to the wide front door with its stained-glass panels on either side, and rapped on the door. Before it opened, there was the sound of bicycle tires on gravel and a young female voice said, "Hello."

He turned, smiled, and inwardly cursed. A pretty young woman, with a touch of Otherness, he suspected, smiled back.

"Good afternoon," he said. Why had she chosen this moment to pedal up that hill?

"Here to see Mrs. Burrows, are you?" She dismounted and wheeled her bicycle. "Better come around to the back door. She usually has the wireless on when she's working and doesn't always hear the door."

Of course. His friend was Pixie. He walked with her round to the door, tempted to give her a compulsion to leave—but maybe she was expected. And he'd come to dispose of Vampires who hindered mortals, not become one of them.

She opened the door as if she knew her way. "Mrs. Burrows," she called. "There's a visitor for you." The aroma of baking wafted though the open door.

"Oh, Mary, lovely to see you, and who is it? Oh!" She broke off as she saw him. "Mr. Clarendon! You are an answer to prayer." He'd never been welcomed quite that way before. "Come in. Come in," she insisted, stepping forward and brushing her hands on her apron, before clutching his in her slightly floury one. "It's a joy to see you. I thought you were in France."

Indiscreet of her. Surprising. "I am here."

She sensed his caution. "Don't worry about talking in front of Mary. She knows what's going on. Mary, this is a good friend and ally. Mr. Jude Clarendon. He's on our side."

Mary gave him a sharp look but took his hand. "I'm Mary LaPrioux. I teach at the village school."

"Now, now, no false modesty, my dear. She does a lot more than that. Mary, I just made a fresh pot. Be a love and pour me a cup, please. Mr. Clarendon, have a seat. You don't know how glad I am to see you."

"I'm beginning to understand, my dear Mrs. Burrows." As he took off his coat and Mary crossed to the other side of the kitchen, he asked in a low voice, "Is she privy to all?"

"Oh! Yes! She killed one of them on Friday evening. She knows."

He should have guessed. The women around here, at least the ones who were Other, made a habit of it. They made fierce enemies. Rather reminded them of his dear Sylvia, who'd been as steadfast as any man on the King's side during the Civil War. "I see." It was almost the truth.

Mary brought three cups over to the table. "Do you take sugar?" she asked.

"Oh, Mary, my love, I should have told you. Mr. Clarendon doesn't drink tea. Doesn't drink anything. He's Vampire."

The poor girl almost dropped the other cup. Half of it slopped into the saucer. She went pale and stared. He half expected her to reach for a stake from the stack by the back door.

She stared at Mrs. Burrows, who stood up and took the spilled cup. "Never mind, my love. I should have told you first thing. Mr. Clarendon is on our side. He helped us a lot at first. You sit down. I'll get you a fresh cup, and then we can talk."

A stiff drink might do her more good, but she sat down, giving him a distinctly wary look. "What does Mrs. Burrows mean by *on our side*?"

He'd take Mrs. Burrows's word that she was to be trusted. "I go back and forth to France, doing to the Germans what your Vampires are trying to do to you." Baynes and Parish and his respected controller would have kittens if they heard that.

She gave a cautious smile. "I hope you're a lot more successful than this lot have been."

"I don't have the opposition they have."

"Here you are, my love." Mrs. Burrows put a fresh cup in front of Mary. "Best tell him about yourself too."

She took a sip. Then a deep breath and exhaled slowly. He couldn't remember being able to do that. Had it helped him gather courage and marshal his thoughts back in his mortal days? Hell if he could remember that either.

She smiled. "I'm Mary LaPrioux. I teach at the village school. I was evacuated with some children from Guernsey. I'm a Water Sprite."

That took him back a bit. "A Sprite, eh? You're the first I've met in years. Centuries even. There used to be a colony here in Surrey, down near Frensham."

"You said *used to be*?"

He nodded. "Cromwell's lot burned them at the stake as witches."

"It happened at home too. I heard stories from my grandmother and great aunts. Makes me glad I was born when I was, even if I am in the middle of a war."

"They're doing nasty things to Others over there. Terrible stories are drifting out." He stopped himself. He hadn't come here to pass on bad news. "So, you've had yet another infestation in Brytewood?"

"We have," Mrs. Burrows said. "Two, from what we can make out. One is done for, thanks to Mary." She smiled at the younger woman. "The other one we're having a bit of trouble with."

"I congratulate you," Clarendon said to Mary. "Not many could do what you did."

She really had a lovely smile. "I had help." She paused, glancing at Mrs. Burrows, who nodded encouragingly.

"He knows about Gloria, my love."

"Gloria helped me. We sort of got him front and back, after Alice repelled him and sent him staggering."

"These Germans picked the wrong village. So, one more?"

"We think so." Mrs. Burrows's tea went cold as she told him what had happened the past couple of weeks.

He was beginning to think life was quieter in Occupied France.

Chapter Forty-Two

Gryffyth Pendragon was thrilled to sit down after a morning spent mucking out the stables and picking brussels sprouts. Even if it meant polishing silver.

"Here we are," Molly said, as she handed him a saucer of pink plate powder mixed with water, and a cotton rag. "I've got to get this lot done for tomorrow. Here, let me show you what to do."

Looked easy enough: rub on the pink stuff, then polish it off until there was nothing left and the fork shone. He picked up a soup spoon and started rubbing.

"Thanks ever so, for pitching in," Molly said. "I've got to get this done for the guests tomorrow, and get dinner started, as Miss Aubin is out this afternoon so I'm on my own."

"No trouble, honest. Makes a nice break and it's nice to be able to sit down."

She gave him an odd sideways glance. "Does it bother you? The leg I mean. Don't want to sound rude."

"You're not. And no, doesn't bother me. Not most of the time." He wouldn't tell her about waking up with a cramp in his nonexistent foot, or toes that weren't there, itching. "Doubt I'll be able to get a job as a ballet dancer or a professional footballer, but most things I can manage. Took a while to get used to it though."

"My brother got hurt." She paused to rub at the handle of a teaspoon. "Wasn't in action though, like you. It was down in Suffolk; he fell off the back of a lorry and broke his leg." She shook her head. "Honest, makes you wonder, doesn't it?"

"You can have bad luck wherever you are."

"Our dad said, if he'd done that in the last war, they'd have shot him."

"I'm not so sure about that."

"Maybe. They'd nicked the lorry to go down into town for a beer and it happened coming back. The rest of his pals lost all their leave forever. He ended up in hospital."

"Is he alright now?"

"Yeah, only now he's going overseas any day. I think Mum wishes he'd break something else."

What could he say? Platitudes about coming back in one piece seemed worse than facile, coming from him. "Write to him," he said, "as often as you can, and send him little things. They might not always arrive but when they do, it's like Christmas."

"Really?" She looked at him. "I will then. Or I'll try. Never was much at writing letters. Not much goes on here."

"I don't know. Disappearing gardeners. Kidnapped people found naked in the stables. Sounds to me there's more going on here than in London." She looked a bit blank. Was he probing too hard? "They say you found him." He hoped she didn't ask who they were.

"That's what's so queer." She gave him a repeat account of what she'd told Alice yesterday. He learned nothing new. Wasn't sure why he expected to. He added another fork to the polished pile. "Hey, you're good at this."

"Thanks. Maybe I'll ask Sir Gregory for a job polishing silver."

"We used to have a butler, Mr. Whorpleston, but he retired just before the war and they never replaced him. Fancy being a butler?"

"Don't think I could be snooty enough. Besides, not sure where I'll end up once this is over. Time will tell." He was saved from what time might tell, by the phone ringing in the hall.

"Drat," Molly said, putting down her rag and forks. "Better get it. Probably Mrs. Worthington-James from over in Dorking wanting Lady Gregory to play bridge." She made a face and went out, to come back right away. "Message for you, from Doctor Watson. Said she'd be up in half an hour or so if that was alright."

"You told her it was?"

She grinned. "Why not? Miss Aubin's gone. Who's to know if you're here or not?"

"Half an hour? Let's see if we can get this done between us."

"Want another cup before you go? I'm dry as a bone."

He might as well. All he'd gained so far was a sore back and aching shoulders. This undercover gardener lark was a dead end.

"Thanks for your help," the villager said, as Weiss put down his pickax.

"Glad I could. Must be on my way though. Promised I'd meet a friend."

Howell Pendragon kept up shoveling rubble into the back of the open lorry. He might appear busy but his ears caught every word. It was him. He'd take an oath to it. Had to be. He was Other and yes, might be a stray Pixie or Elf but really, what were the chances?

What now? As the creature (who'd never given his name

within Howell's hearing) walked down the end of the lane and turned away from the village center, Howell made up his mind.

"Damn!" he said, looking at his watch. "Didn't realize it was so late. I've got to go, lads. Need to get along to Whorleigh's before he sells out. Gryff'll be wanting dinner."

"Time you got yourself married and had a wife in the kitchen," someone called good-naturedly.

"He's already snatched a good cook for himself," another voice said.

"But until then, lads," Howell responded, "yours truly has to shop and peel the potatoes."

And tail suspected Vampires.

He should, perhaps, call and alert Helen and the rest of them. Trouble was, he had no idea where the thing was going. Up to Wharton Lacey made sense, but was he? Anyroad, no point in calling The Gallop. Alice would be out on her rounds, and he wasn't having Helen racing down on her bicycle to join the fray.

Weiss scowled. This was not how things were supposed to be. Any witnesses he might have coerced into divulging information appeared to have perished in the raid Saturday night.

Time to have a word with the cook, and maybe that servant, Molly, needed a little more interrogation. If she had any brain left, that is. He had wiped rather deeply.

Keeping to the road, he began to run at vamp speed, racing past a female on a bicycle at a speed too fast to be seen by mortals. Until he realized who was riding.

A gust of wind made Edith Aubin wobble. Odd, that. She steadied her bicycle and continued, until a hand on her handlebars made her stop short and almost pitch over them.

"What do you think . . ." she began, then recognized the man blocking her way. "You!"

"At your service, Miss Aubin. Are you totally at mine?"

What had they instructed her to do? She slipped her hand into her coat pocket. An unpicked seam gave her access to her skirt pocket. Took a little fumbling to find and activate the switch with gloved fingers.

It was done. Did he suspect? Seemed not.

"I asked you a question, woman!"

"Yes, you did." She took a deep breath and reminded herself she now worked for the Secret Service. "And I have one of you. Where's Mr. Smith? And what was he thinking about, abducting Mr. Whorleigh?"

"What business is it of yours, woman?"

"Plenty, since the place has been humming with policemen ever since."

That caught his interest. "How many?"

"Three or four on Saturday."

"And what did you tell them?"

Time for a little judicious falsehood. "What could I tell them? They kept asking me where I thought Smith had gone. Wanted to know where his parents lived. That lie about him being a nephew has caused me no end of bother."

"You're right." What a nasty smile the man had. "And there is no end to the bother. You tell them . . ."

"I'm finished with telling lies that will get me into trouble."

"Do you no longer care for your ailing mother and elderly father? They won't last long in a camp."

"How do I know you're telling me the truth? That you can really protect them? You told me that Paul Smith would be no trouble. He was just to work quietly until the new year. Working quietly doesn't include abducting respectable people and keeping them tied to a bed! Downright nasty, that was. The police won't be giving up. I don't care if they find him. I'm not taking the blame." Maybe she'd overdone it a bit. His eyes seemed to flare at hers, but she wanted to goad him into saying something. "Do you know where Smith is?"

"How many police in the house right now?"

"One. Where's Smith? They keep asking me."

"Tell them he's in hell."

"He's dead?" Maybe she would get the truth.

"Yes," he replied, grabbing her by the front of her coat. "He's dead. Has been for centuries and now, Miss Aubin, it is time to make yourself useful."

She screamed as he lifted her off her bicycle and tossed her on the ground. The fall knocked her out for a few seconds. As she blinked her eyes open, he was astride her, his face leering, as a wave of horror all but choked her.

He was going to rape her, right here in the middle of the lane. She clawed his clothes, poked at his eyes and tried to bump him off by jerking her hips, but she might as well be trying to lift a ton of bricks.

He didn't even move. Just looked down at her and smiled at her futile efforts.

"Do you know how much better you will taste, after fighting me? Terror always makes the blood sweeter."

His words made no sense, but his meaning was clear. She might not be able to physically fight him, but she could scream and let out the loudest she could, before his hand clamped on her mouth and muffled her.

At least this was being recorded. If he killed her, the record was there.

She bit his hand. He lifted it, just enough to hit her across the face and send her head crashing back on the ground.

"Scream like that again, and I'll break your neck. After I've finished with you."

He would anyway, no doubt. He'd be a fool to leave her here to identify him.

Then he leaned close, his breath rank and fetid. For one hideous moment, she thought he'd kiss her, but instead he put an arm under her shoulders and lifted her. "Not a sound," he said, as his other hand opened the top of her coat and ripped the collar of her blouse.

She couldn't help the cry as his teeth tore into her neck. Then her mind blacked out in a great wave of horror, pain and fear. She was past struggling, past fighting. She wanted oblivion and an end to the hideous pain that tore through her veins.

Seemed time stopped and all she knew was agony, but the screams wouldn't come, just stayed jammed in her throat as she lay limp and unable to move. When he finished, he let her drop. As the back of her head hit the road again, she gasped.

"I told you to be quiet!" he said through bloody lips, as he stood and placed a foot on her stomach. "You mortals never learn but you'll never forget me." He stepped back but grabbed her ankle before she could even try to move. Taking her foot in one hand and holding her leg above the knee with the other, he twisted her ankle. She screamed as the bones cracked and he let her broken leg fall. "That'll stop you riding off and giving warning."

Leaping over her and the fallen cycle, he ran.

In the direction of Wharton Lacey.

Chapter Forty-Three

Alice swerved to avoid the bicycle lying in the lane, then stopped, intending to move it out of the way. It could cause a nasty accident after dark. Then she saw the woman, a few yards off, dragging herself along the road.

The bicycle could wait.

She drove a little further, then stopped. As she got out of the car, the woman looked back. "Help me," she said, her face covered in blood.

Alice grabbed her bag and ran toward her and recognized her. "Miss Aubin, what happened?"

"He got me!"

Alice knelt beside her and realized the bleeding was from her neck. "How did he get you?" Miss Aubin shuddered and let out a weak mewl, like a hurt kitten. "Did he knock you off your bicycle?"

She nodded. "My leg. He broke it."

Took Alice about three seconds to agree with that diagnosis. The foot hung sideways at an odd angle and she could see the end of the tibia as a bump under the skin. At least it wasn't pierced, or it would be agony. She opened her bag and wiped Miss Aubin's face and neck with a gauze saturated with peroxide. As she cleaned it, the blood oozed a little, and Alice saw the marks.

"Did he bite you?"

"Yes." A weak hand clutched Alice's wrist. "Oh, Doctor, it hurts so."

She was sure it did. But remembering the ripped throat in poor old Farmer Wilson's bloodless body, Miss Aubin had been lucky. Not that Alice was going to share that. Explaining this to the hospital was going to be tricky enough.

She'd worry about that once she got her to hospital.

"Look, I'm going to have to get you an ambulance, but rather than leave you here, I'm going to try to get you down to the village and call." Seemed the best choice. None of the cottages between here and the village had phones, and Wharton Lacey was further than the village. She gave her a shot of morphine. "I'm going to bring the car as close as I can."

It wasn't easy but with Alice's hands under her arms, Miss Aubin pushed on her good leg and stood. Leaning on Alice, she hopped to the car. Every step was paining her and she all but collapsed in the back of the shooting brake. Moving her into a sitting position had her grimacing and moaning.

"Doctor." Miss Aubin clutched at Alice's sleeve. "I think he's going up to the house."

"Who is?" she asked, guessing the answer but wondering how Miss Aubin knew him.

"I don't know his name, but he was the one had me say Paul Smith was my nephew. He started all this and they want me to help catch him."

The first bit didn't surprise Alice, although Miss Aubin's involvement did. But the latter worried her. "Who wants you to help catch him?"

"I mustn't tell."

"People on our side? People against the Germans?"

She nodded. "I have a recorder. They told me to tape him if I saw him again."

And no doubt she was taping this conversation too, drat. No point in worrying. "I'll drive as carefully and as smoothly as I can. It's not going to be comfortable I'm afraid, but the morphine should help until you get to hospital."

Alice was torn over going up to Wharton Lacey and warning them that a Vampire was headed their way. Gryffyth was there, and he'd repelled it before. Might need a bit of explaining later but they'd cope with that as needed.

"Another call for you," Molly said, returning from the phone a second time. "Says he has to talk to you. It's your dad. Better tell him we're not supposed to use the phone except in an emergency."

If Dad was calling it was an emergency, but that, he'd keep to himself.

"Dad?" Gryffyth said.

"I'm calling from the ARP post, so must be brief."

For that Gryffyth understood. Cryptic and cautious. "Fine, Dad. What's up?"

"I might have sighted what we're looking for."

"I see."

"Could be coming your way any time now."

"Thanks, Dad. I'll see what I can do."

Cripes, what now? He had stakes in the lining of his coat, Alice and Mrs. Burrows had seen to that. Mary might have staked that other one in Gloria's kitchen but he couldn't see doing it in Miss Aubin's. Even if she wasn't there this afternoon. Besides, he put his faith in Dragonfire. Couldn't do that in the kitchen though, or he'd burn the place down.

Best get on the road and keep his eyes open. Was Whorleigh still out there, and had he seen anything?

Darn, he'd all but forgotten about the grocer. He should have checked on him.

Damn.

"Bad news?" Molly asked, as he went back into the kitchen.

"Not really. Tell you what, I think I'll go out and have a quick smoke, then head on home. See you tomorrow."

"Cheerio, and thanks for the help with the silver."

He loosed the two stakes hidden in his sleeves—insurance, he told himself—and went outside, coat unbuttoned.

He walked behind the stables where he'd last seen Whorleigh and waited and whistled.

Whorleigh stepped out from behind a wheelbarrow that was far too small to hide him.

"Brought me something to eat? I'm famished."

Gryffyth didn't doubt it. "No, sorry, but I have news. Dad called. He spotted our chum in the village, headed in this direction."

Poor old Whorleigh paled, swallowed, and said, "I've got that stake they gave me."

"There may be an easier way but we need to be away from the house." Wouldn't do for mundane humans to see disintegrating Vampire on the drive.

From his perch on the roof, Weiss smiled. Handy little spot this, and the old bitch had told the truth. One single, solitary policeman, or whatever he was, talking to the current lord of the (soon to be Weiss's) manor. They were so engrossed in their nonsense, they hadn't noticed Weiss peering in the window from overhead.

What now? Should he force that younger servant to admit

him to the house? No. This was not the time to show his hand. Better wait until the visitors arrived, and anticipate a little timely carnage. Alone, he'd abandoned thoughts of suborning and controlling anyone, but a nice bit of bloodshed wouldn't come amiss. Even if they were just petty civil servants.

Pity he hadn't coerced names from that cook when he had her under him.

He shouldn't have lost his temper, but he'd been hungry and she was so annoying. She deserved it. And with Schmidt gone, what use was she?

Better concentrate on the other servant. Her fear had been quite appetizing.

Pondering that prospect as he surveyed the parkland, he saw a sight he could scarcely credit. Standing behind the stables was the Fairy grocer. Brazen as can be. What was he doing up here again?

And he had company too.

Making a move too near the house would be a mistake. He wasn't quite ready to draw attention to himself. He could be patient. Sooner or later they'd move. Walk off home and he'd take them undisturbed on these quiet country roads.

He chuckled. As far as injuries and attacks went, they were busy country roads.

"What the blazes are we doing?" Whorleigh asked, in a tight voice.

"Looking for a Vampire."

Were all Elves this skittish? Whorleigh's anxiety came off him in waves. "I don't know why I ever agreed to come up here. I've been attacked. I should be in bed recovering."

Gryffyth ignored that. Yes, he'd had a awful experience but

really, he was a proper wet dishrag of an Other. "Thanks for staying. Did you see anything?"

"Not a blessed thing, but I might have caught a cold. It's no time of year to be outdoors."

He wouldn't argue with that. The afternoon was dank and cold and light was failing. A big contrast to the warmth of the kitchen. "I want to get a good look around." He doubted that policeman in the house was armed to defend the premises against Vampires. "Then let's take a stroll toward home. Dad said he suspected it was coming up this way."

Alice met Sergeant Pendragon just outside the village. He was red in the face from pedaling uphill fast. "Want a lift?"

"I need to get up to Wharton Lacey. I called and warned Gryff, I think the bugger's headed up there. Sorry, Alice, that slipped out."

"Don't apologize. I assume you mean the Vampire?"

He nodded. "Had to be him. Sensed he was Other right away. Came nosing down Bell Lane like a ghoul. Asking who lived there and who'd had flowers delivered Friday. Now I ask you?"

"It was him and he came this way and you're right that he's headed for Wharton Lacey."

"Well, then let's turn around and go after him."

"Can't." She explained about Miss Aubin's attack. "Got to get her at least to the ARP post. They can get an ambulance."

"Right you are, Alice. I'll go on. Can you take my bicycle and clothes up to The Gallop?"

"What?"

"I'm shifting. Don't usually do it in daylight but it's the fastest way and I'll be ready to attack."

Good thing Miss Aubin was halfway to unconscious. The

sergeant moved her to the back seat, something Alice hadn't had the strength to do on her own, and put his cycle in the back.

His clothes he put in a pile on the passenger seat and closed the door. She knew it was rude to look, but she was a doctor and he wasn't the first naked man she'd seen. Not that she saw much: a pale streak across the field, then a flash of light and a shape like a giant bird streaking across the sky.

She hoped no one took a pot shot at him.

Weiss watched the two figures walk down the driveway. He considered letting them go their bucolic way, but decided the grocer merited attention. If he wasn't the murderer, which now seemed apparent, he was Other and, as such, a menace. And as for that cripple walking awkwardly beside him, he'd be easily dealt with. Weiss's attention was so fixed on the ground below, he never gave a glimpse to the sky.

He climbed down from the roof, ran across the sweep of lawn and leapt the wall that bordered the lane. And waited. Hearing the grocer squeal would be a nice beginning.

As they turned into the lane, he leapt and landed fifteen feet or so in front of them.

This was it.

Gryffyth Pendragon stared into the eyes of the Vampire and saw malevolence, hate and loathing. Whorleigh screamed and turned to run. Before Gryffyth could react, the creature had Whorleigh by the scruff of the neck. "Thought you'd escaped me, did you?" His laugh was icy cold and sent a shiver down Gryffyth's spine.

Whorleigh appeared to have fainted.

"Let him go!" Gryffyth shouted, not having much hope that he would.

"Very well," the Vampire said, letting Whorleigh drop. The fall appeared to have revived him so Gryffyth let the Elf take care of himself and hoped he had sense to move or do his invisibility thing.

Gryffyth stepped back as the Vampire smiled, revealing fangs and bad breath.

The smile faded to a scream as the sheet of flame hit him in the chest. Last time had been a warning gust, now he'd put all his Dragonpower behind it. The Vampire reared back as Gryffyth sent another wall of fire that engulfed him from head to toe. He stumbled, and screamed as he ran in circles. Not the thing to do when your clothes are on fire, but apparently his parents had never taught him about fire safety.

Just as Gryffyth was wondering how to end what he'd started, a dark shape swooped out of the sky. "Dad!" It could only be, and he was in full Dragon shape. With a toss of his great head and a little spark of fire in greeting, his father came low, seized the flaming Vampire in his jaws and flew off, a burning speck in the late afternoon sky.

Gryffyth vaguely wondered where he was taking the thing, but Whorleigh needed help right now. Dad would see to what was left of the Vampire.

Whorleigh looked pathetic, shaking by the hedge. "What happened?" he asked. "Where is it?"

"Gone for good."

Now they had a long walk home.

Alice met them half a mile down the road. "Hop in," she said.

He noticed clothes that looked very much like his father's on the front seat.

Alice met his eyes with a smile. "He said he'd meet us at The Gallop. Everything taken care of?"

"Yes. Better drop Mr. Whorleigh off at his own home. I think he needs a nap."

Chapter Forty-Four

"Gryffyth!" Mary enveloped him in a hug, as he walked into The Gallop. He'd have been even happier to greet her alone, and with fewer clothes on. Attacking Vampires did things to a Dragon, but they had an audience, and one of them a man (or maybe Other) he'd never seen.

"Is Dad back yet?"

"Yes," a voice said from behind the door. "Got my clothes, son? I'm not sitting around in Helen's dressing gown all afternoon."

"I have them here," Alice said, then caught sight of the stranger. "And hello, Mr. Clarendon. You're here because of . . ."

"Yes," the man, or whatever he was, replied, interrupting. "Best get the good Dragon his clothes first. Then we can talk."

"Bring 'em here, son," Howell said, reaching a pink fleece-covered arm around the door.

Mrs. Burrows introduced the mysterious Mr. Clarendon, and Dad was back, in his own, rather rumpled clothes.

"So. What happened?" Alice asked. "Gryffyth told me his end of it."

"Not much more to tell. I picked him up after Gryff started

a good job of incineration. Flew around a bit as he burned out, then dropped what was left in the woods up on the heath. Just a mouthful of ashes by then. He won't trouble us anymore."

"Are you alright?" Mary asked Gryffyth, her arms still around him.

He kissed her. Darn the audience. "Fit as a fiddle. All Vampires safely disposed of. We can get married."

"Actually not," Mary said.

"Eh, what? Not get married?"

"I'm all for getting married." That was the nicest thing she could have said in a month of Sundays. "We have another Vampire." If so, why she was grinning like a flipping Cheshire cat was beyond him.

"You're funning, right? April fool's come early?"

"Heavens no!" That was Mrs. Burrows. "Mary's right. We do have another but he's on our side. Meet Mr. Clarendon."

"Jude Clarendon," the man, no, the Vampire, said. "I was sent to dispose of the Brytewood intruders but seems you've taken care of everything."

"With help from Dad. And Mary, she got the first one."

"So I just heard," he said, a wry smile on his face. "I am so delighted my Other friends have prevailed. The war's not over. Not by a long chalk, but I think they lost this battle."

"Can you stay, Mr. Clarendon?" Alice asked.

He shook his head. "I have a report to make. I hope you will forgive me if I take credit for the kill. Both of them. Not trying to steal the glory but I think it would be better than mentioning all of you."

No one argued. Much, much better. Who wanted their Other nature made public?

"No, you keep mum about us and we'll let things ride," Dad said. "Best all around."

"There is the matter of Miss Aubin's injuries," Alice said.

"I hope they write her account off to nerves, shock and the effects of morphine. She had the presence of mind to activate a recorder she'd been given. I didn't know what to do about that."

"What happened?" Jude Clarendon asked.

Alice explained as much as she knew.

"Simple," he replied. "A little verisimilitude never hurts. I found the creature just as he was attacking her, and disposed of him. He was therefore dead and evaporated by the time she was found. I think my superiors in the Service can take care of any inconvenient questions the hospital might have." He reached for his coat from the back of the chair.

"They're all gone, but what if there are more?" Mary asked. Gryffyth had been asking himself the same question.

Mr. Clarendon smiled at her. "There are more, but after four prized agents disappear without a trace, I imagine they might avoid Brytewood. I sincerely hope so." He pulled on his coat. "I bid you all, a good afternoon."

"Well," Mrs. Burrows said, after the door closed behind Clarendon. "Now that's over and done, who'd like a nice cup of tea?"

Chapter Forty-Five

A farmhouse in Southern Germany

"Another one died!" Bela whispered to Simon as they sat side by side, shredding cabbage for their host's wife.

"What?"

"They are all dead! The last one has died. I can feel his power in my veins. It's as if I could fly."

"Forget about flying, I couldn't keep up. But how about getting out of here? Whatever Fritz, outside milking the cows, says about sitting out the winter, I've a bad feeling about this place."

She agreed, but they needed warm clothes, supplies and good skis if they were going to get any anywhere in this weather.

"Two days." She hoped they were safe that long. "Then we go. I'll go down into the town and take what we need. They've taken enough from me, it's no theft."

"It's too dangerous to go out after curfew."

"No one will see me."

She was one stubborn Fairy, and he spent a long night worrying. She was back a little after four.

"I have everything. And I was right. I can truly fly. It won't last long, but it got me what we needed. There have been several robberies in houses and shops, and in the morning when they discover the loss, there's not a single footprint to be seen. Tomorrow night we leave. It's all hidden up in the high meadow."

It was one of the longest days of his life but the soft snow that started after dark was a gift from heaven worth waiting for.

They ran through the night, snow covering their tracks as if they'd ordered it as part of their escape. Bela had been more than efficient. Her cache was stacked in an abandoned sheep-cote. The run had exhausted Simon but Bela was as lively and alert as ever.

"Better spend the day here," she said. "They'll think we headed for the station. If they care. No one in their right mind would travel in this direction."

Maybe they weren't in their right minds but they had skis, boots, warm clothes and rucksacks of food.

With a couple of weeks of travel and a little more larceny on Bela's part, they might even reach Switzerland.

Try the other books in Georgia Evans's
fantasy series . . .

BLOODY GOOD

In the first of a supernatural trilogy, one Dr. Alice Doyle finds that the power to fight evil comes from places she'd never believe . . .

While the sounds of battle echo through the sky, a lady doctor has more than enough trouble to keep her busy even in a hamlet outside London. But the threat is nearer home than Alice knows. German agents have infiltrated her beloved countryside—Nazis who can fly, read minds, and live forever. They're not just fascists. *They're Vampires.*

Alice has no time for fantasy, but when the corpses start appearing sucked dry, she'll have to accept help where she can get it. If that includes a lowly Conscientious Objector who says he's no coward though he refuses to fight, and her very own grandmother, a sane, sensible women who insists that she's a Devonshire Pixie, so be it. Indeed, whatever it takes to defend home and country from an evil both ancient and terrifyingly modern . . .

Alice Doyle was exhausted. Staying up half the night and all day to deliver twins will do that to you. The elation and adrenaline of her first set of twins had carried her this far home, but as she turned into the lane that ran through Fletcher's Woods, weariness set in. It had been a good night's work, though. She wouldn't easily forget the rejoicing in the Watson farmhouse and Melanie's happiness through her fatigue as she breast-fed her lusty sons.

"A fine brace of boys. Gives one hope for the future, doesn't it, Doctor?" Roger Watson said as he smiled at his grandsons. "If only Jim were here to see them."

The Watsons' only son, Jim, was somewhere in Norfolk with the Army and Alice couldn't help worry how Melanie, a Londoner born and bred, would fare with her in-laws in a farm as remote as any you could find in Surrey.

Still, Farmer Watson was right: Whatever the politicians did or however many bombs fell, life went on.

The numerous cups of tea she'd consumed through the night were having their effects and she still had several miles to go over bumpy country roads. She pulled over to the verge and got out. Other traffic was unlikely out here. Few locals enjoyed the supply of petrol allocated to doctors. Even so, Alice climbed over the gate and ventured into the woods for a bit of privacy.

She was straightening her clothes back when she realized she was not alone. Darn! A bit late to be worrying about modesty. Deeper into the woods, someone crawled toward her. Assuming injuries, Alice called, "I'm coming. I'm a doctor."

It was a stranger. One of the workers from the hush-hush munitions camp up on the heath, perhaps? What in heaven's name was he doing rolling on the damp ground? As Alice bent over him, he looked up at her with glazed eyes. Drunk perhaps? But she didn't smell anything on his breath.

"What happened?" As she spoke, she saw the stains on his sleeve. Blood loss might well account for his weakness. She looked more closely at him and gasped. Part of the branch of a tree was embedded in his upper arm. How in heaven's name? Had to be drunk. If there wasn't enough to do, she had to cope with boozers who impaled themselves on trees. Seemed that was his only injury. No bleeding from the mouth or nose. Heartbeat was abnormally slow but steady, his breathing shallow, and his skin cold to the touch. Shock and exposure would explain all that. Best get him out of the damp.

"Look," she said, trying her utmost to keep the fatigue out of her voice. "I need you to walk to my car. I've my bag there and I'll have a look at your arm. Then I'll take you down to my surgery in Brytewood and call an ambulance."

The odd, glazed eyes seemed to focus. "Thanks," he croaked.

"What's your name?"

He had to think about that one. Definitely recovering from a wild night. "Smith." Really? Aiming for anonymity perhaps? "Paul Smith."

Alice got behind him and propped his shoulders until

he was sitting. "Come along, Mr. Smith," she told him. "I'm going to give you a boost and you have to stand. I can't carry you."

They succeeded on the second go and made slow progress toward her car, Alice supporting Mr. Smith from his good side. He was a lot lighter than anticipated as he slowly staggered toward the road. He supported himself against the hedge as Alice opened and closed the gate, but once they emerged from the shade into the thin afternoon sun, he collapsed.

Thank heaven for her father's old shooting brake. She got her patient into the back so he was lying against the sack of potatoes the Watsons had insisted she take with her.

"Mr. Smith, I'm going to examine your arm. I'm afraid I'll have to cut your shirt sleeve."

Taking the nod as agreement, Alice snipped off the sleeve. The shirt was good for nothing but rags anyway. Her first observation had been right: Several chunks of fresh wood had penetrated the flesh of his upper arm. "How did you do this then?" she asked as she opened her bag and reached for sterile swabs and Dettol.

And cried out as he grabbed her free hand in a viselike grip and bit her wrist.

He was more than drunk. He was insane. Alice tried to push him away but he held on, digging his teeth into her flesh. She finally grabbed his nose until he gasped for breath and released her.

"Behave yourself! I'm a doctor. I'm here to help . . ." She broke off when she saw he'd passed out.

Something was really wrong.

BLOODY AWFUL

In the second of Georgia Evans's supernatural trilogy, Gloria Prewitt must reveal her greatest secret to have any hope of saving the people she loves . . .

As the district nurse for a country village outside London, Gloria has the respect of the town and the satisfaction of helping those who need it most. She'd lose both if anyone discovered that she turns into a furry red fox and runs through the Surrey hills by moonlight. But what she sees on those wild nights suggests Brytewood is under attack—from a saboteur with superhuman powers and the force of the Nazi Luftwaffe behind him.

What can one Were-fox do against a predator with devastating weapons at his command—and the strength of the undead besides? What can a woman with a secret reveal without losing all she has? With the help of a couple of Devonshire Pixies, a Welsh dragon, and two men too stubborn to admit they're outnumbered, Gloria might just find out the answers . . .

She'd been longer at the Grayson's than she'd realized. Now the days were drawing in, it was almost dark and Gloria hated cycling the lanes with the miserable shaded light that the blackout required. As if an enemy plane up how many hundred feet would see the flicker of light from a bicycle.

But she wasn't about to break the law.

Keeping as close to the edge as she dared, without risking landing in a ditch, Gloria followed the lane as best she could. A long gap in the hedge showed she'd reached the heath, and when she sensed the trees ended, she guessed she was somewhere near the munitions camp. They were keeping a very tight blackout after the trouble a few weeks back.

Soon the road pitched downhill sharply and Gloria readied for the first bend. She wobbled a little in the dark, even considered getting off and pushing her cycle but the sooner she got home the happier she'd be.

The second bend undid her. If she hadn't been so engrossed in avoiding the hedges, she'd have heard the car engine coming behind her. As it was, by the time the narrow beam of shaded lights caught her, it was too close. The driver steered sharply to avoid her, but clipped her back wheel.

She went over the handlebars and ended up in the damn ditch after all.

The car stopped, narrow slits of headlight angled in her direction.

"I'm frightfully sorry," a voice called in the darkness.

So was she.

And damp and muddy into the bargain. She was going to have to wash her uniform when she got home and dry it in front of the stove. "Can you help me out?"

"Absolutely! I've a torch in the car. Hang on a tick."

He was back in moments, the unshaded beam of light wavering in his hand, in complete contravention of blackout regulations. As the light glanced over her face, the man gasped. "Stone the crows! It's Nurse Prewitt!"

Her rescuer (and attacker come to that) had the advantage there but his voice was familiar. "Yes, it is. Could you give me a hand?" The ditch was deeper than she'd expected.

"Righto! Let's get this off you first."

A weight was lifted off her shoulder and she realized her bicycle had landed on top of her. "That feels better."

"You'll feel a whole lot better still when we get you out of there." She grabbed a pair of strong hands and scrambled up the side of the ditch on her knees but when she tried to stand, her right leg buckled under her and she cried out in pain.

"Damn!" She forgave herself swearing. "I think I've done in my ankle."

Before she barely finished speaking, he'd scooped her up in his arms. Nice strong arms at that. Rubbing her face against the twill of his mac wasn't part of the plan, but she did it anyway, leaning into him as his arms held her close. He smelled of hard working male and fresh air. Her heart gave a little flip and another.

Come off it! This feeling helpless had to be affecting her nerves. She was used, quite literally, to standing on her own two feet and was most definitely not going whoosy over the first strong man who picked her up. Ridiculous!

She gave a little giggle, which he probably took for impending hysterics. He stiffened and held her very carefully. "Better get you on dry land."

Good point, her legs were cold and wet and she was probably dripping all over him. Whoever he was.

He sat her on the bonnet of his car and in the weak light from the torch still somehow in his hand, she looked down at her ankle. Her foot hung crooked at the ankle.

"It's broken." Just what she did not need with new evacuees due any day now. And she'd torn her stockings. Where was she going to get another pair? She couldn't cycle into Dorking with her leg in a cast.

"You look bad. Is the pain awful?"

She looked up at his face. Small wonder his voice sounded familiar! It was the supervisor from the plant. The absolutely dishy man that half the single women in the village (and a few of the married ones) were constantly mooning over. And he'd had his arms around her! "Mr. Barron!"

"Guilty as charged." In the beam of light he smiled. It was a very nice smile. Sexy even. No, it was not! Sexy was not what she needed right now. Helpful, strong, responsible, thoughtful. Not sexy.

"Mr. Barron, I hate to bother you, but would you mind driving me to the hospital?"

He hesitated. For all of three seconds. "That bad, is it?"

"Afraid so." She lifted her leg a little. "Look."

"Crikey! I'll get you there. And I'm sorry! Let's put you in the car then. Back seat might be best, you can prop that leg up then."

It wasn't the most luxurious back seat in the world. The stuffing was coming out of the cracked leather in a couple of places, but with a rolled up blanket behind her and what was left of her nurse's cape over her legs, she was as comfortable as she could hope to be.

With her battered bicycle on the roof, they headed down the hill. "Won't take us long, I hope," he said. "I feel terrible about this. I should have seen you."

She knew just how limited human eyes were in the dark. "Don't worry about it. I'm not dead yet." Crippled and disabled maybe.

"I should hope not! I'd never be able to show my face in Brytewood again if I'd dispatched the nurse to the hereafter."

"I'm not heading there any time soon, I hope. Assuming you make it down this hill safely."

"I'll get you there, don't worry."

It sounded very much like a promise.

Balderdash! More like an earnest hope on his part.

Or hers.

Sitting in the dark, she had a serious talk with herself. She was in shock. That was it. She'd seen the symptoms in patients. Confusion went along with it. Her chest was tight because she was suffering from shock. She'd had a nasty tumble and broken her ankle. That was why her heart was racing and she was feeling like jelly inside.

It had absolutely nothing to do with Andrew Barron up in the driver's seat. She was out of her mind. The man hauls her out of a ditch (after putting her there in the first place) and she goes all wobbly. Ridiculous! The utter last thing she needed was involvement with a human male. It was bad enough Sergeant Pendragon suspected she was a bit more than she appeared.

But she'd brushed him off and everything was fine.

She'd be fine.

Just as long as she never, ever, felt Andrew Barron's arms around her again.